SAY IT LIKE YOU MANE IT

BOYS OF THE BAYOU GONE WILD

ERIN NICHOLAS

ISBN: 978-1-952280-27-6

Editor: Lindsey Faber

Cover photo: Wander Aguiar

Cover design: Najla Qamber, Qamber Designs

THE SERIES

Boys of the Bayou-Gone Wild
Things are going to get wild when the next batch of bayou boys falls in love!

Otterly Irresistible (Griffin & Charlie)
Heavy Petting (Fletcher & Jordan)
Flipping Love You (Zeke & Jill)
Sealed With A Kiss (Donovan & Naomi)
Head Over Hooves (Drew & Rory)
Say It Like You Mane It (Zander & Caroline)
Kiss My Giraffe (Knox & Fiona)

Connected series...

Boys of the Bayou
Small town, big family, hot-country-boys-with-Louisiana-drawls, crazy-falling-in-love fun!

My Best Friend's Mardi Gras Wedding
Sweet Home Louisiana

MAIN AND RECURRING CHARACTERS

Bennett Baxter: partner in Boys of the Bayou, married to Kennedy, millionaire/philanthropist/politician. (Hero-Crazy Rich Cajuns)

Caroline Holland: heroine, heiress, interior decorator with a criminal justice degree, wildlife animal advocate. (Heroine-Say It Like You Mane It)

Charlotte (Charlie) Landry: granddaughter of Ellie and Leo, cousin to Josh, Sawyer, Owen, Kennedy, Fletcher, Zeke and Zander. In love with Griffin Foster. (Heroine-Otterly Irresistible)

Cora Allain: Ellie's best friend and business partner, Maddie's grandmother.

Donovan Foster: Hero. Griffin's brother. Wildlife rehabilitation expert. Former reality TV star and current internet sensation. (Hero-Sealed With A Kiss)

Ella Landry: Josh and Tori's baby daughter, Ellie and Leo's great-granddaughter.

Ellie Landry: owner of Ellie's Bar, matriarch of Landry family, married to Leo.

Fiona Grady: Griffin's friend, met him while they were both working in Africa, runs an animal park in Florida, exotic animal supplier for the Boys of the Bayou Gone Wild. (Heroine-Kiss My Giraffe)

Fletcher Landry: Married to Jordan. Zeke and Zander's older brother. (Hero-Heavy Petting)

Griffin Foster: wildlife veterinarian, Donovan's brother, in love with Charlie Landry. (Hero-Otterly Irresistible)

Jillian (Jill) Morris: wildlife veterinarian, specializing in penguins, in love with Zeke. (Heroine-Flipping Love You)

Jordan Benoit: Fletcher's wife, educational director for Boys of the Bayou Gone Wild. (Heroine-Heavy Petting)

Josh Landry: Sawyer and Kennedy's brother, cousin to Charlie, Owen, Zeke, etc., partner in Boys of the Bayou, married to Tori. (Hero-My Best Friend's Mardi Gras Wedding)

Juliet Dawson Landry: married to Sawyer, lawyer. (Heroine-Beauty and the Bayou)

Kennedy Landry-Baxter: Josh and Sawyer's sister, married to Bennett, Mayor of Autre. (Heroine-Crazy Rich Cajuns)

Knox: city manager, friends with Fletcher, Mitch, Zeke and Zander, etc., works with Kennedy. (Hero-Kiss My Giraffe)

Leo Landry: Grandfather of Landry clan, married to Ellie, founded Boys of the Bayou, ran it with his best friend, Danny Allain (deceased), until he sold it to his grandsons

Maddie Allain Landry: married to Owen, partner in Boys of the Bayou, Cora's granddaughter. (Heroine-Sweet Home Louisiana).

Max Keller: Caroline's best friend, investigative journalist.

Michael LeClaire: Naomi's brother, family friend. Town fire chief and paramedic.

Mitch Landry: cousin to Charlie, Fletcher, Zeke, Owen, Sawyer, etc., works for Boys of the Bayou, handyman, dating Paige Asher. (Hero-Four Weddings and a Swamp Boat Tour)

Naomi LeClaire: friend of the family, grew up in Autre, high school friend of Charlie and Jordan. (Heroine-Sealed With A Kiss)

Owen Landry: Cousin to Sawyer, Charlie, Zeke, etc., partner in Boys of the Bayou, married to Maddie. (Hero-Sweet Home Louisiana)

Paige Asher: dating Mitch, from Appleby, Iowa. (Heroine-Four Weddings and a Swamp Boat Tour)

Sawyer Landry: Josh and Kennedy's brother, cousin to Owen, Charlie, Zeke, etc., majority partner in Boys of the Bayou, married to Juliet. (Hero-Beauty and the Bayou)

Spencer Landry: Zander's cousin, FBI agent.

Theo: Spencer's best friend growing up, game warden, one of the "badges" protecting Autre.

Tori Kramer Landry: married to Josh, veterinarian, Griffin's friend and business partner. (Heroine-My Best Friend's Mardi Gras Wedding)

Wyatt Landry: Zander's cousin, Spencer's brother, coast guard.

Zander (Alexander) Landry: town cop, Brothers Fletcher and Zeke (twin), cousin to rest. (Hero-Say It Like You Mane It)

Zeke (Ezekiel) Landry: Brothers Fletcher and Zander (twin), cousin to the rest. Owns local construction company (also works as family accountant). Engaged to and father of Jill's baby. (Hero-Flipping Love You)

ABOUT THE BOOK

A run-away bride, wearing a freakin' tiara, and carrying a stolen lion cub, of all things. This was *not* how rowdy, bad-boy-turned-small-town-cop, Zander Landry expected his day to go.

He *really* didn't expect his night to end with her sleeping in his bed after her near-kidnapping.
But his intense attraction to her and the feelings of protectiveness she stirs up? Oh, yeah, he knew those were coming.

She's stunning, whip-smart, and trouble with a capital T.

Which means, he needs her to head right back the way she came. ASAP.

His town is exactly the way he wants it . . . crazy and trouble free.

Well, the crazy trouble he's not related to anyway.

Stranded in a tiny town in her half-million-dollar wedding

gown with no money and no place to go . . . today is going pretty much *exactly* the way Caroline Holland expected it to.

But the grumpy, tattooed, oh-my-god hot cop being the answer to all her problems isn't at all what she expected.

Now that she's turned all the criminal (and obnoxious) info about her exotic-animal-dealing ex-fiance over to Zander, she can kick back in a hammock with some sweet tea and relax.

Or not.

Turns out Caroline's not the spoiled heiress Zander thinks she is. The gorgeous hellion wants in on the action and soon discovers just how dirty things can get in the bayou. And the bedroom.

More and more, Zander just wants her safe on the sidelines. But Caroline isn't going anywhere until justice is done.

It's a clash of wills that's gonna get hotter than a crawfish boil in July. And the most fun the Landry family has had watching sparks fly since . . . well, the last book.

1

One thing Zander Landry knew for sure was that moments of peace, when everyone around him was safe and nothing crazy was going on, were few and far between. Which meant that he'd learned long ago to enjoy them fully whenever they occurred.

Which, very specifically, meant going fishing as often as possible.

He gave a longing glance to the fishing rod that was propped against the wall just behind where he sat. *Just a few more minutes, little girl. Just a few more minutes and then it's you and me and the water and the quiet.*

He was seated in his grandmother's bar with the rest of his family and several friends, just waiting for a lull in the action and conversation to sneak out the back door.

Of course, the definition of "lull" was applied loosely around the Landrys because true quiet, calm moments were a fantasy. For Zander, as part of the Landry family and the town cop—so, smack dab in the middle of both family and town drama in all ways—a lull was simply a string of thirty consecutive minutes where no one was likely to die or need to be arrested.

That was it. He didn't need to define it any wider than that.

If he did, he'd never fish again.

He'd just shifted forward in his seat, prepared to stand and head for the back door, when the *front* door to the bar opened. And everyone got quiet.

Well, fuck. No matter how much he wanted quiet, *that* was never a good sign.

Oh, sure, it seemed like it should be. But to stun the entire clan at once took something big.

He braced himself and looked toward what was distracting them all.

Or rather *who*.

Yeah, the woman—or at least she *and* the very wide, very white, very lacy, and very...sparkly dress she was wearing—who had just walked in was big all right.

Dammit.

This woman no doubt drew attention like this wherever she went. She was gorgeous, for sure—like *gorgeous*. As in, *I'll-fight-dragons-for-her* gorgeous.

Which had to be the single most ridiculous thing that had ever crossed Zander's mind.

But yeah, she walked in and looked around with an air that said she expected dragon slayers to be rushing forward, brandishing their swords, and jostling to be the one she chose.

Jesus, dude, you need to lay off the fantasy romance.

His buddy, Ollie, had let him read an early, unedited version of his third paranormal romance and clearly the dragon and princess thing had sunk in. Zander shook his head. That was not good.

But, in his defense, she *was* wearing a tiara. An actual tiara. The thing caught the sunlight from the front window—the only window in his grandma's bar—and sent sparkles dancing across the floor around her like she was moving under her own spotlight. Or disco ball.

Though even without all of *that*, people would've looked. She was carrying a large pet carrier in one hand and dragging a rolling suitcase with the other.

And she was wearing a wedding dress.

A very *big* wedding dress.

The skirt was full and the train was long. In fact, she had to stop, let go of her suitcase, stomp back to the door, push it open, yank the back of her dress across the threshold, and then drag it across the wooden floor of the bar to where her suitcase was parked.

The dress also sparkled. Like really fucking sparkled. It had sequins or rhinestones or something all over it and, thanks to the dragon-and-princess-romance he'd just finished last night, he thought for *a second* that she looked like she might have some fairy magic or something going on.

Zander shoved a hand through his hair. *No*. He needed some sleep. And to fucking fish. And to stop reading Ollie's books.

"Hi. Can we help you?" his grandmother Ellie, the owner of the bar, asked the woman. She stepped from behind the long, scarred wooden bar where she'd been serving drinks.

"I assume so," the woman replied. "I'm looking for Donovan Foster."

Zander's eyes flickered to Donovan. He was standing just to the side with his girlfriend, Naomi. Everyone else's very interested gazes flipped between Donovan and the woman and Naomi.

"Swear I've never seen her before in my life," Donovan told Naomi quickly. Then he stepped forward. "I'm Donovan."

The woman thrust the pet carrier at him. "Here, I brought this to you. I'm surrendering it."

Donovan took the carrier with a frown. "What is it?"

The woman lifted a brow. "It will be very obvious when you look inside."

"Right." Donovan set the carrier on the table to his right and bent to look inside. He straightened a moment later and turned to stare at the woman, his shock evident. "No way."

She lifted one slim shoulder, bare in the strapless dress, and a creamy white that nearly matched the silky fabric.

Zander rolled his eyes at himself. He was really noticing her skin tone in such a cliché way?

No more romance for awhile.

But there's that one...

No!

"He's all yours," the woman said to Donovan. "I brought him here specifically to you. I know you are an expert and that you have a sanctuary here."

Donovan was an expert in wild animal rescue and rehabilitation. And they did have a sanctuary here for wild and abused and abandoned animals.

Zander sighed. He did not want to know what was inside the pet carrier.

The woman turned and started for the front door.

"What is it?" Naomi asked Donovan.

"It's..." Donovan clearly decided it was easier to show than tell. He opened the carrier, reached inside, and pulled the animal out, holding it up for everyone to see.

"I kind of feel like that opening song from *The Lion King* should be playing right now," one of Zander's cousins said.

Donovan was holding up a lion cub.

An actual real, live lion cub.

Because of course he was.

"Come *on*," someone groaned.

Yeah, Zander felt the same way. But it was a *minority* opinion that having the local petting zoo turning into an animal park and wildlife sanctuary was a little over the top.

Of course, he was one of only a few who was actually inconvenienced by things like the increased number of visitors to the park causing increased traffic and commotion in town. All of which generally meant more phone calls and paperwork for Zander.

It also meant far fewer fishing trips.

Zander slumped down in his seat and pulled his hat down over his eyes. Any minute someone was going to think that he needed to go after the stranger who had just left the building in a wedding dress after dropping off a lion cub.

But for now, they were distracted by the baby animal. Maybe by the time they realized that there was a *human* acting unusually, she'd be gone and he wouldn't have to worry about looking into what the hell *that* was all about.

Though he probably should check on it. Because later *he* would wonder what the hell it was all about.

Still...she hadn't done anything wrong. And she hadn't asked for help. And, while he generally was all about helping people, he also believed in leaving them alone when they didn't need help and weren't hurting anyone.

"I guess...we have a lion now," Donovan said to the room at large.

"Just like that?" Knox, their city manager—who was also often inconvenienced by things having to do with the animal park—asked. He turned to Fiona Grady. "People besides you are going to be bringing stuff here?"

Fiona owned and operated an animal park in Florida. She was also an animal advocate and rescued animals from abuse and neglect situations on a regular basis. She was the reason that the Boys of the Bayou Gone Wild had gone from a petting zoo with goats and alpacas and a few otters to a park that had lemurs, red pandas, and even a sloth.

Fiona shrugged. "She surrendered him to Donovan. He is a

wildlife expert and we are an animal sanctuary, so she can do that."

"Without knowing where she got it? What if she stole it?"

Yeah, that thought had crossed Zander's mind as well. Which meant he had a *real* reason to go after her. Dammit.

"Why would she be bringing him to Donovan if she stole him?" Fiona asked.

"Why would she just have it in the first place?" Knox shot back.

"Well, those are really good questions to ask *her*," Fiona said.

Knox and Fiona both turned to look at Zander.

He didn't say anything. Those *were* really good questions.

"Did anyone else notice she was in a *wedding dress*?" another cousin asked.

"And pulling a suitcase?" one of Zander's sisters-in-law added.

"Might be a good idea to just *ask* if she's okay too. You know, if there's any particular reason she's here in that dress without, you know, a *groom*," *another* cousin agreed.

Zander closed his eyes and tried not to groan out loud. God, he had a lot of relatives. And they tended to all hang out together in one big, loud, all-talking-at-once, opinionated group. It was no wonder he had so many headaches.

"Maybe he's outside waiting," Zander's brother offered.

"Why's she pulling her suitcase around then?" yet *another* cousin—who happened to be Zander's boss—asked. "He could at least hold her bag."

Maybe he's an asshole, Zander thought to himself.

"And he's sending her into a strange bar alone? With that tiara on her head?" Zander's other sister-in-law asked.

Damn, there were a lot of people here right now.

"No way. Either he is a huge asshole, or he's not out there," someone said. It didn't really matter who.

"Somebody really should probably go find out," another voice agreed.

Now they *all* looked at Zander.

He really should have snuck out of here twenty minutes ago.

He sighed. "What?"

"This kind of seems like something maybe you should follow up on, doesn't it?" Fiona asked him.

"Wearing a tiara and a wedding dress isn't illegal," Zander told her. Which was true. He probably didn't need to worry about the woman at all. If she could afford a tiara like that, which he doubted was fake, she was going to be fine.

"Zander!" about twelve people said at once.

He sighed again. More heavily this time. Not that his sighing ever got to anyone around here. "I just wanted to go fishing today."

"Alexander Raymond Landry," his grandmother said, taking a step toward the table.

Yeah, now he *had* to get up and go after her. Even at age twenty-six and in uniform, he didn't mess with Ellie when she used that tone.

"Okay, okay, *geez*." Zander shoved to his feet and straightened his hat. Hell, he'd been going after the woman anyway. Not that he was going to admit that to them. They all needed to mind their own business.

He almost laughed out loud at that concept.

"Let's not all go gettin' all worked up," he said dryly, as he stepped around the end of the table. "We wouldn't want *that* to happen."

"Worked up" was pretty much the constant state of the Landry family.

He started for the front door after the woman, muttering about how any one of *them* could've gone after her, and how being an only child born to only children parents was probably heaven, and how they were all huge pains in his ass.

No one moved to stop him and no one asked him what he was muttering. They knew better.

Zander stomped to the door and jerked it open, stepping out into the late afternoon.

He didn't know how the woman had gotten down here, but surely she'd returned the same way. Whether she'd driven herself or had hired a car...

But nope. Of course not.

He was definitely not going fishing today.

She was sitting by the road on her suitcase with her fancy-schmancy wedding dress dragging in the Louisiana dirt that covered his grandmother's parking lot. Her head was bowed, and her shoulders were slumped. She looked sad and alone and dejected.

Well...fuck.

He looked up and down the road as he started toward her.

No sign of a stalled car. Why couldn't she have had car trouble?

No unconscious body either. Why couldn't her groom have had too much to drink at the reception and she'd pulled in here for help when he'd passed out in the car on their way to their honeymoon suite?

No, it wouldn't be anything easy like that, would it?

But, he knew exactly what to do with a woman who'd been left at the altar.

Take her back inside Ellie's.

There was plenty of booze just inside. And other women. He could easily pawn her off on any of the girls, who would tell her all about what a dumbass the guy was and how she deserved better and how she'd come to the right place to drown her sorrows.

She'd be shit-faced and laughing in no time. Then he'd take

her over to the B & B, have Heather put her to bed and feed her in the morning, and then he'd drive her wherever she wanted to go when she felt better.

Feeling a little more optimistic, he approached her.

He had a lot of women in his life, but they weren't the cry-over-being-dumped types. They were more the cut-off-his-balls-and-feed-them-to-the-gators types. Now that he was in law enforcement, he couldn't cover for them like he would have at one point, but they all also knew better than to tell him flat out about anything like that. And he knew what questions to *not* ask.

"Ma'am?"

Her head came up as he approached, and Zander realized that she hadn't been crying at all. Her head had been down, strands of hair falling over the side of her face because she had been hunched over her phone.

She seemed confused when she looked up at him. "Yes?"

When her eyes met his, Zander had to take a second.

Goddamned romance novels.

That was his first thought. Well, after cataloguing that her eyes were a stunning aquamarine blue, her hair was at least three different shades of gold all streaked together in thick waves, and her skin was smooth and creamy.

All of those were descriptors that came straight from the pages of the books he read with his friends in their romance book club. No way would he have noticed all of that before he'd started reading those damned books. *A fucking hot blonde* would have done it.

But she *was* gorgeous. Not just from across a dim room with a tiara-halo on top of her head, but right up close along a dirt road too.

And that was all the most clichéd shit he'd ever heard.

Thought.

Whatever.

Still, he had to pry his damned tongue from the roof of his mouth.

Because of all the stupid romance novels he read. And movies he watched. And country love songs he listened to.

And because he was a Landry.

He sighed. *Mostly* because he was a Landry.

He might not have actually thought the words "aquamarine blue" without the books, but he would have had the *wow, she's something special* thought trip through his head because of his DNA.

The Landry family had as much romance in their blood as red blood cells. They were genetically programmed and then nurtured from the crib to believe in love and fate and soulmates and romance.

Some of them just went with it. Some of them fought it.

But none of them were immune.

He cleared his throat and ignored the voice in his head that whispered *she's extraordinary.* See? Even the voice in his head was romantically dramatic.

Good God. She wasn't extraordinary. She was *new.*

She was a beautiful blonde. He loved blondes. And he'd hooked up with all the eligible ones in Autre. That's all this was. She was new. And hot.

He cleared his throat again and put his cop voice on. "I was just wondering if I could be of some assistance."

"Unless you have some unused hotel points, probably not."

He blinked at her. "Hotel points?"

She wanted him to take her to a hotel? Just like that?

She nodded. "What I need right now is a hotel and he's already cut off my credit cards."

She's in a fucking wedding dress, asshole, Zander reminded himself. If that didn't make a woman off-limits, he didn't know what did. Not to mention the gigantic diamond ring on the fourth finger of her left hand that glinted in the sunlight as she lifted it to tuck a strand of that thick, silky, golden hair behind her ear.

Thick, silky, golden hair? You need to get a murder mystery in your head ASAP.

That ring cost more than his truck. Both of his trucks. Put together.

Focus. You're a cop and she's... What was she? Gorgeous and in need of a hotel room. Okay, that he could do.

"What's your name?"

"Caroline."

"Caroline, I'm Officer Landry. So, you need a place to stay?"

She sighed and dropped her phone to her lap. "Well, I guess I need a pawn shop first." She frowned. "How did he cut those cards off already? *That* was his first thought after everything went down?"

"Your new husband?"

Her frown deepened. "I don't have a husband."

Awesome.

What? No. That's not awesome. That is not even relevant. To anything.

It was simply an answer to one question. Or maybe part of one question. The wedding she was dressed for hadn't happened. "So your fiancé."

"My *father*. I was expecting to be cut off eventually, but I didn't think it would be number one on his to-do list." She chewed the inside of her cheek, looking past Zander, clearly lost in thought.

"So you don't have any money?"

"I had to give the rest of my cash to my driver for bringing me down here."

"You had a driver bring you down here, but he left?"

"Well, I guess technically he's Brantley's driver."

"Your father."

"My fiancé. Ex-fiancé. Brantley Anderson."

Right. There were a lot of people in this scenario. "So the driver brought you down here, but didn't wait for you?"

"No, the bastard. And I'm sure he's going to tell them all where I am too."

"And you don't want them to know where you are?"

"No. I need...a break."

Okay, he was not going to delve into this any further. She was not crying, she was not hurt in any way, she had left her wedding, seemingly on purpose and not under the influence, and now she was more or less stranded here in Autre. That meant his job was fairly straightforward.

"Is there anyone I can call for you? To come help you?"

She shook her head. "No."

"Then how can I help?"

"Is there anywhere around here that would take me on my word that I would pay them back at a later date?" She wiggled her left hand with the enormous diamond ring on it. "I have the ability to get some money, I just don't have it on me at the moment."

Hence the pawn shop reference. So she was planning to sell the ring. He knew lots of jilted women did that and honestly, he couldn't blame them. Maybe she'd found out her fiancé was cheating right before walking down the aisle. Maybe she'd been faced with a church full of people and realized that she simply couldn't promise to love this man for the rest of her life. It wasn't really Zander's place to judge why she'd left without even changing her clothes. She had, and that was her business. What she did with the ring on her left hand was also her business.

But he felt something he almost never felt: curious.

They did have a motel in town a few blocks away and there was a chance they'd let her stay if he acted as a reference. But there was another place that was a sure thing.

"My cousins' aunt actually owns the bed and breakfast here in town. I'll take you over there."

She looked puzzled. "Your cousins' aunt? She isn't *your* aunt?"

"She's their aunt on their mother's side. We're cousins on their dad's side."

She went over that in her mind, then shook her head. "It's really like that in small towns, huh? Related to everyone somehow?"

"It is here."

"And she'll let me stay just because you ask her to?"

"Yep."

"I kind of thought it was just TV movie stuff." Caroline seemed charmed by the information.

Zander shrugged and pushed away how charming he found her being charmed by his town and family connections. "Well, it works that way around here."

"You'd really vouch for me?"

"Worst-case scenario, you skip out without paying your bill and Heather makes me scrub a few toilets in exchange. I've done worse."

At that, she gave him a bright smile and Zander felt like she'd punched him in the gut.

Yeah, he needed to avoid having this woman smile at him.

She wasn't technically taken, but she'd literally walked out of her wedding mere hours ago. She came with baggage—literally—and he *really* tried to avoid baggage.

He wasn't looking for anything serious. At all. No way. No thank you.

And wearing a wedding dress and an engagement ring big enough to knock out a guy's front tooth if she punched him just right, was an obvious sign that the woman was ready for something serious. With someone.

Did he believe in love? Absolutely. It was all around him.

Everyone in his family had, or would, fall in love. A couple of them more than once.

Did he believe in love at first sight? Again, yes. Not only had he read about it over and over again—and enjoyed the hell out of it for reasons he couldn't explain and had given up pondering a long time ago—but he'd seen it in real life around him in friends and family as well.

Did he think that he and this woman might actually have some kind of connection that was real? Sure, maybe.

But he didn't care.

Believing in something and wanting it for himself were two different things.

"Here, let me help you with your bag." He took a step forward as she stood and he was about to grasp the handle on her suitcase when he heard the sound of a car approaching.

This road had definitely not always been a major road in town. It ran past several Landry family businesses—mechanic, construction, Ellie's bar—and it brought tourists to the Boys of the Bayou Swamp Boat and Fishing Tours office and docks. In the past year though, it had become much more heavily traveled. Not only had the swamp boat company's business grown, but now the family's petting zoo and animal park brought in lots of visitors.

So Zander didn't think much of the sound of the car. Until he looked up.

And a black stretch limo screeched to a halt right in front of them.

The next thing he knew a man in a tuxedo jumped out of the backseat and stalked toward the woman.

Oh good. The fiancé was here.

Zander hated the guy on sight.

Which was not okay.

He was feeling jealous and possessive? *No.* Just no. It would actually be fantastic if his soulmate was married to someone else. Very off limits. Way out of Zander's way and reach.

Good for the guy coming to win her back.

You need to immediately download a book about investing and then do a re-read of To Kill A Mockingbird. *Get off the romance, man.*

"Dammit, Caroline! What the *fuck?* Get your ass in this car. We're going back to New Orleans!"

Okay, *that* was not all right.

Zander frowned and took a big step forward.

Instead of screaming or running, however, the woman faced the man with her hands planted on her hips. "*Chris?* What the hell are you doing here? How did you even find me?"

"Don't worry about that. Just get in the car. Everyone is pissed but they said if you come back now, we can still do it. They're all just waiting."

Caroline crossed her arms. "I'm not going back. You can tell them all to go to hell."

"You *are* going back." The man wrapped an arm around Caroline's waist and lifted her off the ground, starting back toward the car.

She immediately started kicking and hitting and pummeling him with both fists. "You asshole! Put me down!"

Yeah, okay, *now* Zander was getting involved.

"Hey!"

The man turned and looked at him.

"Put her down."

"Stay out of this. This is just between us."

"It stopped being between just the two of you when she said no and you didn't listen."

"Look, man, I understand if she batted her eyes and made you some promises, but she's got an appointment in New Orleans."

Zander drew to his full height and shifted so that guy could see his badge clipped on the front of his belt. "This isn't about batting eyelashes."

The guy sighed and put Caroline down. "You got the cops involved?"

Caroline shoved him back. "I didn't get anybody involved. He came out to see if I was all right."

"Well, tell him you're fine. And get your ass in the car."

"No. Because I'm not fine. I'm not getting in the car. And I'm not getting married today."

"Caroline—"

Zander took another big step that put him right beside Caroline. "I believe she said no."

"So this is going to be a problem?" Chris asked Zander.

"It doesn't have to be. If you get in the car and leave. Without her."

Chris looked from Zander to Caroline. Then back. "Fine." He looked at Caroline. "But you know this isn't over." He straightened his jacket, muttered a curse, then stomped to the limo, got in the back, and a moment later the car drove away.

Zander turned to look at the woman with a brow up. "Anything else you'd like to tell me?"

She met his eyes directly. She studied him, seemingly thinking over his question. Finally, she nodded. "Yeah, I think so."

"Okay. What's going on?"

"It might take a bit. Want to buy me a drink?" She glanced back toward Ellie's.

Did he want to take the gorgeous woman in a wedding dress with another man's ring on her finger who had almost been kidnapped right in front of him back inside his grandmother's bar where most of his family and a lot of the town was gathered?

He most certainly did not.

"No," he said simply.

Caroline looked surprised. "Can we"—She looked around —"at least go somewhere else?"

That seemed like a good idea. She was very conspicuous here and his family could, at any moment, come out. And start asking questions. Not to mention that the would-be kidnapper now knew where she was.

"Is there a chance your fiancé is going to come back?" Of course there was. A man didn't just let this woman go.

She bit her bottom lip and looked up the road. Then she nodded. "Yeah, there's a chance. Or that he'll tell someone else where I am." She looked at Zander again. "But that was my brother. Not my fiancé."

Oh, that was interesting.

No, it fucking isn't. Knock it off.

"So, will your fiancé be coming after you?"

"Ex-fiancé."

Right. She'd mentioned that.

"Okay. Will he come after you?"

She didn't answer right away. Which Zander also found interesting. Though he shouldn't. He did *not* want to be interested in this woman. At all. He didn't want anyone getting kidnapped while they were in Autre, though, either. Okay, he didn't really want anyone getting kidnapped, period. But *especially* while they were in Autre.

"There's a chance," Caroline finally admitted. "Or my dad might come. Or my ex-fiancé's dad might come."

"And you don't want to go back with any of them? Is that right?"

"Yes."

Well, fuck. He had to at least be sure she didn't get taken anywhere by anyone against her will.

And he would feel that way about *anyone*. It had nothing to do with the crazy stirring in his gut that seemed new. Different. More intense.

She studied him for a long moment. "So, you're willing to help me, Officer Landry?"

Her question—and her *voice* and her eyes and her everything, if he was being honest with himself which he decided to *not* be—sent a shot of *something* through Zander's chest.

It was the familiar streak of adrenaline he often felt with his work. It primed his gut to act on instinct when necessary, it made him ready to take on people intent on doing bad things and face potential danger, and it focused his mind. But he also recognized the sliver of trepidation. It wasn't fear or reluctance. It was...awareness. Like knowing he was about to open a big old can of worms.

But he nodded. "Helping people with problems is kind of my job."

"Then I would love to tell you what's going on."

He wanted that. And it wasn't the cop in him thinking that.

Fuck. Dammit. Hell. Sonofabitch.

"Okay. Let's go...someplace your brother doesn't know about."

"Like your place?"

Yes. He wanted her at his place. That was the safest. He could definitely keep her safe there. His property was at the end of a dead-end road so the only traffic was trucks he knew. His neighbors were his brothers and cousins. His backyard butted up to the bayou.

But *fuck no*. He wasn't taking this woman anywhere near his house. Where his bedroom was.

She was dangerous. He couldn't sort through all the reasons why at the moment, not while looking into her eyes and wondering how soft her skin was and how silky her hair was, but he had enough self-preservation instinct to keep her *away* from his house.

"I'm thinking the B & B."

He grabbed her suitcase and started for his truck.

"But he might think to look there," she protested. She gathered up her enormous skirts and followed him though.

"I'll tell Heather not to tell anyone anything about you," Zander told her, storing her bag behind the front seat and then turning to face her.

Fuck.

Again with the eyes. And hair. And lips. Okay, he hadn't included the lips in the earlier inventory, but they were great too.

So he liked female lips. Big deal. These were *not* that exceptional. What the hell was wrong with him?

She's probably your damned soulmate or some shit and the second you touch her hand you're going to feel sparks.

I'm not going to feel sparks. That's a stupid cliché. But I have to get some war biographies. Or maybe something about Ruth Bader Ginsburg. Something about women who are amazing but not sexy. It doesn't have to be about sexy all the time. Get away from those romance novels.

The thing was, smart, bold women like RBG *were* sexy in their own way and if Zander had been Ruth's age and run into her at a bar when she was single, he absolutely would have hit on her.

"Are you okay?" Caroline asked, stepping forward with a slight frown.

He jerked out of his stupid thoughts. "Yeah. I'm fine. You're the one with the problem."

Well, that had sounded rude as fuck.

Her eyes widened, but then she nodded. "Yeah. I am. We should definitely work on my problem. It's going to keep getting bigger if we don't."

Zander sighed. He didn't even know what that meant but... of course it was.

2

As she made her way across the parking lot, Caroline studied the big man who was currently her favorite person in the world.

Which was not easy. Not the studying him part. That was very easy. He was incredibly good-looking.

Walking across a dirt parking lot in this *monstrosity* of silk and tulle and lace with three-inch heels, however...*that* was torturous.

This damned dress. Who had thought this was something she would ever in a million years pick out and wear?

Was she being dramatic?

About the dress, maybe.

About thinking this small-town cop was her new best friend?

No.

Caroline had one true friend in the world, who was in San Antonio on some work assignment for the next few days. Max Keller was the only person Caroline trusted one hundred percent. Max had kept Caroline's secrets for twenty years. The really juicy ones—like the ones that would get her disowned from her family and maybe even thrown in jail—for the past thirteen. So yeah, Max was her ride or die.

Max would hit the road immediately if Caroline asked, but wouldn't be as much help as someone in law enforcement. Max was an award-winning investigative reporter and would love to tell the world about what Caroline had uncovered. Sometimes...okay, most of the time...that was exactly what went down. Caroline got the dirt, Max exposed the dirt. But this was something that needed someone with a badge.

And *this* badge was something. Caroline *really* liked a good guy and this one was giving her very nice tingles on top of the omg-yes-be-my-hero relief she was feeling.

He had to be six-four and had broad shoulders, big biceps, a flat stomach, and a tight ass. He was in fighting shape, no doubt about it. He had long hair and tattoos that ran from under the short sleeve of his uniform shirt to his wrist.

Damn, he wore that uniform well. There really was something about a guy with all that authority. He had a holster around his hips and carried himself with the I'm-in-charge air. But the long hair and the tattoo made her wonder if he wasn't quite as perfectly pressed and buttoned up as he appeared.

She was intrigued.

"Where's the B & B?" she thought to ask as she finally got to the truck.

He stepped back as she got close, presumably so she could get into the truck. She should maybe text Max about what was going on at least, right? Before getting into a truck with a strange man with a gun?

The guy just made her feel safe.

And she had excellent instincts about smarmy, lying, manipulative assholes. Spending the last thirteen years surrounded by them—and manipulating them right back— had made her an expert.

This guy wasn't any of those things.

He jutted his chin to his left, indicating somewhere generally north of where they were standing. "Just up the road." He
paused a beat, then as if reading her mind, asked, "You want
some references?"

She looked him up and down. "Do I need them?"

"I'm just saying, you don't know me. Would make sense if
you wanted to be sure I was safe."

"Who would I get references from?"

He grinned and Caroline had a flickering thought of *I don't
really care if you're safe*. Which was absolutely the opposite of
safe.

"Well, most everyone I would get a reference from is inside
the bar. And they're all relatives. But—and you'll have to take
my word for this—they would be the hardest on my character.
My grandma, for instance, would tell you I can be a damned
grump and that I don't give people the benefit of the doubt
enough."

"And is that true?"

"Yep."

She had no reason not to trust this guy. If he didn't give a
shit, he could have just let Chris take her back to New Orleans.
And he wouldn't be concerned about putting her somewhere
safe now.

And she really did need someone to get on this problem
Chris and Brantley had revealed. She'd hoped to have a little
more time to dig up information, but Brantley—and more
likely Brantley's father—had decided that a surprise wedding
was the way to go and she'd run out of time.

"Okay, officer, I guess you're stuck with me for a little bit."

He narrowed his eyes. "Define *a little bit*."

She gave him a half smile. "As long as it takes."

He lifted a brow. Clearly he didn't love that answer.

"I plan on getting you tucked away and then informing
whoever shows up looking for you that you've moved on," he

told her. "You're going to tell me what your problem is, I'm going to fix it, and then you *are* going to move on." He said it all firmly. Like *very* firmly.

It was almost as if he thought she was planning on sticking around and wanted to be certain she understood she was *not* welcome.

Well, geez.

"By the way, you can call me Zander," he told her. "No need for the officer stuff."

She squinted at him. "Zander?"

"It's short for Alexander. But no one calls me that but my mother. And my grandma when she's pissed."

"What if I get pissed?"

"You can leave."

Wow. Okay, then. "Well, I'm Caroline. Caroline Holland."

He gave her a single nod. "Okay." Then he paused and frowned. "Wait. Holland? Not as in Holland Shipping?"

Terrific. He was familiar with her family name. "You've heard of my father's company?"

"I was a cop in New Orleans for a couple years. Detective for one. We...ran into your dad's...associates once in a while."

She laughed. "You can say it. You ran into criminals who worked for or around my father."

Zander just stood studying her for a long moment. Finally, he nodded. "Yeah. Your dad has some interesting friends."

Caroline shook her head. "I know this probably sounds ridiculous, but those weren't his friends, and my dad didn't really know what he was getting into."

"What do you—" Zander shook his head. "How about we go up to the B & B? We can keep talking but we might as well get you settled. I'd like to have you up there before anyone decides to come back for you. Are they coming from New Orleans?"

Yes," she confirmed. "That was where my wedding was supposed to happen."

"I'd love to know more about that too," Zander said.

"Would you?" Caroline asked. "And why is that?"

"Well, now knowing that you're Charles Holland's daughter, everything got even more interesting. But I was intrigued before."

"Intrigued?"

"Absolutely. I love some good gossip. I can tell you all about what's going on with Jason and Vivian or Kelly and Brett."

She was trying to get up into the truck with her huge stupid dress.

When he didn't say anything more, she looked up and realized that he seemed to be waiting for her to respond. She shook her head. "Sorry. I have no idea who Brett and Kelly or Jason and Vivian are."

Zander sighed as he held a hand out toward to her. "Guess I'll just have to keep gossiping with my grandma."

That distracted Caroline long enough that she put her hand in his without thinking.

She felt the connection like a jab of heat to her lower belly though and she quickly looked up into his eyes.

"Well, fuck," he said softly.

She wasn't sure what that was about. But she somehow knew that she didn't want to ask.

He helped her up into the truck, even gathering her massive skirt and tucking it in around her on the truck seat. It felt stupidly considerate. Maybe even intimate. Almost as if he was tucking her into bed.

Caroline shook her head at that and forced herself to concentrate. She didn't need him taking care of her. That wasn't why she was here. She was here for assistance, sure, and him being a cop could be handy, but she didn't need him for anything personal. Well, unless you considered keeping her brother from pursuing a life of crime and her personal vendetta against nearly all of her father's friends personal.

She cleared her throat. "So you're telling me you're a gossip?"

Zander tucked the final bit of shiny bejeweled fabric around her feet and then nodded. "Of course."

"Are Kelly and Brett people from here in Autre?"

He laughed. "Country music singers."

"Oh, so *celebrity* gossip, not local gossip. And here I was picturing you sitting around the coffee shop downtown with the little old ladies talking about who got caught sneaking out of whose house early this morning."

"Oh, I definitely gossip about that stuff too. And this building right here"—He nodded toward the bar—"is one of the best places in town for it. Being a cop, it's pretty handy to keep my ears open and ask a lot of questions. Helps that I was born and raised here. People know I'm always up for a good story or tall tale. They forget that now some of that stuff can be incriminating."

Caroline snorted. "Convenient."

"Very." He stepped back and slammed the truck door.

She watched him round the front of the truck and wondered what she was getting herself into. That had seemed like a warning. How much should she tell him?

Then she thought about the lion cub she'd surrendered inside the bar. She was in Autre because of Donovan Foster. She'd seen him on television recently and knew that he was doing wildlife rescues and rehabilitation right here in Louisiana. Social media had been blowing up with the news that he was starting a new TV show that was going to be filming right here in Autre. It made sense to bring the lion cub to an expert. She figured that if Donovan couldn't take care of it, he would know someone who could.

In any case, the lion cub was much better off here in Autre

than it would've been with her fiancé, his family, or any of his friends. And now she needed to figure out a way to save the rest of the animals.

Zander climbed up into the truck and started the engine. She studied him as he pulled out onto the main road and turned north. They bumped along the dirt road for only about a mile before they pulled onto pavement.

"So we need to go over some realistic possibilities of where you might go."

She looked over at him. "What do you mean?"

"If someone shows up here looking for you, we're going to convince them you already left town. Where would you go?"

Oh, right. Were they going to come back looking for her? Yeah, it was really possible. How fucking annoying was that?

"How about you just say you don't know where I went? Why would I tell you that? You can tell them you gave me a ride back to New Orleans and dropped me at the airport," she said.

"Do they have the ability to track things like you checking onto a flight?"

Dammit. She wouldn't be able to do that without a credit card and her dad would know that.

"Okay, you tell them that you gave me some cash and the last time you saw me, I was at the gas station on the corner. You don't know anything about where I headed or who I went with."

"That kinda makes me sound like an asshole. Why would I not be more concerned? Why would I not personally take you somewhere safe?"

She lifted a brow. "Just tell them that I insisted on not involving you."

"I'm a cop, Caroline. I have an obligation to make sure people in distress are no longer in distress when I leave them."

"They don't know how I was when you left me."

"After your run-in and the way I stepped in with Chris, I

26

think 'distressed' is a good way to describe your emotional state."

Caroline sighed. Running away from home as an adult should be easier than this. "Okay, you took me back inside the bar and got me something to eat. I went to the bathroom, and never came back out. As far as you know I snuck out the back door and disappeared. No one has to know any different."

He thought that over. Then nodded. "Okay."

She was a little surprised. "Do we need to set it up with everybody inside? Maybe actually go in and eat something? I can go to the bathroom and then sneak out the back. You can meet me later, but at least the people inside will have a real story then."

He shook his head. "I'll tell them what to say. No big deal."

"You're gonna tell everybody their story, and they're all going to stick to it and nobody will have any problem lying?"

"Pretty much."

"How can you know that? You know every person inside?"

He nodded. "Yeah. I told you I'm related to most of them."

"And they would just lie for a stranger?"

"If I asked them to. "

"And you would do that?"

"Yeah. If it keeps you safe. If you don't want to go back to New Orleans and they come down here and try to force you to, then I'll do whatever I need to do to keep them from causing trouble. And the sooner they think you're not here, the sooner they quit coming around. That seems like a good thing for the town and for me."

He was trying to make this sound like he cared about this not becoming a problem for him and the town, but Caroline got the impression he was more than intrigued by her and whatever was going on. He was worried.

Max was the only one who worried about her.

Because Max was the only one who ever really knew what was going on in Caroline's life.

What would it feel like to have someone else in on her secrets? Someone else to talk to? Lean on? Someone who could actually *do* something about some of this?

Caroline was still thinking about how damned tempting that was when he pulled up in front of a huge two-story brick house. They'd only driven for about five minutes, but they were clearly on the edge of town. The wooden sign at the start of the drive read "Hebert Bed and Breakfast".

"This is it," he said, shutting off the ignition.

"Do you need to go in and see if there's a room?" Caroline asked, peering through the windshield at the house.

There were flowers everywhere—in the beds in front and along the paved path, hanging from baskets and on multiple surfaces—including tables, ledges, and even the floor—of the front porch that was eight steps up from the ground.

"There will be a room," Zander said. He got out without any further explanation. A moment later, he opened her door.

"Do you think—"

Caroline didn't have a chance to complete her question because Zander reached out and grasped her around the waist, pulling her off the truck seat. He turned and set her on the grass a moment later, but all thoughts and rational questions had completely fled her mind.

He stood just looking at her for a moment. "Do I think what?"

She shook her head and wet her lips. She had no idea what she'd been about to say. "Oh, um, never mind."

He shrugged and pulled the seat forward so he could reach behind for her bag.

With that in hand, he started up the front walk and Caroline followed. Not that she really had a choice. She was here now. For better or worse.

But the fact that this guy could touch her, whether it was her hand or helping her out of the truck, and affect her the way he did, was starting to freak her out.

The skin on her waist still tingled where he'd touched. In spite of the *layers* of material that had been between her and his hand.

What the *hell*?

She avoided personal relationships because of the work she needed to do, but that was relatively easy considering she was never tempted. In general, she had spent so much time around men that made her skin crawl and her general hope in humankind shrivel, that it was hard for her to think about dating or letting anyone get too close. She had a healthy and well motivated lack of trust for most men and Max told her that she put off a very effective *I'm too-much-work-move-right-along* vibe that made most men quickly set their sights on the women who were easier to impress.

In fact, studying those women and the way they interacted with men was one of the most enlightening and helpful things that Caroline did. She could channel those women in any situation that called for it. Men were easy to manipulate. When you gave them exactly what they wanted.

"Heather? Hey, it's Zander!" Zander opened the front door, pushing it open, but standing back so Caroline could step through in front of him.

She started to move past him, but her dress caught on something on the threshold, pulling her up short. She heard something rip and she swore. "Fucking sonofabitch."

Zander gave a soft snort. "Everything okay?"

She grabbed the skirt and yanked. "This damned dress. Who the fuck would wear something like this?" She yanked again and realized it wasn't the threshold holding her up, but something clear back on the top step. The fucking train was so long that she'd gotten hung up way back there.

"May I?" Zander asked, reaching for the train.

"Please."

"You don't care if it rips?"

"Well...I do need to try to resell it."

He gave a nod. "Right. Okay." He set her suitcase inside the door and then went back to the steps. He examined the problem, loosened the train from whatever had caught it, and then gathered it up in his arms. "I take it you didn't pick this out?" he asked as he came toward her.

"Definitely not."

She preceded him into the house and he waited until they were both clear of the door to drop the bunch of white silk.

"How's a girl end up wearing a wedding dress that she didn't pick out to a wedding that she then leaves before saying I do?"

Caroline lifted a hand and scratched at the back of her neck and then tried to reach the spot between her shoulder blades where the lace rubbed against her skin. "It was a surprise wedding."

Zander looked startled. "They threw you a surprise wedding?"

"Yeah. And they definitely got the surprise part right."

"How's that even work?"

"Well, you tell the bride that it's a surprise birthday party, and you get her to the country club before you spring it on her. Then you lay on a lot of guilt and plenty of reasons why she might as well just go ahead with it since it was in the plans anyway."

"So it worked...long enough to get you into the dress," he said. "But then you bolted."

"Oh, I had zero intentions of walking down the aisle with Brantley. Ever."

He narrowed his eyes. "Yeah. Intrigued."

She shrugged. "I just hadn't gotten around to calling it all off yet." That was mostly true. She'd needed to get more details about the illegal exotic animal buying and selling before she lost access to Brantley's house and home office.

"So how'd they get you in the dress?" Zander asked.

"I got into the dress on purpose."

"Why?"

"It's worth three hundred thousand dollars. Give or take."

He made a choking sound. "You're shittin' me."

"Nope. And it was big enough to hide this." Caroline reached up under her skirt and watched as Zander's eyes widened. The white silky material bunched high on her thighs as she reached, but there was just too damn much of it for him to really see anything.

She unclasped the fanny pack—yes, she was able to wear a small fanny pack under this stupid skirt—and pulled it loose from under the layers of white. She unzipped it and then turned it upside down. A huge diamond necklace, diamond earrings, a bracelet, and two more sets of earrings fell out onto the hardwood of the B & B's front foyer. She reached up, pulled the tiara off her head and tossed it on the pile.

"Are you confessing to a jewelry heist?"

"Oh, these were all gifts. So they belong to me. And I wasn't leaving without them. I knew when I left he would cut off my credit cards. I didn't expect it to be immediate, but I knew it would happen eventually. This is my insurance plan."

"You know that you can't buy burgers and stuff with diamond earrings, right?"

"This tiara," Caroline said, pointing. "Is worth fifty thousand dollars. I'll pawn it and use that money to...do whatever I need to do." She looked down at her dress. "Just like I'll sell this thing." She held up her left hand and wiggled her fingers. "And this monstrosity? Half a million."

Zander tucked his hands in his pockets "But you know

you're not gonna get half a mil for that from a pawn shop, right?"

"What do you mean?"

"I'm guessing you've never pawned anything before."

She stopped at that. "Well, no. But I know the general gist. You go in and give them valuable things and they give you money in exchange."

"But they're not giving you full value. They might not even take some of this stuff if they don't think they can resell it. People who are lookin' for, and can afford, wedding dresses like that aren't shopping in pawn shops, princess."

Caroline knew she was staring. No, she'd never pawned anything before. And knew nothing about how pawn shops worked.

Well, fuck.

And he was right. She couldn't just go to the front desk of a hotel, or an airline, or through a grocery line and offer a diamond tiara in exchange for a room, ticket, or bag of apples.

"Well, how much do you think I could get for this stuff?"

"Thousands, sure. You can get a great hotel room. A plane ticket to probably anywhere. But you're not buying a new mansion or starting a brand new life."

Caroline stared at the diamonds laying on the floor. Then she looked up at Zander. She believed him. "I'm in so much trouble."

Z ander started forward as Caroline crumpled.

Literally. She seemed to just curl into a ball and slump to the floor. She was one big blob of white satin and sparkles. And this time he was very sure she *was* going to cry.

Shit. Fuck. Damn.

Protective instincts surging, he went to one knee in front her.

He didn't miss the irony of that. Within an hour of knowing her, he was on one knee in front of her. Cute. She was even already in the wedding dress.

Knock it off. He wasn't sure if he was talking to the voice in his head, or Fate, or just the universe in general. But they all needed to knock it off.

"Hey, hey, you're okay," he told her.

She sniffed. "I'm really not."

Dammit. She'd *sniffed*.

"You are. You've got a place to stay, no fee. We'll...figure the rest out."

"I'm rich," she looked up at him. "I really am. How can I be so fucked?"

See, responding to *that* the way his brain did at first was not cop-like, or gentlemanly, or at all appropriate. Or helpful. To either of them. She was in trouble and sad and in need of help. And she was *not* going to be...

Zander pulled in a deep, sharp breath. "You are *not* fucked," he said firmly. "I'm gonna need you to take a deep breath. We're going to fix this."

Those blue-green eyes shimmering with tears and fear and then hope...hope that *he* would help her...made Zander's chest tighten and his stupid palms itch.

He wanted to hug her.

Fucking hell. He wanted to hug her.

She took the deep breaths he'd insisted on. Then said, "I know how this is going to sound so just bear with me for a minute. But I'm rich. Like my dad has *millions*. Many, many millions. I have whatever I want. I don't intend to live like that forever, but for right now it's kind of a necessary evil. I have to pretend that I'm living that lifestyle so that I can get the intel I need. So I pretend that I don't know how to make my own money and how to get along in the world. Which means, for now, I'm completely dependent upon him for money and clothing and shelter and food..."

Her voice slowly rose to a near panic level and Zander found himself leaning in and taking her face between his two hands.

"Caroline. Breathe." He said it softly, but firmly.

She stared at him. Then she breathed. Deeply. Twice.

"I've..." He really didn't want to say this. But those eyes. "... got you," he finally finished.

And then she combined looking up at him with those eyes with another of those smiles and Zander realized that *he* was very much the one who was fucked.

3

"Zander! What's going on?"

Zander pulled back from her as a woman stepped into the foyer.

Caroline could imagine how she looked, sitting on the floor in a wedding dress, jewelry scattered all over, and Zander crouched in front of her trying to keep her from having a panic attack.

Actually, for a second there she'd really thought he'd been about to kiss her.

Wow, she could play the damsel in distress so well she'd fallen into that habit without even realizing it. Oops.

And dang, she regretted doing it to this guy. It clearly got to him. Because he was a good guy. Tears even got to some of the assholes she dealt with, but she might have turned this on too much for an actual nice guy who legitimately cared about other people.

She swiped at her cheeks and looked up at the woman with a smile, working to get to her feet.

Of course, she needed help because of the fucking dress.

There was so much damned material, she couldn't get her shoes on enough solid floor under her to get up.

The hot-chemical-whatever-it-was connection between them broken, Zander wrapped a big hand around her upper arm when he saw her struggling and hauled her to her feet.

"Hey, Heather," he greeted the other woman. "I called out. You must not have heard me."

"Oh, I had the mixer running in the kitchen." Heather approached with a smile. "What do we have here?"

"This is Caroline. She's having...a day. She's going to need a room."

Heather looked her up and down and nodded. "We can do that."

Caroline decided to answer the un-asked questions upfront. "Yes, this is a wedding dress. No, I didn't get married. Yes, I'm hiding out. No, I don't have any money."

Zander sighed. And let go of her arm.

She hadn't realized she'd been able to feel him through the fabric of the dress, but now her skin felt cool where he'd been holding her and she missed his touch instantly. It was stupid, but she felt safe with this guy. And...comforted. Wow, that was new.

He obviously thought all of this was a little crazy, but who wouldn't? The wedding dress alone was surely not an average Friday afternoon occurrence in his small-town bar. But paired with the lion cub in the pet carrier and her near-kidnapping, she could imagine the small-town cop was wondering what the hell had rolled into town.

"We're gonna work out the financial situation," Zander said. "It's a favor to me, okay?"

Heather shook her head. "I'm not worried about that. Are you okay, honey?" she asked Caroline.

That was sweet. And Caroline gave her question some real thought. Maybe for the first time since leaving the church, actually. She took a deep breath and noticed the hint of cinnamon in the air as well as the scent coming off of Zander Landry. She couldn't quite place it. It was an outdoorsy, woodsy scent. And she wasn't so sure that it was cologne. She thought it was more likely how he smelled. She loved a good cologne, for sure, and had been close to many an expensive one, but the urge to put her nose against this cop's neck and breathe deep was incredibly strong.

In any case, the cinnamon-and-man scent, combined with the quaint, cozy foyer of the bed and breakfast, the bright smile of the woman looking at her, and the solid, steady presence of the man next to her, made her nod. "Actually, I think I am. Or will be."

"Are you a tea or coffee drinker?" Heather asked.

Oh, an easy question. "Tea."

"I'll get some ready. There's an open room, third door on the right. En suite bathroom. Toiletries are in there. Linen closet is right across the hall. Let me know if there's anything else you need."

"And if *anyone*"—Zander emphasized the word—"whether we know them or not, asks if you've seen her, you haven't."

Heather lifted a brow, but nodded again. "And I'll call you right away."

"Thanks. Is Beau around?"

"Down in his workshop. But he'll be here later, of course." Heather looked at Caroline. "Beau's my son. He owns his own woodworking business. He makes furniture. He's built most of this furniture." She gestured to indicate a gorgeous oak table that sat just inside the foyer under a large mirror, an ornately carved wooden bench, and Caroline assumed the table and chairs in the dining room just off to their right. "But he also does all the repairs around here."

Caroline studied the furniture. She was impressed. It was bulkier than anything her mother would put in their house, but it was definitely as beautiful as anything her parents' interior decorator ordered.

"He also lives out back in one of guest houses," Zander added. "So it will be great having him around."

"*One* of the guest houses?" Caroline asked.

"This place used to be a pecan plantation," Heather said. "I own and run it with my sister, Hannah, and my best friend, Crystal. We've restored the main house and a couple of the other buildings, including the carriage house, where Beau lives, into additional quarters. And then we added a few cottages. We have ten rooms here in the main building in addition to my room and Crystal's rooms—she's our chef—here on the first floor, and six bungalows on the property with room to add more. We have a central flower garden with paths that connect them all with the main house where we serve the meals and a gorgeous walking trail that circles the entire property. We also have a stable with a few horses for trail rides, and a chicken coop where we collect fresh eggs, and a big vegetable garden that has a few fruit trees that we use."

It was clear Heather was very proud of their...estate. Caroline honestly didn't know a better word to describe a bed and breakfast that included a main house with so many additional buildings and grounds.

"Wow. I'd love a tour," Caroline told her. The place sounded amazing.

"I'm happy to show you around."

"You need to stay inside," Zander said firmly.

Caroline looked up at him. "Seriously?"

"Yes, seriously. The idea is to lay low so no one knows you're here if they come back looking for you."

"How would they even know I was here?" Caroline asked.

"They might have someone following you. And make a plan in case they do. Or in case they come back now that the first attempt at...persuading you...to go home didn't work." His jaw ticked at the memory of the limo rolling up and her brother grabbing her.

That was sweet. She'd like to think that the men in her life would care if she was actually being kidnapped, but obviously, no one would care if Chris came to grab her. She was sure his failed attempt to bring her home was earning him some pretty stern words.

But would they send someone to follow her?

It didn't take her long to get to the "yep" on that one.

Oh...crap. Caroline gave a shiver at that. She was acting very out of character, which would make them suspicious. Running out of her wedding to one of her father's best friend's sons was *not* what anyone would have expected from her. What had she been thinking?

Oh, yeah, that she didn't want to be married to Brantley Anderson. Though she could have had it annulled. Or divorced him after she sent him to prison, she supposed.

But she'd panicked.

Crap.

Still, Zander had a point. They would be very suspicious now. And would they send someone to follow her when Chris went back and reported that she'd refused to come home, fought him, and had a cop on her side now? Uh...yeah, maybe.

She usually appeared very...compliant. Submissive even. She inwardly winced at even using that word in her head. She rebelled against everything the people in her father's inner circle did, stood for, and believed in, but she gave every indication *to them* that she went along with it all. Or, more accurately, that she just didn't care about any of it.

She played the part of the ditzy, shallow socialite much more concerned with how her spray tan had turned out than any business talk or political gossip or deals being made over the hors d'oeuvres platters at the parties in her parents' living room.

"Fine," she finally said to Zander. Because what else was she going to say?

"Why don't you go upstairs and get into something more comfortable?" Heather suggested. She gave a soft laugh. "I imagine traipsing around in that thing hasn't been easy."

Someone who understood. Caroline smiled at her. "It weighs a ton."

Heather looked at Zander. "You should help her get upstairs."

Zander stiffened next to her and Caroline felt the tension emanating from him suddenly. She looked up at him and saw his jaw was tight again. But she didn't think this was about her almost-kidnapping.

Oh, he didn't want to go upstairs with her?

Well, too bad. There was no way she was getting up a staircase in this damned dress without tripped on it in her heels and possibly breaking her neck.

Plus, she kind of liked seeing the big, broody cop uncomfortable. That wasn't very nice of her, probably, but she couldn't help it.

She smiled up at him sweetly. "I'd really appreciate it."

He looked down at her and she actually batted her eyelashes. He rolled his eyes.

She almost laughed. Zander Landry wasn't quite as easy to wrap around her finger as the other men she spent time with. She liked that about him.

Men were so simple. And exhaustingly shallow. Money and power and sex. That was what she could reduce the interests of ninety-percent of the men she knew down to. At one time, before her father had gotten rich and she'd met a whole new group of people, she'd assumed most men were like her dad.

She'd been wrong.

Men in general were kind of awful. Rich men were terrible. And there were a lot more of them than she'd ever realized.

"Fine," Zander said. "But I've got work to do. So let's go. I need to head out."

He was just going to leave her here? She had things she needed to tell him about. Things she needed his help with.

"I was going to fill you in on—"

He reached to grab her suitcase and then grabbed a big handful of wedding dress train with his other.

"Let's go."

Heather gestured at the jewelry laying on the floor. "Anything you'd like me to do with this?"

"Can you...just put it in something?" Zander asked.

He suddenly seemed very fatigued.

Yeah, well, welcome to my world.

"Of course. I'll put it in a Tupperware for you."

Zander actually snorted at that. "Thank you."

He looked at Caroline expectantly.

"What?"

"After you, Your Majesty," he said jutting his chin toward the stairs.

She lifted *her* chin, picked up the front of her skirt and did her best to flounce up the stairs.

Flouncing was difficult to pull off in three-inch heels and the heaviest wedding dress in history, though.

Four steps up, she let out a frustrated groan and leaned on the banister to reach under the layers of fabric for the shoes. She managed to get one shoe off, her bare foot meeting the runner that carpeted the steps just before she heard Zander mutter, "For fuck's sake," behind her.

Suddenly she was swept up in two strong arms and cradled against a broad, hard chest.

"Hey!"

"It's going to take forever for you to get up these steps even if you manage it without breaking your neck," he told her as he started up the stairs.

41

He didn't look down at her. But she definitely looked up at him. And wrapped an arm around his neck.

He had a point, after all. And she'd never been carried like this. At least not as a woman by a man. Maybe as a kid after she'd skinned her knee or when she was sick or something, but never like *this*.

She liked it.

He wasn't even breathing hard when he got to the top of the staircase. He also didn't put her down. He strode to the bedroom, leaned to twist the doorknob, pushed the door open, and carried her into the room.

Huh. Across the threshold, into a bedroom, while in a wedding dress.

He set her on her feet next to the bed. She wobbled slightly on her one high heel, bracing her hand on the mattress.

"You're heavier than you look," he said.

Her eyes widened. "Hey! It's the dress. I told you it weighed a ton."

"Uh-huh." He turned on his heel and walked out.

Caroline blew out a breath and pressed her lips together. She was *not* going to call after him and ask him when he was coming back. Or *if* he was coming back. He'd better be. And if he didn't, she was going to show up at the police station. She needed his help. He wasn't going to just dump her in the bed and breakfast, penniless, and let Heather deal with her.

She looked around the room she could only describe as charming.

There were white lace curtains on the window, a large white wooden dresser with an enormous mirror hanging over it, a four-poster bed covered in a beautiful multicolored quilt, and a matching side table with a lamp that she could already imagine casting a warm glow over the closest pillow to read by.

There was also a rocking chair in one corner near an honest-to-goodness wardrobe.

She took a deep breath and actually felt some tension leave her shoulders.

This was going to be okay. She could hang out here. Heather was nice and had tea. And would know how to find Zander. He had work to do, he'd said. Fine. She'd showed up unexpectedly. She could understand that he might have some other things to take care of now that he'd ensured she was safely hidden away for the time being. But if she didn't see his big, broody...

He came back through the door before she'd even completed the thought.

She felt her stomach swoop and she thought she might have caught her breath.

She was glad to see him.

It hadn't even been two freaking minutes, but she was happy he was back.

And not just because she really did need his help.

She wasn't sure what to do with these feelings. These tingles of awareness and attraction were foreign. She spent so much time playing men. She was constantly putting on a little show. With her father she was sweet and innocent and just wanted to please him. With his friends she was flaky and superficial and silly. With guys her age she was flirty and oh-so-interested in them and willing to let them close...but not *too* close. She was the sexy-but-I-don't-know-it virgin that just seemed to be so many men's kryptonite.

She was always close to men for a purpose—to get information from them. She never *wanted* to be closer to them just to be close.

But she wanted to step forward into Zander Landry's arms and have him hold her.

Holy crap.

He dropped her suitcase to the floor with a thunk. "Do you need anything else before I head out?"

A hug.

She was *not* going to say that.

"I, um..." She looked down at her suitcase. "I didn't even pack that. I have no idea what's in it. Or not."

He grabbed the handle and flipped the bag up onto the bed. "Check it out."

He was being short, but she somehow knew it was because he did *not* want to be in this bedroom with her and not because he didn't like her.

She liked having an effect on him. And not because she was going to get him to slip up and tell her some secret he didn't mean to spill, but because...he was affecting her too.

Caroline turned her attention to her suitcase. She opened it and started digging. She tossed the contents out onto the bed one item at a time. "What. The. Hell." She straightened with a garment in each hand. "Who packed this? Where exactly were we going for our honeymoon?"

Zander looked at the soft peach-colored teddy dangling by a strap from her right index finger to the floor-length, spaghetti strapped red evening gown draped over her left palm. "I'm guessin' your fiancé packed that."

"This is all I have," she said, motioning with the skimpy teddy to the rest of the clothing on the duvet. "Lingerie and evening gowns. I've got two bras and like three thongs. That's it. There's no make-up, no blow dryer, no shampoo. Just clothes. And only sexy clothes."

Zander tucked his hands into his front pockets and nodded. "Like I said, a guy packed that bag. With the stuff he wanted you wearing."

She huffed out a breath. The idea that Brantley had put this together and thought *this* was what she was going to be wearing for him made her roll her eyes. She tossed the teddy and dress back into the bag. "Is there a clothing store here? Better yet, a place that will deliver something over here?"

"Nope."

"Great." She held out her arms. "Well, I'm homeless, penniless, transportation-less, and now..." She reached for an ice blue nightie that was completely sheer. "I'll basically be walking around naked."

Zander shifted his weight and cleared his throat. "You can borrow some clothes."

"Oh?" Caroline used the opportunity to run her gaze over him from head to toe. "Don't think we're quite the same size."

He didn't even smile. "I've got cousins and sisters-in-law. You can borrow something from one of them."

"Okay." She sighed. She was going to be stuck in this damned wedding dress for awhile longer. "Let's go."

"You're not coming."

"I'll have to try the stuff on."

Now *his* gaze ran over her. There should have been way too much fabric in the way for it to have any effect. But she still felt tingly when his gaze came back to hers. "I'll bring you something that will work."

"You think you can just eyeball me and decide what size I am?"

Oh damn...the corner of his mouth curled up and he gave her a cocky nod. "Bet I can get pretty close."

That simple phrase clearly said the man had seen a lot of women, of various shapes and sizes, naked. And had taken careful inventory.

She believed him. She also knew those women had been just fine with his up-close study.

The jittery feeling in her stomach—and lower—intensified and she took a deep breath. She didn't like being off-kilter. When she dealt with people they always *thought* they had the upper hand. But they were wrong.

With Zander Landry, she had a feeling he had the upper hand. And they both knew it.

"Well, let me help you out with that," she said. She reached behind her for the zipper on her dress, drew it down, let the heavy material fall down her body, and stepped out of the mound of silk and sequins.

Then she stood in front of him in her strapless bra, white panties, and sheer slip. She propped a hand on a hip and tipped her head. "Now you can get a better idea of my size and shape."

He didn't react. At all.

He didn't blink. He didn't shift. He didn't cough. All he did was the take-in-every-little-detail thing again. And her nipples and stomach and a sweet, achy spot between her legs that had been asleep for a *very* long time all said, *please notice me, me, me!*

Then he gave a single nod and said, "Yep. Very helpful. Thanks." He pivoted on his heel and started for the door.

What?!

"Wait!"

He looked back.

"I need your help, Zander."

She knew she had to look like she was about to cry again. She really needed him to listen.

Suddenly he was back, standing right in front of her, towering over her. "Don't push me, Caroline."

She felt her eyes go wide and round. "Wha—what?"

"One minute you're all ballsy and bold walking into my grandma's bar. The next you're crying and all desperate on the floor in the foyer. Then you're awkward and sweet and can't even get up the damned stairs by yourself. Then you just strip your clothes off." He leaned in. "I know you're trying to figure out which one I'll react to—the boldness, the tears, the seduction...well, the thing is, it's *all* working. I'm here. I'm going to help. Stop. Playing. Me."

Caroline knew she was staring.

He'd figured her out.

At least in part. Not *all* of those moments had been specifically planned out and she hadn't been playing him consciously every one of those times. But...that was what she did. She figured people out and then did whatever it took to make them trust her, or feel sorry for her, or ignore her, or, yes, sometimes want her. Whatever got her close enough to get what she wanted from *them*.

She wet her lips. "Pushing you is the last thing I want. I want to...pull you."

His eyebrows slammed together.

Yeah, that had sounded stupid.

"I mean...as in...I want to pull you closer. Keep you close. Stay close. I don't want to push you away, that's for sure. I need your help and you make me feel..." She frowned, but what was the harm in admitting it? She wasn't playing this guy. It was true. "Safe," she finally finished. "I feel like I can trust you."

He studied her face for a moment, his eyes intent on hers. "Trust me for what?"

"There's a group illegally buying, selling, and transporting exotic endangered animals. I can...tell you all about them." Okay, she couldn't tell him *all* about them. That was the problem. She'd needed more time being engaged to Brantley and in his family's inner circle to get all the details. But she had some. "I need help breaking it up." Actually, she needed to give the information to someone who would do the breaking up. That wasn't her role. She gathered the intel and passed it on.

Zander scowled. But said nothing.

"I can even give you documents."

Fine. It was two emails and two texts. But she had to give this information to *someone* and she'd—clearly—burned her bridge with the Andersons today. She was going to have to hope that Zander Landry was not just a good guy...that he was a good *cop* too.

"Later," he finally said shortly.

"But—"

"Clothes first." Then he walked to the door, pulling it shut behind him. But before it latched, he leaned back in. "Stay here." The door shut firmly as he disappeared through it.

Caroline stood staring at the heavy wood for several long seconds.

Crap. Now what?

She looked around. She didn't have a whole lot of choices. She felt safe here. And what was she going to do? Hitchhike in the hot pink corset? And where was she hitchhiking *to* exactly? Because she was pretty sure she'd get a ride. She was equally sure she would not want that ride.

At least she wasn't currently standing in the bridal suite of some stupidly expensive hotel as Brantley Anderson's new wife.

But she had no plan.

She'd always known this day would come, and that she'd have to figure something else out when it did, but she'd really thought it would be her choice. When she'd woken up this morning and gotten ready to go to Wallace Anderson's would-be surprise birthday party, she really hadn't prepared for this to be the day that everything fell apart.

She'd always known there would come a time when she would be ostracized from her family's social circle and cut off from access to the information about their corrupt, greedy ways.

But she'd really thought she'd have clothes on when it happened.

4

Yep, that was definitely Caroline Holland.

  Caroline Camille Holland. Age 26. Interior designer. Daughter of Charles and Gretchen Holland. Engaged to Brantley Austin Anderson. Age 23. Engaged three months ago.

Zander blinked at that. They'd only been engaged for three months and their families had thought that throwing her a surprise wedding was a good idea? And Brantley was only twenty-three. A younger man.

Zander should not be this interested. Or annoyed. He was looking her up to see if there was more to her story than what she'd already told him. There was *always* more than what people told him. Well, except his family. The Landrys typically told him, and everyone else, more than they needed—or wanted—to know. There was no such thing as a filter for the Landrys.

But as far as he could tell, Caroline was who she said she was. She was Charles Holland's daughter, she'd been engaged to be married, the guy who had tried to pull her into the limo was her brother Christopher, who was apparently Brantley's best friend, and she'd been wearing that huge-ass diamond ring on her left hand for the past three months.

Zander slammed the top of his laptop shut.

That ring was fucking ugly.

And the fact that he had an opinion about her engagement ring was fucking annoying.

There was nothing new in any of the information he had dug up. Caroline had no arrest records, not even a parking ticket. There were no scandals around her. The only social gossip was her engagement. Which was really more fact than gossip. It might have been more of a story if Brantley hadn't been a friend of the family and if Caroline's family wasn't just as rich as the Andersons were, but this looked every bit the combining of two wealthy families in the age-old tradition of marrying to merge assets.

As if either the Hollands or the Andersons needed any more assets.

He would have been digging into this even if Caroline hadn't showed up with a lion cub. And hadn't cried. And wasn't gorgeous. And hadn't taken her clothes off in front of him.

He really would have.

She'd almost been kidnapped. And she'd dropped that bit about people buying and selling illegal exotic animals.

She also hadn't denied that she'd been testing him to see which Caroline—the ballsy one, the desperate one, or the sexy one—would do it for him.

They all fucking did it for him.

And he'd admitted that to her.

Zander scrubbed a hand over his face. He needed to focus.

She was the only daughter of Charles Holland and she was in Autre. Zander would have checked that out. There was no reason for the heiress to a multi-million-dollar inheritance to ever be this close to muddy water and alligators.

Charles Holland was still the CEO of Holland Shipping. He

still had shady business associates. Some of them had been indicted on things like embezzlement. Some had been taken to court by their ex-wives because of cheating, and in one case, domestic abuse. A couple had gone to court but had escaped jail time by setting someone up lower in the company as a scapegoat. It was all very typical, greedy, corrupt, elite bullshit carried out by greedy, corrupt, elite assholes. It was stuff that Zander didn't get his hands in anymore.

Even in his time as a cop and his very short stint as a detective in New Orleans, he tended to deal with the grittier side of things. Not so much the CEO level, but the guys who were doing things like transporting goods stolen from the big shots' warehouses or the guys who were sent out to get money back from people who were late on debt payments to those bigwigs.

Guys like Charles Holland and his friends didn't get their hands dirty. They didn't touch the stolen merchandise, they didn't bloody noses, they didn't even make the direct threats or direct *deals*, for that matter. They knew better than to be involved face-to-face and have their fingerprints on anything. There were middlemen who did the dirty work. *Those* were the guys Zander had dealt with.

But he definitely knew who Charles Holland was. And the fact that Holland's daughter was now in Autre, Louisiana, having run away from her wedding and telling Zander that she needed help was far more intriguing than Zander wanted it to be.

Dammit, he had to find out what was going on. He'd hoped he could look up her name and something would've jumped out to him that he could call up to New Orleans and pass off to someone else. He'd hoped that something would've stood out in the gossip pages about her fiancé or in the business pages or even the *front* page about her future father-in-law that would be worth looking into but wouldn't require Zander's assistance.

The thing was, he couldn't find anything obvious, and he

had the nagging feeling that even if he had, passing this off wouldn't have been that easy. Which really pissed him off. He did not want to be involved. Not with this woman.

Okay, not with any woman.

He was very happily single. Very purposefully single. He had a lot of people to take care of and he wasn't interested in adding any more. The additions to his family kept happening and would keep happening. And he was happy about that. He wanted his cousins and brothers to be head over heels in love and find their life partners. And he would welcome them into the family with open arms and protect them with his dying breath.

But because he knew that was going to keep happening and his family was going to keep growing and they all wanted and needed Autre to continue to be a happy haven, it was going to be more and more important that Zander was able to keep things stable and steady and safe.

None of them knew how close the bad guys really were sometimes. None of them knew how close things had gotten to shaking the very foundation of Autre, Louisiana, two years ago. They didn't know what it took to keep the perimeter solid.

There was a band of badges—guys who had gone into various types of law enforcement and civil service—keeping Autre safe. And keeping the things they did to keep it safe out of the public eye.

Everyone thought Zander, Michael, Theo, Wyatt, Spencer, and a few other friends who had vowed to keep their work a secret, were just fishing-and-beer-drinking buddies. And that worked great. The fishing cabin deep in the bayou that was accessible only by boat and only if you knew exactly where it was, served as the perfect place for them to plot and plan.

And they did catch some pretty great fish there too.

Everyone thought Autre was a fun, easygoing, safe, relaxed place to be. They thought the badges came to Autre as a break from all the other places in the world where they were called upon to protect and serve. But the truth was, they all came to Autre to fight the good fight when needed to keep this corner of the world safe. And it was needed far more than anybody in Autre really wanted to know.

So the last thing Zander was interested in was adding anyone else that he might need to worry about. Especially someone like Caroline Holland. Caroline had *I'm gonna be a huge, gorgeous, sweet, lose-your-mind distraction* written all over her. And Caroline had a direct line into a bunch of shady characters.

That didn't mean *she* was shady. That would remain to be seen. But Caroline hung out with some people who had proven that they were not above stepping on people, bending the rules, pushing boundaries, and flat out putting themselves above everyone else when it benefited them. Zander wasn't bringing that into Autre.

And he'd already felt the spark that absolutely made every self-preservation instinct kick into high gear.

Caroline Holland, of all the fucking women who could have gotten stranded in Autre, had to give him a spark.

He didn't want it, but he wasn't about to blow that spark off as nothing either. In fact, he was going to treat it with care and respect.

Like a bomb.

But he wasn't stupid enough to think that would be easy. He'd seen Landry men go gaga in the blink of an eye. Like magic. Not just the romantic ones, or the ones getting a second chance with a woman they'd loved before, or the ones who were ready to settle down. Oh, no. Landry men set on being bachelors, Landry men who were *happily* single, Landry men who were dead-set against falling in love had gone and lost their hearts.

And then there were the men who weren't Landrys, but who fell for Landry women.

Some of 'em had put up a fight.

But they'd all gone down.

Being loud and obnoxious was the second best thing Landrys did.

Loving was the first.

With a heavy sigh, he pulled his phone out and dialed Fiona Grady's number. Normally, he wouldn't have any trouble calling, but she wasn't at home in Florida right now. She was just a few blocks away at Ellie's with all of his family and friends.

She answered on the second ring. "Hey."

Zander appreciated the fact that she didn't use his name. Fiona was one of those people who understood that sometimes phone calls needed to be under the radar.

"Hey, don't let anybody know who's calling."

"You got it."

"Has Donovan or Griffin said anything about the state of the lion cub?"

"Yeah. Good to go."

He also appreciated the fact that Fiona knew how to have a conversation without giving anything away on her end. "So he's healthy?"

"Seems that way."

"Still illegal for her to have him."

"Yes."

There was a slight hesitation at the end of Fiona's answer and Zander knew she wanted to add more. He heard her murmur something on her end and a chair scrape. He assumed she was excusing herself.

Fiona worked with multiple animal rescue groups. She was the most knowledgeable person he knew about animal rescue and captivity laws and regulations.

She was in Autre at the moment, because she'd joined the Autre gang in Alabama recently following Hurricane Clare. She'd met up with the group to do rescues and they'd ended up bringing home a zebra, tiger, and a harbor seal confiscated from a man who had kept them in a private zoo that had been ruined by the hurricane.

The animals were now living in Autre and Fiona had been preparing to return to Florida. Zander was glad that if a lion cub had to show up, at least it had happened while Fiona was still in town.

"Okay, I'm outside now," she said. "So the lion cub is healthy, but young. They don't know if he was born in captivity or bought and taken from his mother immediately, or what. This happens all the time, Zander. There are so many cats in captivity. But yes, it is illegal in Louisiana for him to be here at all in private possession. The thing is, if she illegally purchased him, or was given him, or however she came to possess him, she did the right thing turning him over. It's up to you what you do with that information, but I'm very curious where he came from."

"Yeah, I'm curious about a lot of things."

"Do you have any idea who she is or where she went?" Fiona asked.

Zander debated telling her the truth. But there was something about Caroline that made him especially protective. Maybe it was just the mystery around her. Maybe it was the fact that, actually, as far as he could tell, she'd been completely honest with him about everything and said she needed his help. She said she felt safe with him. That she wanted to stay close. That messed with a guy who took protecting people very fucking seriously.

Maybe it was the fact that for just a brief moment in Heather's foyer he'd been about to kiss her. In spite of knowing full well that the sparks with her were to be *avoided* at all costs.

But he definitely needed to get some answers.

"Yeah, I think I'm going to be able to track her down and get some more information from her," he finally said. "She hinted that there might be more animals. Exotic, endangered animals being bought and sold."

"Fuckers," Fiona muttered. "Find her and find out what she knows."

"This is a little out of my jurisdiction, don't you think?" Zander asked.

He wanted it to be out of his jurisdiction. The thing was, nothing *really* fell out of his jurisdiction. Sure, as a cop he had his territory and what he was in charge of and expected to do. But honestly, when it came to keeping people safe and keeping bad people from doing bad things, he felt like there was a wide berth and his friends who always had his back and helped him out when he needed it—and vice versa—agreed. Criminals played in the gray area, so sometimes the good guys had to too.

"Zander," Fiona said firmly, and he could imagine her with her eyes narrowed, hand on her hip, cheeks pink. Nothing got Fiona fired up like animals in need. "Find. That. Woman."

"Fine. I will get as much...information...from her as I possibly can," Zander finally said.

The amount of information that he wanted from Caroline Holland was immense.

He wanted to know everything about her. He wanted to keep her right by his side, and he wanted to make sure that no one would ever hurt her.

And that no one would ever come after her and throw her a surprise wedding...that she might end up sticking around for.

Fucking sparks.

His complete overreaction to all of that was a huge red flag. But he couldn't stay away from her. Not just because he couldn't quit thinking about her eyes and her lips and her hair and her curves, but because he literally couldn't stay away from her. She was in trouble and he was the local law enforcement officer. And there were a whole bunch of questions he needed the answers to.

He and Fiona disconnected and Zander let out a long breath.

His fishing pole was still leaning up against the wall at Ellie's bar. Someone would tuck it away for him. It would be fine.

But he had a feeling it was going to be a very long time before he and that fishing rod hit the water for anything even remotely resembling peace and quiet.

Caroline kicked her wedding dress toward the corner of the room, but with the weight of the silk and jewels it took three kicks to get it wadded up into the corner satisfactorily. She glared at it. Then stomped over and picked it up with a sigh. She draped it over the rocking chair. She did want to try to sell the damn thing, after all.

She turned to the bed and regarded her suitcase. So lingerie or evening gowns. What was best for lounging around and waiting for Zander Landry to come back?

Lingerie. Obviously. It was more comfortable and she wouldn't mind meeting him with only a little lace in a few strategic places. Seeing the heat and intensity in his eyes like she'd seen when...

She frowned. Interestingly, she'd seen even more heat when she'd told him she felt safe with him than when she'd been standing in front of him in just a bra, slip, and panties.

Hmm...

She focused on her suitcase again. If she wasn't starving, she'd consider the lingerie on the bed thing. A nap didn't sound terrible either. But the smell of cinnamon in the air seemed to be coming from an actual food item, which she assumed was in the kitchen and which she hoped was full of butter and sugar and was available to the guests.

Tossing the pieces of lingerie aside—far more pieces than she actually owned, which led her to wonder who exactly had shopped for her—she worked on taking deep breaths like she did in yoga.

But no, it didn't matter how far down she dug, there was not a regular pair of underwear anywhere in the suitcase. Every pair was a thong. She didn't hate thongs but she really just wanted some plain old underwear right now. Was that so much to ask?

Apparently yes.

Again the frustration and the feeling that maybe she was in over her head started to rise up in her chest.

She took another breath, but it was still shaky. She wanted to be *steady*. She wanted to be sure of what she was doing. She wanted to know that even if things sucked at the moment or were uncomfortable, it was for a greater good. The way playing the ditzy blonde interior designer who needed her daddy's friends to give her jobs decorating their offices had been for the past four years. The way being engaged to Brantley had been.

Suddenly an image appeared behind her eyelids.

Zander Landry's face.

Even in her imagination his jaw was tight and he looked a little annoyed, but his gaze was intent, unblinking, and a feeling of security swept over her just thinking about him.

He was clearly competent and had multiple resources. He knew her situation, knew who she was—mostly—and even if he hadn't stuck around to hear her whole story, he knew that she was more or less stranded and he'd made sure she was somewhere safe and had given Heather instructions to keep her that way.

She opened her eyes, surprised to find that she felt less

agitated. Zander might not be an ally exactly, but he certainly was more on her side than anyone else at the moment.

Which made her think of Max. Her only true friend. She needed to call Max.

Caroline quickly reached into her suitcase for the least bulky and uncomfortable of the evening gowns—a silky, spaghetti-strapped red dress that hugged her curves and had a slit that went nearly all the way to her hip on the right side.

It wasn't practical in the least. She really didn't have a choice here, though. The other gowns either had sequins, sleeves, or were an ugly purple color. Okay, only one was an ugly purple color, but she knew that dress had been stuffed to the back of her closet after the one and only time she'd worn it. Whoever had packed the suitcase had done a shitty job in general and in particular for including that dress.

She didn't even bother to look for shoes because there was no way in hell she was putting heels back on. She also bypassed all the thongs and undid the strapless bra and tossed it on the bed. She was wearing that dress and that dress only. That was as close to comfortable as she was going to be able to get.

Oh wait...there was one more thing. She reached up into her hair and pulled out the few bobby pins that were holding up the sides, easing the beginnings of a headache. Or so she hoped.

With her hair falling around her shoulders and now dressed in an only slightly less ridiculous dress, Caroline padded to the door, opened it, and peeked in the hallway. The entire upper floor of the bed and breakfast was quiet and she wondered if there was anyone else staying here. She needed to call Max but was also very curious about Heather, the town of Autre, and yes, Zander Landry. Maybe she'd step outside to give her friend a call and have a look around the neighborhood.

She grabbed her phone and started down the stairs.

Heather must have heard her coming because she met Caroline at the bottom of the grand staircase.

"I didn't know if you prefer your tea hot or cold, or sweet or unsweet, and you were busy upstairs so I didn't want to ask so..." Heather held out a large glass of iced tea with a sprig of mint at the top and a long green bendy straw. "I just brought you my specialty."

Caroline wasn't sure what to make of the fact that Heather didn't even blink at her being dressed in a red, slinky evening gown now. "I actually like it both ways." She took the glass with a smile. "Thank you."

"I'd offer to let you drink it out on the front porch, but I'm thinking that you will attract some attention and it seemed that Zander was wanting to avoid that."

Caroline sighed. "Yes. It's safe to say that Officer Landry wasn't expecting to have to deal with me today and I might have thrown a wrench into some plans."

Heather laughed softly. "That's his job. To take care of things that are difficult. And he takes it very seriously. Don't let his attitude put you off. He wears exasperated instead of cologne."

Caroline grinned. "Really? He smelled pretty good to me."

Heather winked at her. "He's growly. But mostly that's because he really wishes everybody would just behave. He says it's because it would make his job easier, but it's mostly because he worries."

"He worries?"

"He knows everybody in this town. He's probably related to more than half somehow. The other half is made up of people he's gotten into trouble with, gotten into fights with, gotten drunk with, gotten into bed with or...people who are related to someone he's done one of those things with."

Both of Caroline's brows arched. "Wow."

"Taking care of us is really important to him."

Caroline took a short draw on her straw. She thought about that. "He does seem the protective type."

"Oh, he is that."

"And if he thought somebody was going to cause trouble for the town or some of the people, he would be even growlier."

"Absolutely."

Yeah. He was worried she was going to be a problem for his people. Great. "Well, I really don't plan to cause trouble for anybody."

"Does he know you need help?"

Caroline nodded.

"Then he'll be back."

"You think so?"

"Zander solves problems. Fixes things. Takes care of trouble. Badge or not. So yes, he'll be back."

"Then why did he just leave so suddenly? Why didn't he let me explain?"

Heather studied her for a long moment. "Must have been something he needed to figure out first."

"Like what?"

The older woman shrugged. "Maybe how much trouble you were going to *be* versus how much trouble you were *in*."

Caroline should possibly feel offended at that, but it was probably fair for him to wonder about her. Even if he didn't know who her father was. What kind of cop would see a woman walk into a bar with a lion cub, wearing a wedding dress, and not at least ask a few questions? Oh plus, she'd almost been kidnapped by her brother.

But she liked the idea that he might be looking into things more thoroughly right now and would be back over to question her later.

Maybe he'd been too distracted by the zing of whatever-that-had-been when he'd taken her face between his hands the way he had.

"So you guys don't like strangers coming to town?" Caroline asked Heather.

Heather motioned for Caroline to follow her as the other woman turned and started down the hallway that led from the foyer to the back of the house

"Oh, that's not the problem. Strangers come here all the time. Tourists are in and out every day. And lots of visitors of other kinds too. And we keep a lot of 'em." Heather laughed. "The Landry boys—one of Zander's brothers and a bunch of cousins—have fallen in love with girls who aren't from here. And some of *them* have brought friends who have stayed and become a part of the family."

"Me being a stranger isn't the red flag for him then," Caroline mused.

"No. More people in town just means more people to take care of. Once you're in Autre, until you leave, you're Zander's responsibility. At least that's how he sees it. Been that way ever since he was a teen. Saw personally a bunch of people he loved get hurt, lose people they loved, and he determined to do whatever he could to keep that from happening again."

"Wow, that's a lot for one guy to take on," Caroline said. She'd been right reading Zander as an intense guy, it seemed.

"It sure is. I'm not sayin' it's rational or healthy. But it's Zander. We just make sure to support and love him extra hard while he works to keep us all safe."

Caroline liked the way Heather said that so matter-of-factly. Like love and support were just a given here.

"So, anyway, no, I don't think his instincts are jumping because you're a stranger," Heather said.

Caroline took a seat on a stool at the breakfast bar across from the counter where Heather had clearly been in the midst of some kind of food preparation. Whatever was bubbling on the stove smelled amazing.

"But you think he is feeling jumpy?" Caroline asked,

curious about the way Heather had phrased her comment.

"Definitely." Heather added pasta to the pot and stirred.

"I really don't want to be a problem. And I don't intend to stay long."

"He'll probably be glad to hear that."

Well...ouch. "So if he's a cop and doesn't mind strangers and is into fixing things and will be glad I'm not sticking around, why would he think I'm a problem?" Caroline asked.

"Because he looked at you the way he looked at his new fishing rod his grandpa got him for Christmas."

Caroline just stared at Heather. She had no idea what that meant.

"And you looked right back at him. And he noticed."

"How did I look at him? I've never been fishing in my life."

"No, you looked at him like...he was a plate of my shrimp and crab mac-n-cheese."

That made no sense either. "I've never had your shrimp and crab mac-n-cheese," Caroline pointed out.

"Oh, you're right, I'm getting things out of order." Heather laughed. "We'll talk about how you looked at Zander *after* you've eaten dinner."

"And we're having..."

Heather grinned at her. "Shrimp and crab mac-n-cheese. And cinnamon crumb cake for dessert."

She *knew* she'd smelled cinnamon. Caroline laughed and her stomach growled at the same moment. She realized that Heather might just have a way of reading people. Because not only was she hungry, but she wouldn't be surprised at all to find out that she was looking at Zander Landry as if he was something very tempting that she'd like to put in her mouth.

She almost blushed at that thought.

Almost.

But she was too busy thinking about Zander putting his hands all over his new fishing rod.

5

Zander walked around the edge of the bed and breakfast to find Caroline on the back porch just as Heather had said she'd be.

But Heather hadn't warned him what he was going to find exactly. And some warning would have been really fucking nice.

Caroline Camille Holland was sitting in a rocking chair with her bare feet propped on the wooden railing that ran the length of the porch that wrapped around two sides of the enormous main house. She was sipping a tall glass of sweet tea with a bright green bendy straw and she looked the very epitome of laid back and relaxed.

But nothing was quite as straightforward and boring as that. Which was usual for Caroline, as he'd already learned in the short time he'd known her.

The cherry red evening gown she wore was slit on the side up to her hip and, because of the way she had her heels up and ankles crossed, the silky material had fallen away from two very long, smooth, toned legs, leaving them completely bare. Right up to where her panties would show. If she was wearing any.

There was no way she was wearing any.

She also had that damned tiara on her head.

It was sitting askew on her blond waves that fell loose and free around her face and shoulders. She looked a little... tousled. And sexy as fuck.

Torn between amusement, desire, and exasperation— because really, how hard was it to *stay inside* and just look normal?—Zander schooled his features and approached as if nothing was out of the ordinary at all.

"Evening, Ms. Holland."

She rolled her head to look at him and gave him a slow smile. "Well, she was right."

He climbed the back steps. "Who's that?"

"Heather. She said you'd be back."

"Did you doubt that?"

"Yes."

A simple answer to a simple question.

"I told you I'd be back."

"Did you?"

"I at least implied it."

She lifted a shoulder. "Well, a lot of people tell me a lot of things. And insinuate a lot of things. And *suggest* a lot of things. And most of it's bullshit."

He believed her. He knew the people who spent time close to her father. He didn't know how close *she* was to any of them. But he intended to find out. "Fair enough."

Zander knew that getting closer to this woman—physically or intellectually—was dangerous. But he didn't have a choice.

Steeling himself against his mind and body's tendency to respond to Caroline with things like *look at the way the sunlight makes her hair turn a burnished gold*—what the fuck did that even mean?—and his body basically just getting hard and hot, Zander dropped into the matching rocking chair to her left.

He didn't quite keep his eyes from scanning up and down

the length of her long, bare leg, but he did pull his gaze from the smooth skin to look into her eyes.

Which was no less impactful. Damn, was it the color? He just couldn't figure out what it was about looking this woman in the eye that always made him feel like he'd taken a shot of his grandpa's moonshine. The heat shot through his chest and burned all the way into his gut and made his head felt fuzzy instantly. No other booze did that fuzzy-head thing so fast. Leo's moonshine though? Definitely. No other woman did this to him either. But Caroline Holland? She mixed him up. He didn't like it.

"Did you look into my story about the endangered animals being bought and sold?" she asked.

"I looked into *you*," he told her truthfully.

"What did you find?" She actually smirked slightly as she took a draw on the green straw.

She knew he hadn't found anything. "That you're Charles Holland's only daughter. That you were engaged to be married to Brantley Anderson. That there's an APB out on you because you're transporting a stolen lion cub through the state of Louisiana with the intent to sell it."

Her feet dropped from the porch railing and she sat up straight, nearly spilling her tea. "*What*? I did *not* steal that cub! And I turned him over to a wildlife sanctuary! Brantley *gave* me that lion! He was a gift. So he's *mine*. And I, of course, don't *want* to own him. People should never own big cats! I had him in my possession exactly the amount of time it took me to get from the hotel to your grandma's bar!"

He waited for her to take a breath. When she finally did, and looked over at him, he said, "So that's how you ended up with him."

She opened her mouth, then snapped it shut. And glared at him. "You could have just asked." She sat back in the chair. Then, watching him, she lifted her feet back to the porch railing, letting the red silk slide over her leg and drop to the floor, baring a whole lot of smooth, creamy skin all over again.

Dammit. Zander tore his eyes away. "This was more fun."

"So there's no arrest warrant."

"No."

"Do you believe me? About how I got the lion?"

He thought about that. "I don't have a reason not to believe you. Yet."

She nodded, as if that answer didn't surprise her. "You think I might be trouble for your town, or the people here."

He leaned forward, resting his forearms on his thighs and studied her. He wondered how much he should tell her. Then he decided *what the hell?* There were plenty of guys that he'd said flat out, "Don't fuck with me or my people" to. Caroline might look like a refined, sophisticated woman, but he still wasn't going to let her mess with anybody. Including him.

"You're not going to be trouble for this town or anybody in it," he told her. "I won't let you be."

She lifted a brow, and took a long pull on her straw. After she swallowed, she said, "I was going to say that I don't want to be trouble for anybody, but that's not true."

Well, he very much appreciated open communication. "Who do you want to be trouble for?"

"Whoever's behind the animal buying and selling."

"The Andersons are involved with the animals?"

"Yes."

"Is that in the documents you have?"

She hesitated. "Yes."

Zander narrowed his eyes. "Caroline. What do you know?"

She sighed, took another drink of tea, then rested her head against the back of the chair. "Not enough."

"What's that mean?"

"I was planning to be engaged to him for at least another six months. I was hoping to stretch the whole engagement to a year. I know gathering this kind of information takes time and the slower I take it, the easier it is to get it all. But...I don't know what happened." She frowned off into the distance. "I don't know if someone got suspicious or what. Why did they decide to do a surprise wedding?"

"Because Brantley was madly in love and didn't want to chance losing you?"

Now see, *that* was the kind of shit that Spencer and Wyatt and Theo would never say. Because they didn't read romance novels. Spence and Wyatt were Landrys, so they had some of that romantic predisposition, but they would never *say that* out loud.

But Caroline just snorted softly. "Don't think so."

"Brantley isn't in love with you?"

She looked over. "Brantley thinks he is. He's had a crush on me since he was about twelve. But he would have waited. Long engagements are the norm in our circle. Gives everyone the chance to throw multiple parties and the bride-to-be gets to show off her ring and her doting fiancé and have at least three showers and fuss over everything from the flowers to the exact shade of the ribbons around the centerpieces at the reception." She rolled her eyes and tipped her head back again. "It's all ridiculous. But everyone revels in it. So, I figured I easily had nine months, if not twelve."

"You weren't eager to be married and start living your life of wedded bliss?" Zander asked dryly.

He recognized that being jealous of Brantley Anderson was the stupidest thing he'd ever felt. Feeling sparks with Caroline was dangerous, but not stupid. But being jealous of a man he'd never met, over a woman he'd never have—and didn't want— was stupid.

Caroline looked over again. "Oh, I never intended to marry him."

Zander frowned. "What?"

"The engagement was just my way to get closer to the family and get into the house more often. I was going to call the whole thing off as soon as I had the information I needed. Long before the wedding day."

Okay, he needed to focus here. She'd said something about information before. What the fuck was he doing?

It had to be the bare legs. And the fact that he was not only ninety-nine percent sure she wasn't wearing panties now that the dress had shifted again and he could see a whole lot of hip, but he was one hundred percent sure she didn't have a bra on. The dress dipped low in front and he'd seen no flashes of anything but silky skin. And yeah, he'd looked.

So what? He didn't like it, but it hadn't happened before and as far as he knew from Landry family lore and the fucking romance novels, he was a little bit powerless to resist *all* of this.

And yeah, her nipples were showing through the bodice of the dress.

"Look," she said. "I know you didn't ask for this. It's not like I came here to tell you all about it. But I don't really know who to tell about it. I was going to tell Max. I always tell Max everything. But I just feel like this is something a little bigger."

Well, who the fuck was Max? Zander sighed. So she wasn't in love with Brantley and was somehow just using her engagement to him to spy on his family. But now there was a Max? And she told him everything?

Yeah, Zander didn't like Max.

"Usually Max takes care of it. I turn the info over and that's it. But this is something that's happening *now* and needs to be stopped. The animals are being hurt and exploited and...I guess it was seeing one of them that really got to me. Usually I have some distance. And it's all business and politics and it doesn't bother me that it takes time to uncover it all. But this feels so much more immediate. Someone needs to *do* something. So when I got the cub, after

I recovered from my shock, I immediately thought of Donovan Foster because I'd seen the stuff online that he's been doing down here and that just recently they brought a rescued tiger here to take care of. And I thought, okay, so that's something I can actually *do*. And then you—" She looked over at Zander again. "You walked out of the bar with your badge and uniform looking all big and strong and confident and concerned and asked if you could help and...I just felt this *feeling*." She laughed softly. "I mean, obviously I felt a feeling. But I had this sense that I could tell you and trust you and just turn it over to you. And then Chris showed up and tried to take me back and you stepped in and I just knew that you were someone who would step in and do the right thing and help and—"

"Caroline."

Zander stopped her with that firm, simple use of her name.

She looked over at him.

"Take a breath," he ordered.

She did.

"We need to back up." He needed to know who Max was.

No, you don't. You need to focus on her, right now, right here, and then get her the hell out of this town.

She nodded. "You'll help me?"

The thing was, he would probably say yes to anyone in this situation. She'd landed in his town. The minute someone crossed the city limits into Autre, for however long they were there, Zander took responsibility.

If they were here to cause trouble, he was on their ass. But if they needed help, whether it was a flat tire, directions, transport, care because of heat exhaustion, or protection from some guys who were illegally buying and selling exotic animals, he was going to say yes.

Still, in that moment, with Caroline Holland's beautiful turquoise eyes on his, and that question hanging between them, Zander knew that she could ask him for *anything* and he would say yes.

Though that was information that he was going to keep very much to himself.

"I am going to help you. If I can do something directly, I will. If I need to pass this on to someone else, I will." Exotic animal transport and possession *was* outside his jurisdiction. But, of course, he knew people who would want and need to know about it. All about it. Everything Caroline could give them.

But now that he knew Caroline was mixed up in this somehow, if she needed to be extricated from it, he was going to be involved.

It was a truth that he didn't exactly welcome, but he accepted.

"I would very much like for you to not be sitting outside on the porch, though," he said. "Some of these people probably aren't exactly the nicest guys. Your own brother already came down looking for you and said that everyone was pissed. I'd really like to make sure that you stay safe. And sitting out here, looking gorgeous in a bright red evening gown with a tiara on your head is maybe not the best way to be inconspicuous."

She gave him a little, almost wobbly, smile. "You said gorgeous."

He shook his head. "That's a newsflash, that you're gorgeous?"

"It's news that you think so."

"Bullshit," he said, his voice gruffer than he'd intended.

"You changed your clothes too," she commented, her eyes moving over him.

He'd gone home and changed into a pair of jeans and a simple black t-shirt. He still had boots on his feet, but he always had boots on his feet. Boots were prepared-for-anything footwear. He was always prepared-for-anything. But these weren't his cop boots, these were his general kicking-around boots. Just like the gun he now carried was his personal firearm.

He nodded. "I'm technically off the clock."

"But you're still over here checking on me? I'm not something that could wait until eight o'clock tomorrow morning?"

Again, he thought about how to answer that. He felt like being too transparent with all the things that were swirling through him since this woman had come to town would be dangerous for some reason. But he ended up nodding. "Yeah. You seem like you're a twenty-four-seven kind of issue."

Her brow wrinkled between her eyebrows. "I don't really want to be an issue. But I guess that's one way to put it. I definitely need help and I don't know where else to go. I also don't really have the resources to go anywhere else. You saw me turn the lion over to the local wildlife expert so it seems like you are the most involved law enforcement officer."

"I am. And I'm going to coordinate this. You don't have to worry."

The smile she gave him was bright and beautiful, but it was the relief in it that really grabbed him in the chest.

Fuck. If she was playing him somehow, she was good.

She'd clearly convinced Brantley Anderson that she wanted to marry him. She'd convinced Zander that she was bold, lost and alone, and the sexiest woman he'd ever met as well.

But he had the craziest impression that she was, actually, all of the things she'd shown him today.

"Maybe you should put on some of the clothes I brought you," he said, his eyes again drifting to her legs.

He was a professional. He was also grumpy, stoic about his emotions, and absolutely determined not to get sucked into any kind of heart-eyes-warm-fuzzy-feelings for her. But covering up as much of her skin as possible wasn't a bad idea.

"You brought me something?"

"Yep. And I think they'll be the perfect fit."

Dammit. Why had he said that? Why did his tone sound flirtatious? Why could he feel the corner of his mouth tipping up in a cocky smirk?

She returned his little teasing smile that was full of flashback to the bedroom where she'd stripped so he could, literally, size her up.

His cock reacted.

Worse, his chest got a little warmer and tighter too.

Fuck.

"Let's find out." She held out a hand.

He reached for the cloth tote of clothes. Charlotte "Charlie" Landry was his cousin and the closest in body type to Caroline. Charlie was shorter and a touch curvier, but Caroline was taller than all of the girls and had fuller breasts and hips than petite Jill and slim-built Jordan. Paige was probably a close second. She had great curves too, but was also shorter than Caroline's five-seven or five-eight. He could have checked with Tori, Maddie, Juliet, or Kennedy too, but he'd known within a few seconds of seeing Caroline that Charlie was the best fit.

Yes, he was good at this. What could he say?

Though he'd kind of wished Jordan had been the best match, because the food at Jordan and Fletcher's place was the best to "borrow" as well. Still, the sandwich he'd pilfered from Charlie and Griffin's had been really good.

Caroline took the bag of clothes and something that looked a lot like mischief danced through her eyes.

Zander felt the resultant kick in his chest and tightening below his belt.

He didn't welcome mischief in his life. He wanted a lot less of it. At least in his head. But he did react to it.

He had caused and enjoyed plenty of mischief before he'd become a law enforcement officer, and the only reason he'd been called into this line of work was because his protective streak happened to be larger than his troublemaking streak.

He also believed that people who liked to cause trouble and were good at it were very good at recognizing *other* people who were the same.

And Caroline Holland was a troublemaker.

It just remained to be seen if it was good trouble or bad.

She dropped her heels from the porch railing and leaned over to set her drink on the porch floor, which caused one of the straps of her dress to slip off her shoulder.

Zander actually had to tighten his fist to keep from reaching over and sliding that strap back up. Slowly. While running his roughened fingertip over what was sure to be silky, smooth, pampered skin.

She looked up at him, then rose to her feet, unfolding gracefully like a cat.

She turned, presenting her back to him, and lifted her long hair with one hand. "Would you unzip me?"

Would he? Fuck yes.

Fuck no. Keep your damned hands to yourself.

"You get into that dress yourself?" he asked, cursing the rough note in his voice.

She looked over her shoulder. "I did. But I've only got one hand now." She wiggled the tote bag.

"Caroline," Zander said.

"Yeah?"

"You're pushing me again."

She grinned. "Just teasing."

"Testing."

She regarded him for a long moment. Then she dropped her hair and turned to face him, her smile gone. "Yeah."

"Why?"

"It's...instinct. It's what I do with men. Well, probably all people, but especially men."

"You flirt and tease them?"

"I try all kinds of things. You called me on it before," she said. "I try to figure out what will work best."

"To wrap them around your finger."

She seemed to think about his words for a long moment. "To get them to let me as close as possible. Sometimes the flirting is best, yes. But sometimes it's playing the damsel in distress. Sometimes it's playing the dumb blonde. Sometimes it's just trying to blend into the woodwork."

"Why?"

"So they say and do things around me that I can use against them."

He hadn't expected that, honestly. "You're trying to find things to use against me?"

She shook her head. "No. Like I said, it's instinct. I try different things to try to get a read on people when I first get to know them."

He gave her a long, steady look. Then said firmly, "Stop it."

She pressed her lips together, but nodded.

"I want to know that the things you say and do with me are honest. Or I won't be able to help you." He added that last sentence for himself as much as for her. He really just wanted to know that what she said and did, how she acted and reacted, were all genuine because he wanted to know her. He wanted to read her too. He wanted to be close to her and know that he affected her as much as she did him.

And that was dangerous as hell.

He needed to concentrate on the helping her part.

That was true as well. He couldn't help her if he didn't know that what she was telling him was legit.

"Got it." She nodded again. "Sorry."

"Change your clothes."

She stepped behind the rocking chairs, dropped the tote, and reached back for her zipper.

"*Inside*," he said, through partially gritted teeth when he realized she was about to strip on the porch.

"Why? Keep facing forward, Officer. This will take two seconds and we can keep talking."

Bold. Practical, even. See, that seemed true to her character as well. She was just going to change her clothes right out here in the open.

"There might be other people staying in the cabins," he commented. They were on the back porch, away from the road that, honestly didn't have much traffic anyway. But they were facing the huge flower garden and the large circle of six "bungalows", as Heather called them, that made up the rest of the bed and breakfast.

"Well, I'm sliding the shorts up under the skirt of the dress before I take it off," she said. "Then I'll pull the shirt on before I slide the straps of the dress down. And I'm behind your chair. They might catch a flash or two, but it's not going to be anything worth getting worked up about."

Really? Because he was feeling pretty fucking worked up just imagining it.

Do not ask her about panties and a bra. Do not ask. Don't you fucking ask.

A minute later, she stepped back in front of the rocking chairs, draped the red dress over the porch railing, set the diamond tiara on top of it, and leaned back against the railing as she reached up to gather her hair at the back of her head.

She watched him as she wove her hair into a thick, long braid and secured it with an elastic band she pulled out of seemingly nowhere. Zander had spent enough time around women, however, to know that elastic hair bands seemed to just appear when needed.

And, with her arms up, hands behind her head, wearing a soft, light gray t-shirt, it was *very* obvious—painfully so—that she was most definitely not wearing a bra.

Her nipples were hard points behind the soft cotton and Zander was having a hell of a time keeping his gaze on her face.

But damn, he really was pretty good at sizing up a woman's body and figuring out which size clothes she needed.

Unfortunately, he'd made a big mistake. Now Caroline Holland was dressed like a regular girl. And it turned out that made her seem even more approachable. And touchable.

Finally she finished with her hair and leaned over to pick up her iced tea. She dropped into the rocking chair again, propped her feet up on the porch railing, and gave a long, contented sigh.

Yeah, those long legs were as bare in the shorts as they had been in the evening gown. He wanted to run his palm from her ankle to her hip and see if he could elicit some goose bumps.

He gripped his fist tightly and shook himself. For fuck's sake. He was acting like he was a horny thirteen-year-old.

He'd just been out with someone last weekend. Or maybe it was the weekend before that. Or the one before that. He couldn't remember for sure. But it had been fairly recent. It wasn't like he was going without.

Fuck, maybe he needed to call someone tonight. He needed to get rid of these ridiculous primal urges where this woman was concerned.

In his work in Autre, he'd felt frustrated, exasperated, pissed off, and protective. But intrigued? No. Not in a very long time. If ever, really. But beyond intrigued, she made him feel like he needed to stay on his toes.

And then there was the temptation. Temptation he didn't need. Being a little challenged, having a mystery to solve, that might be a little fun he could admit. Certainly, coming to the rescue always fired him up. But tempted, to the point where he was having trouble focusing on the job? No. He didn't want that.

She looked over at him. "Now what?"

He worked on seeming nonchalant. "Now you start at the beginning. Who are you exactly? What do you do *exactly*? And why are you in my town getting me mixed up in your trouble?"

"I've been trying to tell you that since I got here."

"Well, now I'm ready to listen."

She huffed out a breath and Zander could only hope that she was feeling a touch of the exasperation he was feeling. If he was going to be all worked up whenever he was in her presence, she could feel a little bit too.

"Why don't you start with why your fiancé thought giving you a lion cub was going to be such a great wedding gift. If you're so offended by buying exotic animals, what made him think that that was the right thing to do?"

"Because he doesn't actually know me at all."

See, that right there was exactly the kind of thing he didn't want to be interested in.

But he definitely fucking was.

6

D *on't push me.*
    His words kept playing in Caroline's mind.

Zander Landry was dangerous. He was sharp and skeptical and he'd figured her out. And she'd confessed. Her usual tactics for getting men to let down their guard weren't going to work with him.

She might as well spill her guts.

The urge to do just that was crazily overwhelming. She just wanted to dump it all out there and have him say, "I'll take care of it."

She dropped her feet from the railing to the porch floor and pushed with her toe, starting the chair rocking.

"Brantley thought I would like a lion cub because I told him I wanted one. I was trying to get him to take me where they're keeping them."

"Where they're keeping them? Who's keeping them?"

"The people Brantley's working for. He and my brother are transporting the animals from the sellers to the buyers. I actually don't think Brantley has anything to do with getting the animals from wherever they're originally coming from. And he has nothing to do with setting up the sale. He's just the transporter. But still, I thought the more information I could get out of him, the closer Max could get to figuring out who was behind it."

"Who's Max?"

Zander's question was short and curt and Caroline glanced over at him. He was scowling at her. He almost seemed angry.

"Max is...the person I usually tell about this stuff."

"This stuff?"

Caroline stopped the chair rocking and sat forward. But that didn't quite give her the direct eye contact she wanted. She set her tea down, grasped the seat of the chair, jerked it around it so she was facing Zander more directly, then leaned in so her forearms rested on her thighs, mimicking his position.

"Yeah. Stuff like embezzlement. Like tax evasion. Like fucking underage girls." She watched his perfectly stoic gaze flicker at that. "The stuff I find out about the horrible people my family now hangs out with. Though the underage girl thing Max and I turned directly over the cops. Tax evasion and embezzlement takes a little more investigation and the public exposure is as bad for them as the legal implications. But the truly evil shit, like rape and animal abuse, we know can't wait around for headlines."

A muscle tensed along Zanders jaw. "Who the fuck is Max?"

"Max is the journalist that I give information to. That's where the big breaking stories in the newspapers come from. It's how Paul Dixon was brought down in the big embezzlement case three years ago. It's how the feds ended up raiding Arthur Taylor's mansion and offices last year. It's how Heath Connor ended up divorced and in jail because of his affair with his seventeen-year-old daughter's best friend."

"Max is a reporter?"

"Yes."

"How did you meet?"

Caroline studied Zander for a moment. It didn't matter who Max was, or how they'd met, for the story she was telling Zander. It was interesting that he wanted to know. She had the impression that it had to do with more than just what she was telling him. "We met in second grade in public school. Stayed friends even after my father inherited the shipping company and became an overnight multimillionaire and was pressured to put me into private school. Max has kept me grounded all these years. It started with my stories about how incredibly crazy, vain, greedy, and out of touch with reality my new circle of friends were clear back when we were in seventh grade. I was the new girl in school, had no idea which fork to use at the fancy dinner parties, couldn't have cared less about my wardrobe or going to their ridiculous, petty social events. But Max insisted I play the part and get as much dirt on these people as I could because the people I was in high school with would someday be CEOs of big companies and running for office. We joked that having documented secrets about them could pay off someday. It took me a while to realize that it wasn't actually a joke. But when I figured it out, it was...really awesome."

"What happened?" Zander asked.

He was listening and watching her intently.

"You really want to hear all of this?"

"I really do." His reply was simple. And resolute.

"Okay. Our senior year, I was at a party and I overheard two of the rich kids trying to talk our star running back into throwing the homecoming football game so they could win some bet. He didn't want to do it. He had a huge scholarship riding on his performance and a scout was going to be there. They told him if he didn't do it, they would plant drugs in his locker and make sure the coach found them before the game. His entire *season* would be over and he'd *never* get to play in college. I was furious that they thought they could manipulate someone like that and not even give a shit about hurting him. It was all just a stupid game to them. I told Max about it and we decided I should dig back through everything I'd been documenting about everyone. Sure enough, six months before, I'd overheard someone else talking about how one of those guys had slept with the other one's girlfriend. So, we told him if he didn't leave the football player alone, we were going to tell his friend and everyone else."

Zander's scowl deepened. "You confronted this asshole?"

"Well, Max did. With an anonymous text. Then a message on Instagram. Then a letter to his house. Then a glitter bomb to school. Then a singing telegram to the country club. Just so he knew that we knew, for sure, who he was and to keep reminding him in the days leading up to the football game."

Zander seemed unsure how to respond to that.

"Max was great at research even back then. We found him easily. These guys are always so full of themselves, they never worry about letting everyone know who and where they are, but it wouldn't have mattered. We would have gotten him eventually."

"Seems a singing telegram to the country club kind of spilled the whole story, didn't it? Why would he leave the football player alone after his secret was out?" Zander asked.

"Oh, it didn't tell the secret. It was just the chorus from that old song 'Somebody's Watching Me'."

For just a flicker of a moment, Caroline thought Zander was going to smile. He didn't. But the hint was there.

"So what happened?"

"The player had the game of his career, got the scholarship, was a huge star in college, even played in the NFL for a few seasons."

Zander gave a single nod. "And the assholes?"

Caroline sighed. "They became the CEOs of their daddies' big companies and one's a state senator."

"Damn," he murmured, his eyes on hers.

"Yeah. But..." She shrugged. "I still go to parties where those guys show up and I have even more dirt on them now. If they ever become more than the average spoiled, rich pricks, I can give something to Max."

"You think you're keeping them all in line?"

"No. But I'm doing *something*. I stay close. I collect info. And I turn it over if it's something that's going to end up hurting someone. Or *something*." She leaned in. "Like an animal. Or *animals*."

"So you still do this. The spying thing."

"I'm just accepting invitations to social engagements. It's not my fault if people think the pretty interior designer is too dumb to understand what they're talking about, or if they don't notice that I'm standing there, or if they don't lock their home office doors."

"You sneak into their offices and look at private papers?"

"They invite me into their homes, and I might happen to walk through unlocked doors once in awhile. These houses are huge. I can't be expected to remember where all the bathrooms and bedrooms are, Zander," she said, with a little eyeroll.

He rolled his right back. "And they've never caught on? Even when people have gone to prison for things that had to have been traced back to paperwork from inside the company."

"*Exactly.*" She gave him a little grin that she was sure seemed pleased with herself. Because she was. "The info *had* to come from *inside* the company, right? I'm not inside any of those companies. They've never suspected me. At all." She sat back with a shrug. "It's their own stupid egos that get them into trouble. Which is truly sweet justice. They think that everyone they socialize with somehow admires them or owes them or is intimidated by them and would never betray them. Or they think that a young woman would never have the brain or the balls to do it. Either way, they're wrong. And it's their downfall."

"You let them think you're dumb and docile," Zander summarized.

She nodded.

"Doesn't that get old?"

"Yep. About the time I showed up to a surprise birthday party and found a wedding dress and marriage license waiting."

"Right." He sat back in his chair. He was still watching her thoughtfully, his jaw tight and his eyes unreadable.

"I have two options now," she said. "One, I burn this bridge entirely, move in with Max, and do something with my criminal justice and pre-law degrees. Or, two, I figure out a great story about why I ran out, I go home and make up with everyone, and get back to work."

His scowl was back. "You have criminal justice and pre-law degrees?"

"Yes."

"Thought you were an interior designer."

"That's what everyone thinks. And they're happy to let me decorate their offices and homes."

"Your dad's friends give you jobs decorating their offices and houses?"

"Some of them are my mom's friends."

"If they're paying you for this, why don't you have any money?"

She smiled. "They don't pay me. They're...letting their friends' silly daughter play around. It's 'for my portfolio'," she said, using air quotes. "And everyone, my dad especially, considers it just a hobby."

"But you *don't* actually have a design degree so you can't be too offended."

She shrugged. "I'm making it work."

"Because that's one way you get into their private files and computers—" He held up a hand before she could respond. "You know what, never mind. I don't want to know."

"Thankfully, nepotism is alive and well," Caroline confirmed. "And poor, silly little Caroline needs all the help she can get."

"But you do have to actually redecorate their offices and homes, right? How do you pull that off when you don't have a design degree?"

"Seriously?" She gave a short laugh. "I can put any damned thing in these people's houses. All they care about is that it costs more than everyone else's. And if they're the first to have something, no matter how crazy or ugly, they're a trendsetter. It's the easiest fucking gig in the world."

She knew Zander heard the disdain in her tone. She wondered if he was surprised by the f-bomb though. The lift of his brow made her wonder what he was wondering about.

"Why'd you get the criminal justice and pre-law degrees?"

"It was what I was interested in."

Finally, he actually had a *reaction*. He didn't just sit there, watching her, clenching his jaw. He blew out a long breath, closed his eyes, and shook his head. "Of course you have a criminal justice and a pre-law degree."

Now *she* raised her brow. "Excuse me?"

He opened his eyes. "You need to stay out of the way of... whatever this is. Give me the information and I'll...look into it."

The pause there at the end made her narrow her eyes. "What does looking into it entail?"

"It means, tell me the rest of what you know. Or I'll walk off this porch and you're on your own."

Right. He had the power here. She was, literally, out of options for...anything...except what Zander Landry gave her. A place to stay. A ride to that place. Protection. Help.

Caroline sat back in her chair and crossed her arms. "Fine. Like

I said, Brantley and Chris are transporting the animals. They get a text from someone—I haven't been able to figure out who yet—and that person tells them where to meet. I was hoping that I was going to be able to get one of those incoming texts to Max to try to figure out where they were coming from. Or, that I was going to be able to talk Brantley into taking me along on one of the transports."

Again, Zander scowled. "You were going to go along? To God knows where, to meet up with God knows who, to do God knows what?"

"I just told you, no one is ever there. So it wouldn't be meeting up with anyone. But I thought..." She sighed. "I don't know. Brantley's an okay guy, but he's not the brightest bulb. And he doesn't care. Or pay attention. I thought there might be something about all of it that he was missing that I could catch."

"He's an okay guy?" Zander growled. "Really? The guy who's transporting animals to be sold to private dealers?"

She winced. "Yeah. Okay. He's...kind of an ass. But I think he's just..." This was going to sound bad. Like she was defending him. And she wasn't. Exactly.

"He's just what?" That muscle in Zander's jaw was ticking again.

"Bored."

Zander didn't respond to that. But she saw his hand curl into a tight fist.

"These rich guys do stupid shit all the time. They're pricks, I'll readily admit that. My brother's not much better. Things come too easily to them. They never really have any challenges. So they do really dumb stuff. They race motorcycles and cars. They gamble. They drink too much and mess with drugs. And they get involved with really stupid, shady stuff because it gives them a thrill."

Zander still said nothing.

"They're just—"

"I know exactly what they are, Caroline."

Zander's firm, flat tone stopped her.

"You...do?"

"I do. Tell me more about the animals."

She took a breath. "I know they've transported another lion. A cheetah. And some monkeys."

Zander just listened.

"The addresses change all the time. But they're always in Louisiana or Texas."

Zander sat forward at that. "Sometimes they're in Texas? So, they're taking them across state lines?"

She nodded. "I know that whoever they've been in touch with has asked them if they're willing to go into Alabama, Texas, even Oklahoma."

"Fuck," Zander muttered.

"Crossing state lines makes this a bigger deal, right?"

"Of course it does."

"So who do we call? Do you have contacts?"

"*We* don't call anyone. You're going to finish telling me everything you know. Then *I'll* figure this out."

It was essentially exactly what she'd been hoping he'd say. She'd wanted him to say that he'd just take over. But suddenly, Caroline didn't want to just dump it in Zander's lap.

She paused. What? Why? It wasn't because she didn't trust him. Even though it was clear that Zander didn't want to be involved with this. Why would he? This was hardly what he'd woken up this morning expecting to be doing with his day. Transporting exotic animals was illegal in Louisiana. Add *endangered* species to that and it was an even bigger deal. But if there were other states involved this became a much grander scheme. She knew that this was beyond what a small-town cop would be dealing with, but she sensed that Zander knew exactly what to do.

And she wanted to be a part of it.

That was it. It hit her suddenly. It wasn't because she didn't trust Zander to take care of it. It was because she really cared what happened and she wanted to be a part of this. A bigger part. Bigger than just turning over the tiny bit of information she had.

The other time she'd felt this way had been when she'd given Max information about Heath Conner having the affair with Molly Evans. The girl hadn't been physically hurt or even coerced, but she'd been underage, and Heath had been cheating, and everything about the situation had been wrong. Caroline had had no qualms turning that information over and had been thrilled when Max had told her it had all been immediately given to law enforcement.

But Caroline had felt a strange restlessness. Once the information had gone to Max, Caroline had been out of the loop. She'd felt good about her part in the whole thing. Especially when Heath had been arrested, but there had been a part of her that had wanted to do more, to be more directly involved. The embezzlement and tax evasion and other business schemes that she'd uncovered and turned over hadn't been the same. The affair had been directly hurting other people. People she knew. She knew Molly as well as Heath's wife, Laura, and his two daughters, Steph and Stacy. She'd known the people he was hurting personally. And even if she hadn't, knowing there were direct human victims was different than understanding a multilayered business scheme.

It was the same here. There were animals being directly terrorized, abused, and exploited by what was going on. She had direct knowledge of this. She wanted to put a stop to it and she was aware in that moment with Zander that she was not going to be satisfied just turning the information over. She wanted to see the animals rescued and justice done firsthand.

"That's what I know. That's why I wanted our engagement to go on longer. I didn't want to actually marry him, but I wanted to stay close enough that I could overhear phone conversations, see text messages, see any paperwork or emails that came through. And maybe even work up to the point where he trusted me enough to tell me something more or take me with him."

"Well, thankfully it never got to that point."

She frowned. "I appreciate your concern, but it's unnecessary."

"Is it? I understand that you're trying to do the right thing here, but trying to talk the man you were tricking into marrying you—"

"I only tricked him into being *engaged* to me," Caroline corrected.

"Trying to convince the man you *tricked* into having a close, *intimate* relationship to take you along on a criminal interaction isn't smart."

Caroline noticed the way Zander said *intimate* and couldn't help but wonder what that was about.

"Well, Brantley was my most direct way of getting the most information as quickly as possible."

"Let me see what I can dig up from what you told me."

"It might not be much. Max has tried."

"Well, no offense to your superstar journalist best friend, but I might have a few more resources."

"You *might*," Caroline muttered.

The lift of Zander's brow told her that he'd heard her clearly.

"If you think of anything else that you didn't tell me tonight, let me know." Zander stretched to his feet. He reached into the front pocket of his blue jeans.

It was really unfair that he looked so good in blue jeans. She'd really liked the way he looked in his uniform, but the blue jeans and casual shirt did nothing to diminish her attraction to him.

89

The man was not only extremely good-looking, but his confidence and sternness did something to her. She was used to being around spoiled, rich playboys. Guys who didn't take much seriously and who always got their way. Guys who threw around their money, reputations, last names, and privilege and who very seldom, if ever, looked thoughtful about anything.

"Here." He held something out to her. "This should give you a few options."

Caroline rose and held out her hand. Zander placed a stack of bills in her palm.

Caroline knew her eyes were wide as she looked up at him. "What's this?"

"I'm buying some of your jewelry."

"Excuse me?"

"I can't give you what they're worth, but no one else is going to either. This will get you a plane ticket, rent money for a couple months. Some new clothes." His mouth actually tipped up at the corner.

Caroline felt the flip in her stomach in response. "You're giving me money to run away?"

"I'm giving you that option at least."

Caroline felt her throat tighten. He didn't approve of her family and friends, or probably how she'd been conducting herself with her social circle, and he certainly hadn't planned on having her on his list of issues today, but he wasn't just doing the minimum here. He was not just giving her cab money to get back to New Orleans. He was actually giving her an escape.

She hadn't counted it, but she'd guess she was holding at least five thousand dollars. She doubted that five grand cash was easy for a small-town cop to come up with in a couple hours' time. He'd called in favors or raided a stash somewhere or borrowed it from someone. She wondered if he'd told that person what, or who, it was for.

She swallowed hard and looked up at him. "And you're just giving me this money?"

"Like I said, I'm taking some of the jewelry in exchange."

"And you're going to go to the pawnshop with it," she guessed.

He nodded. "I'll have better luck getting a good price than you will."

She had no doubt of that.

"This is really sweet of you."

"I just..." He stopped and blew out a breath. He tucked his hands into his back pockets. "I really need you out of my town."

Caroline blinked at him. Oh, okay. Ouch. But she got it. She'd come to town, stirred things up, and definitely brought at least the hint of trouble. Heather had told her that Zander didn't like that. He was protective of the people in this town. Caroline might not be a direct threat, but she knew bad people. One who had sent someone after her and might again.

She just really didn't want to leave.

Yes, it was because she wanted to know what was going to happen with rescuing these animals. But it was also because she felt safe here.

The only other place she would consider going was to be with Max.

She really had nowhere else *to* go that she wouldn't be alone.

She really didn't want to be alone.

She should probably be stronger and more independent than that, but she wasn't. She could admit that.

Besides, Max was coming *here*. Eventually. After the story in Texas was finished. Caroline was going to stick around long enough for her friend to get a read on the situation as well.

Max always knew what to do. If Max thought Zander was handling this correctly and that everything would be fine, Caroline would leave. Maybe then she'd go back to Max's apartment, buy some new clothes—her mouth curled slightly as well—and lie low for a while.

She looked up at Zander. Was she going to see him again? She wasn't sure. Just because Max was coming to Autre in a couple of days, didn't mean that *her* path would cross with the hot cop's again. So she took a step closer to him, put a hand on his chest, stretched up, and pressed a kiss to his cheek.

She felt his entire body tense and the sharp intake of breath near her ear.

When she leaned back, she looked up into his eyes.

Now they were readable. They were stormy, filled with heat and enough desire that she actually felt the electricity zipping along her nerve endings.

Whoa.

She wet her lips, and Zander's gaze dropped to her mouth.

Whoa, doubled.

She swallowed. "Thanks," she managed. "For everything."

"You need to leave. Tomorrow." His voice was gruff.

And in that flicker of a moment, she understood.

The longer she stayed, the more he'd want her to stay.

Because she was feeling the same thing.

"I can call you when I get where I'm going so you know that I'm—"

He took a huge step back. "No." He shoved a hand through his hair. "No, you don't need to call."

If it hadn't been for that little moment of awareness between them, her self-esteem would be lying on the porch of Autre's bed and breakfast in tiny shattered pieces.

But she'd seen it. He wanted her. He didn't want to want her. But he did. And he was fighting it very hard.

And he was afraid it was a losing battle.

Which not only kept her girly ego intact, but actually pumped it up just a little.

"Okay, no calls," she agreed.

"No. Call if you have trouble. If you need anything," he said quickly.

Right. Don't call just to say hi or to tell him where she was if she was fine. But if she needed him, he'd be there.

Dammit. Her ego wasn't the only thing that liked all of that. A lot.

Don't push me, echoed in her mind though and she decided not to poke at him with a *when you say anything, do orgasms count?*

Instead she said, "Hey, do you want to take my wedding dress along with the jewelry?"

"I definitely don't want your wedding dress."

"Guess I'll just keep it then. Maybe I'll need it—"

"I'll burn it tomorrow," he said. "No problem."

Her eyes widened. As did her smile. Gotcha.

She nodded. "That's all I needed to know."

Zander held her gaze for just another second and she wondered if he'd figured out what she just figured out.

He hated her wedding dress because he liked *her*.

But he turned on his heel and stomped across the porch and down the steps before he said anything more.

As he disappeared around the corner of the house, Caroline returned to her rocking chair and picked up the best sweet tea she'd ever had in her life. She propped her feet back up on the railing of the porch and took a long draw on the green bendy straw, feeling the strangest sense of satisfaction and contentment. Especially considering her life was a big fucking mess right now.

She just couldn't help thinking that perhaps this day had turned out very well after all.

7

W hy had he only picked shorts when he'd gone through Charlie's clothes for stuff for Caroline to borrow?

Sure, Louisiana was sweltering in July, but he really should've thought through the fact that Caroline Holland dressed in short denim shorts would be a bad idea. If not for his own sanity and ability to sleep at night, then for the traffic hazard she would create were she to, for example, decide to walk down one of the main streets of Autre in a pair of those short denim shorts.

He sighed. He was on his way to the bed and breakfast to see if she needed a ride back to New Orleans. Whether she was going home or to catch an airplane or whatever, he didn't care. Or so he told himself. But he was willing to offer her transportation to get her outside of the parish borders where he felt responsible for her.

He pulled up nearly on the back bumper of Hank Bast and flashed his lights.

Hank stuck his hand out his driver's side window and waved for Zander to pass him.

Yeah, that wasn't happening. Hank was driving fifteen miles

an hour in a thirty mile-an-hour speed zone and while, technically, it wasn't illegal, the fact that he was doing it to ogle the blonde who was walking along the shoulder was a problem. Maybe not for cop Zander, but certainly for man Zander.

Zander leaned out his window and yelled, "Move along, Hank!"

Hank just gave him a thumbs up.

With an even heavier sigh Zander grabbed his cell phone and dialed Hank's number.

He picked up a moment later. "Hey, Zander."

"She's too young for you. And too good for you. And you're blocking my way. Move."

"This is what's wrong with you youngsters," Hank said with a chuckle. "Always in such a hurry, you miss a lot of the beauty in the world."

Yeah, Zander wasn't missing a bit of the beauty of Caroline Holland. It was irritating as fuck.

"Seriously, Hank. It's creepy."

"Yeah, yeah, fine." Hank hung up on him. But then stepped on his gas pedal and drove on past Caroline.

Then, realizing that he might come off just as creepy as Hank, Zander pulled up next to her and rolled down his passenger side window.

"So the part about leaving tomorrow—which is now today —didn't really register?"

She looked over at him with a smile as she continued to walk and he rolled along beside her.

"Is there anyone currently being booked into any prison system for the illegal transport, buying, or selling of exotic animals in Louisiana?"

"Not that I'm aware of."

"So also no one is specifically being booked in connection with the lion cub I brought yesterday?"

"No."

"Then no, I'm good here."

"You're going to stay until we arrest someone for the lion?" That was *not* going to be good for his sleep. Or for the people around him when he was sleep deprived.

"I'm going to stay until I'm satisfied with the results of your efforts."

Well, that was vague as fuck.

Probably on purpose.

He watched her walk for a few more steps. "Where you headed?"

"To get coffee."

"I'm quite certain that the bed and breakfast offers coffee as part of your stay. Want me to talk to the management?"

"Oh, I had a cup of Heather's coffee this morning and it was delicious. But—and I'm sure this will shock you—I like my coffee a little more..."

"High maintenance?"

She shot him a grin. "I was going to say interesting."

"Potato. Potahto."

She actually laughed at that. And Zander had to fight a smile.

"Where exactly do you think you're going to get this froofy coffee?"

"I was going to head downtown and find your local coffee shop."

"We don't have a local coffee shop."

She stopped and faced the truck, a hand on her hip. "There's no place for people to get coffee in this town besides the gas station or their own homes?"

"Nope," he lied.

"Your grandma's restaurant doesn't serve coffee?"

Dammit. "Well, she sure as hell doesn't serve coffee with any kind of caramel syrup or nutmeg or whipped cream."

"Huh. Maybe I'll chat with her about adding a cappuccino

machine. It could increase her morning bottom-line substantially. Especially with all the tourists."

As much as Zander would enjoy watching Ellie shoot Ms. I-Always-Get-My-Way Holland down, the last thing Zander wanted was Caroline in his grandma's bar. Because Ellie would enjoy getting to know this woman, as would the other dozen or so family members who would be there.

He did not need for them to find out about her ex-fiancé and brother dealing in illegal animals, or her brother trying to kidnap her, or her father's various, questionable business practices or how Caroline spied on, stole from, and lied to nearly everyone she knew.

Almost worse, it would only take them about five minutes to realize how charming and funny and smart she was. And to invite her to the next crawfish boil. Which she would, of course, say yes to because his damned family was just as charming and funny as she was.

And, of course, at some point someone would definitely mention that Charlie had a cappuccino machine—along with caramel syrup, nutmeg, and whipped cream—in the office she shared with Jordan in the education center at the Boys the Bayou Gone Wild Animal Park.

Charlie and Jordan would love Caroline. Hell, they'd probably get Fiona on a Zoom call and would be planning a middle-of-the-night sting operation to take down the animal buyers and sellers themselves before they finished their first caramel macchiatos.

He really had no other choice here.

He stopped the truck. "Get in."

She turned toward the truck, and planted her hands on her hips. "Excuse me?"

"You need froofy coffee and I need you to not walk around town causing traffic accidents." He didn't include the part about not getting to know his family. "I'll take you over to the next town. They have a coffee shop that'll make whatever you want."

She was clearly surprised, but a second later gave him a bright smile. "That is the nicest thing that you have said to me since we've met."

"I think I've actually been quite nice to you."

She climbed up onto his passenger seat. "Oh, no doubt. But you taking me for froofy coffee, when that is clearly absolutely the last thing you want to do right now, is awesome."

"Well, I hope you brought some of that money I gave you last night. You're paying."

She laughed and pulled a hundred dollar bill out of the front pocket of the shorts.

And again, Zander had to hide a smile.

They drove to the main highway that led out of Autre and he turned east. After about two miles, Caroline pivoted on her seat and tucked a foot underneath her.

"You should sit straight."

"My seatbelt's on."

"Seatbelts work better when you're sittin' right."

"Yeah, Heather mentioned that you were super protective. That even extends to people you've just met?"

"I'm a law enforcement officer. I appreciate safety laws."

"You're cop in the town where you grew up. Where your family still lives. I'm guessing they have some interesting stories about you when you were a kid. Have you always been buttoned up or do you have some wild times in your history that you'd rather people not know about?"

"You don't need to be asking my family for stories about me."

"Is this one of those towns where everyone knows everyone? I wouldn't have to technically ask family, right?"

"You don't need to know stories about me."

"You know a lot about me, I think I should get to know about you."

Zander looked over at her. He stoically avoided looking at her legs and met her gaze instead. Not that her face was any less tempting. She had her hair pulled back in a ponytail and very little if any makeup on. Interestingly without all of the stuff around her eyes and what had to have been fake eyelashes last night, her blue eyes were even brighter and more stunning.

Fucking hell.

"We're not going to be friends. There's no reason for you to know my history."

She sighed. "Fine, then tell me some stories about someone else."

"What makes you think there any interesting stories here?"

"There are interesting stories everywhere, Zander. I know very well that the sweeter and more idyllic something looks, the more chances there are layers and layers of intrigue. Remember I come from a world where people spend lots of time, energy, and money covering things up. The prettier something is, the greater the chance it's working really hard to cover something up."

He glanced over at her. *"You're* very pretty."

She tipped her head. "Thanks." Then she nodded. "And I lie to my family on a daily basis, spy on them, and expose their friends' secrets whenever possible. Plus, there's a very high likelihood that I'm driving a car, wearing clothes, living in a house, and even eating food that was paid for with money that was... obtained by nefarious means."

"Your father has never been implicated in any crimes."

She nodded. "Well, so far so good. It *is* fair to say, though, that the money isn't exactly earned by my father's hard work and skill." She paused. "I mean, I suppose a case could be made that my father earns the money by overseeing the company, making deals, and managing what goes on. But the people doing the *actual* work are far removed from him and they're certainly not paid anywhere near what he puts in the bank. And, obviously, none of what I spend is earned by *my* own hard work and skill."

Zander frowned. There was a bitter edge to her tone and he couldn't help but ask, "It bothers you that you're not making any of your own money?"

"Of course it does. I'm twenty-six. And I'm completely dependent on my father for everything."

"You could change that."

"Yeah. You'd think. I mean, I've been staying where I am because I think that there's a purpose for it. But this is the first time I've been aware that my life isn't really my own. I feel like I'm choosing to be there, but am I? And what I'm contributing to the world at large is questionable."

Wow. He really should just turn the truck toward New Orleans. What would she do? Now that she was in his vehicle, she couldn't really stop him from taking her home.

But now there was no way in hell he was going to make her go back to all of that.

Jesus.

They were quiet for nearly a minute. Then she said, "So tell me what you do. Do you feel like you're serving a greater purpose? Are you fulfilled by your work?" She asked it with a tone that indicated she expected him to say no.

So he nodded. "Very."

"There's a lot of crime to fight in Autre, Louisiana?" she asked.

"Well, like you said, the prettier and more idyllic something looks, the more chances there are layers underneath."

She turned a little further in her seat, suddenly looking very interested. "Really? There's a dark underbelly to Autre?"

"No. Because I'm here. With a few friends. But if we weren't, yeah, there could be a darkness."

"So the charm isn't fake?"

"No. But that's what makes me even more determined to keep it in place. There are people who would love to use the real charm to cover up a bunch of dark shit. I won't let that happen."

"Tell me more." She leaned to prop her elbow on the middle console and rested her chin on her hand. "Seriously. You can tell me. I don't know anybody here." She laughed. "And I'm amazing at keeping secrets. Like, my whole life is a bunch of secrets."

"Why do you care?"

"Honestly? Okay. This will probably sound bad, but it's because it actually makes me feel a little more normal. It's not that I want bad things to happen everywhere, but the idea that they do, kind of makes me feel a little better. I feel like I'm surrounded by it. I feel like I'm constantly having to be vigilant about who's doing what bad thing today and I'm suspicious of everyone I cross paths with if they have anything to do with my family. It's a terrible way to live, frankly, and knowing that my family isn't some kind of unique magnet for horrible, awful people and behavior is my morbid way of feeling like maybe my life isn't so strange."

"Oh, trust me, Caroline, your life is pretty strange."

She laughed. "I know that. And like I said I don't actually want bad things to be happening everywhere. That's a terrible reality." She paused. "Honestly, I want to hear your stories because you're succeeding."

"Succeeding?"

"Yeah, you said you're fighting to keep Autre charming and safe and happy and that it's working. That's what I want to hear about. I want to hear that there are good people out there fighting these fights and winning."

And just like that, Zander decided he was going to spill his guts to this woman.

Dammit. He wished he could blame it on her blue eyes. Or the shorts. But he knew it was more than that. He *was* fighting the fight and they were winning, at least mostly, for now, and telling her about it in that moment, seemed like a good idea. He wasn't sure if it was to make her feel better or to make himself feel good. Or maybe both.

"Okay, let's get our coffee and then I'll tell you."

They pulled up in front of the coffee shop in Bad, the next town up the bayou from Autre. Bad, Louisiana was nothing if not quirky. The original German name for the town—something long and hard to pronounce and including B-A-D in it—had been shortened over a hundred years ago to simply Bad and the town now leaned into the name. The hair salon was *Bad Hair Day*, the bar was *Bad Brews,* and *Bad Habit* was the quaint little coffee shop that was painted a sunny yellow and had white wooden shutters and a white wooden front porch.

Over the years people had tried to make Autre and Bad rivals, and they certainly had been in things like high school football and baseball, but when it came right down to it, the two towns got along and Carter, the cop in Bad, happened to be one of Zander's good friends.

Zander also really happened to like this coffee shop.

They went inside and placed their orders. Zander's regular —which made Caroline smirk, both because he had a regular order that the barista knew automatically and because it involved cinnamon dolce syrup, heavy cream, and a dusting of cinnamon over the whipped cream on top—and her concoction with at least four ingredients that he wouldn't have been able to repeat if he had to. But he steered her back out to the truck once they had their cups in hand, rather than to one of the tables or booths.

He had to work today and couldn't spend all morning sitting in the coffee shop in the next town telling Caroline all of his deepest, darkest secrets.

Even if he wanted to.

Still, as they drove back to Autre, sipping their drinks, he told her far more than he'd ever told anyone.

"Little over two years ago, Theo was out patrolling the bayou," Zander started when they were about a mile out of Bad.

"Who's Theo?" Caroline interrupted.

"One of our game wardens. My best friend since we were kids."

"Okay, got it." She lifted her cup and seemed to settle into his truck seat.

"He found a cabin deep on the bayou, that had been abandoned for years, was suddenly occupied. Along with the one half a mile to the north and another one a quarter mile east."

"And that's weird?"

"A little. Those aren't vacation homes. The only way to get out there is by airboat. There are no roads. Gettin' supplies out there isn't easy. There's no cell service out there. People who live or even stay out there to hunt and fish have to know how to rough it."

She nodded. "Okay."

"So Theo kept his eye on things. He had to be sure they weren't hunting or trapping without licenses or violating any environmental regulations. Having a bunch of guys suddenly show up in abandoned cabins is just worth looking into."

"Agreed." Caroline sipped again, clearly intent to just listen.

"Over the next couple of weeks, he noticed that boats kept showing up with supplies. But not fishing and camping equipment. Tech equipment. Computers and stuff. Plus lots of guns and ammo."

"Wow."

"Yep. So he asked some questions. And took some photos. Of course, the guys wouldn't say much and he didn't have a warrant to search the cabins so he didn't get inside, but he passed the photos and info he had on to Spencer."

"Who's Spencer?"

"FBI agent. My cousin. The one I've been in touch with about the lion."

"Okay. And he found something?"

Zander nodded. "Two of the guys are regulars on message boards that the FBI watches."

Her eyes were round when he glanced over again. "Um...wow."

"Yeah." He sighed. "They haven't *done* anything, but we're keeping a very close eye on them. And when a few of them started venturing into town, talking to people about making really good money by helping them out with machine parts and transportation and contract work—welding, and electrical work, and stuff—we told them that they were not welcome in Autre."

"You and Theo and Spencer?"

"And Michael and Wyatt."

"Who are they?"

"Michael's our fire chief and chief paramedic. Autre boy all his life. Wyatt is Spencer's brother. Coast Guard. Their grandparents were from Autre, so they know and love the town."

"You made it clear that you're protecting Autre as law enforcement officers?"

"No. As men who weren't going to let anything happen in or to our town."

"And your brothers and cousins, they all feel the same way, right? You have a huge number of people to protect Autre."

"No," he said quickly, and firmly. "Just Michael, Theo, Spencer, and Wyatt."

"Your brothers don't know? And your other cousins? Isn't one of your cousins the mayor?"

Yeah, clearly Heather had filled Caroline in on his family tree over dinner last night.

"Yes, the mayor of Autre is my cousin. But no, she doesn't know about this."

"Shouldn't she?"

"She would be the first one to get on an airboat and head out there to kick their asses," Zander said.

"But seriously—"

"I'm being serious. My family is very protective of this town too. They're all strong and stubborn and fiercely loyal. They would want to run these guys off."

"So why not let them in on all of this? The more people the better right? I'd love to have a bunch of people on my side helping me with my stuff."

"It's not that easy. One of my brothers is a third-grade teacher. One does construction. My cousins run a swamp boat tour company. Others are veterinarians and lawyers and TV stars and..." Zander ran a hand through his hair. "Kennedy and her husband run a foundation that's working to save the coast-line of Louisiana. They're involved in politics and have the ear of people who can get important things done. Fletcher teaches little kids to read and about science and about being kind. He's literally helping make good future citizens. My cousin, Charlie, has taken the little otter exhibit and, with the help of everyone else, has turned it into a sanctuary for abused and endangered animals."

He blew out a breath, feeling the familiar tightness in his chest that was a weird mix of pride and anxiety. "They drive me crazy. But they are amazing people doing amazing things and I can't risk them getting hurt or even losing sleep or spending their energy or time worrying about some assholes camping out on the bayou. That's *my* job. That's what *I* can do. I can keep that shit away from them so they can do the great stuff they do to actually make the world a better place."

There was no sound but the tires on the pavement for several seconds. Then she said. "Got it."

"Do you?" he asked, glancing over. He sincerely wanted to know if she understood.

He and the guys wore their badges proudly and believed in what they stood for. But sometimes, it came down to him just being a guy who was willing to do whatever it took to keep his family, friends, and town safe. He didn't work with kids or animals or the environment, but he sure as hell could keep the people safe who did.

"Of course. I've been living a double life for almost a decade in an attempt to keep my family safe from the threats I perceive around them."

He thought about that. What she'd been doing seemed very different than what he did, but she had a point.

"Did it work? I mean, do those guys leave Autre alone?" she asked after a moment.

"They don't come into Autre. They don't try to recruit or do business here. That we know of, anyway. But it's possible they got smarter. Or sneakier. Or both. And they still use those cabins. They're several miles out, but they're still way too fucking close for my liking," he admitted.

"But you're keeping them at bay."

He nodded. "For now."

"That's big."

"It's what you're doing, right?" he asked. "Your dad and brother haven't been directly implicated in any crimes. No matter how close stuff gets to them, it's never affected them directly."

She sighed. "Yeah. I mean, that or they're *really* good at covering."

"Which do you think it is?"

"I think they're staying just this side of that line," she said after a moment. "But I hate how close they get."

"I understand that."

They both sipped, lost in their thoughts.

"Anything else?" she asked. "Other bad things happening in your sweet little town?"

"There are the usual things. There was a guy who was abusing his dog. We took care of that. There's a guy who was hitting his wife. Took care of that. Bar fights. Couple guys with some addiction issues we help out when things get bad."

"You help them out?"

"Make sure we're checking on them. Make sure they're eating. Make sure they don't have any weapons around. Make sure they know they've got people who care. Sit with them. Talk if they want to."

She was staring when he glanced over. "What kind of addiction issues?"

"One's an alcoholic. One's addicted to pain killers."

"And you just...let them get drunk and high or what?"

"Sometimes. We just make sure they're not driving or messing with guns or getting into things with anyone else." He blew out a breath. "One's a vet. He's got bad PTSD. He deals with it. Goes to therapy. Has a therapy dog. But he struggles and some days he loses the battle. So, we're just there when that happens. The other one lost his kid to cancer and his wife left. He really tries. He's been to treatment twice. But again, some days are just too much and the best we can do is just be there until he's through it. Make sure he doesn't hurt himself or someone else."

He was actually keeping a closer eye on Lionel "Sharp" Sharpton. He was a local guy, about thirty-eight. Zander was afraid he was getting mixed up with the guys who'd taken over the bayou cabins. Guys like that preyed on the desperate and Sharp definitely fit that description.

Caroline was quiet for a long time. Zander looked over. She finally just said, "Wow."

"Bad things happen everywhere, princess. To good people who don't deserve it often."

She nodded.

"The guys I work with most—Michael, Spence, Wyatt, and Theo—all lost someone in a big explosion that happened here in Autre when we were teens. My cousins, Sawyer, Josh, and Owen, lost their friend and business partner, Tommy, to a bull shark attack on the bayou. A lot of people have been through a lot of bad shit. And they still turn out to be good humans who want to help others and have happy lives. I want to help them do that."

"So you work to make Autre as safe and happy as you can. For them."

"Yep."

Neither of them said anything else until the sign for Autre came into view. Zander didn't know what she thought of all of that and it didn't really matter. It was all just what it was.

"Well, you missed otter yoga," he said dryly as they pulled up to the stop sign at the corner where he needed to make a decision about where they were going. "Should I drop you back at the bed and breakfast?" He knew her answer would be no.

The smile she shot him told him that she knew that he knew her answer would be no.

"You know what I'd really like to do? I'd love to go see the lion cub."

Now see? That was sweet. He liked that she was actually concerned about the animal beyond just wanting it out of her possession because it was illegal or wanting to get her not-beloved-ex-fiancé into trouble.

"Donovan should be around somewhere. I can get a hold of him and have him fill you in on how it's doing."

"That would be really nice."

He sighed. "I guess I'll take you up to the petting zoo. You can check out some of the other animals."

"Yes, I'd love that."

He was not, however, going to drop her at the barn where the goats, potbellied pigs, and alpacas—along with various other furry and feathered creatures—were. She would, for sure run into Jordan and Charlie there and he wasn't quite ready for that.

Instead, he took her to the enclosures where the red pandas and sloths were housed. Those were far more fascinating than the goats and potbellied pigs anyway. And along with the red pandas and sloths were a collection of peacocks, a few porcupines, and if she continued up the path, she'd find their flock of flamingos as well as the colony of penguins. In fact, she could walk this entire loop and visit their camels, donkeys, and zebra as well as their tiger.

Out here it was also a little less crowded with Landrys. She might run into Jill, the primary caregiver for the penguins, but Jill was far less chatty than Jordan or Charlie. He also had no trouble with Caroline spending some time with Donovan and likely Naomi. They were not blood or marriage related to the Landrys. Though they were family in all the ways that counted. Still, Naomi was very respectful of other people's privacy and Donovan didn't know nearly as many family stories as the girls at the main barn would.

Zander pulled up next to the sloth enclosure and pointed. "I'll have Donovan meet you by the sloths."

"Oh my gosh! I see these guys online." Her eyes were bright, her smile wide.

"Well, have fun," Zander said honestly. The animal park had been kind of a pain in the ass for him. It brought a lot of strangers to town. But it made his family happy. Not to mention making them additional revenue. And now looking at Caroline's face, he definitely felt a little more tolerant toward the whole thing. Dammit. This was what the stupid falling-head-over-heels-in-love-at-first-sight would do to a guy.

Resisting the urge to lean across her and shove her out of the truck, Zander said, "Have fun."

"Are the penguins around here?" she asked, looking like a little kid on Christmas morning.

"Right up there. Just follow the path." He pointed through the windshield.

"Oh my gosh, this is so exciting." She pushed her door open and looked back. "You sure you can't come with me?"

He wanted to. He freaking wanted to walk around the petting zoo that he saw every damned day and that gave him a huge headache most of those days. "No. I gotta go to work."

"Well then, thanks for the coffee. And the ride. And for spilling all your secrets. They made me feel better. In a really macabre way that I should probably apologize for."

"Caroline, get out of my truck." *Before I kiss you.* He did not add that part, of course, but he had the strangest impression she knew what he was thinking.

"Okay, see ya, Zander."

She slid off the seat, slammed the door shut, and he watched her walk toward the sloth enclosure.

He had a feeling that she *was* going to see him. And that that was an even worse idea now than it had been last night.

And last night it had been a very, very bad idea.

Caroline had only been at the sloth enclosure for about five minutes marveling at the quirky, interesting animals when she heard someone approaching. She turned expecting to see Donovan Foster. Instead, it was a beautiful woman with long, dark hair, carrying a baby on her hip.

"Good morning," the woman greeted.

"Hi. I'm Caroline. I'm just waiting for Donovan."

"Yes, I remember you from yesterday. The wedding dress and lion cub in the bar."

"Yep, that was me," Caroline said with a wince.

The woman laughed. "I'm Tori Landry. I'm one of the vets here and my husband is part owner in the swamp boat tour company. And this is our daughter, Ella."

Caroline smiled at them both. "It's nice to meet you."

"Thanks. I see you've met Slothcrates and Slothparilla." Tori came closer. "I'm here to do a little checkup. Do you mind?" She started to hand the baby to Caroline, and Caroline reached out instinctively.

Ella gave her a big grin and a little, "Hi" as Caroline took her into her arms.

"Well, hi, sweetie."

Tori laughed. "This kid has been passed around more than any child, probably in the history of the world. There's absolutely no stranger danger on her radar. But considering that she's never more than two feet away from a relative around here, I'm not too worried at this point."

"She's adorable."

Tori gave her daughter a smile that was full of pride, love, and a touch of awe. "Thanks. I'm madly in love with her if you want to know the truth."

"I think that's exactly how you're supposed to feel," Caroline told her.

Tori ran a hand over Ella's head, then turned toward the sloths. "Well, let's see if we can help Slothparilla get used to this mom thing too."

"Her name is Slothparilla?" Caroline asked, grinning.

"Yep. Sarsparilla is a climbing vine that's found in the rainforest in South America, among other places." Tori laughed. "So it has a lot in common with sloths."

Caroline moved closer to the enclosure as Tori opened the door and stepped inside. Both sloths looked toward her, blinking slowly. She talked quietly to them as she approached and reached out to stroke first one, then the other.

"What's that?" Caroline asked as Tori withdrew what looked to be a small teddy bear.

Tori held up the stuffed animal. "Slothparilla is pregnant. Sloths take about four months to gestate and she is right about two months now. We're going to have her hang onto this little baby sloth so she gets used to the weight and sensation of it on her body, as well as having us moving around and handling it so we can more easily care for the live baby once it's born without causing her stress."

The little stuffed animal was indeed a sloth rather than a bear. "That's so cute. Is that the size the baby sloth will be?"

"Yes, almost exactly and it weighs about eight ounces which is what a newborn sloth should weigh." Tori reached over and gently laid the stuffed animal on the belly of the female sloth as she hung from the branch. "Baby sloths are born with full fur and their eyes open and the ability to climb from the very first minute. They cling to their mothers for the first few months and they actually stay with their mothers for the first year or two before moving off on their own but usually only to a nearby tree."

Tori repositioned the stuffed sloth and stroked her hand over Slothparilla a few times. "You're going to be a good mom, aren't you, sweetie?"

Caroline watched the interaction, completely enchanted. "It's amazing that in this tiny town in Louisiana you get to work with sloths."

"Oh, believe me, I think about that every day. I came here from Iowa. I used to work with horses and cows and dogs. I came down here and we went from fairly normal things like alpacas and goats to having a family of otters and then Charlie showed up and suddenly we have red pandas and sloths and peacocks and penguins." Tori shook her head, laughing. "It's amazing and I already felt lucky living here, but adding in all of these animals is like a dream come true."

Caroline watched her, and then looked down at the baby in her arms. She thought about what Zander had told her about how bad things even happened to good people in nice places like Autre. She thought about how close the mysterious guys in the bayou cabins had come to Autre and how determined Zander was to protect the town and the people here. Tori was a Landry. So was baby Ella. They were part of his family, and his life included them and all of these animals and this amazing little petting zoo that was actually a haven for abused animals behind the cute sloths and endangered penguins. She completely understood why he felt protective.

"Well, I can't wait to see *all* the animals and see what all you do here," Caroline said as Tori came out of the enclosure and shut the gate behind her. "I've been watching the animal park grow online."

Tori grinned. "It's been amazing. Thankfully we've grown with people just as much as we have animals. I don't know how we would possibly be doing this without everybody on board. It's truly a family project and that makes it all so much better and even more meaningful."

"Hello, ladies!"

They turned to find Donovan coming up the path toward them. Ella immediately starting pumping her legs and reached out her arms, opening and closing her fists as he came closer. "D! D!"

"Ella Bella!" Donovan took the happy baby and brought her up to his face for a big wet kiss on her cheek. She squealed happily and kissed his cheek in return.

Tori laughed and rolled her eyes. "She's got every single man in this town wrapped around her finger."

"You're a motherfucker!"

Tori winced as Caroline spun around at the voice that had just come from behind her.

"Shut the fuck up!"

"Except for the swearing parrots," Tori said.

"You have swearing parrots?" Caroline asked. Stupidly. Obviously the voices were parrots and she spotted them immediately. The brightly colored birds were now perched between the sloth enclosure and the lemur enclosure next door.

"We do," Donovan said, settling Ella on his hip. "But they're only naughty with new people. They test to see if they'll get a laugh. If they do, they'll keep going. If not, they stop. They like the attention."

"Are you worried Ella's going to pick that language up?" Caroline asked, trying not to laugh and egg the birds on

Tori lifted a shoulder. "If she doesn't hear it from the birds, she'll hear it from her uncles down on the swamp boats. Or at Ellie's." She grinned. "Either way, I intend to blame it on the birds when my mother hears it for the first time."

Caroline laughed and the first parrot repeated, "You're a motherfucker!"

"Shut the fuck up!" the second responded.

Donovan rolled his eyes. "Zander said that you were interested in seeing the lion."

"I'd love to, if that's okay?" Caroline asked.

"It's more than okay. I'm gonna need some help naming him and thought you'd be the perfect person to consult."

Caroline felt a little flip in her stomach. "Really?"

It was so easy to get caught up in all of the good vibes and excitement and craziness around here.

"Of course." Just then a phone started ringing.

Donovan groaned, and Tori laughed as she reached for Ella.

"But first, Donovan needs to deal with the Goat Phone," Tori said.

Caroline frowned. "The what phone?"

Donovan pulled a phone from his pocket. The phone case had an up-close photo of a goat's face on it.

"The Goat Phone," Tori said. "We have a herd of goats at the petting zoo that gets out on a regular basis. Our border collie, Benny, rounds them up and herds them but she hasn't quite figured out how to herd them back to the *barnyard*. She'll just herd them into the nearest building or structure. It's now become a game around town. When you see the goats, you mark the location on your Goat BINGO card. When you get BINGO, you bring the card into Ellie's for free fried pickles."

"Oh my God. That's...hilarious," Caroline said, still trying to process it all.

"Except for the guy who carries the Goat Phone and has to go up and actually retrieve the goats from wherever they are." Donovan lifted the phone to his ear. "Yeah."

He listened for a moment, frowned, and started laughing. "Yeah, I'll be right there." He disconnected. "Well, this is a new one."

Tori gave a little groan. "That's never a good phrase around here."

"Oh, this is pretty great. Caroline, how would you feel about making a stop with me on the way to see our lion cub? We just need to swing by and pick up a unicorn."

Caroline looked at him, then at Tori, then back at him. "A *unicorn*? You're not serious, right?"

Donovan laughed. "It's Autre. Never ask that question."

8

Zander wasn't sleeping well.

That wasn't unusual. Being a worrier made deep, peaceful sleep hard to come by many nights. Being a secret keeper in a family that kept no secrets and had no filters added another layer of guilt and pressure that often made sleeping deeply even more difficult. So fully relaxing anywhere other than in his fishing boat out on the bayou alone was unusual.

But with Caroline Holland in town, and just a few blocks away, Zander had found it completely impossible to not lie awake for hours every one of the past four nights.

He was annoyed that she was *still* in town.

He was annoyed that he'd actually made almost no progress on the issue of the lion cub that was keeping her in town.

He was annoyed by the case that was keeping Spencer too busy to come down and give him a hand.

And he was especially annoyed by the regular Caroline reports he'd been getting from everyone. Every day. All day. They made it impossible to forget, even for an hour, that she was in town.

She'd not only helped Donovan name the lion cub,—

Mwanzo, which apparently meant "new beginnings" in Swahili —she'd also helped him retrieve an escaped pony that had been dressed up like a unicorn for a birthday party. Then she'd put on her horrible-huge-gaudy-what-the-hell wedding dress and tiara, of course, and pretended to be the princess who owned the unicorn to bring it back to the party. Charlie and Jordan would *not* shut up about how amazing that was.

She'd also attended two otter yoga classes with Paige, been out on a swamp boat tour with Maddie, and had, of course, eaten and drank at Ellie's several times. So, basically, she'd completely charmed his entire family.

Which meant he was avoiding Ellie's.

Even if she wasn't there, everyone who *was* there at any given time—including Ellie herself, who was *always* there— couldn't wait to tell him all about Caroline and what she'd been up to. So not only was he annoyed and sleepless, he was also pretty hungry. He was definitely gumbo-deprived. He could fend for himself when needed, but his gumbo sucked.

It seemed clear from the gossip, however, that while Caroline had learned a few stories about him after all—mostly from Jordan and Naomi, who had grown up with him and his brothers—she hadn't spilled much about herself other than the fact that she'd decided she couldn't marry her fiancé and had bolted in a panic.

He appreciated that his family and friends had no idea that her family rubbed elbows with white collar criminals or that she was actually hanging out in Autre because she was insisting he investigate alleged crimes against animals. That alone would have riled up his animal-loving family.

He'd even thanked her for that when he'd brought her coffee from Bad Habit Sunday morning.

He hadn't done that to be *nice*. Or to start his day with one of her smiles. Or because showing up as yoga was ending just happened to coincide with seeing her stretching in yoga pants.

He'd done it, both Sunday morning and today, to keep from having to put up with her chattering, and long legs, and blue eyes in the cab of his truck for the trip to Bad.

Yeah, so she'd discovered the cappuccino/espresso machine in Charlie and Jordan's office mere hours after he'd dropped her off at the sloth enclosure. Still, he'd had to touch base with her, didn't he? He was obligated to ask if her brother or fiancé had tried to contact her. Or if she needed a ride to the airport to use the five grand she now had on a ticket to somewhere far away. Or if she had plans to *ever* leave his town. And his life.

She'd simply asked if he had plans to *ever* put anyone in jail for ripping a baby lion away from his mother or to help free the other animals that were being bought and sold as playthings and trophies for rich, entitled assholes who didn't care about anything or anyone but themselves.

Since he was waiting on Spencer to get his ass to Autre and actually help him with that very issue he'd simply sighed and walked back to his truck.

Which was *all* why he wasn't sleeping tonight. Again.

Which was why he was upright on the edge of his bed with his phone to his ear before it even rang a second time.

"Zander."

"It's Beau."

Zander's heart slammed against his rib cage. It wasn't completely uncommon for Beau Hebert to call him. It was, however, fully out of the ordinary for him to hear from Beau at two a.m.

"What?" Zander was already on his feet and pulling the blue jeans he'd kicked toward the chair in the corner of his bedroom up over the boxers he slept in.

"There's someone here who wants to talk to Caroline."

A sharp coldness swept through Zander. "Where is she?"

"Upstairs. Asleep as far as I know. He didn't get that far."

"Who is he?" Zander swore if it was her brother again, this time he was going to punch the guy.

Hell, he was going to punch whoever it was. It was two a.m. No one was there to see Caroline for a friendly chat.

He yanked a t-shirt over his head, shoved a hand through his hair, and started for the stairs.

"Says he's her fiancé."

Zander paused halfway down the steps. Brantley Anderson was in town? Interesting.

Honestly, Zander hadn't expected the rich, playboy asshole to come after Caroline himself. He didn't get the impression that this was a deep, abiding love affair between two soulmates.

No shit, she's your soulmate.

Zander shoved that voice very firmly to the back of his mind. The last thing he fucking needed right now was his own subconscious talking about what Caroline meant to *him*.

Zander continued down the stairs. Brantley Anderson just seemed like the type of guy to have other people do the hard things. And surely coming to Autre, Louisiana in the middle of the night to convince his runaway bride to come home would seem hard.

If it didn't seem hard, it would mean that Brantley thought he had a compelling argument, or a tantalizing bribe, or enough force to get Caroline to come back with him easily.

The idea of Brantley forcing Caroline to leave Autre had Zander's gut clenching and he grabbed his boots from beside the front door and stomped out across his front porch, down the steps, and across his yard to his truck without even putting them on. He threw the boots onto the front seat and climbed in and started the engine.

"I'm on my way now. Where do you have him?"

"We're in my kitchen."

Zander liked that. Beau lived in the first cottage behind the bed and breakfast. That meant Brantley was not inside the main house causing a commotion that Heather or Crystal would get involved with or that Caroline might come down to investigate.

"You okay for a few minutes?"

"Oh, we're fine." Beau said it confidently and Zander had to wonder if there was rope, a shotgun, or Beau's dog Bear involved. Or all three.

He wasn't worried about Beau. Beau was built big, wide, and tough. He was a bayou boy. He hunted gators and played football and could absolutely hold his own with any of the other bayou boys. Which meant that handling a pampered millionaire from New Orleans should be a piece of cake.

Still, Zander found himself speeding through the sleepy streets of Autre, glad that Brantley had decided to sneak down when everyone else was tucked in bed.

He pulled up alongside the B & B and stomped around the side of the house, still without boots.

He let himself in through Beau's front door.

Beau and Brantley—it was indeed Brantley Austin Anderson sitting at the handmade kitchen table—both looked over.

Brantley wasn't tied up, but Bear was sitting next to Beau between Brantley and the front door. And Beau apparently hadn't needed a shotgun to convince Brantley to sit still and wait for local law enforcement.

Brantley did have a bleeding lip though.

It wasn't enough.

Zander was shocked by how badly he wanted to hit the man and make him bleed more.

And he was not happy about it.

He wasn't into getting worked up over women or jealousy. He also wasn't into hitting first and asking questions later.

So he'd ask a couple questions first.

"How'd you find her?"

"So you know who I am," Brantley said.

"Of course."

Brantley looked him up and down. "You're the cop?"

Zander glanced at Beau. Apparently, Hebert had told Brantley he was calling the cops. "I am."

"You're the one that kept her from coming home with Christopher."

Zander braced his feet apart and crossed his arms. "I'm the one who kept him from taking a woman against her will."

Brantley rolled his eyes. "Whatever."

"How did you find her?" Zander repeated.

He swore to God that whoever had told Brantley that Caroline was staying here was going to have a pissed off Landry, out of uniform, breathing down his or her neck.

There was an unspoken rule in Autre. Zander got answers. Sometimes they were official, and in those cases he wore his uniform to do the questioning. If he showed up without his badge, people knew whatever they talked about was off the record.

Sometimes that was good for them. If they wanted him to know about something that wouldn't be officially investigated or wouldn't necessarily lead to their own entanglement with the law.

Sometimes, it wasn't so good for them. Because that meant Zander didn't necessarily have to operate within the confines of the badge either.

He took his oath to his badge seriously. He'd become a law enforcement officer because he believed in what they did. But he was first and foremost an Autre boy. A Landry. He would use whatever resources and tools he had to keep Autre and the people here safe. Usually it was best with his uniform and badge. But not always.

"I tracked her down," Brantley said with a shrug. "That's all you need to know."

"That's not all I need to know. I need to know exactly how you found that she was staying in this location."

"I have my ways."

"You're pissing me off, Anderson. You really want to do that?"

"Are you threatening me?"

"Are you refusing to answer questions from law enforcement? If you have nothing to hide, that's pretty stupid."

"Why is law enforcement questioning me?" Brantley returned. "Am I being investigated for something? Am I under arrest?"

Zander looked at Beau. "Was he trying to break in?"

"I got to him before he did anything like that," Beau said. He narrowed his eyes at Brantley. "Maybe unfortunately." He looked back to Zander. "He tripped over some stuff on the back porch and I heard him. I don't think he'd even gotten as far as the door."

Zander focused on Brantley again. "You're trespassing on private property. That's a start. Then there's the lion cub you gave her."

Brantley's gaze wavered. "My fiancée is here. I'm concerned about her. We were supposed to get *married* a few days ago. I'm here to check on her."

"You didn't talk to her brother? The one who came down to 'check' on her before, and who she told to leave her alone?"

"Well, obviously I have a different relationship with her than she does with her brother," Brantley said with a slimy smile. "What kind of guy would I be if I didn't come down and see if she was okay?"

"At two a.m.? Four days later?"

"I've been trying to call her. And we were all thinking that she'd come to her senses and come back. I guess I finally got tired of waiting."

Zander felt rage sweep through him.

He would've been concerned about anyone who had someone stalking them in the middle of the night, of course, but the idea that someone was coming after Caroline, while she was sleeping and completely vulnerable, in the place where *he'd* put her to keep her safe, made his blood boil.

When he protected someone, he fucking protected them.

He wanted to lock Brantley up so he knew exactly where the asshole was and what he was doing at all moments.

"Maybe we should go downtown."

"Maybe you should back off," Brantley said. "I haven't done anything wrong."

"Owning a lion in Louisiana is illegal."

"I don't know what you're talking about."

This was how they were going to play this? "She said you gave it to her."

Brantley scoffed. "I gave her a lion cub? On our wedding day? Why would I do that?"

"Because you're mixed up in a ring that's illegally buying and selling them to private owners."

"Wow, that's quite a story. Do you have any proof? Other than my estranged fiancée's word?"

Fuck.

Brantley was a prick.

But he also wasn't wrong. Zander didn't have any proof.

And he also wasn't objective where Caroline was concerned. Dammit.

He didn't think Caroline was lying to him. He knew Brantley was doing exactly what she said he was. But he couldn't prove it. Yet.

And that "yet" promised to be a huge, giant pain in his ass.

Brantley paused. "Yeah, I didn't think so." He sat back in his chair. "You know, my lawyer would have a really good time with police harassment from a small-town cop." He put his wrists together and extended them toward Zander. "But by all means, cuff me. Drag me downtown."

Zander just stared him down. Trespassing was the worst he had on the guy right now. Stalking or harassing Caroline would even be tough to make stick. After all, Caroline had been engaged to the guy. And Zander definitely didn't want a bunch of high paid lawyers descending upon the town. The mayor would not be happy with that. Even if she was his cousin. Hell, the lawyers would have a really good time with *that* too, he was sure.

"You need to leave town. You're not going to see Caroline."

"I just want to talk to her."

"I'll give her a message. Tomorrow. If she wants to call you, I'm sure she has your number."

"What if I don't hear from her?"

"Then you'll just have to move on, man. There are plenty of fish in the sea," Zander said dryly.

Brantley sat, just staring at him through narrowed eyes. After nearly a minute, he must have realized Zander wasn't budging. "I'll make a deal with you. I'll leave tonight if *you* make the call while you're with her. That way, I know she's still here, and you can make her talk to me."

"No."

Brantley finally had the sense to look annoyed. It meant he was getting the fact that he wasn't going to win here. "You don't know what's going on," Brantley told him. "This is none of your business."

"It became my business when a woman came to my town and asked me for help getting away from her fiancé. Not to mention when a guy showed up and tried to physically stuff her in a car."

"Christopher could've handled that better," Brantley said, clearly trying to placate Zander now. "But this is personal. A family matter. Caroline got upset with me about something.

But couples have problems sometimes. I can't just let her disappear without speaking to her and never see her again."

"Actually, you can. If that's what she wants."

"Why do you care so much?" Brantley asked him. He narrowed his eyes, studying, Zander from the few feet that separated them. Then, it seemed understanding dawned. "*Oh. Yeah, she's pretty, huh?*"

Fuck.

If fucking Brantley Anderson could guess Zander had feelings for Caroline, his grandmother was going to sense his I've-got-a-soulmate-itis from a block away.

"Actually, caring about other human beings is something some of us just do," Zander said, putting his don't-fuck-with-me face on.

"Sure. Okay. Well, the thing is, Caroline has something of mine. If we're breaking up, I need to get it back."

"You want the engagement ring back?"

"Actually, no."

"Tell me what it is, I'll see if I can help."

"No way," Brantley said. "Thanks anyway. But I can promise you that if she gets it back to me, I'll leave her alone."

"You were going to marry her for whatever this is?" Zander asked.

"I was gonna marry her because my dad wanted me to."

"Wow, how manly," Beau muttered.

Brantley gave him a bored look. "Banging a hot, rich chick for the rest of my life? Yeah, poor me."

"Oh, sorry, manly *and* romantic," Beau said.

Brantley laughed. "Have you met Caroline? She's awesome. I've known her my whole life. She's funny and sweet and yeah, hot. Sue me for wanting to fuck my fiancée."

Zander was across the space between them with Brantley's shirt in his fist and his chair tipped back on two legs in a split second.

"She's not your fiancée anymore," he growled.

Brantley stared up at him. Then he said, "Yeah, she's just another human you care about, right?"

"Get the fuck out of my town."

"Have her call me."

"She will no longer be staying here in the bed and breakfast. Pass the word."

"Have. Her. Call. Me," Brantley repeated.

Zander stared down at the man. Clearly, Brantley wasn't here for Caroline. Not exactly. But Zander wanted to make it very clear that Caroline was no longer an option. For phone calls, visits, or walking down the aisle.

"You're dealing with me now."

"If I get what I want, I can handle that."

Zander let go of him, the chair thunking back to the floor. Brantley straightened the front of his shirt.

"Leave." Zander told him shortly.

Brantley stood and Zander backed up only enough to let the man pass.

"I'll expect a phone call tomorrow," Brantley told him.

"You'll hear from me when it's time."

"Look, I don't have a lot of that. Time."

"The more you enlighten me, the more help I might be able to be."

"I might believe that, except for the shiny badge you normally wear."

"That badge can be helpful."

"Not with this. A five-minute conversation with Caroline and I can be gone from her life for good."

Zander wasn't naïve enough to believe that. Not that Brantley would hang around and try to get her back. That was not the vibe he was getting at all. But their families were obviously close and Brantley wasn't the type to really move on with his life. He was going to be living off mom and dad as long as that gravy train was on the tracks.

Of course, Caroline was the wild-card here. What were her plans? He'd given her the option to truly run away. Was she going to take it? Once he solved this lion problem? If so, where would she go? Would she cut herself off completely from her family?

No matter who her family was, and how she felt about them, that was a big ask.

And, in spite of himself, in spite of his self-awareness and better judgment, Zander felt the getting involved reaching out and wrapping around him. Yes, he'd given her money. And obviously, the woman had some moxie. But even if she could run away and start over, would she? All alone? Would she be okay if she did that?

Suddenly he needed to know that. And know that she would be safe. In spite of the fact that he told her no phone calls.

First things first, he had to make sure she was safe and away from her old life. If she really wanted to be. And if she didn't want to be, he needed to know that.

He wasn't going to spend time delving into *why* he needed to know that.

He'd chalk it up to general frustration over people being unable to break bad cycles and get away from toxic situations. He saw it all the time as a cop. It was human nature to go with the familiar and comfortable, even if it was painful and toxic.

He would not think about the fact that if Caroline didn't leave her old life, it would mean she'd probably end up Mrs. Brantley Anderson at some point.

He really was going to burn that wedding dress if nothing else. She'd have to get a new one if she reconsidered walked down the aisle with Brantley.

"You'll hear from me," Zander finally told Brantley. He

wasn't willing to give the other man more than that. He wasn't really *able* to give the other man more than that. He needed to talk to Caroline. He needed to figure out if she knew what she had that Brantley needed. He needed to figure out what *her* plan was. And yeah, at some point he was probably going to have to think about what he hoped her plan was.

"Fine. But even if you move Caroline and I can't find her, I know where to find *you.*"

"Are you threatening an officer of the law, Mr. Anderson?"

"No. I'm threatening the man who's hiding my fiancée from me."

"I might worry more about that if I thought you really gave a shit about your fiancée."

Brantley shrugged. "Like I said, she's pretty."

Zander's hand clenched into a fist and he took a step toward Brantley but the man was smart enough to immediately head for the door.

Zander waited until he heard Brantley's car start and pull out of the drive. Then he swung back to look at Beau. "Thanks for the call."

Beau was watching him with interest. "Of course."

"I'm taking Caroline to my place. You're the only one who knows that. I expect it to stay that way."

"No problem. Though, do you think that's a good idea?"

"It's the only place I can keep her safe."

"That's absolutely not true and you know it," Beau said. "You're willing to wake her up in the middle of the night and drag her across town?"

"Yeah, I am. I could stay here, make sure that no one else comes back for her, but that puts your mom and Crystal, you, and any other guests in the way of anything they might do."

"Anderson doesn't exactly strike me as a bloodthirsty criminal. He just wants something Caroline has. Maybe you should let him talk to her."

"No. He's never talking to her. And this is the second person who's come after her since she's been in Autre. Maybe he's not bloodthirsty, but we don't know who's coming next."

"What makes you think anyone else is coming?"

"I think her dad might actually care about her." He hoped so. And that annoyed him. He shouldn't care about the woman's family dynamic after knowing her for only a few days. "Charles Holland inherited his shipping company. The previous owner, James Horner, didn't have any children and took a huge liking to Charles. He became Horner's right-hand man quickly and Horner trusted Charles with everything. When the old man got cancer, he put Charles in charge of the whole company. It was an unprecedented move in such a huge company with so many assets. But the old man hung on like three years and was able to train Charles and introduce him to all the important people. Charles stepped right into his shoes the day the old man died."

Zander shook his head. He remembered hearing the story before. Horner had even agreed to change the name to Holland Shipping before he passed.

"Ever since then, Charles Holland has been one of the most powerful businessmen, not to mention richest, in Louisiana," Zander said. "Probably the entire South. He's never been directly linked to any criminal activity, but plenty of his associates have. So he's either lucky, smart, or has actually maintained a little of his moral compass. Still, the crowd around him is full of people who have been prosecuted for things and plenty more that has just been whispered about for years. Brantley might not want Caroline and maybe she does just have some little trinket that he wants back, but I can't imagine that their fathers are fine with her just walking out on this wedding. It's gotta be embarrassing at least."

"So you're suspicious?"

"Always."

"Or are you..."

"Don't say it."

"Someone has to ask it," Beau said with a grin. "Let me say it."

Beau was related to Zander's cousins, Josh, Sawyer, and Kennedy on their mother's side. Hannah was Heather's older sister. Technically Beau and Zander were really nothing more than friends, but they were tied together by family. In a town the size of Autre, everyone who was a friend felt more like family anyway, but they did have family members in common, which, as far as Zander was concerned, basically made Beau a cousin.

"Fine." Zander braced himself.

"Are you suspicious, concerned, or just jealous?"

Zander blew out a breath. "Why can't I be all three?"

Beau chuckled. "As long as you're good with it."

"I wouldn't say that." Zander glanced toward the door. "Can you let me into the house?"

"Sure." Beau shoved his chair back from the table and stood. Bear came off his haunches, clearly ready to go with his master.

They followed the path to the back porch and Beau unlocked the door that would lead into the kitchen. It was the farthest from any bedrooms, including Heather's and Crystal's.

"Thanks, man," Zander said quietly, shaking Beau's hand. "I appreciate everything tonight."

"Any time."

"Keep an eye out for anything else. I think Anderson will spread the word that Caroline won't be here and definitely won't be alone, but just in case."

"I think I'm gonna let Bear sleep out on my front porch the rest of the night," Beau said. The dog's ears perked up. "He'll let me know if anyone else drives in."

Zander patted the dog's head. "Good plan."

Zander crossed through the kitchen and crept up the back

stairs to the second floor. He approached Caroline's room carefully. He didn't want to startle her or put himself in the path of any fists that might come flying in his direction. At least he hoped that the woman had enough self-preservation to swing at anyone who came into her room in the middle of the night unexpectedly.

If she didn't, he was going to have to give her some self-defense lessons. He opened the door quietly and waited.

There wasn't a sound from the other side. He peeked in. He could see her head on the pillow, and the muted light from the streetlamp outside the window illuminated the lower half of her face.

He slipped into the room, closed the door quietly behind him, and crossed to the bed.

Of course she was gorgeous sleeping. She looked soft and vulnerable and very, very touchable. Then again, he'd thought a lot about touching her when she'd been wide awake too.

And all of that was pretty creepy, considering she was completely unaware he was even here.

His gaze drifted from her face down her neck to her bare shoulder that was crossed with a simple pale blue spaghetti strap, then started to travel down her arm. But then it hit him...

Bare shoulder. Spaghetti strap.

Of course, because his luck was what it was, he realized belatedly that he hadn't included any pajamas when he'd brought her clothes to borrow.

Which meant she was sleeping in some of the lingerie that had been packed for her.

Thankfully it wasn't one of the teddies or corsets. But the pale blue silk camisole was still tiny. She was, thank God, covered with the sheet so he couldn't see the matching panties. But he remembered them from when she'd tossed them on the duvet a few days ago.

His body heated and hardened and he averted his eyes and took a deep breath.

This had just gone from pretty creepy to creepy as fuck.

He really should just camp out on the floor in front of her door. Then he wouldn't have to wake her up. Or look at her dressed this way. But it still would mean Brantley and anyone else that might come looking for her would potentially put other people in jeopardy.

In the back of his mind, he knew that the chances of that were small. He didn't judge Brantley or even Caroline's brother Christopher to be hardened criminals. He didn't think they would get violent with anyone other than maybe him and even then, it would likely be provoked by him swinging first.

He also recognized in another tiny part of his brain that he was making up excuses to stay close to her.

Yes, as Beau had said, there was some suspicion and concern, but there was also attraction. Those three combined made it so that he felt the need to stay close to her. He wasn't going to worry about which of those three things was the strongest.

It was the middle of the night and Caroline was a stranger in town. Whether she was the one *in* trouble or the one potentially causing the trouble didn't really matter. For the time being, keeping Caroline Holland in sight and reach seemed the best course of action.

Zander knelt next to the bed and reached to brush her hair back from her face. Not because he wanted to touch her, but because it seemed the nicest way to wake her up gently.

That was his story and he was sticking to it.

"Caroline," he said softly.

She gave a little sigh and wiggled slightly but did not open her eyes.

"Caroline," he said a little louder, again brushing his hand over her cheek. "Wake up. It's Zander."

Her mouth curved into a smile. But her eyes stayed shut. "Zander," she said sleepily.

Well, that was a nice reaction. Whether she was fully conscious—which he doubted—or not, at least she wasn't freaking out.

"Wake up, Caro, I need to take you to my house."

She moved her cheek against the pillow and took a little breath in and out. "Okay."

Still, her eyes were shut, and Zander doubted she was actually awake.

"Come on, belle, need to wake up."

Her eyes fluttered then and slowly opened. He was kneeling so they were face-to-face. She frowned slightly. "Zander?"

"Yeah. It's me. I need you to wake up and talk to me."

He liked the fact that she recognized him so easily. He also liked the fact that she'd been sleeping so peacefully. He'd brought her to the bed and breakfast to keep her safe, but he loved the idea that she was comfortable enough here that she'd been able to fully relax. Now he felt bad about waking her up.

Well, maybe he didn't need to wake her *fully*. "Will you come with me?" he asked softly.

She nodded, her cheek brushing the pillow again.

"I'll just carry you out to the truck and take you to my place for tonight, okay?" Zander clarified. "Just you and me. We'll come back here tomorrow. Your stuff can stay here." In the light of day, with more people awake and around—and with his cousin Spencer in town *finally*—he'd feel better about her being here at the B & B. Until then, he needed her with him.

"Okay," Caroline said. She started to sit up.

It took Zander a second to respond. Partly because she'd agreed so easily. He liked that her natural instinct was to agree to trust him. He was practically a stranger, but in the middle of the night, she was still inclined to let him take care of her. But part of his hesitation was the way the sheet slipped down her body.

The camisole was...well, not meant to stay on the wearer's body for long.

It was thin and silky, clinging to her breasts and showing off the hardened tips clearly. It also wasn't long enough to meet the top of the matching thong, leaving a wide strip of smooth, pale skin between the lower lacy edge and the lace that trimmed the top of the low-cut thong. Even her belly button was sexy.

Then one of the straps slipped off her shoulder and Zander's hand shot out just in time to keep the silk from falling away from her left breast.

She sucked in a quick breath as his hand suddenly cupped her entire shoulder. Her eyes flew up to meet his.

He quickly scooped the strap back into position. "Here." His voice was harsher than he meant it to be as he yanked on the top sheet and wrapped it around her.

She didn't say anything, but she let him bundle her up like she was a little girl and then urge her up off the mattress.

"Okay, cher, here we go," he said, trying to gentle his tone. And not touch her again. And not think about her breasts and nipples. Which he hadn't seen and yet could imagine clearly.

He escorted her to the door, but she tripped over the bottom of the sheet.

With a muttered curse, Zander bent and swooped her up in his arms. Having her warm, barely dressed body against his wasn't going to help him get his thoughts into good-guy territory but it was going to get her into his truck and across town faster...and without any physical injury to her. He needed to focus on *her*. He could deal with himself later.

He got her into the passenger seat and even managed to get the seatbelt around her without further dirty thoughts.

They were pulling into his driveway when she finally spoke. "Is everything okay?"

He looked over at her as he shut the truck off. "It is now."

"Something happened?"

"Brantley showed up looking for you."

She frowned. "Really?" She seemed genuinely surprised.

"Yes. But I don't think he'll be back."

"Oh." Her frown deepened.

"Did you...want to talk to him?" Zander asked. That hadn't occurred to him. In fact, he'd been very certain that she would *not* want to talk to him.

"No. But why did you let him leave?"

"Because I want him out of my town and away from you."

"Why didn't you arrest him?"

Zander sighed. She was wide awake now. "For the lion cub?"

She nodded.

"I can't arrest him for that. He was not in possession of the cub...or any other animals...when I saw him tonight."

"But I *told you* that he gave me the lion."

"And I've been in touch with the proper authorities." Spencer really needed to get his ass down here. "They're going to investigate. They'll ask you all about it. But it's not my juris-diction."

"When?"

"When what?"

"When are they going to talk to me about it?" she asked.

"Tomorrow. My cousin, Spencer, is with the FBI out of New Orleans. He's going to come down and talk to you."

She chewed on her bottom lip for a moment. Then nodded. "Okay."

"You still okay staying here tonight?"

She glanced toward the house and then back to Zander. "You're really worried about Brantley?"

"I guess..." Fuck. He'd overreacted. He knew that. But he still felt a hell of a lot better with her sitting next to him in the truck than he had with her across town at the B & B even before he'd known Brantley was in town. "I don't want him messing around over there with Heather and Crystal and the other guests there. If he wants to talk to you, and you're okay with that, then he can do that *away* from anyone else."

She thought about that, then nodded. "You're right. It's not fair to wake anyone else up. I'm sorry you got pulled out of bed."

"I'm not," he told her honestly, his voice gruff.

He got out of the truck and rounded the front, pulling her door open and scooping her into his arms without giving her another option. She didn't have shoes on and his driveaway was covered in rocks. That was a good enough reason in his mind.

She didn't protest. In fact, she seemed to cuddle into him as he carried her into the house. He stopped inside the front door only long enough to lock it. Then he headed up the stairs and to his bedroom.

"I have another bedroom, but no furniture," he told her, depositing her on his bed. It was unmade and the sheets were still rumpled from where he'd been trying to sleep just before Beau's call. "Everyone I know has their own beds here in town, so I don't host guests."

That included the men that came to town to help with any covert protective actions. They preferred to pretend they were in town to visit family and stayed at the B & B or they slipped into town and stayed out at the bayou cabin they all used as their headquarters. No one needed to crash at Zander's place.

"I'll take the couch," he added.

He'd love to have his eyes on her all night, in more than one way, but he doubted very much that Brantley could climb the outside of his house to get into his bedroom window and that was the only way he'd get to that room with Zander on the couch. If Brantley was even going to try again tonight. Or could find Zander's house. Both of which were very unlikely.

"I..." Caroline wet her lips. Then she lifted her chin. "I'm not going to put you out of your bed, Zander. You're trying to protect me. Just...sleep in here."

Bad, bad, tempting idea.

"I don't know if that's such a great idea."

She rolled her eyes. "We're both grown adults who are capable of making our own decisions. I trust you. If we decide to sleep in here, in the same bed, together, and only *sleep*, then that's what will happen, I'm sure."

"Trusting a man you just met that much is maybe also not such a great idea."

"If you wanted to hurt me or...whatever...you could have done it a dozen times already," she said. "If you have nefarious intentions, you saying you're going to sleep on the couch doesn't keep me any safer than you being right here in the bed with me."

She made some very good points. So he decided to be honest. "I might actually get some sleep if I'm on the couch instead of right here in the bed with you."

She gave him a little smile. "Or are you going to be lying down there wondering what every bump and squeak is and wondering if I'm sleeping and wondering if *I'm* wondering what every bump and squeak is?"

He wanted to sleep up here with her. He did. For all those reasons, and more that he didn't want to go into. "Will you at least wear one of my shirts to sleep in instead of what you're wearing?"

This time her smile was a little more sly. "Whatever you want."

The punch of heat in his gut at that little bit of acquiescence was a huge red flag. Still, he crossed to his dresser and pulled a t-shirt from his third drawer. One that was a little big even on him.

"Bathroom is the next door to the right."

She just grinned as he handed her the shirt and let the sheet fall.

Right. This was the woman who'd changed clothes on Heather's back porch. He sighed and turned away. And gritted his teeth through the sounds of clothes and sheets rustling and then blue silk hitting the floor by his foot.

"You can turn around now," Caroline told him.

He did and seeing her in his shirt did absolutely nothing to quell the feelings of wanting to make her *his*.

Fuck. Fuck. Fuck.

9

Caroline scooted to the opposite side of the bed. "Or is this your side?" she asked as she slipped under the covers.

"It's...fine." It was not fine. Her in his bed was not fine.

"So this *is* your side." She grinned unapologetically.

"I sleep all over it," he told her honestly.

She laid on her side, putting her head on his favorite pillow, and tucked her hands under her cheek. Watching him.

Zander accepted his fate.

He *was* a grown man. So he wasn't going to pretend this was anything other than what it was. A gorgeous woman he felt very protective—and possessive—of was in his bed. And he was going to sleep next to her. And he hated the idea of any other man sleeping next to her, in the past or the future. And he was just going to have to deal with those feelings. Tonight. And tomorrow. And after she left town.

But for right now, he was going to get in bed.

He lifted the covers on the near side of the bed.

"Really?" she asked.

"What?" He got in bed, hoping like hell the mattress dipping on his side wouldn't cause her to roll into him.

"In your clothes?"

"Yep." He reached over and shut the lamp off.

The room plunged into darkness and it took a second for his eyes to adjust to the faint light that filtered in from the tall yard lights his brother had put in at this end of the dead end street.

This strip of homes was now known as Bachelor Row since Fletcher, Mitch, and Zander had moved into the old family homes clustered down here near the bayou. Zeke had remodeled them all and then built his own house. There was one house that had been in the Landry family but not yet claimed by the younger generation. That house had been Jill's, kind of, for a couple of months, but now served as a general guest house for the family members of all the girls—well, there were a couple guys too—who had come to Autre and ended up falling in love and staying. But for the most part, Landry family homes got handed down.

"You're going to be comfortable sleeping in jeans?" Caroline asked.

"I've slept in much less comfortable circumstances. At least I've got a bed and blanket here." Though lying next to her, knowing those curves and that silky skin was very much within arm's reach, was going in the top three worst situations he'd tried to sleep through.

"Like when?"

He rolled his head toward her. "Really? You want to chat? It's the middle of the night. Go to sleep."

"I'm interested in you."

"Don't be."

She laughed. "That's not how interest works."

"I'm a cop. I was a detective. I grew up on the bayou. I've slept in cars, tents, old shacks, boats, outside. In the cold, rain, with animals roaming around that might like to take a chunk out of me. I'm fine lying here in a pair of jeans for a few hours."

"The most uncomfortable place I've ever slept was upright in the backseat of Max's car while we were on a stakeout."

Fuck. Yeah, just telling himself not to be interested was definitely not how interest worked. "Max took you on a stake out?" He wasn't sure how he felt about that. He didn't really like it. And he did know that he didn't like not liking it. He shouldn't give a shit what stupid, possibly dangerous stuff she'd done in the past. Or that she might do in the future.

But telling himself wasn't how *that* worked either, apparently.

He could see her smile in the faint light. Or maybe he just sensed it.

"We were in tenth grade. Max was trying to find out who Derek Robbins was dating so we followed him all over one Saturday night."

"Did you find out?"

"Nope. He went to a ballgame, then out for pizza, then to a friend's house to play videogames. He didn't see a girl all night. We fell asleep across the street from his friend's house and totally got busted the next morning."

Zander chuckled in spite of himself.

"Just so you know," she said softly, a moment later. "Brantley's never seen me in lingerie. We've never slept together."

Let it go. Just let it fucking go.

He did not let it go. "That's good to know."

See, that was *not* the kind of thing he should be admitting.

She nodded. "I don't know why, but I wanted you to know that. Maybe so you won't feel bad about arresting him. I'm not in love with him. We're not a *real* couple."

"You were going to get married."

"No."

"Brantley thought so."

"Brantley was just going along with what he thought everyone wanted him to do. Like he always does. Do I think he was *upset* about the engagement? No. He's always flirted with me. When he and Chris were fifteen, I overheard him telling Chris he had a big crush on me. It's how I came up with this whole plan. But it's not *love*. And I really doubt he's broken-hearted now. Or even surprised." She paused. "I guess that's why I can't believe he came after me. Maybe my dad or his dad made him."

"He said that you had something he needs back. He came to get it," Zander told her. "Any idea what that might be?"

She seemed to give that some thought. But then shook her head. "The jewelry? The lion? I mean, I suppose he'd want those back for the money he could get for them?"

Zander nodded. "I wondered about that. He wants to talk to you tomorrow."

"Oh great! He can come back tomorrow when your FBI friend is here and he can arrest him."

"It doesn't work like that," Zander said. "They have to investigate. They have to have a *reason* to arrest him. Proof. Evidence."

"But *I told you*—"

"I know," he cut in. "And you can tell Spencer everything, too. But it will take more than that."

She deflated. "There are more animals in trouble, Zander. This can't take weeks or months or years."

"The more information you can give them, the faster they can work."

"I've got some more stuff," she said. "Some documents."

"Great. We'll give it all to Spencer."

"Okay."

She got quiet and Zander clenched his jaw.

You don't have to comfort her. You don't have to make her feel better. There might not be anything that will be better. Spence might not be able to do anything. Just let it play out. She's a grown woman.

He had no chance of resisting reaching out and squeezing her arm, though. "Spencer will do everything he can."

"Okay."

"Caroline—"

"That lion cub isn't old enough to be away from his mother, Zander. Think of how scared he is. And is he even going to be healthy? And how many more are there?"

Zander felt his chest tighten. "The vets and people running the sanctuary here are very good."

"I know. I've followed Donovan Foster for awhile."

Don't be jealous of Donovan and her clear admiration. Donovan's a great guy. She should definitely admire him. The self talk didn't work. *He* wanted to help her. He wanted to fix this. He wanted to be the one making this better.

Yep. He was in a lot of trouble here.

"They'll be very good to him," Zander finally said.

"It's not as good as him being left with his mother."

No. It wasn't.

Then...she sniffed.

And his chest tightened again. As did his hand on her arm.

Fuck.

But he gave in to the inevitable. As he tugged her closer, he wasn't sure why in the hell he'd tried to resist this from the very beginning. He should have just kissed her in the foyer of his aunt's house. He'd known even then that he was trying to prevent something from happening that was absolutely going to happen no matter what he told himself, tried, or did.

Caroline came across the few inches of mattress easily. Almost eagerly. Zander wrapped an arm around her as she curled into his side, resting her head on his chest.

At least he hadn't undressed. Not taking his pants off was

the one really smart, rational decision he'd made where this woman was concerned.

Her body heat soaked through the soft cotton of the shirt she wore and the scent of her floated up to him as her hair tickled his upper arm.

"I'm sorry I'm being pushy," she finally said softly.

"I'm sorry I can't make it go faster." And he was. Because yeah, there were animals potentially being harmed, but also because he wanted to fix this so Caroline would move her sweet ass on down the road and out of his orbit.

Here he was, four days after meeting her and telling himself all the reasons he was going to ignore his natural inclination to wrap his arms around her and tell her everything was going to be okay, holding her...in his bed...and wanting to make it all okay.

"I guess I'm not used to this part," she said.

"This part?"

"I usually just turn the information over to Max. I don't talk to the cops or other sources or anything."

"And everything happens fast?"

"Yeah. I guess. I mean, it feels faster because I'm not right in the middle of it." She sighed. "I'm not always waiting on a criminal investigation either. I'm mostly happy with the story exposing the person as a piece of crap that my dad and other people shouldn't trust."

Zander frowned. He was trying very hard to ignore how perfectly she seemed to tuck against his side. They barely knew each other. They'd never hugged, danced, fucked. How did it feel like he'd held her like this before and that their bodies knew exactly how to fit together? He cleared his throat. "Why's that?"

"I do it to remind my father that the people he associates with aren't good people and that if he's not careful he could get pulled into their corruption and cheating and lying and problems."

Zander let that all roll over in his mind. "You gather information about your father's colleagues and expose it to keep your dad in line?"

"I guess. He just...I know he's a good man down deep but this world he's in...it's like poison. I've seen it working on him. He's changed. And I just don't want him to think that any of these people are his real friends or can be trusted." She was quiet for a moment. "He won't just listen to me *tell* him that. He doesn't think I know what I'm talking about. So...yeah. I guess I do it to be that voice of conscience for him."

Zander couldn't blame her. And he couldn't deny that he was a little impressed. It was passive-aggressive, sure, but it was also effective. If her goal was to remind her father of the man he was and what he could become if he wasn't careful, then this was a creative way to do it. Being aggressive and direct could have been a problem anyway. She could have put herself at risk —if not physically, then at least her plans, reputation, or financial standing—if she tried to confront any of these people personally.

Zander believed that her father wouldn't have listened if she went directly to him with any secrets about his cronies. And unless she wanted to blackmail one of these people into doing something for her or giving her something, what good would it have done if she'd gone to them and told them she had dirt on them or their business?

Leaking secrets and scandals to the media, and occasionally to law enforcement, certainly proved to them all that someone was watching and they weren't immune to trouble if they crossed certain lines.

"So why's this different? With the animals?"

"It really doesn't have anything to do with my dad," she said. "At least as far as I can tell. I don't think he's had anything to do with it at all. In fact, I'm not sure any of *his* friends have. I think maybe Brantley and Christopher got into this on their own. But once I found out about it, I wanted to stop it, of course, and I wanted to show Dad that getting involved with these people has led Chris down a bad road. But now I'm more concerned with the animals than teaching my dad a lesson. Even if I could go back and take more time to get more information about what's going on from Brantley or Chris, I wouldn't. I just want someone to stop this."

And then she had to be sweet? That was going to be an even bigger problem for Zander. But that was stupid.

He was already attracted to her and it wasn't like women who loved animals were a major weakness or anything. He was around sweet, animal-loving women day in and day out. Both of his brothers were married to women who worked for the animal park. Jordan, Fletcher's wife, was the educational director for the park. She was not only sweet and cute with animals but with little kids too. Would he have dated Jordan? Maybe. Would he have ever gotten serious with Jordan? Nope.

Zeke's wife, Jill, just happened to be a world-renowned expert in endangered penguins and was caring for a colony of Galapagos penguins. Had Zander flirted with Jill when she'd come to town? Unapologetically. Would he have gotten her naked given a chance? If Zeke hadn't fallen head over ass for her the first night, sure, maybe. Would Zander have gotten serious with her? Nope.

He wasn't looking for serious. It was that simple.

And women being beautiful and having soft spots for animals hadn't shaken him before.

There was also Charlotte, and Naomi, and Tori, and Juliet, and Maddie. All gorgeous. All amazing. All animal lovers.

He hadn't felt one prickle of "uh, oh, she could be trouble". His heart had never been in jeopardy.

So Caroline Holland being soft for these animals shouldn't be a turn-on.

But Caroline wanted someone to shut down this animal trafficking thing...he wasn't sure what exactly to call it...and Zander knew that he would give Spencer all the information and then insist on helping.

He was fascinated by her and he might as well just accept that and be honest with himself about it.

"You never worried about victims in any of the other cases you've gathered information about?" he asked Caroline. "The animals are the first time you've felt like you needed to advocate?"

She didn't answer immediately. Then he felt her shift against him. He willed his body to not react. She felt good against him. She was soft and warm and smelled amazing. Was his body urging him to do more? Of course. He could easily roll to the side, pin her beneath him, and kiss her.

But he liked this too. He never cuddled. It wasn't that he *never* spent the night with a woman beside him, but he wasn't much of a hold-them-all-night guy. And he really wasn't the chatty type. He supposed he could chalk that up to knowing most of the women he took to bed at least well enough to know that their fathers weren't criminals. But he also just wasn't that interested in backstory and opinions.

"Sometimes the victims were the company's board of directors or their shareholders," she finally replied. "Like in the embezzlement cases. Or the government if it was tax evasion or something. So no, I didn't *worry* about the victims. There were a few cases where I exposed them cheating on their wives and that affected their families. And I felt bad for their wives and kids. But I also felt like they were better off knowing and, in the case where they divorced, they were better off without him. But..."

Zander felt her hand move. Her arm had been slung across

his stomach, but now she pulled it back, her hand resting on his abs just below his diaphragm. His muscles tensed and he had to consciously relax.

"But?" he prompted, knowing his voice sounded strange, but needing her to *talk*.

"I don't think I really let myself think that much about victims. I told myself that the person who was doing the bad thing—whatever it was—should get in trouble and it would make the victims happy that they were punished."

"But the animals are different."

Her hand moved back and forth across his shirt but he didn't think she was truly conscious of the motion. He felt her cheek move against his chest as she nodded.

"Yeah. The animals are innocent and helpless. And…"

She sniffed again and Zander tightened his arm around her even as he moved his hand to rest on the top of hers to stop it moving. The strokes were sending jolts of awareness straight to his cock and it was very interested in doing more than talking.

"…I realize there were innocent, maybe helpless, people involved in some of the other stuff and I *should* have cared more about them and I should have pushed harder and gone faster and there's no doubt more going on that I should dig into here. I need to focus on more than just how this affects my father and my family. But I ran out of the wedding and pissed everyone off and getting back in and getting them to trust me is going to be hard. I might have blown it all up."

Zander's focus shifted from the ache behind his fly to the clear ache in Caroline's voice.

Without really thinking, he rolled toward her. She looked startled when her head tipped up so she could meet his eyes but she didn't pull back.

"Hey," he said, his voice husky. "No. Stop. I didn't ask that to make you feel bad. I find what you've been doing for and because of your dad interesting and I was poking. But I'm not judging you."

"*I'm* judging me," she said softly.

"You left your wedding because it was the wrong thing for you. You don't really believe that you should have stayed and married him just to stay in that inner circle, do you?"

Something twisted inside of Zander at the idea of her leaving Autre and potentially going back to New Orleans to her family and to that world. To Brantley.

"I was in a position that not just anyone has access to. The ones who *do* don't use their power and privilege that way. They take advantage. They enable. They look the other way. Or they don't think what these people do is a problem. I thought I was a rare combination of aware, appalled, and able."

"You were." He agreed with her. It was unusual for someone who benefitted from a system to want to dismantle that system.

"So, if I'm not there, accessing that inner circle and keeping watch, who will?"

"You can't go back and marry Brantley because you think they need a watchdog."

"I..." She pressed her lips together. Then continued quietly. "I don't know what else I can contribute."

"Contribute to what?"

"The world. Everything."

The emotion that had twisted itself in Zander's gut tightened again, and he realized it was *like*. Along with a hefty dose of concern and I-want-to-take-care-of-you and tell-me-all-your-stories and I-want-to-help-you-feel-fulfilled.

Yeah, he liked her.

She was slightly misguided. She *was* privileged. She was naïve about how the system really worked. But she wanted to do the right thing, she was willing to put herself out there, take some risks, and give up some of her privilege to get justice. She wanted to be a champion for animals that didn't have anyone else looking out for them.

"What?" she finally asked after he'd stared down at her for several long moments.

He was fighting with himself.

And he knew he was going to lose.

"You're..."

"I know."

He huffed out a soft laugh. "What did you think I was going to say?"

"Annoying. A pain in the ass. Some variation of that."

"No."

She did look surprised then. "No?"

"You're...remarkable."

Her eyes grew rounder. "Oh."

"Yeah."

"You probably shouldn't have admitted that." Her breath was warm against his lips.

"I'm actually aware of that."

She smiled. "You remember what I said about how Brantley and I weren't really in love. How we weren't sleeping together. All of that?"

"Yeah."

"Good." She leaned in and pressed her lips to his.

Caroline half expected him to pull back or push her away, but Zander leaned into it. Immediately. He also dropped a hand to her ass and brought her up fully against him, then rolled her to her back, pinning her pelvis between his hand and his cock. She immediately felt how hard and thick he was.

She gave a breathless little gasp and arched into him. Her

hands went to the back of his head, holding him close, and she opened her mouth, letting him sweep his tongue in to taste her.

He pressed her deeper into the mattress and she brought a knee up, cradling his hips between her thighs.

They kissed, lips, tongues, and breath mingling in a sizzling mix of lust and discovery that was easily the hottest kiss of her life.

It wasn't a *really* high bar, but this kiss was...*everything*.

It was going to end. Zander Landry, the gruff, bossy, put-upon small-town cop, did *not* strike her as the type to make out with a near stranger he felt equally protective of and frustrated by without eventually, and probably abruptly, coming to his senses and ending it. And probably making the whole thing a big deal.

So, Caroline slipped her hands under his shirt, her hands running up the bare skin of his back. She wanted to touch as much of this man as she could in whatever amount of time she had. His muscles bunched under her palms and she felt a shudder go through him. The groan and the way he deepened the kiss made her think the shudder was a good one.

He again pressed the deliciously large bulge between her thighs against her sweet spot. Her clit ached for more pressure and friction and she shifted restlessly against him, lifting her hips and circling them.

"Jesus," he rasped as he dragged his mouth along her jaw to her ear. "You feel so fucking good."

"Ditto," she managed.

She hadn't had sex in a *long* time. Hadn't even wanted to, honestly. But she didn't remember *needing* a man against her like this. They weren't even undressed.

She was mostly very happy to take care of her own needs. It was just easier. And less complicated. She was always aware that the people around her were constantly making deals and using absolutely everything they had as leverage and that no one ever *really* trusted anyone else.

But right now, with Zander, she didn't care. She would have done anything as long as he'd promise to put his hands and tongue in *all* the places she suddenly needed them.

He kissed down her neck as his big hand slipped from under her butt to slide under the bottom of the shirt. She missed the pressure lifting her against his cock, but she loved the feel of his hand on her stomach. His skin was rough against hers. He had calluses on his palms and his touch was hot as he rubbed back and forth over her waist and up over her ribs. His thumb grazed the bottom curve of her breast and she moaned.

God please keep going.

She arched her back, encouraging him.

He did. He cupped her breast, running his thumb over her nipple.

She actually whimpered at the touch.

He paused. "You okay?" His breath was hot against her ear.

"So okay," she promised, again arching closer. "More. Please."

He gave a little groan but he took her nipple between thumb and forefinger, rolling then tugging gently. A heavy throb started between her legs and she lifted her hips against him more firmly.

"Caroline," he rasped.

She turned her head and met his mouth. She knew he was going to say they had to stop. And they did. This was crazy. But she just wanted his hands on her for as long as she could have them.

He kissed her hungrily, teasing her nipple, pressing his hips against hers, the friction against her clit so damned good.

Her hands went to his ass, gripping firmly, wanting to hold him close and wishing he'd taken the jeans off.

He skimmed his hand down her side to her hip, squeezing,

and she held her breath, hoping he was about to whip her thong off. But that was when she sensed the shift. He kissed her deeply, then he pulled his mouth away, resting his forehead on hers.

They were both breathing fast and they just stayed like that, her hands on his ass, his hand on her hip, the other elbow bracing him above her, their breaths mingling, their noses touching.

Finally, he said, "We need to stop."

She nodded. "I know."

He squeezed her hip one more time, then rolled to the side. But he kept his hand on her. She breathed out.

"I like you touching me." She wasn't sure why she said that. Surely that had been obvious. But she didn't mean it sexually. Not just sexually. She put her hand on top of his. "I like your hands on me."

"I like them on you too." His tone was slightly amused, but the huskiness was sexy and there was a touch of affection as well. "Too much, probably."

"Is it?" she asked. She looked over at him. "Is there a reason we shouldn't do this?"

"Probably several."

"And you never do things you shouldn't?"

"Didn't say that."

That made her feel better. She didn't really want to be something he shouldn't do but did anyway. When he thought about her in the future—and she did hope he would, which was a weird thought to have—she didn't want him to have regrets.

"You should go to sleep." His voice was soft, but there was something in it that made her wonder if he knew what she'd been thinking.

Yeah, she probably should. Sex with Zander would have been a nice distraction, but now that was off the table, her options were sleep or lie here and think about all the decisions she was going to have to make now.

Did she try to go home? That would require apologies she didn't want to make. But if she didn't go home, what was she going to do? She could start over but what would happen to her dad? If she wasn't around, keeping track of the corruption around him and pointing it out, would he get truly sucked into it? What about Christopher? What was he getting into? And she'd been doing this for a few years now. Was it really making a difference? Were these people—

"Caroline," Zander's voice rumbled. "Go to sleep."

She felt her mouth curve. Yeah, she needed to do that.

His hand still rested on her hip, his forearm a warm weight on her lower belly.

"Okay," she finally agreed.

She closed her eyes and took a deep breath and focused on Zander. She breathed in his scent, absorbed his heat, focused on the solidness of him next to her. She thought about how he'd come back to the bed and breakfast with clothes and money—and options—for her, how he'd believed her story, how he'd taken her for coffee, how he'd brought her more of that same coffee the last two mornings, how he'd come for her again tonight when Brantley had shown up and brought her here.

She felt more cared for by this almost-stranger, who didn't feel like a stranger at all, than she had by any other man.

She also felt more thoroughly kissed by him than by any other man. His hands on her set her nerve endings on fire. His voice, his eyes, his gruff-protective-but-annoyed attitude made her smile. But it was him just showing up again and again, even when this was the last thing he'd expected or wanted on his doorstep, that made her really *like* him. He was a good guy and she was really damned glad she'd walked into his grandma's bar.

10

_Z_ ander's phone ringing awakened them the next morning.
But neither of them jerked awake. Caroline's eyes blinked open and she realized that she had slept deeply for several hours. And Zander's hand was still resting on her hip, his forearm across her lower belly.

She was warm and felt a sense of contentment that she couldn't recall ever feeling before.

She rolled her head to look at him and found his sleepy gaze studying her.

His phone stopped ringing.

"Hi," she said.

"Hi."

He seemed different this morning. He'd been gruff and intense and bossy, but also protective and funny and sexy. Now he seemed relaxed and almost thoughtful. She liked _all_ of those sides of him.

His phone started ringing again.

"I should probably get that." His voice was sleep roughened, but he made no move to get out of bed or even reach for the phone.

"Okay."

They looked at each other for a long moment. Her gaze dropped to his mouth and the memories from the night before flooded through her.

She came toward him at the same moment he leaned in, their mouths meeting.

The kiss was instantly hot and deep. Zander's tongue swept into her mouth, stroking against hers as he rolled her back, bracing himself on his elbows on either side of her head. She bent one knee, cradling him between her hips and arching her pelvis up toward his morning erection.

He ground into her and they both moaned.

But when his phone started ringing for the third time, he lifted his head and stared down at her. "Now I really need to get it."

She nodded. She hadn't been expecting this to progress any further. Zander was...honorable. She supposed that was the best word for it. She wasn't used to being around men who put other people's needs in front of their own.

That wasn't entirely fair, she told herself the next moment.

Her dad *used* to be that way. Charles Holland had been a hard-working family man at one time. She had every reason to believe that he'd taken extreme pride in his work, and had done everything he could to impress his superiors. Eventually, that had all been rewarded when James Horner left Charles the entire company in his will.

She knew that everyone in their social circle, his business circles, and even outside of the business still talked about it.

But his change from hard-working family man to wealthy CEO trying to impress people who didn't deserve his respect or earnestness made her sad.

Zander stared at her for another long moment before pushing off of her and rolling to the side of the bed. He reached for his phone, glanced at the screen, then tapped a few buttons before lifting it to his ear. He listened for a moment, she assumed to a voicemail.

She sat up, pulling the sheet around her waist, and wondering what exactly her next step should be.

"Spencer's in town," Zander told her, lowering the phone a moment later.

"Oh good." The cavalry. Finally.

"He's up at my grandma's bar for breakfast with everyone. Wondering where the hell I am."

"You're not the type to sleep in?" She gave him a little smile. She already knew the answer.

"That's one way to put it." He glanced at the clock. It was 9 a.m. "I'm gonna shower and change. I'll run next door and get you some more clothes to borrow. Then we can head up and talk to Spencer."

"Great," Caroline said, perking up. She couldn't wait to give the FBI all her information and get this moving. She did understand jurisdictions and the fact that there might be limits to what Zander could do, but she refused to believe that *no one* could do anything about Brantley.

Zander seemed to want to say something more, but pushed up off the bed and strode from the room without a word.

Caroline took some deep breaths and thought about what her next step was. But really, she didn't have a lot of choices. She didn't have any clothes here, her phone was still back at the bed and breakfast, and she was dependent on Zander for... everything at the moment. She had a vague recollection of driving from the bed and breakfast to his house, but she wasn't exactly sure where she was in town.

Not that she felt the need to strike out on her own and walk back to the bed and breakfast. Zander was going to take care of her. She knew that and it felt good. She was a very independent person. She'd felt on her own for years now. She played the part of the needy, dependent-on-her-daddy socialite, but it was an act. She was resourceful and knew how to take care of herself. If she had a plan.

But she didn't mind having Zander Landry looking out for her.

She just had this nagging feeling that he felt obligated and didn't want to have this responsibility.

He liked her. At least she was pretty sure he did. He definitely wanted her physically. Their attraction was undeniable.

But she was an unexpected complication and she'd dumped a further problem in his lap when Brantley had shown up last night. She couldn't blame Zander for wanting to get her out of town as soon as possible.

Caroline frowned. What the hell had Brantley come to town for? Zander had said he was looking for something that he needed back.

The jewelry and lion cub were truly the only things that came to mind. But why was he skulking around in the middle of the night for those things? He could have his damn jewelry. But she would *never* let him near that animal again. Maybe that's why he had come sneaking around in the night. He had to know how upset she was.

But it made no sense that he'd been trying to sneak into her room. Obviously, she wouldn't have the lion cub literally *with her* at the bed and breakfast. It wasn't like Brantley was the brightest bulb in the light string, but that all made her think that it wasn't the lion, he was after. Unless he'd just been planning to make her tell him what she'd done with it.

Caroline blew out a breath. She really didn't know what Brantley was thinking. She'd known the guy most of her life. Brantley and Christopher had been friends since they'd been five. But all she really knew about Brantley was that he was spoiled and thought she was hot.

She gave a little shudder. She couldn't go back and pretend they were madly in love. She couldn't go back and pick up where they'd left off with their fake engagement. Well, fake on her side anyway. Any groveling or apologizing she did would simply not be sincere and even Brantley would probably be able to see through it.

What was she going to do?

Zander strode back through the bedroom door just as she was starting to get worked up about her future plans again.

Her heart gave an extra hard kick in her chest when she saw him and her thoughts immediately shifted and her heartbeat suddenly wasn't racing because of anxiety.

His hair was damp though he'd already pulled it back again. He wore gray athletic shorts and was shirtless. Which meant now she could see all of his tattoos. The ink went from his left wrist to his shoulder, then crossed his broad chest, where her head had rested last night, and wrapped around his right shoulder and biceps. She wanted to explore every one of those lines and swirls. And she really hoped some of them extended onto his muscular back.

She took in every inch of his chest, shoulders, the thick arms that had held her and made her feel safe and sexy at the same time, and the planes of his flat stomach that ended at the elastic band of the loose shorts that sat low on his lean hips.

Her tongue seemed stuck to the roof of her mouth and she had a hard time swallowing.

"Come on," he said.

"What?" It came out as almost a croak.

"Coffee's in the kitchen. Are you a coffee drinker?"

"Yeah. In the morning. If you don't have tea."

"No tea."

Yeah, he didn't seem the hot tea type.

"You can get tea at my grandma's when we get up there though."

"We're going to Ellie's? Together?"

He hadn't been up there even once when she had been over

the past few days and she'd heard one of his brothers—or was he a cousin? There were *a lot* of Landry men—comment that Zander never stayed away from Ellie's like that. She'd concluded he'd been avoiding her.

He sighed. "That's where Spencer is."

She smirked. Now he *couldn't* avoid her. Ha. "You don't have to make me coffee. I can wait until we get up to the restaurant."

"Caroline," he said firmly. "I need you to get out of my bedroom." His expression was partly amused and partly pained. "I need to get dressed and having you half-naked in my bed isn't doing me any favors."

Without meaning to, she looked down at the front of his shorts. He was hard. Her body reacted to the evidence of his desire immediately. She felt her nipples tighten and a warm swirl danced through her lower belly as she remembered his hands and mouth on her and how his body, particularly *that* part of his body, had felt against hers.

"I've been half-naked in your bed all night," she reminded him.

When the heat flared in his eyes and his jaw clenched, she thought that maybe she should not poke the bear.

The heat swirled faster through her and dipped between her legs as he approached the bed.

Or maybe she should *absolutely* keep poking the bear. God, he looked hot when he got all growly and intense.

Sleeping with Zander was a bad idea. She knew that. On some level anyway. It would be a fling at best and would lead to nothing, and... Yeah, that was all she had.

But having it leading to nothing was a good thing. The last thing she needed was a long term...anything. She didn't know where she was going to be or what she was going to be doing in a week, not to mention a month or more from now.

But he wasn't proposing. Why couldn't she have a fling? He was a good guy and she was probably never going to see him again. She hadn't done something irresponsible and fun in a very long time. Too long for her to really remember. She was always too caught up in worrying about the greater good and saving her father and brother from themselves and making sure justice was done and a whole bunch of other high-and-mighty-greater-purpose thoughts and intentions.

Why couldn't she blow all of that off just one time?

A hot fling with Zander Landry sounded like a great idea.

Max would be here in the next day or so and could help Caroline get her thoughts in order and get a plan in place. Then maybe she and Zander could spend a couple of hot sweaty hours together right here in this bedroom before Caroline packed up and left town.

"You need to go down to the kitchen, Caroline," Zander told her, his voice low and firm.

"Could I use your shower first?"

He shook his head. "Nope."

She widened her eyes. "I can't shower now while you get dressed?"

"I can't have you naked while I'm here," he said as if it was obvious.

She felt a smile teasing her lips. "Oops. That's awfully close to admitting that you lack some self-control, Officer Landry."

He simply nodded.

She raised both eyebrows. "You're willing to admit that?"

"You're willing to play dumb and pretend you don't already know that?"

"So we can talk openly about the fact that we have an incredible attraction that's very hard to resist?"

"I don't think we should pretend that our physical attraction isn't very strong and real. We both need to acknowledge it and that it could be a problem, so we can deal with it."

"It could be a problem? How?" She liked the way he made

her feel and liked that he was willing to admit that she made him feel things too.

"Well, last night I brought you here to protect you, but instead of just letting you sleep safely and watching the door and being ready to take care of any threats, I kissed you, touched you, and spent the night thinking about all the ways I wanted to make you come."

Her breath caught in her chest, as lust zinged through her body. She stared at him, thinking about his hand on her breast and how he'd felt pressing between her legs and how hungrily he'd kissed her.

She wanted more of all of that.

But he had a point.

"And you really don't want to do anything about it?" she asked.

"I didn't say that."

"But you're not *going to* do anything about it," she clarified.

He looked at her for a long moment. "I don't think I said that either."

Her stomach swooped and her lady parts gave a little *whoop!*

She wet her lips. "So what *are* you saying?"

"I'm saying that we don't have time for that right now."

That was not a *we're never going to get naked together.*

"Will we have time later?"

"Do you want to have time for that later?"

Caroline wet her lips and thought about the question. It was a fair question. And if they were going to be open and honest about everything it was one she needed to answer. "Yes."

He studied her for a long, hot, tension-filled moment. Then he nodded. "Go downstairs."

Feeling suddenly light and happy in a way that she could only compare to how she'd felt as a kid knowing that the next day was her birthday and her family was planning a big party,

Caroline whipped the covers back and scooted to the edge of the bed.

Zander didn't look away as she stood, covered only to mid-thigh in his t-shirt. He didn't back up either. He was just *right there.*

She stood, looking up at him, waiting for him to say or do something.

Finally, he lifted a hand to the back of her head, tipped it back, and sealed his mouth over hers.

He kissed her thoroughly, melting her bones and making her stretch up on tiptoe, grasping his biceps, and giving one of those needy little whimpers that only this man could elicit.

He let her go many hot seconds later and looked into her eyes as he said, "Later."

Caroline wasn't sure if it was a promise *to* her or if he was looking for a promise *from* her, but she nodded.

He stepped back and she took a deep breath.

"Go," he said simply.

She pulled the shirt down, then padded across the room to the door. She had no idea where the kitchen was but figured it couldn't be that hard to find. But she glanced back over her shoulder and found him watching her go, his hot gaze on her ass, and she tripped over her own feet, nearly falling.

She braced her hand on the doorframe and looked up to find him smirking at her.

"*Later*," he said.

That also caused an arrow of heat to jab her. Intense, amused, cocky...this guy didn't have an emotion or expression that didn't turn her on.

She was falling over herself, literally, because of this guy. She never did that. And she should be appalled.

But she wasn't. She felt playful and flirty and sexy and fun. God, that felt good.

She never had fun with men. *Never.* Not anymore. Maybe at

one point she'd flirted and had fun with guys in high school and college, but it felt like she'd been playing the part of the silly socialite for so long that none of her interactions were real anymore.

She *pretended* to flirt and to have fun and to enjoy the company of the men she spent time with, of course. But none of it was genuine. And when they flirted back and seemed to enjoy her company, they were responding to the fake her.

Mostly, it didn't bother her. She didn't wish for a boyfriend or more. Her concern for her father and brother and her disgust at what some of their associates did and got away with were bigger than any desire for her own social life. The role she was playing was important. She had to convince everyone she was no threat. It made her father's friends and business associates complacent. Which meant they said and did things in front of her, that they might not otherwise. It was very important that everyone feel that she was superficial, blithe, not paying attention, and certainly not smart enough to be interested in what they were doing. Or to understand it even if she did overhear something.

Flirting with, being playful, feeling sexy, and making out with Zander Landry was not just fun...it was like diving into a cool swimming pool after baking in the hot sun all day. It felt delightful, delicious, and, strangely, like a huge relief. She could be herself and just enjoy it all.

"Caroline."

His firm, slightly amused voice pulled her out of her thoughts.

She met his gaze. "Yeah?"

"Do I need to physically throw you out of this room?"

His hands would have to be on her again for that to happen...

He took a step toward her. His voice was a low, almost growl. "Caro."

And a damned nickname? She remembered in that second that he'd called her that last night when he'd awakened her. Yep, everything about him, this, *them,* was sexy and sweet and fun and tempting.

"I *really* want later to happen," she said.

He stopped coming toward her. His body was tense. His eyes were hot. His nostrils flared.

"I also really like being able to just say that," she said. "I never get to be blatantly honest with anyone." She sighed. "God, it feels good."

His jaw clenched, then he asked. "Okay. What else?"

"What do you mean?"

"What else do you not get to do? What else can you not be completely honest about?"

She just stared at him. "I..." She pulled her lip between her bottom teeth.

"I'm guessing, from what I've read and you've told me, and now getting to know you better, there are things that you'd like to do but can't because of this persona you put on," he said. "What else do you want to do? Drink moonshine? Country dance? Skinny dip? Fish?"

Caroline knew her eyes were wide. "*Yes.*"

All of that sounded like a whole bunch of letting-loose-and-having-fun and suddenly, just being in Autre with this man, she wanted all of that.

Zander gave a little chuckle and shook his head. "I'm going to regret all of this."

She frowned at that. "I don't want that."

"Don't worry about me."

"No, seriously. If you don't want to do...any of that..." Damn, that would suck. She really wanted the naked time. "You don't have to. I'm not your responsibility. I don't want you to hate having me here."

He blew out a breath. "That's not the problem. At all. And I don't think there's any way I can *not* make sure you get to do all of those things if you want to. And I want to be there to see it."

"Yeah?"

"For sure."

"Why?"

"Because, against my better judgement, I like you. And I've resigned myself to the fact that as long as you're here, you're... mine. To take care of. To entertain. To...enjoy."

Heat, and something that felt like *more* somehow, again arrowed through her.

She swallowed hard. "Then why would you regret it?"

"Because it's a big deal to take someone's virginity. Whether it's sexual virginity or crawfish boil virginity or skinny-dipping virginity. Showing someone something they're gonna really love is special."

She felt melty again. Wow. "I'm, um, not a...you know...an *actual* virgin. Just so you know."

"You ever been fucked by a bayou boy after drinkin' moonshine at a crawfish boil while skinny dippin' when you're supposed to be fishin'?"

His drawl had just gotten very deep and pronounced and Caroline felt her clit actually tingle in response. "I..." She cleared her throat. "...have not."

"Then you're a virgin in all the most fun ways."

She really didn't know what to say to that.

And he clearly saw that. And he smirked again.

He had the upper hand here. It was obvious to them both. He'd not only given her food and shelter and protection, but he was also making sure she knew that he could be the best time she'd ever had. He was going to let her let loose. He was going to encourage it.

She wasn't used to not being in control of her interactions with men. She prided herself on figuring them out and using their egos or their weaknesses—which were often the same thing—or whatever else she knew about them to manage the situations she was in.

Not so with Zander Landry.

And she loved it. The feeling of freedom. The feeling of anticipation. The feeling of...being a little naughty. Other people got to be naughty. They got to be downright terrible people. She felt like she always had to be the good girl. The rule follower who made sure others were following the rules too.

And again, the words *not so with Zander Landry* tripped through her mind.

He not only made her want to be naughty, but he was also clearly able to handle any out-of-control situation. She could relax with him.

His phone chimed as a text came in, breaking the moment of silence that stretched between them full of lust and expectation and, yes, fun.

He crossed to the bedside table and picked the phone up, glancing at the screen. "Paige says you're welcome to use anything of hers. Clothes, shampoo, whatever."

"I love Paige," she said with a smile.

"She's the best," he agreed. "And you can shower over there."

"It's okay for me to shower at Paige's but not here? I'll still be naked while you're there."

Again, the muscle along his jaw tensed, but he nodded. "I'm not saying I'm not going to be hard the entire time with some *very* dirty thoughts going, but I'm not going to do anything about them in someone else's house."

She *loved* the blatant admissions but also the fact that he had *some* self control. He had rules, an idea of how things were supposed to go, principles. Lord, she did *not* spend a lot of time with people with principles.

Plus, this building tension was fun too.

"Because that would be weird?" she asked, poking a little.

"Because if we break a table or knock over a lamp or something, I'd feel bad."

She felt a little bubble of laughter rise in her chest and she grinned. "Wow, I'm a table-and-lamp-breaking-sex virgin too."

He didn't smile. He gave her a nod. "Good."

Whew. How did he pack so much heat in one word? He was right. If he wasn't going to do anything about this ache that kept growing in her, she needed to get some space.

"I'm going down to get some coffee."

"Good."

She looked down. "Can I go to Paige's like this?" She was covered, but she didn't have pants or shoes on.

"Yep. No one's around this time of day. They're just two houses over."

"Piggyback ride?" she asked, wiggling a bare foot at him.

"Or I'll throw you over my shoulder," he said without blinking. "But you don't have to worry, Caroline. I'll take care of you."

Hot shivers went through her. "I believe you, Zander."

Then she turned on her heel and finally left the room.

Somewhere between kissing Caroline Holland in his bed—the first time—and sunrise, Zander had finally, fully given into fate.

Honestly, he was proud he'd lasted as long as he had. His draw to her had been nearly instantaneous and powerful. Better Landry men than him had fallen this fast. Why he'd thought he'd win the battle, he wasn't sure. He had very good reasons not to let himself get tangled up with a woman, especially one like Caroline. But Fate and the Landrys had a long, serious relationship and he was sure they'd *all* been laughing the entire time he'd tried fighting.

Now she was down in his kitchen and her eyes had actually lit up when he'd mentioned a crawfish boil and moonshine. And of course, the fucking.

She wanted him. She wanted the hot, dirty sex he was promising. She was very open and honest about it. And he was more turned on by that than he had been by anything else he could remember. Ever.

From the start, he'd known that Caroline tried on different identities when she met people. She looked for what worked best to get what she wanted. She'd told him about how her family and their social circle worked. He knew that she was never *real*.

But in that bed last night she'd been fucking real. And standing in his bedroom door, lighting up about the idea of moonshine-country-dancing-bayou-fucking, she'd been real.

She didn't like having to play parts. She wanted to just say what she thought and do what felt good.

And as much as he wanted her out of Autre and his life and away from his heart, he wasn't going to send her away before he gave her the chance to feel as good as she ever had.

He got into his uniform and headed for the kitchen.

He'd take her to Paige's to clean up. He *could* take her back to the bed and breakfast, but he liked having her here, on this end of town, borrowing stuff from his cousin-in-law, and then going to breakfast with him in his truck. It was crazy, but he liked that she didn't have any of her own stuff here. Nothing from her life in New Orleans, nothing that had anything to do with the Holland family or Brantley Anderson.

It was a little controlling and it wouldn't last. He couldn't keep her from her phone, her purse, and her belongings forever. But he liked the idea of providing what she needed and taking care of her. And yes, cutting her off from all of that for a while.

It was going to be short-term so he was going to lean into it.

As soon as Spencer took care of this illegal animal situation, Zander could kiss Caroline goodbye.

He found her sitting at his table, his favorite mug cradled in one hand, reading the romance novel he'd started three nights ago.

She looked up as he came into the room. "Is this yours?"

He nodded. He didn't care if people knew he read romance. He enjoyed it. So what?

She tipped her head. "You are...fascinating."

"That's a bit of a stretch," he told her, crossing to the coffee pot. He poured himself a cup and turned to face her, leaning against the counter.

"It is?" she asked. "You're a cop who reads romance novels and keeps up on Hollywood gossip."

"My grandma loves Hollywood gossip."

"You keep up with it for her?"

"It started that way. Now I love all the drama."

"Not enough drama here?"

"I like the stupid, meaningless drama. I like the idea that people can get worked up over someone's shoes on the red carpet or get into putting two total strangers into imaginary relationships. People need silly outlets for their emotions sometimes, and to pretend that all of that superficial bullshit actually matters, because real life is tough and often sucks."

She nodded. "Is that why you read romance?"

"Yep. The world needs more happy stories, and there's nothing happier than love stories."

Her eyes widened. He sipped from his cup to hide his smile. She was so easy to surprise. She was from a cutthroat world of arrogant, greedy pricks who would do anything for power and she was ballsy enough to try to take the big dogs down, but she had a sweet air about her. Almost an innocence. Which reminded him of what she'd said about being a virgin. She might not be an *actual* virgin, but she hadn't been properly fucked. Not the way she needed to be. He was sure of it. He didn't know why, but he was.

And he intended to fix that.

She was going to take a piece of his heart with her when she left, but he couldn't let her leave his world untouched. He was *not* that noble of a guy. He wasn't sure he was all that noble at all, really.

"So you believe in love stories?" she asked. "You read romance because you like pretending there are happily ever afters and people finding their soulmates and all of that?"

"I definitely like reading love stories, but there's nothing pretend about it. I've seen them in real life all around me my entire life. People here fall hard and fast and forever."

"Wow. Really?"

"All the time."

She narrowed her eyes as she took another sip of coffee. "That's another reason it's important that Autre stay...happy, right? So they can all fall in love and build their lives and families."

He narrowed his eyes back at her. "Why do you say that?"

"Because I've met them, Zander. Tori and Josh and Ella. Paige and Mitch. Donovan and Naomi. Jordan and Fletcher. Charlie and Griffin. Ellie and Leo." She sighed. "*All* of them. It's taken only four days around them for me to totally get it." She laughed lightly. "It didn't even take that long. I've seen exactly what you're protecting."

He stared at her. His heart was hammering. His gut was tight. His nerve endings were tingling.

Theo, Michael, and the others got it. He knew that. But to have this woman, this outsider, this stranger, get it and *say it* like that did something to him.

But it shouldn't surprise him that his family's love and happiness was so evident.

He cleared his throat. "I'm glad."

She finished her coffee, still watching him. "That's a lot of pressure on you, isn't it?"

He lifted a shoulder. "Someone's gotta do it."

"Why you?"

"Because I can. And because I care more about them being happy than anything else."

She studied him as she rose from the table and brought the coffee mug to the sink next to where he was leaning. She washed it and set it on the drainage rack. Then she turned, propping her hip against the counter. "So you're willing to give up all the happy-falling-in-love-family stuff for yourself to make it happen for them?"

She'd nailed it. He nodded. "Me and a few other guys."

"You don't want what those romance novels talk about?"

"I get some of it." He reached out and snagged her hand, tugging her close. "You should read chapter six." With his cup still in one hand, he slid the fingers of his other hand into her hair and tipped her face up to his. He kissed her slow and deep, tasting the coffee on her tongue, and absorbing the way she willingly leaned into him, accepting his kiss and pressing close for more.

He let her go a moment later, studying her eyes as he held her head.

She ran her tongue over her lips and his cock twitched, wanting that pink tip on it. "I noticed that you read some pretty dirty stuff," she said, a little breathless.

He gave her a slow grin. "I sure do."

She took a deep breath and he let her go. He couldn't *not* touch her, but he really couldn't keep going. They needed to get up to Ellie's. He wanted to get Spencer working on this case, for one thing, but the longer it took for him to get Caroline up there, the more curious his family would get about what he and the gorgeous heiress were getting up to. He wanted her and intended to have her before she left, but he did *not* need to get his family all riled up about how he might feel about her.

In their minds, the *perfect* Autre meant *everyone* in the family was deliriously happily in love. That was the one thing he wasn't going to give them and he hated that anything would feel *less than* to his parents or grandparents. But he had to put them first and he was already distracted as hell with Caroline in town. She'd been here for less than a week and he could already feel how his attention and loyalties and time would be pulled in different directions if she were to stay and become a true part of everything.

"Let's get you dressed and then see what Spencer can do about Brantley," he said, reminding them both of the most important focus of their day.

She nodded, but her gaze dropped to his mouth and Zander liked the realization that he could distract her from pursuing the criminals behind the illegally bought and sold animals. He knew how important that was to her.

He led her to his back porch, then bent and swept her up into his arms. She gave a little giggle that punched him in the gut. He loved making her laugh and smile and flirt. He got the impression all of that was uncommon. Or if she did it with other men, it was forced.

He carried her and her bare feet to his truck ignoring the fact that she felt amazing in his arms and that her legs were smooth and that if he ran his hands over that silky skin he wouldn't run into any barriers until he got to that thong.

Mitch and Paige didn't live far enough away to actually drive usually, but after Caroline was cleaned up and dressed, they'd be driving up to Ellie's anyway, so he pulled into his cousin's driveway a minute later. He carried Caroline inside and set her down in the living room, pointing her up the stairs.

"Bathroom is at the top of the stairs. Linen closet is to the right. Help yourself to everything. She said to tell you that the third drawer down in her dresser has shorts in it. Fourth drawer is jeans. Shirts and shoes are in the closet. Grab whatever you like."

Caroline shook her head. "This is really nice. Remind me to send her a gift basket or something."

He chuckled. "Sure."

She started up the stairs and Zander didn't even try to pull his gaze from her ass. Damn, he was going to be sorry when she was no longer wearing his shirt. She looked sexy as hell in that. But he needed to get work done today. They *had* to talk to Spencer. And if she stayed in that shirt, he wasn't going to be able to resist putting her up against a wall much longer.

While she showered and changed, Zander made himself return a couple of calls and emails, trying to keep his mind off the noises coming from the second floor and the images of her showering that kept teasing him.

But then she came back down those stairs in some of Paige's denim shorts, a red tank top, and red flip-flops with sparkly stones along the straps. She also had her hair back in a braid.

Zander could easily picture her sitting on the tailgate of his truck with a jar of moonshine in hand and he realized the up-against-the-wall was absolutely still on the table.

"We need to go." He pivoted toward the door immediately.

With the flip flops on her feet, he didn't have to carry her. Thank God.

She followed him out but once they were in the truck, the scent of soap and shampoo drifted to him and he wanted nothing more than to put his nose against her neck and breathe it all in.

"Are you okay?"

He looked over at her as they rumbled down the dirt road toward Ellie's. "Yeah."

"You look stressed." She looked pointedly at his fists gripping the steering wheel.

"Tryin' to keep my hands to myself," he said honestly.

She gave a surprised laugh. "Oh. Well, no need on my account."

His gaze dropped to her bare legs and then shifted back to the road. "You could have chosen jeans."

"No way," she said. It was clear she found all of this amusing. "I don't even own a pair of denim shorts so I have to wear these as much as possible. I'm getting some of my own as soon as I can."

He couldn't keep his eyes from running up her legs again. Her skin was pale and creamy. Definitely not sun-kissed or tanned. "You spend a lot of time indoors?"

She nodded, not offended. "I do."

"We'll have to be sure you don't get a bunch of bug bites."

"Am I going to be outside a lot?"

She really shouldn't be a lot of anything here. She should only be here for another day or so. "Crawfish boils and skinny dipping happen outside," he said anyway.

"Does *everything* you mentioned earlier happen outside?"

He looked over and found her watching him. "Fishing happens outside, yes. Or are you asking if we're going to...drink moonshine outside?" He watched her cheeks get a little pink and found that turned him on as well.

She nodded. "I'm asking about all of that."

"Yep. Moonshine in the moonlight is the best."

"Okay."

He grinned. Was he going to fuck her in his truck bed? Yep, maybe. But he also wanted to have her in his bed. And maybe his shower. And on his kitchen table. And...

This woman was getting to him in a way that was unprecedented and now that he'd just decided to go with it, he was having a hard time reining anything in.

He pulled up in front of his grandmother's bar and took a quick inventory of the other vehicles. It looked like Jill was there, as was Griffin, and Donovan. Fiona was back too. Or had she not left? Maybe the info he'd given about big cats being illegally dealt in the state had given her a reason to stay.

Spencer's truck was parked along the side too. Good. The animal experts were here and could give both Spencer and Caroline a lot of useful information.

Zander shut the truck off and looked over at Caroline. "Even if you don't have denim shorts, you're still a grits girl, right?"

She nodded. "Love grits."

He wasn't sure that was a good thing actually when she gave him that grin. It would be easier to resist her if she was the stuck-up rich girl he'd first assumed. But there were layers to this woman. She was softer, sweeter, and more real than he'd guessed.

And fuck, he wanted her.

Her gaze dropped to his mouth and he made himself turn away and push his door open before he leaned over and kissed her. He had to quit doing that. They were going to get things going with Spencer and then he'd take Caroline out tonight, they'd burn up his truck bed, and he'd send her sweet ass on out of town.

That was the plan and it was a very good one. Even if there was a niggle in the back of his mind telling him that one night wouldn't be enough.

Too fucking bad. He was in no position to have multiple nights.

11

As Zander pulled open the door to Ellie's and let Caroline step through in front of him, he was reminded of why *he* didn't get to have multiple nights with anyone. The sights, smells, and sounds were the most familiar of anything in his life. This *was* his life.

Ellie's was the hub of...everything. It had been here since his parents had been kids. The family gathered every night for dinner here as if this was the dining room at Ellie's house. She claimed she kept the restaurant and bar going because she couldn't fit them all into her house and she'd never give up feeding the whole big group. He knew she also loved being a staple in this town that meant the world to her, but Zander believed that a lot of what kept her behind that bar was that it was the perfect place for her kids and grandkids to stop in during the day for food, drink, gossip, advice, and just to be taken care of for a little bit.

It was late enough in the morning that the majority of the people in Ellie's were relatives. The regulars from town who came in for breakfast had come and gone and a lot of the family had headed out to work as well. The guys who ran the swamp boat tours would be out on the bayou already, Mitch would be working on whatever projects he had today, Paige was teaching class, Zeke would be at a construction site, and Jordan would be at the petting zoo. There were a few tourists at tables closer to the front, but the back tables were full of Landrys and adopted Landrys. As always.

But everyone present at the moment was here for Zander. Jill would usually already be up at the penguin enclosure, Griffin would be at the vet clinic, Charlie would be at the Gone Wild offices working on whatever next big promotional project they had coming up, and Naomi and Donovan would be at the wildlife rehab center with whatever animals Donovan had under his care currently. Like the lion cub.

They'd all come in this morning because Zander had asked for their input. And to reassure Caroline, *again*, that the lion cub would be fine. With Spencer here too, they could also assure her that the whole situation with Brantley and whatever he was into was going to be handled.

Yesterday Zander would have said he wanted to reassure her because he wanted her to be willing to leave Autre as soon as possible. Now he was pretty sure it was because he just wanted her to be happy. And to trust him. He wanted her to know that he'd take care of what he said he'd take care of. He didn't want her to worry.

Jesus. He was on day six. Only day six.

This Fate stuff was crazy.

Ellie was refilling coffee cups while Leo set down a new plate of bacon in between Griffin and Donovan as Zander and Caroline approached the table.

"Mornin', everybody," Zander greeted.

They all looked over with smiles, greeting Caroline as if she'd been a part of the group for years instead of days. Donovan gave Zander a knowing wink.

Yeah, yeah, Caroline was gorgeous and was fitting right in

and Zander had called a bunch of people together for her sake. So what?

But Zander was glad his brothers weren't here. Especially Zeke. There was no way he'd get anything past his twin. They had that weird connection identical twins always talked about having. It was why it felt so fucking strange that Zander was keeping secrets from his brother.

Hell, Zeke was one of the reasons Zander had been determined to keep that darkness from encroaching on Autre. Even before Zeke had met Jill, Zander had wanted love and family and a happily ever after for his brother. Both of his brothers. And now that Fletcher was married to Jordan and talking about babies and Zeke and Jill had their twin girls, Poppy and Allie, Zander would do anything to keep Autre the haven they deserved.

Zander gave Donovan a lifted brow. Donovan just smirked. He knew Zander had feelings for Caroline. Zander sighed inwardly and looked at his grandmother. Ellie gave him a smile and a little nod. Yeah, Ellie had noticed the vibe between him and Caroline too. Of course. Ellie Landry saw everything. The rumor was that nothing happened in Autre without Ellie knowing about it. Or sensing it. Or guessing it. Zander believed it. He'd witnessed it all his life.

He and Ellie had never talked about the group that had set up camp deep in the bayou that he, Spencer, and the other guys kept tabs on, but he somehow knew that Ellie knew about it. He suspected that she helped keep the family distracted from anything that might tip them off to any unrest or that Zander was working on anything beyond a cooler of beer or a fishing expedition when those guys were in town.

More than half of his "fishing trips" were actually meetups with his little posse of protectors.

God, he missed *actually* fishing.

"'Mornin'," Ellie greeted as the others shifted around and

pushed chairs out for Caroline and Zander. "Do you need anything other than grits, bacon, eggs, and biscuits?"

"Caro?" Zander asked. Then winced. The nickname came out too easily.

He avoided looking at Donovan.

"Nope, that's all really good with me," she said cheerfully, taking the seat next to Naomi and giving the other woman a big smile.

"Glad you're here," Naomi said. "We've got news. Tell her," Naomi said, nudging Donovan with her elbow.

"Tell me what?" Caroline asked.

"We have an idea for Mwanzo." Donovan looked excited.

So did Griffin. Which was *very* unusual. Griffin was a wildlife vet and much preferred animals to people. Except maybe Charlie. But he was a very stoic guy. Excited was definitely not a norm.

"What kind of idea? Is he okay?" she asked.

"He's a little underweight, but he's eating well," Griffin said. "But we're concerned about his socialization."

Caroline frowned. "Concerned?"

Zander slid his arm along the back of her chair. He didn't touch her, but he leaned toward her slightly. "It'll be okay," he said. "Griffin and Donovan are experts."

She looked at him and he saw her shoulders relax. She nodded.

"It's just that lions are the only wild cats that live in groups," Donovan explained. "Most wild cats are solitary. But lions live in prides and they depend on that group dynamic," Donovan said.

Caroline nodded, a tiny line wrinkling the space between her eyebrows. "And he doesn't even have his mom."

"Right," Griffin said. "He's going to need some kind of group."

"Can he be with the tiger you have?" Caroline asked.

Donovan shook his head. "Tigers don't function in groups and he's an old guy who we think has been alone most of his life."

Caroline's frown deepened.

Zander felt his own tension in his neck. The last thing any of them needed was *another* headstrong woman getting worked up about animal welfare. They had plenty with Fiona and Charlie and Jill and Naomi.

"He's pretty set in his ways," Donovan continued. "But..." He looked excited as he glanced at Naomi, then Griffin.

"*What?*" Caroline asked, leaning in.

"We're thinking that Brinkley might be good for him."

"Who's Brinkley?"

"Our dog," Naomi said. "She's a German shepherd and we think she's had puppies in the past. She's so sweet. She's a rescue and really seems to need socialization herself."

"You want a dog to become a surrogate mom to a lion cub?" This came from Charlie, who had leaned in to join the conversation.

"Oh my God, I love that," Fiona added from the end of the table.

"That can happen?" Caroline asked.

Griffin shrugged, but Naomi nodded. "Definitely."

Donovan laughed and explained. "Dogs are pack animals naturally. Like wolves. And like lions. They do best in groups. They love to be a part of a family. If Brinkley had puppies but wasn't allowed to mother them—"

"Why wouldn't she have been allowed to mother them?" Caroline broke in.

Realizing Caroline was not going to focus on food as long as they were talking about the lion cub, Zander reached for a couple of plates and started filling them from the serving bowls in the middle of the table.

Ellie, Leo, and Ellie's best friend and business partner, Cora, waited on the rest of the tables like a normal restaurant with menus and individual dishes. But for family it was more like they were all sitting down at a table in her home and she served up whatever she wanted to. It wasn't as if any of them would turn down any of her food anyway.

"We rescued Brinkley from her asshole owner," Naomi said with a frown. "It's possible he didn't want to deal with a bunch of puppies so when she had them, he probably took them away from her. Hopefully he gave them away but...who knows."

It was clear that other possibilities occurred to Caroline right away. She looked shocked, then angry, then sad, and Zander had to keep from snapping at them all to watch what they said.

Holy shit.

"Eat," he told her, sliding a plate in front of her.

She didn't give a specific indication she'd heard him, but she picked up a piece of bacon.

"So that could work?" Caroline asked. "Brinkley might mother a *lion cub*? I mean...seriously?"

Donovan nodded. "He needs someone to cuddle and comfort him, to keep him company, to teach him to do things like play appropriately. He won't need to learn to hunt if he stays with us, but—"

"*If*?" Caroline interrupted again. "You're not going to keep him for sure?"

"We're working on the paperwork," Fiona explained. "It shouldn't be a problem, but nothing is for sure until it's all signed."

Caroline frowned and looked at Zander. "But—"

"It will be okay," he said again. He made his tone firm. She seemed to respond to that best. Firm reassurance.

She took a deep breath as she looked at him.

He nudged her arm and she lifted the bacon to her mouth.

He smiled even as a shaft of heat hit his gut. He did like

being in charge and having people do what he told them to, especially when he was trying to take care of them. He loved to give orders that were immediately obeyed simply because the other person knew he had their best interest at heart. It made protecting people so much easier when he could simply bark out, "Stop!" or "Get out now!" or "Everyone inside!"

That Caroline so easily trusted him and listened gave him a sense of primal satisfaction that he couldn't deny.

It was the weirdest damn thing but when she took a bite of that bacon, it made him want to make her come hard, screaming his name. What bacon and orgasms had in common he couldn't have explained, except that it all fell under the category of taking care of her and making sure she had whatever she needed.

"So Brinkley can give the cub what he needs to be happy and healthy," Zander summarized as Caroline ate. "And physically, he's in decent shape and you have reason to think he can improve."

Griffin and Donovan both nodded.

"We might even get Brinkley and the cub another couple dogs to add to the pack," Donovan said. "Maybe a couple of other puppies too so he has some brothers and sisters his age to play and grow with."

"He'll outgrow them pretty fast, but if we get the right breed —something bigger but with a good temperament—it could work," Griffin said.

"There are others who have done this," Jill said, adding to the conversation for the first time. "Griffin and I are waiting for some calls back from colleagues."

Zander liked all of this. This was absolutely the right group of people for this. He really wanted Caroline to see that.

He was equally pleased when Caroline picked up a spoon and took a bite of the grits. Just like he'd enjoyed clothing her, he liked feeding her. Okay, Paige had clothed her and Ellie was feeding her, but he was arranging for those things to happen and that still gave him more pleasure than made sense.

It was a little caveman, he knew. He'd love to ask his brothers if this was how they felt about Jordan and Jill. But even as he thought it, he knew it was. He'd seen how his brothers looked at their wives. There was a possessive-affectionate heat in their eyes that he'd never seen in them before those women had come into their lives. He'd seen it in his cousins, Josh, Owen, and Sawyer too. The guys had all dated and had their share of flings and fun, but when the women who had settled them down and made them into husbands had shown up, the guys had become more open and more protective at the same time.

Not that Caroline was going to make him into a husband. That wasn't in his plans. It couldn't be. But she was showing him exactly what he was protecting for his brothers and cousins. Life with these women that made them better men and made them happier than they had ever been.

"Why do I have the FBI asking about stolen animals being kept at the animal park?"

Zander looked up to find that Knox had joined them. The city manager was perpetually annoyed by the animal park's existence.

Zander was right there with him. He'd written more parking tickets and been called to more fender benders in the past year since the petting zoo had added the sloths and lemurs —and had kept growing—than he had in the two years prior put together. People in Autre loved and hated having more strangers coming to town and wandering around. The visitors brought more business and money with them, but they also brought more congestion and noise.

Zander hated dealing with stupid stuff like people parking where they shouldn't and getting into arguments over who should have yielded to who at the four-way stop. But more, he hated that with so many strangers coming in and out of town, it was easier for troublemakers to get lost in the crowd. He didn't know who was here to see the alpacas and who was here checking out weaknesses in the security around town. And there was plenty of that. Autre was a sleepy little bayou town where everyone trusted one another. They didn't lock their back doors and they didn't look at one another with suspicion. And Zander didn't want that to change.

So he just had to be more vigilant and couldn't get distracted. He cast a glance at Caroline.

But Knox wasn't looking at Zander for an explanation about the FBI inquiry anyway. He was focused solely on Fiona.

"Hey, Zander called Spencer," Fiona told Knox, her hands up in surrender.

Knox narrowed his eyes. "You know Spencer?"

"Just met him today," Fiona said with a nod. "But we're best friends now." She batted her eyes at Knox. "I'm going to introduce him to some of my other contacts that could be helpful to him in investigating illegal animal buying and selling."

Knox crossed his arms and looked at her. "Is that right?"

He was a big guy, with longish hair, tattoos, and a bad attitude. At least when it came to things that made his life more difficult. Zander didn't really need to accompany the Viking lookalike when he needed to confront someone about...well, just about anything—property line disputes, someone who wasn't cleaning up their yard, or paying their water bill—but he often tagged along. The two of them could be damn imposing.

It didn't seem any of the women involved with the Boys of the Bayou Gone Wild thought so though. And Fiona Grady definitely didn't.

"Yep." Fiona grinned. "You know how *passionate* I get about guys who want to do right by animals."

Fiona poked Knox. All the time. It was very clearly one of her favorite things about visiting Autre. And the fact that Knox *could be* poked was also surprising. And amusing. He was easily annoyed, but Fiona didn't annoy him. She...got him worked up.

Zander cast a glance at Caroline. He knew exactly what Knox was feeling for Fiona.

"Spencer is here now?" Caroline asked, now leaning to look past Zander to Fiona.

"He's just back in the kitchen chatting with Cora," Fiona said, gesturing toward the swinging door behind the bar that led into the kitchen. "He's been waiting for you two."

Knox focused on Caroline. "You're the one who brought the lion cub."

He'd been in the bar Friday, but Zander understood why he hadn't immediately noticed she was the same woman. She looked very different today.

Caroline nodded. "Yes. With the hopes that someone would look into the whole situation."

Knox frowned. "There's a whole situation?"

"There are more animals where that cub came from," Caroline said with a nod. "I wanted him to be safe of course, which is why I chose Autre and Donovan." She shot the other man a smile. "But I'd hoped someone would be willing to take on the criminals behind it too."

"There are criminals?" Knox looked at Zander. His expression was one of concern tinged with exhaustion.

"Of course there are."

"It's under control."

Caroline and Zander spoke at the same time. He gave her shoulder a squeeze as he addressed Knox, giving his friend a look that said, *I've got this.* "Spencer is here and is taking it over. It's nothing for Autre to be worried about."

Knox gave him a nod. "Good to know."

"Well, Autre *should be* concerned that there are animals being illegally possessed by people who are using them as trophies and don't really care about them and aren't taking good care of them," Caroline protested.

"Of course," Zander said. "But Spencer is the best one to be taking this on."

"Wait, so you know something more about all of this?" Fiona asked. "I thought you just grabbed the lion and ran."

"My ex-fiancé gave me the cub. He's been transporting the animals from seller to buyer," Caroline said.

"Just lions?" Fiona asked.

"Oh no."

"You know the seller?" Naomi asked.

"Not for sure," Caroline told her. "I was trying to get that information, but I hadn't gotten that far when they suddenly sprang the wedding on me."

"They *sprang* the wedding on you?" Jill asked, now leaning in as well.

Knox and Zander sighed at the same time.

The last thing they needed was *all* the girls getting worked up.

Zander *was* going to take care of this. Or he was going to help Spencer take care of it. But he did *not* need the Autre women—the women who were willing to do anything and everything to save every puppy, squirrel, and injured sparrow they ran across—involved in trying to save exotic animals from being sold to private owners.

Of course that needed to be shut down.

But *these women* didn't need to be the ones doing it.

"Okay, we need to talk to Spencer," Zander said, shoving his chair back from the table.

"Yeah, you and I need to have a chat," Knox said, stepping toward Fiona.

"We do?" she asked.

"Yep. Let's go."

It didn't take a guy who read romance novels to understand

the sexual tension between them. It was palpable. Zander wasn't so sure anything had actually happened between them. Yet. But it seemed inevitable.

Fiona stared Knox down for about ten seconds. Then she rose.

It was then that Knox noticed the ankle brace she wore.

"What the hell is that?" he demanded, frowning. His arms dropped to his sides and he took a step forward.

"I twisted my ankle," she said, lifting a shoulder.

"Doing what?"

"Work."

Knox sighed. "Fi, what happened?"

Yeah, he liked her. A lot. The nickname slipped out when he was concerned or feeling protective. Zander had enjoyed feeling smug and teasing his friend about it. Knox always shut it down with a "Shut the fuck up" pretty quickly but it had been funny to see the big grump getting twisted up over the pretty brunette.

Now Zander felt a lot more sympathy. Caroline's scent drifted up to him and Zander felt a stirring that was a combination of desire and resignation.

He owed Knox an apology.

"I was trying to get out of the way of one of the giraffes and I stepped in a shallow hole and twisted it." She shrugged. "Just an accident."

"You were at home?" Knox asked.

"Yes."

"You weren't rescuing something?"

"No."

"You were just doing regular things? Well, regular for you."

She grinned. "Yep."

He studied her, but seemed to decide that she was telling him the truth. "Why didn't Colin fill the fucking hole in?" he finally asked. Grumpily.

Fiona rolled her eyes.

Zander almost laughed. Knox was protective of Fiona so he couldn't *not* be pissed about her ankle even if it was a normal, everyday routine thing that had caused it. Which meant, lacking anything else to blame, he was going to blame her friend and business partner, Colin.

"Colin isn't responsible for what happens with my holes, Knox," Fiona told him.

Knox froze and there was a beat of silence before there were a few snorts around the table.

While Knox was clearly still trying to figure out how to respond to that, Fiona took his hand and started toward the back door, limping slightly.

After three steps, Knox seemed to snap out of it and he bent, scooped her up, and carried her out the door.

Caroline turned wide eyes to Zander. "What's with them?"

"That is a very...big question."

"Zander! Finally!"

Zander looked over as Spencer stepped out of the kitchen.

Zander blew out a breath. That was good. He was glad to see his cousin. Spencer was going to take care of...all of this... and Caroline could hit the road. Tomorrow. That was good.

No matter how it felt.

"Hey, Spence," Zander greeted, rising as his cousin came to the table. They shared a quick one-arm hug, then he gestured toward Caroline. "This is Caroline Holland."

"Hi, Caroline," Spencer said, offering his hand.

"Hi."

They shook hands and Spencer gave Zander a quick glance.

It was the same knowing look Donovan had given him. These guys thought they knew him so well. And they did. In *other* aspects of his life. He trusted Spencer with his actual life. But they couldn't just look at Caroline and know Zander had feelings for her. He didn't have a type. He did, however, have an aversion to getting worked up and turned upside down for no reason. Which was very much how this all felt, and he was sure *looked* from the outside.

He resisted responding to Spencer's look.

"Where do you want to go to talk?" Spencer asked.

Caroline scooted back from the table and Zander had to clamp his mouth shut to keep from pointing out that she had barely eaten anything. That was none of his damn business or his problem. She was a grown woman who would be out of his life as of tomorrow morning.

"We can go to your office, right?" Caroline asked, looking at Zander.

"I was thinking we'd head to the rehab facility. That way you can hang out with Donovan and the lion after you tell Spencer what you know."

"Donovan won't mind waiting around?" Caroline glanced at the wildlife rescuer.

Zander gave her a smile. "It won't be long. You don't really have that much to tell Spencer."

She blew out a breath. "You've got a point."

Spencer arched a brow. "Don't tell me I drove down here for nothing."

Ellie smacked him on the back of the head as she came up behind him with the coffee pot. "You had breakfast."

Spencer chuckled. "Best I've had in a long time," he agreed.

Ellie gave him a grin and a wink as she went to refill mugs around the table.

Donovan held up a hand as she reached for his. "I'm good. Looks like I'm heading out."

"All of you?" Ellie asked as everyone started getting to their feet.

"Yep, see you later," Charlie said, dropping a kiss on her grandmother's cheek.

"'Bout time. I didn't think I was gonna get these dishes done by lunch," Ellie said, watching them all gather their things and start for the front door en masse with a look of affection.

Zander looked down at Caroline. She was frowning, watching them all go.

"What's wrong?"

"I hope I'm not inconveniencing everyone."

She was inconveniencing *him*. But he liked it.

He shook his head. "They're fine. And Donovan would be going to the rehab center anyway. Come on, I'll take you up there."

"Okay, let me just duck into the ladies' room." She headed for the restrooms at the back of the bar.

"Please tell me she really does have *some* useful information," Spencer said.

"You're just going to have to—"

"Excuse me!" a voice called, cutting off Zander's reply.

A stranger was striding through the bar, toward them. Her red hair was swinging as her ankle-high black boots hit the wooden floor with intent. She was slim and wore a sleeveless black blouse with a short black and gray plaid skirt, yet Zander had the impression she was willing, and maybe even able, to kick somebody's ass at the moment. She looked completely pissed off.

Both he and Spencer straightened. It was their natural instinct to react to anyone being upset but yes, women probably caught their attention a little more easily.

Maybe especially gorgeous redheads.

Spencer took a slight step toward the woman and Zander glanced at him. Zander couldn't help but smirk after all the shit Spencer had been giving him about Caroline.

"Can I be of some assistance?" Spencer asked.

"If you can tell me where my friend is. She checked into the bed and breakfast, but she isn't there this morning and no one seems to know where she is or when she left. All her stuff is still there. Including her phone. She never goes anywhere without it. So anyone want to tell me where she disappeared to?"

Zander frowned. She had to be talking about Caroline. He didn't like that at all. The first stranger to show up looking for Caroline had tried to stuff her into a car. Okay, he'd been her brother, but Zander still didn't like it. The second one had tried to sneak into the B & B while she'd been asleep. He *definitely* didn't like that.

Was this woman the next person they'd sent to bring Caroline home? Was she going to pretend to be a friend to get information about where Caroline was? Or was she actually someone Caroline knew who would pretend to be a concerned ally until she got Caroline into her car? Or alone somewhere she could keep Caroline until Brantley, or Christopher, or someone worse showed up?

Zander spread his feet and crossed his arms, keeping an eye on the woman and keeping his body between her and the bathroom.

"It's gonna be okay." Spencer held up a hand. "Just take a deep breath."

The woman's eyes widened and she took a step toward him. "A deep breath? My friend was nearly kidnapped the other day, then checked into a bed and breakfast in *this* town, and is now missing. And you want me to *take a deep breath*?" The woman looked Spencer up and down. "Who do you think you are?"

Clearly Spencer's attempt to be soothing wasn't working and he seemed confused by that. In spite of his suspicion of the woman, Zander had to cough into his hand to cover his laugh.

"How about you tell me who *you* are first," Spencer said.

"I don't need to tell you anything."

"Well if you want help, that's kind of how it works."

The woman's eyes narrowed as she studied Spencer. Zander opened his mouth to intervene.

"Wait, are you the hot cop?" the redhead asked Spencer before Zander could say anything.

Zander paused at that. Caroline's brother could have told this woman that there was a cop involved, of course, but he doubted Christopher had used the word "hot".

Spencer lifted a brow. "What makes you say that?"

"She told me she'd met a cop. He was the one who took her to the bed and breakfast in the first place. And you have cop written all over you." The woman pointed a finger and circled it as if to encompass all of Spencer.

"And you think I'm hot, huh?" Spencer gave her a cocky little grin.

"You're not exactly her type, though." The woman looked puzzled.

"No?"

"No. She goes more for the bad boys. Tattoos and stuff."

Spencer glanced at Zander.

Yeah, this sounded...off. Not that Zander was going to argue about Caroline's type. But because he didn't have the impression she was close to any of the women in the wealthy social circle her family was a part of. Not close enough to talk about what kind of men they were attracted to, anyway. Sure, this woman could be a total stranger to Caroline, sent here just to get information, but that just didn't feel right.

"You don't know that I don't have tattoos," Spencer told her. "But maybe if you're nice, I'll show you."

The redhead lifted both brows. "So my friend comes here, you put her up in the bed and breakfast, and now she's *missing*, but you're here having coffee, and hitting on total strangers? What the hell?"

Spencer stuck out his hand. "Special Agent Spencer Landry. I'm not your friend's cop. For the record."

The woman looked at his hand. "Special Agent?"

"FBI."

"Are you here investigating her disappearance?"

Spencer withdrew his hand when it seemed clear she wasn't going to take it. "I am not."

The woman's eyes flickered to the table behind him again. "Not done with your pancakes yet?"

"And who are you again?"

"Max Keller. Investigative journalist for the *New Orleans News*."

Surprise slammed into Zander. Wait a second. *This* was Caroline's Max? Her only friend? The reporter she fed info to? The one she'd gone to grade school with?

The Max Zander had been stupidly jealous of ever since he'd first heard the name and how close Max and Caroline were?

Holy shit. Max was a woman. A very attractive, feisty, clearly-protective-of-Caroline woman.

Spencer's mouth curled up. "Investigative reporter? So you're really good with details and stuff like that?"

The woman propped a hand on her hip. "I am. And holding people in power accountable."

"People in power. Right. Like him?" Spencer pointed at Zander.

The woman looked over, took note of Zander's uniform, and straightened. Then understanding dawned. "*You're* Caroline's cop."

Zander nodded. He sure fucking was. As problematic as that thought was. And *this* was Caroline's best friend. A woman. Who was not here to do her any harm. Or take her back to her family in New Orleans to marry Brantley Anderson. "Zander Landry."

"Landry? You two are related?"

"Yes."

"So it's safe to say the FBI is not here investigating *you* and the fact that you might've been the last person to see my friend alive?"

"Caroline is fine," Zander said.

"Caroline is not where she's supposed to be. Her phone is still in her room rather than *with* her and there's no sign of her."

"Were there signs of a struggle? Blood? Any witnesses hear or see anything strange?" Zander asked.

"No. But I know Caroline better than anyone. She wouldn't just up and leave without letting me know. She would never leave her phone behind unless she had a very good reason. And the people that she deals with probably wouldn't leave behind the signs of a struggle or blood."

That was interesting. Max was clearly not a fan of the circle Caroline usually ran in and he could appreciate that. She was also extremely protective of her friend and even ready and willing to fight with law enforcement to find Caroline. He liked Max.

"Well, gee, maybe there are things you don't know, Ms. Keller," Spencer said.

Zander shot his cousin a look. Why was Spencer poking this woman? She was clearly concerned about her friend and that wasn't inappropriate, considering the circumstances.

But when he looked back at Max and saw the spark in her eye and the pink in her cheeks, he understood. She was stunning and it was possible that Spencer just wanted to see her riled up.

"Look, Special Agent," Max said, derision dripping from her words like hot sauce from a crawfish. "I know Caroline, and I promise you that I'm going to get to the bottom of whatever is going on down here."

"Well, Ms. Keller, I can promise *you*—"

"Max!"

They all turned as Caroline came out from the back of the bar.

"I'm so glad you're finally here!" Caroline hurried forward with her arms out and a huge grin.

But Max didn't react immediately. She looked taken aback. It was clear she didn't recognize her friend at first.

Caroline came up short in front of Max, dropped her arms, and gave her friend a grin. "Hey. It's me."

Max started shaking her head. "Holy shit. What are you *wearing?*" Max stepped forward and pulled Caroline into her arms, hugging her tightly. But then she set her back and swept her gaze from head to toe. "What the *hell*? Where have you been? And I would have walked right past you looking like this."

"I'm sorry. I left my phone in my room last night. And I should have thought of you trying to call but I was..." Suddenly Caroline's cheeks got pink and she looked at Zander before dropping her gaze to the floor. "Busy."

Max gasped. "Caroline Camille Holland!" But then she grinned and hugged Caroline again. "Good for you." Her eyes met Zander's over Caroline's shoulder. "Yeah, he's definitely your type." She let Caroline go again and looked her over. "I seriously did not recognize you."

"Is it really that different?" Caroline looked down at herself.

"Girl, you're wearing...*denim*."

"I've worn denim."

"You've borrowed jeans from me. Like single digit times. You don't own your own jeans. And you've never worn cut off shorts in your *life*." Max lifted her hand to one of the braids that hung against Caroline shoulder. "And your hair is in braids? I have never seen your hair in braids."

"Never?" Caroline asked.

"I have known you for twenty years and I have never seen

your hair in braids. But, girl, you are rocking this denim. *Damn, you make a good country girl.*"

Caroline blushed slightly, and Zander felt his body stir. Of course, the woman could sneeze and he would feel his body stir.

Caroline ran a hand over the front of her tank top and jeans shorts. It was the most basic, most common outfit seen in Autre, Louisiana, and yet she was acting like she was wearing a ball gown.

"You really think so?"

"You always pull everything off," Max told her. "You make everything look beautiful. And I love and hate you for it. But yes, if you're going for blending in down here, you are spot on." With her hands on Caroline's shoulders, Max turned her, checking her out from all directions.

Zander certainly didn't mind and took the opportunity to do the same. But when he noticed that Spencer was also appreciating the various angles, he elbowed his cousin hard in the side. Spencer only laughed.

Max nodded. "Yeah, you need more shorts like this. Your ass looks great in those."

Caroline laughed and covered her butt with her hands, but she looked pleased.

Zander shook his head. Was it possible that this woman didn't know how fucking gorgeous she was? Or that other people never told her this?

"I concur," he told her, knowing his voice sounded husky.

"Same," Spencer said with a nod.

Zander punched him in the side this time and got a little *oof* before Spencer chuckled.

Caroline's cheeks were bright pink now, but she met his eyes and he felt the heat flicker between them.

"Yeah, I *knew* he was your cop," Max said, watching them.

"Stop it," Caroline told her softly.

"What? Long hair, tattoos, big, and willing to punch other guys? Totally what you go for." Her gaze flickered to Spencer. "That one is too buttoned up for you."

"You don't know a thing about me, darlin'," Spencer told her, drawling the last word for good measure.

"I know that if you do have tattoos, they're only in places where you can cover them up. Wouldn't want the FBI seeing any ink peeking out underneath your starched white sleeves, right?"

Spencer was, in fact, wearing a button-down white shirt with the cuffs rolled up. The tattoos on his upper arm and his left shoulder blade did not show. On purpose.

Spencer's gaze tracked over her now. "I'm not seeing any ink anywhere on you either."

"Yeah well, thankfully, being big and inked and badass isn't the only way to get girls into bed," she said in a sweet voice while she batted her eyelashes.

Her underlying meaning sunk in a second later, and Spencer straightened, blinking at her.

Zander smirked. It was a Landry male curse to assume that *all* women could be easily charmed by a grin and a drawled *darlin'*.

The problem was that they never learned any better, because it was true for eight out of ten women they encountered. Yes, all Landry men. Of course, those two out of ten women were the ones they ended up settling down with so they did figure things out. Eventually.

"Okay," Caroline broke in. "Max, I'm sorry I didn't tell you I left my room in the middle of the night. Zander came and got me."

"Very glad to hear it," Max said, appreciatively.

"Brantley showed up and Zander was worried about me staying there," Caroline explained quickly.

Max's smile dropped and she wrinkled her nose in confusion. "Brantley showed up in the middle of the night?"

"I left her phone behind," Zander said. "Wasn't sure if Brantley was tracking her through some kind of GPS. Don't know how else they found her."

"Brantley couldn't use his own GPS to find his way home from two blocks away," Max said with an eye roll.

She was protective of Caroline, built Caroline up, could spar with Spencer, and didn't like Brantley. Max was now one of Zander's favorite people.

"So why do you think he showed up?" Zander asked her.

"I have no idea," Max said. She looked at Caroline. "He's never acted like this before. Did you come across something else? Something bigger?"

Caroline shook her head. "Nothing new since the stuff I showed you."

"Hold on," Spencer said. "You know about all of this? The animals and everything?"

Max looked totally offended. "I told you I'm her best friend. She tells me everything."

"Except when she leaves the bed and breakfast last minute with Zander," Spencer said. With a smirk.

Max glared at him. Then she swung to Caroline. "And when you run away from your own wedding."

"I didn't have time!" Caroline protested.

"You weren't there?" Spencer asked.

"It was a surprise wedding," Max told him.

"So? Wouldn't her family invite her best friend?"

The women shared a look. Then Caroline said, "My family doesn't know about Max."

"Why not? Are you and Max secretly lovers?" Spencer asked.

Max rolled her eyes and muttered, "Jesus."

Caroline laughed out loud. "No. We've been friends since we were kids. But we kept it a secret. My family..."

Max tossed her long ponytail when Caroline trailed off. She looked up at Spencer, her hand back on her hip. "I'm from the wrong side of the tracks. They would never have approved of her hanging out with me. So we kept it on the down low. Made it a lot easier for her to sneak around with me and tell me all these secrets anyway. They've never suspected that Maxine Clermont, the woman who keeps breaking open the stories about their friends' corruption, embezzlement, and criminal activities is actually their daughter's best friend."

"You write under a pen name?"

"Maxine is my real name. Clermont is my stepdad's name. It's not my legal name but a lot of people assume it is. But it sounds like an older white lady with a bone to pick with old white men abusing their power, doesn't it?" She seemed pleased.

Spencer just studied her for several ticks. Then asked, "Do I need to do a background check on you?"

"As if I didn't think you were gonna do that anyway."

"Why would I have reason to do it anyway?"

"Because you're gonna try to find out how many women lovers I've had," Max told him, looking smug. "Because it's really bugging you to think that I might like girls instead of boys."

"*Okay*," Caroline and Zander spoke at the same time.

"Let's go to the rehab center," Zander suggested before his cousin could get into some very unprofessional hot water with a journalist. "Caroline, and now Max, can tell you everything they know about the animals and Brantley Anderson and anyone else. And Caroline can see the lion cub."

"Oh, me too!" Max said enthusiastically, her frown instantly morphing into a big grin as she linked arms with Caroline and started for the front door, dismissing Spencer without even another glance.

Max insisted that Caroline ride with her to the rehab center, but they followed Zander and Spencer in Zander's truck.

"Well, they're something," Spencer commented after a couple blocks of silence.

Zander shot him a grin. "Yup."

"You know, there might not be much I can do."

Zander squeezed the steering wheel. He did know that. "I really need you to do whatever you can, man."

"Of course. But without concrete—"

"I know," Zander cut him off. "Just be really confident. Convince her that you've got this covered."

"Which her?"

"Caroline. Though, fuck, you'll have to convince them both now. And Caroline would probably be easier."

Spencer didn't answer but Zander could practically sense him thinking, *No shit.*

They bumped along the dirt road toward the wildlife rehabilitation facility for several yards before Spencer asked. "So, what's up with you and Caroline?"

Zander understood that this wasn't just gossip or Spencer giving him shit. Spencer actually needed to know if his cousin was personally involved with a witness in an investigation he was about to start.

"I need her to leave. And she's not going to until she knows for sure this is being handled. She wants these animals safe. And, I mean, hell, so do I. But I know it can take some time. If you can just convince her that it's all good, that she can just turn it all over to you and go home, that would be great."

"Seems like you really like her, though," Spencer said.

"I do. That's exactly why she needs to leave."

Spencer nodded. "I'll tell her whatever you want."

One thing Zander really appreciated about Spencer and the

rest of the guys he worked with on these down-low ops was that they all understood not getting emotions wrapped up in what they did. And none of them were into deep conversations unless one of them wanted to talk something out.

"Not asking you to lie, man," Zander said. "Just use some of your natural confidence and charm."

Spencer grinned. "Can do. But I'm cool with lying if needed."

Zander looked over at him.

Spencer shrugged. "Hey, I'm not a priest. Or her husband. I'm fine with lying if it keeps her safe. If it also keeps you happy, even better. No struggle with my conscience. Safe and happy is what we do, right?"

Zander nodded. Safe and happy was absolutely what they did.

They pulled up at the rehab center and he watched as the girls parked next to them.

Safe and happy was what he wanted for Caroline. In fact, in the span of six days that had become his number one priority.

And safe had to come before happy.

12

"I 've never dated a guy with long hair and tattoos before."

Max grinned at her. "But those are the ones you always think are hot, whether they're celebrities or guys we met in college. Besides, if anyone needs a little bad boy in her life, it's you."

Caroline laughed. "Zander's a cop."

"Yeah, but he has a definite bad boy air about him, don't you think? Bet he has some stories in his past. Oooh, I bet it has something to do with why he became a cop." Max actually seemed genuinely curious.

Which was common for her. Caroline always chalked that up to her journalistic instincts. Max was curious about everything. Particularly people. And they didn't have to be good people. She didn't *like* bad people, but she was always curious about what made them tick.

"I don't really know. You are so sweet to talk me out of liking him so much."

Max looked at her. "Wait, why would I do that?"

"Because I can't be with him. I can't..." Caroline sighed.

"What? Have a normal life? With a good, normal guy?"

Max sighed. "I know we both take this thing we do with your family and their friends seriously, but you can't do that forever. If you've met a great guy, maybe you need to think about what that means. What your future looks like. I mean, you finally walked away from your family at the wedding. And I'm *so* proud of you. Maybe you just need to make that stick now."

Caroline shook her head. "How do I make that stick? What am I going to do? I panicked. I should've thought it through. I have no job, nowhere to live. I just showed up on Zander's doorstep. Yeah, he likes me. But he's planning on me leaving town as soon as possible. He's certainly not talking about anything long-term. And even if he was, that would be crazy."

"So what? You're going to go home and actually marry Brantley? Come on, Caroline. *That* would be crazy. No. Leaving was the right thing to do. And now you're away from them and now you can find a new path."

"What about you? This affects you too. I've been feeding you all this information all these years. You're the one who encouraged me to start doing that."

Max nodded. "I know. And I've had a lot of guilt and second thoughts about that. Frankly, it's been fun. And I think we've done some good work. But we both knew that wasn't going to last forever."

Caroline wasn't so sure *she'd* known that. She hadn't thought about it anyway. Which was naïve, she realized now. "I suppose I was waiting for my dad to have some big epiphany or something," she said. "Something that would indicate we had accomplished something. That I'd...made a difference."

Suddenly her chest felt tight. Had she made a difference? Really? Some bad people had paid some fines, and a few had spent some time in jail. Not everyone had gotten away with all the bad things. But her father was still conducting his business with these people. Every time one of them got caught, by her and Max or someone else, she became aware of two more doing ugly, illegal things.

"Ugh," Max groaned. "I've hated some of the positions you had to be in and I knew you wouldn't stop until your dad changed and I didn't think he'd ever really change. And I've had inklings that it was getting more dangerous. And when you suddenly told me that you were going to get Brantley to propose to you and you were going to say yes, I realized we'd gotten in too deep. We can't keep playing these games, Caroline. I love getting this information and breaking these big stories, but I can't keep putting you in these positions and there are other ways for me to get information. I'll have to develop new sources."

Caroline blew out a breath. She'd given Max names, dates, relationships, even direct quotes in a few cases. She'd turned over recordings, a video or two, documents and emails, and photographs. She knew she was Max's primary source for the big stories Max broke. But Max had to back up the information or try to at least get someone to authenticate it. She was sure Max would be able to find others who could give her dirt on the people they were trying to hold accountable.

"Caroline," Max said, reaching over to squeeze her hand. "You've been *very* important. I don't want you to think that's not true."

"I know. But you can do this job without me."

Max didn't deny it. She shrugged again. "If it means that you'll go out and fall in love and have a life that doesn't revolve around scumbags, then yes, I can do my job without you. But it won't be as fun."

"Okay," Caroline gave her a smile and nod. She didn't need Max to make her feel better about all of this. The stories they'd broken and the people they had exposed had deserved it. She didn't regret any of the time she'd spent being Max's informant.

Still, she had a niggling, nagging feeling that she was floating, a little lost, without any specific direction now. Her reason for living the life she lived had been to try to protect her family and to help keep them on the right side as much as possible. Now she wondered if she'd actually done that and if she should just leave all of this to people like Zander and Spencer.

"Listen," Max told her, turning back to watch Donovan with the lion cub in the pen on the other side of the fence where they stood. "If you need a place to stay, you're obviously going to be in my guest room. And you have a college degree, Caroline. You're smart and bold and resourceful. We'll figure something out."

"Thanks. I'm gonna take you up on the guest room."

"This is incredible," Max said distracted for a moment as Naomi led a German Shepherd into the pen.

Caroline assumed this was Brinkley. The dog was on a leash and Naomi brought her closer to Donovan, who held out his hand. Brinkley sniffed his hand and then bumped against it, asking for a rub on the head. After he'd loved on the dog for a moment, he brought her around to show her the lion cub. The dog sniffed at the cub curiously. The cub mewled softly, and the dog reared back as if in surprise. Donovan chuckled, and Naomi dropped to the ground next to them sitting crisscross, clearly as fascinated by the scene unfolding as Max and Caroline were.

"At least I did this right," Caroline said, shaking her head. If nothing else, she knew bringing this lion to these people had been the right move.

Max looked at her. "You've made a ton of right moves, Caroline."

"Yeah. I just want to keep making right moves."

"Oh my God, I almost forgot," Max dug in the bag she had slung over her shoulder and pulled out a large manila envelope. She handed it over. "This might be what Brantley was looking for."

Caroline frowned at her. "What do you mean?"

"Didn't you say that Brantley told Zander he came looking for you in the middle of the night because you had something he needed back?" Max asked. "It is not like Brantley to just show up in the middle of the night and sneak around. He's hardly a stealthy kind of guy. Unless there's something that you have that he doesn't want you to know about."

Caroline opened the clasp at the top of the envelope and pulled out a packet of papers about five pages thick. "What is this?"

"Names, amounts, dates, and addresses," Max said. "I'm wondering if these are buyers or sellers. Or both."

Caroline lifted wide eyes to her. "Where did you get this?"

"Outside pocket of your suitcase. I mean, I was worried when you weren't at the bed and breakfast, but I thought that maybe you had left me a clue or a note or something. So I went through your stuff."

Caroline laughed. Of course she had. Max would've had no qualms about going through her stuff if she thought Caroline was actually missing. Or even if she thought Caroline was hooking up with a hot cop across town. Max would've wanted to know what was going on.

"I did not put this in my suitcase."

Max nodded. "Exactly. You said that you didn't pack your suitcase, right? Maybe whoever did, put this in there. Or maybe Brantley just stuck it in there at the last minute. But it makes sense that it's something you had that he needed back and something that he would come sneaking around to get."

"I have no idea what to do with this information."

Max grinned at her. "But I do. I'm going to start running these names and addresses."

Max was a master researcher. She could track down all kinds of interesting information from all kinds of places most people wouldn't think, or even know, to look. But it drove her crazy that she wasn't good at computer hacking and didn't have a lot of the higher tech skills she would kill to have. She'd solved the problem by becoming friendly with several people who existed in the gray area between legal and illegal and had made a few you-scratch-my-back-I'll-scratch-yours deals over the years.

She'd also tried to have them teach her some of their more useful skills, but she didn't have a particularly techy mind and the two times she'd tried it on her own, her hacker friend Diego had made her swear to never do it again. The fixes he'd had to do to keep them from being discovered had been extensive and had made him sweat.

"You mean you can have Diego run them."

"Well, I'm gonna start with the stuff I know. But yeah, if there's anything interesting, he can dig a little deeper."

Diego was just one more way Max could get information that she didn't need Caroline for.

Caroline shook that off though. Max loved her and they were a great team, and it didn't matter if Caroline only gave her half-assed information that she had to further research. Caroline had been useful, dammit.

"You've already taken photos of this stuff, right?" Caroline asked, knowing her friend well.

"Of course."

"Okay, then we should turn this over to Zander and Spencer."

"Yeah, I guess we should." Max's gaze flickered over to the other end of the rehab facility.

Caroline and Max were standing outside where Donovan was working with the lion cub and introducing him to his, hopefully, new foster mom. Zander and Spencer were standing several yards away out of earshot discussing whatever two cops needed to discuss about illegal animal buying and selling in Louisiana.

"Spencer's pretty good-looking, isn't he?" Caroline asked casually.

Max laughed. "Very much so."

"Why don't you like him?"

"He's one of those bossy-in-charge-I-always-know-best guys," Max said. "You know how I am with those."

If you told Max not to do something, it became her number one priority to do exactly that thing. She didn't do well with authority.

"What if he brings down an illegal animal buying and selling ring?"

"What if he does?"

"Would that make you like him more?"

"If he *doesn't* do that, it will make me like him less. It's his *job* to do that, isn't it?"

"Yeah, I guess it is."

Max nodded. "Wouldn't it be nice to just count on the good guys to do *good* things, instead of worrying about the bad guys not doing bad things?"

Caroline looked over at Zander again and found him watching her. "I think that there are a lot of good guys we can count on to do good things."

Max whistled low and shook her head. "Wow, you have it bad."

"He's just been...great."

"I'm glad," Max said, turning Caroline back to face her. "But, sweetie, your standards for great are very low because of the scumbags you spend time with. I just want you to keep in mind that he doesn't really have to try that hard. Keep your wits about you and maybe even more importantly, protect your heart."

Caroline swallowed. Max definitely had a point. Caroline was not used to guys being good, deep down, and doing the right thing. It didn't take much to impress her. She nodded. "Duly noted."

"Now, you go in there and spend some time with your lion cub," Max said.

"Where are you going?"

Max plucked the envelope from Caroline's hand, but was watching the two cops. "To negotiate."

"You're going to convince them to let you in on the story in exchange for this information?"

Max grinned. "Exactly."

Well, at least someone had a plan. And there were three someones who could do something useful in this whole situation.

Caroline looked into the pen where the German shepherd was now lying on her stomach, her nose up next to the lion cub who was rolling on his back and batting at the dog. They both seemed completely at ease and she felt a smile stretch her mouth.

That was good. That mattered. She'd done *that*.

Caroline caught Donovan's eye and he lifted a hand and waved her into the pen. She felt lighter as she unlatched the gate and stepped through.

She just needed to focus on the things she could do and trust Zander and Spencer and Max to do the rest.

Even if that left a hollow ache in her gut.

Zander and Spencer were *finally* doing exactly what she'd been insisting and nagging them about doing for days.

Which meant, three days after Spencer and Max had landed in Autre, Caroline was bored out of her mind.

It wasn't just them, actually. It was everyone. Everyone was working and, as pathetic as it made her, she had nothing to do.

She had no real job. She didn't really have any hobbies other than plotting rich men's downfalls and actively trying to cajole a hot small-town cop into doing an investigation. And a girl could only go on so many swamp boat tours and do so much otter yoga. Mostly because otter yoga only happened at certain times of day and they needed the seats for *paying* customers on the swamp boats.

She'd been helping Donovan out up at the rehab center but he'd gotten a call for an animal rescue—something about armadillos and a collision with a skateboard—so he'd needed to leave. Max had gone back to the bed and breakfast because she had a deadline on another story that she had to meet and she was going to make some phone calls about the lion cub case.

Everyone else in Autre had been sweet and patient about having Caroline around. But they all had actual important jobs to do. Running a petting zoo and animal park and taking tourists out on swamp boat tours sounded like a great time, but it was also a lot of work. Feeding and caring for a bunch of animals, especially exotic—and in some cases endangered—ones, and maintaining all the equipment that went into both the animal park and the swamp boat tours was no small thing.

She could of course have returned to the bed and breakfast. But yesterday she'd helped Heather bake muffins...and had burned three dozen. It was probably no surprise to anyone in Autre that the wealthy socialite wasn't much of a domestic goddess.

Of course, she would've loved to spend the day hanging out with Zander, but Zander and Spencer were busy doing, well, exactly what she'd been hounding them to do. Besides their regular jobs, they were looking into everything she'd given them about Brantley, the lion cub, and now the list of names and numbers they'd discovered in her suitcase.

In short, Caroline was the only one who didn't have

anything to do and would basically be in the way of everyone else working.

Which was why she found herself approaching the front of Ellie's bar. She honestly didn't have anywhere else to go and while, obviously, Ellie was at work, she was also the one most used to people hanging around while she did it.

Caroline took the bar stool next to where Leo was sitting and gave him a smile.

"Well, hey there," he greeted.

"Hi. Mind if I join you?"

"I never have and never will turn down the chance to have a pretty girl sit next to me," Leo said.

Ellie chuckled from across the bar. "That's for sure. And everyone here in Autre knows it. It's how we always end up with dozens of boxes of Girl Scout cookies, at least four of whatever the moms with the PTA are selling for their fundraiser, and why all the guys from all the sports teams send their girlfriends or sisters over to talk to him when they're raising money."

Caroline chuckled. "So you're a soft touch?"

Leo nodded. "No apologies."

"What can I get you, honey?" Ellie asked.

"Coffee, I guess."

Ellie gave her a look. "You're not here to drink coffee."

"What do you mean?"

"I know all about the coffee Zander's been buying you in Bad and that you've been drinking with Charlie and Jordan. How about a Pimm's Cup? Nobody in Bad or around Autre even tries to compete."

"You don't mind not having the best coffee?" Caroline asked with a grin.

Ellie waved her hand. "What you all drink isn't coffee. It's milk and sugar and foam and syrups with a hint of coffee flavor if you close your eyes and concentrate really hard. My *coffee* does what coffee's supposed to do. It warms you up, wakes you up in under thirty seconds, and tastes like coffee."

Caroline laughed. "But it's ten o'clock in the morning. Is that too early for a Pimm's Cup?"

"Are you driving? Taking care of children, sick or old people, or operating heavy machinery?" Leo asked.

Nope. She wasn't doing *anything*. "No to all of the above."

"Then it sounds like Pimm's o'clock to me," Leo said.

Day drinking was not something she did a lot of, but what the hell?

"Well, you've been telling time down here longer than I have," she finally said. "I'll go with whatever you say."

As Ellie mixed the drink. Leo sipped from his own coffee cup. "So, I hear you're an interior decorator."

"I do interior design," Caroline said. She didn't want to lie to these people. For some reason. Probably because they were good, decent people who had been treating her very well since she'd been here. But Zander didn't want his family to know what all she was mixed up in and if she told them that she only played at interior design they might want to know why.

Leo swiveled on his stool and surveyed the room. "So we were thinkin' to redo something in this place."

Caroline felt both her brows rise. "Really?"

She couldn't say why she was surprised, but both Leo and Ellie fit so well inside this bar. They were very laid back and there was nothing elaborate or even remotely pretentious about either of them. They'd both been wearing jeans and a t-shirt every time she'd seen them.

Sometimes Leo's was a Boys of the Bayou t-shirt since, as he'd explained, he drove the bus that went to New Orleans to pick tourists up from their hotels and deliver them to the docks for swamp boat tours. But other times his t-shirts said things like, *So when's this old enough to know better supposed to kick in?*

Ellie wore t-shirts with various sayings and logos from the

fifty states and had explained that she was sent them from tourists who had come in and enjoyed their time in the bar. The one she wore today said, "Maryland! We've got crabs!"

The bar was very much like Leo and Ellie, in Caroline's opinion. Laid back, with a come-as-you-are vibe that was so comfortable and friendly you immediately felt at ease and like you knew you'd be back. It was filled with a collection of mismatched chairs and tables, a scuffed wooden floor, and the décor was very..."we like this stuff and don't really care what you think of it". The walls were covered in photographs—of the family, the town, the bayou, visitors and tourists, events, and holidays—posters, sports team banners, and an odd collection of other paraphernalia that, if it had a theme, Caroline hadn't a clue what it was.

"Yeah, we were thinking of something like this." Ellie wiped her hands on the apron she had tied around her waist and pulled her phone from her back pocket. She quickly swiped her fingers over the screen and then turned it for Caroline to see.

Caroline's eyes widened. "Seriously?"

The site was a bar and restaurant décor website and the photo Ellie had pulled up was for a sleek, modern pub done in blacks and grays with a lot of silver and glass accents. The floor was stone, the bar top looked like granite.

"Yeah. It would modernize the place, right? Now that the grandkids are older and a younger crowd is hanging out here, we thought maybe that was a direction we should consider," Ellie said. "They've got friends coming in and we're competing with the bars in New Orleans—they love to hang out at Trahan's Tavern right down in the Quarter—and the place up in Bad is definitely fancier than we are."

Oh. They were worried about competing for business? Well, she could understand that, she supposed. Caroline studied the photo again. "Well, I mean, you could do this, but I think you need to go with browns instead of grays, at least. The black and glass would still give it a modern look but..."

She couldn't do this.

It hit her all of a sudden.

The bar in this photo was *not* Ellie's. It looked too polished, too cold, too...not Ellie's.

She suspected Leo and Ellie were just being nice. What else were they going to talk to her about after all? But this photo was real and Ellie had pulled it up easily. Damn.

She'd actually been hoping for some more stories about Zander and the rest of their grandkids growing up. She'd been enjoying those a lot the last few days. She had a feeling she would've enjoyed the stories anyway, but hearing Zander's cousins and brothers tell the stories was doubly entertaining.

She'd even gotten a few tales about Zeke and Zander switching places as identical twins. She would've been disappointed if they hadn't done that, but in even the few days she'd known them, they were absolutely the types to do those kinds of swaps.

Her favorite of them all was about the time Zander had been a starting receiver on the football team their senior year. Zeke had been second string, but only because of disciplinary problems like showing up late to practice and not learning the playbook in as much detail as their coach wanted.

They were in the second half of the homecoming game and the team distracted the coach long enough for Zeke and Zander to switch jerseys. When it was time for the big play at the end of the game, the ball had been thrown to Zeke instead of Zander and he'd scored the final big touchdown.

Of course they couldn't celebrate *too much* without calling attention to what they'd done, but just having Zeke and the rest of the team know who'd actually scored had meant a lot.

And Caroline had found herself not one bit surprised that Zander had put his brother ahead of his own moment of glory.

Caroline looked up at Ellie. "You're really interested in doing something new?"

"Well, this past winter, the boys sideswiped the building there on the side," Leo said, pointing to the main wall straight across from the bar.

"Sideswiped? You mean with a car?"

"Airboat."

Caroline opened her mouth.

"It was more than a *swipe*," Ellie said with a laugh. "They more or less crashed through that wall. That's why that wall looks like it's brand new. It is. And we've been needing to repaint it. Which got us thinking about remodeling in general. They're damned lucky Zeke and Mitch do construction."

"And turns out the rest can follow directions and use tools when their grandmother is their foreman," Leo said with a chuckle.

"Bunch of idiots," Ellie muttered, shaking her head.

"I'm sorry. Can we just go back for a second?" Caroline said. "The boys—I'm assuming some of your grandsons—crashed through the wall with an *airboat*?"

They were very close to the bayou. Walking distance. She could see the water that led out into the bayou if she went out the front door of Ellie's. The docks for the Boys of the Bayou Swamp Boat Tours were just on the other side of the road. But they were certainly far enough from the water that accidentally hitting a building with an airboat seemed like a bigger story.

"Well, they had the airboats up on the streets."

Caroline blinked at him. "The airboats can go up on land?"

"It was after the big ice storm. They got the boats up on the ice and because airboats only have big fans on the back and no rudders or anything underneath, they can just slide along like big sleds." Leo grinned. "I mean, it looked like a hell of a good time."

"Something you have to know about Landry men," Ellie

said, bringing her drink over to her, "is that the more guys, the fewer IQ points. So they put these humongous fast-moving 'sleds' up on the ice and forgot that airboats don't have brakes."

Caroline gasped. "Did anyone get hurt?"

"Of course. But they all lived through it. Which, to them, was proof that they should do it again because it would be even better next time. Story of my life."

Caroline laughed. "So they bash into the side of the building and you had to do repairs and now you want to possibly redecorate the whole place?"

"Thinkin' about it," Ellie said with a nod, looking at Leo, who also nodded.

Caroline looked around again. She wasn't really an interior designer and there was no way she was going to haphazardly throw crazy shit up inside this establishment like she usually did. She never really cared about her jobs. The people she "worked" for could afford even the stupidest, most elaborate things she could find. And there was no limit to how ridiculous they would go. But there was no way she was going to do her usual thing here. She *liked* Ellie and Leo.

She took a breath and took the phone, holding it up and looking out at the room. She could definitely help them find fixtures and flooring and a bar top and shelves like this.

Ellie stepped up on the little footstool she kept behind the bar because she was too short to reach across the top. She leaned onto her elbows. Leo propped an elbow on the bar and also focused on Caroline fully.

"Okay, well, we could..." But she couldn't even finish the sentence. She shook her head. "I'm sorry. I don't think you should do this."

Ellie and Leo both looked at her in surprise.

"You don't think we should do what?" Leo asked.

"I don't think you should redecorate. At least, not this drastically. I understand that you want to put that wall back together, but the way you have it decorated is...you. And I think that the spaces where people spend a lot of their time should reflect who they are. Whether it's their home or their business. People should have a space that makes them feel happy and comfortable and like it's where they belong. I know this isn't your house, but this place almost seems more like a home to you and your family than anywhere else."

Ellie was looking at her with a soft smile. "So what do you think we should do?"

"Well, you could paint that wall. It would be nice in a little brighter color. Maybe a lighter tan or even a cream color. But something simple. It's just a backdrop. What I think is important is what you put on it. These are the things that are important to you," Caroline said, indicating the posters, banners, and photos. "The things that make up your life. I don't think you should change it."

"But other bars and restaurants have a theme to their decor. Like sports bars have sports teams. Other bars might have a more local theme like a railroad or a music theme," Leo said. "We talked about maybe putting up a bayou theme in here. Boats and fishing gear and things like that."

Caroline nodded. "I understand that. The bayou is a huge part of your life and the local lifestyle. And people might come in here because of the bayou, but they don't fall in love with it and come *back* because of that. They fall in love and come back because they feel like a part of the family. Because they feel welcome and accepted here. That's what all of this represents." She gestured to encompass all of the photographs they had hanging on the wall. "I think these photographs are key. The posters and sports banners are great, but these photographs need to stay for sure."

"So just repaint the wall and stick this all back up?" Leo said. "That seems easy enough."

Caroline was studying the wall and an idea occurred to her.

She slid off her stool and crossed to the wall. She pulled one of the photographs down. One that she'd been looking at for a couple of days and that she really liked for some reason. She carried it back over to Leo. "Tell me about this photo."

Leo smiled as he looked at it. "Well, that's me and Danny Allain." He pointed to the two men standing on the airboat in the background. "Danny was Cora's husband. My best friend. We started Boys of the Bayou way back in the day. And these boys on the dock are Josh, Owen, Sawyer, Mitch, Fletcher, Zeke, and Zander." He pointed to each one as he named them.

Caroline nodded. "And what do you think about when you see this photo?"

"Same thing I thought about every time we had those boys down on that dock when they were kids. How they reminded us that even though we had to worry about bills, and deadlines and due dates, and things like illnesses and repairs, there was always another day with a bright blue sky and a big warm sun, and more laughter and smiles to come."

Caroline swallowed hard. "See, that's the feeling you give all the people who come down here. Like I said, they come for the bayou, but they leave with *that* feeling. If we were to put a frame around this photo in any color, what color do you think it should be?"

"Sky blue," Leo said. "For sure. That's the color I think of when I look at that photo."

Caroline nodded, feeling strangely emotional.

She turned and looked at the wall again. Then back to Leo and Ellie. "One of the things I love best about this room is all of the mismatched furniture. All the different styles and colors in the furniture is just like all the different kinds of people who come in here and sit down and eat and drink and laugh. It's also like all the different people and personalities in your family who all come together and make one big crazy group. I think you should leave that exactly as it is. And I think we should frame each of these photos in a different colored frame and hang them back up on this wall."

Leo and Ellie stared at her for a long moment. Then they looked at each other, then back to Caroline. Finally Ellie said, "Damn, girl, we were just trying to make conversation with you. But that's amazing."

Caroline felt her cheeks heat. "My God, you don't have to do any of that." She'd gotten carried away. She pressed her hands to her face. "It was really fun just brainstorming. A lot of times people I work for don't get involved in the ideas. They just tell me to go do whatever I want and throw money at it. I never get to actually talk with them about what's important or what they care about. It's never this personal. But you don't have to listen to me at all. No hard feelings."

Leo shook his head. "Don't be ridiculous. We're definitely gonna do all of that."

Caroline pressed her lips together and regarded these two people who were loving and outgoing and completely accepting and had made her feel welcome and taken care of in her time here. "Can I tell you a secret?" she finally asked.

Leo nodded. "Lots of people do."

"I'm not really an interior designer. I didn't study for that in school. It's really just a hobby. I don't actually know what I'm doing."

"Well, can I tell you a secret?"

"Of course."

"I had no intention of painting any walls when you walked in here, but you've convinced me. Now I can't wait." Leo slid off his stool with a chuckle.

"Well, if you're serious, I think this is the first time I've ever actually designed something legitimate. Something that would actually matter to the person I'm doing it for."

"I'd say this is about as legitimate as it can get. You took something that was really meaningful to us and made it even more special."

Caroline grinned, feeling warmth spread through her chest.

"I'm heading up to get paint, you okay with a cream color?" Leo asked Ellie.

"Yep. And I'm gonna call Beau and see if he can make us some custom frames. He's one of the best woodworkers around and he's right here in town," Ellie explained to Caroline. "He's also practically family. His mom is the sister of one of our daughters-in-law."

Caroline shook her head. It seemed everybody in town was connected to the Landrys in some way or another.

"Leo?" Caroline asked. "Can I..."

"What?"

"Can I help you paint?"

He shook his head. "You don't have to do that."

She nodded. "Yeah, I know. But I want to. I never actually *do* any of this. I never get my hands dirty. I order stuff from furniture companies and art galleries. We hire painters and people to put in the new flooring and fixtures. I never actually do any of it or feel a part of it. I think this would be really fun."

"Well, I'm never gonna turn down the offer to spend more time with a pretty girl."

Ellie just laughed and shook her head.

13

Forty-five minutes later they had all of the photos and posters off the wall and plastic drop sheets on the floor and had pushed all of the tables to one side of the room so that Ellie and Cora could continue waiting on customers as they came and went. Caroline and Leo had all of their supplies and had just started rolling cream-colored paint onto the walls.

"This is not exactly how somebody usually vacations here in the bayou," Leo said from the stepstool he was using to reach the upper half of the wall while Caroline dealt with the lower.

She smiled up at him. "Actually, this is so much more laid back and relaxed than what I usually do. At home, I'm usually on all the time, having to worry about what people are thinking and what they really mean by what they say and what they're talking about behind my back. I love it here. Everybody is genuine and says what they think and they truly take care of one another. I'm really amazed by your whole family, Leo. They do really important work here. Whether it's construction or teaching or veterinary medicine or running a petting zoo or taking people on tours and teaching them about the ecology and the history and culture of this area. On the surface, it all seems so light and fun. But what they do really matters. I know you're really proud of them all."

Leo nodded as he rolled paint onto the wall. "Absolutely. I take partial credit, of course. I like to think that I was a good role model and give out some good advice when asked, but they definitely help one another too."

She nodded. "I love that too. They are incredible individuals and as a group they are an unstoppable force."

"I'd say that's pretty accurate."

"It's so great that you all have created this place where people can come and kick back and relax and enjoy life a little bit."

"Yeah, it's a gift to be able to give people happiness."

That was just so *nice*. No wonder all these people had turned out to be so generous and sweet with a grandfather like this.

She glanced down as she stepped to the side and noticed a photo that had fallen under the edge of the tarp. "Oh!" She leaned over and gingerly pulled it free. "This one didn't make it over to the table." They'd moved all the photos and posters to a table on the far end of the room to keep them away from any paint splatters. She studied the photo. "Who's this?" She held it up to Leo.

He looked down, and a soft, sad smile touched his lips. "That's Tommy. Maddie's older brother, Cora's grandson."

"Does he live around here?"

"He did. He was one of the partners in the Boys of the Bayou. Took it over with Sawyer, Josh, and Owen from me and Danny. But he was killed a few years ago."

Caroline gave a little gasp. "Oh, I'm so sorry."

"Yeah. He was out on the bayou alone and was bitten by a bull shark. Lost a lot of blood, and by the time Sawyer found him, it was too late to bring him back."

Caroline studied the photo. "That must've been really hard on everyone."

"Absolutely. Tore us all up pretty good. It's not something you ever totally get over."

She nodded. "He looks so happy in this photo."

"He *was* happy in that photo." Leo got down off the footstool. He crossed to the table. Caroline followed. "This is Maddie's mom. She was killed in a drunk driving accident."

Caroline looked at the picture of the beautiful woman smiling, holding two happy little kids. That had to be Maddie and Tommy.

"This is Michael's son's mother, Lauren." Michael was with her in the photo. She was clearly several months pregnant. They were in front of Ellie's with Naomi and Jordan and several of the Landry boys, hugging and smiling.

"Are she and Michael still together?" Caroline asked.

Leo shook his head. "They weren't really together even then, but they were going to raise Andre together. Then she was killed in a big explosion when Andre was just a baby."

"An explosion?" Caroline repeated.

"Our community center here in Autre was destroyed by a gas explosion. Several people died, many others were injured. Our whole community was rocked by that. It happened back when most of the grandkids were teenagers."

Caroline frowned, feeling her stomach knot. "I'm so sorry to hear that."

Leo nodded. "It was very tough."

He pointed at another photo. Caroline easily recognized Spencer in the photo. A much younger Spencer, but it was obviously him. He was smiling into the camera with another boy next to him and his arm around an older woman.

"That's Spencer and his brother Wyatt with their grandmother. She was killed in the same explosion." Leo pointed to another photo. "And that's Zander and his best friend growing up, Theo."

Caroline also recognized Zeke in the photo. There was another boy as well.

"Zander was always close to all the Landry boys, of course, but Zander and Theo were tight ever since kindergarten. Great man. He and Zander are still close."

Caroline knew what Leo was about to tell her. "And this other boy?" she asked softly.

"That's Theo's older brother, Wade. He was at the community center that night too."

Caroline covered her mouth with her hand. "So much loss."

"Yep. And it was so sudden. For all of us. The people left behind still have huge holes in their hearts and their lives. The crazy thing that a lot of folks still grapple with, is that people came and went from the community center all night. There were people, some of our own family, who had been there earlier in the night. Others who showed up late and just happened to be there when the explosion happened." Leo stopped and swallowed. He shook his head. "Wade wasn't supposed to be there at all. He and two friends snuck in, trying to steal beer. On a dare. They were there at just the wrong time."

"Oh God," Caroline murmured.

"Yeah. That was definitely part of why it was so hard. Zander and Theo were shocked and sad, but also pissed for a long time. If Wade hadn't been taking a stupid risk, he wouldn't have died that night."

Caroline nodded.

"Zander watched Theo go through losing his brother," Leo went on. "They were just kids. Tore Theo up. Watching Theo suffer like that, deal with the idea that he could have, should have, stopped Wade from going in there, all of that was horrible. Then going home to his own brothers and his cousins who were like brothers and realizing how suddenly he could lose them and seeing what that would be like. That changed him."

"That was when he decided to be a cop?"

"I don't know if he specifically decided to be a policeman then, but he was destined to be a protector all along. Ever since he was a little kid. He was always looking out for others. Especially Zeke. But that was when he got really anxious about losing people close to him and wanting to do something tangible about it."

"I'm so glad you have all these photos," she said. She took a deep breath. "Now I'm even more convinced that putting them back up is important. This shows the good times, the smiles and laughter. It's a reminder that even if there are sad and dark times, there are happy times too." She looked up at Leo. "It's like what you said about that first photo I showed you, the one with the sky blue frame—the kids reminded you that in spite of the bills and illnesses and repairs, there were more blue skies and warm sunshine to come, right?"

Leo's smile was bright and sincere. "Yes, Caroline. That's exactly right. And I'm so glad you can look at these photos and understand that. Zander needs someone like that."

She looked at him in surprise. "What?"

Leo nodded. "Zander almost never takes time off. He lives in a town that specializes in vacations, and kicking back, in having fun. His family owns a bar and a tour company and a petting zoo. We throw a crawfish boil every Friday. But where Autre is fun for everybody else, it's a responsibility for him. And the more people come to this town and the more people that we add to this family, the more responsibility he feels. Every time he takes even half a day to go fishing, I pray the whole time that nothing will happen while he's gone because he'd never forgive himself."

"Oh, Leo..."

"But since you've been here in town, we've seen him smiling

more than he has in years. We see him relaxing, slowing down a little. He never does that. He never takes time for himself. But this last week he's actually smiling, laughing, and showing up late, and dawdling. It's really nice to see."

Caroline had no idea what to say. Her throat and her chest felt tight, but now her stomach twisted harder. But...she wanted that for Zander. She wanted him to be able to relax and take time to laugh and enjoy and to look around this town and look at these people around him and realize how wonderful it all was and not just worry all the time. She wanted him to look at these photos and have the feelings Leo had—memories of blue skies and warm sun and laughter instead of the loss and hard times that were to come. Hell, she wanted to see dozens more photos with Zander *in* them, smiling and laughing like he had as a kid. Before he knew about loss and grief and fear and worry.

"Well, that makes me feel really good, Leo. Thanks for telling me all of this."

"You think you might hang around a little bit?" Leo asked.

Could she hang out in Autre? A few days ago she would've said that was crazy. But now, she realized that she hadn't felt this much like herself in years. She nodded. "I just might."

"We might get to add some photos of you up on this wall."

And that felt like one of the biggest compliments anyone could've given her.

They returned to their painting and made amazing progress. An hour later when Kennedy and Juliet came in for a break from their work days, Leo and Caroline had finished the first coat and had painted the first two wooden picture frames. One sky blue and one bubblegum pink.

"What is going on in here?" Kennedy asked as she came from the front of the restaurant.

"We're finally getting that wall painted," Ellie told her from behind the bar.

"Wow." Kennedy focused on Caroline. "Did you talk them into this?"

"No convincing required. She came up with a great idea and we jumped on it," Leo said.

"What idea?" Juliet asked.

Leo held the pink frame up to show Kennedy.

She took it from him, studying it. "You're going to hang this back up on the wall in a *pink* frame?" The photo was of her, dressed in her usual head-to-toe black with heavy eye makeup and her hair dyed purple and styled in two long pigtails. She had black combat boots on and her tattoos and piercings were all on display. She had an arm around Leo's neck in a hug and they were both laughing.

He nodded. "Pink is the color I think of when I think of you."

Kennedy arched a dark black brow. "Seriously?"

"Seriously. I know you try to be all bad, and tough, and scary, but you were the first granddaughter I got after a whole *bunch* of boys and the only one who lived here. For the first five years of your life all I bought you was pink stuff. You're always tryin' to be all dark and mysterious but you've always been my bright spot and so bright pink is how you make me feel."

Kennedy stared at her grandfather for a long moment and then suddenly burst into tears. She crossed to him, wrapped her arms around his neck, and said, "You're crazy, and I love you."

He squeezed her. "Ditto."

She let him go, wiped her cheeks, sniffed, and looked at Caroline. "All these frames are going to be different colors?"

Caroline wasn't sure how the family was going to feel about this. Hopefully they wouldn't think it was silly. She lifted a shoulder. "Yeah. We might have more than one that's blue or orange or whatever, but we'll pick different colors that fit each photo."

Kennedy and Juliet looked over the photographs, nodding. "That's really cool," Kennedy said. "Can we help paint?"

"You would help paint the frames?" Caroline asked, excited. "I think that would be perfect. The family really should be painting these frames and deciding what colors to use and helping put this all together. This is *your* wall."

Juliet nodded. "I agree." She pointed at Caroline's hands. "But after all this manual labor, you're gonna need a new manicure."

Caroline looked at her nails and tucked them under into a fist. "Oh, it's no big deal. I'm not used to actually working with my hands." She gave a self-deprecating laugh. "But it's good for me."

Juliet smiled. "I know exactly what you mean. And I would be honored if you'd let me redo your manicure when we're done with all of this."

Caroline surprised. "Really? You'd do that?"

Kennedy rolled her eyes. "Juliet gives the best manicures. But don't let that sweet offer fool you. She is going to have her level and her measuring tape in here making sure that we put all of these photographs up perfectly. She will drive you crazy first."

Juliet laughed. But didn't deny it.

"Well, actually," Caroline said, carefully, "the beauty of this is letting it be imperfect. This wall is like the rest of the bar. Which is like all of the people who come and go from this place. It's a hodgepodge of different backgrounds and personality types and quirks. No one's perfect and it doesn't all match. But yet when it comes together in this bar, it all just fits."

Again she found herself with two people just staring at her for several seconds.

Then Kennedy started crying again, and Juliet came forward and enfolded her in a big hug. "That's beautiful, and perfect. And I'm going to call everyone and get them up here to start painting and you're absolutely right, I'm not even going to get my tape measure."

Caroline found herself a little choked up as well. But she felt better about this than she had about anything she'd done in a very, very long time.

It felt so good to be *real*. To talk and have people care about her opinion and listen. To influence someone and make a positive difference.

This was just a painted wall with some framed photographs...but it felt bigger than that.

And two hours later when the whole Landry clan had gathered and painted and looked at and talked about and laughed over a bunch of photos they hadn't really paid attention to in a long time and said how cool this project was and the wall was all put together and looked really, really good... Caroline realized it *was* bigger than that. And she'd made it happen.

A man could only live without gumbo for so long. Zander finally gave in and went to Ellie's for dinner. Which was a huge mistake.

For about two minutes he'd believed that Caroline was simply there doing her nails, which had been easy enough to roll his eyes about.

Then he'd gotten the full story from Cora. About how happy she'd made his grandparents, how sweet she'd been with Leo, how earnest she'd been about the photographs and making this place reflective of the *people* who came here, how she'd included the whole family. And how they all now thought she could walk on water.

Then he'd seen her happy, relaxed, smiling face as Juliet brushed new polish onto her nails.

And seen the way she was sitting, in the midst of his family, looking like she absolutely *belonged*.

And seen the wall that was, quite honestly, stunning.

Not in the sense that great works of art or literature were stunning but in the sense that he almost couldn't breathe when he realized how she'd basically framed and displayed all the reasons that he got up every morning and did what he did.

That wall represented why he was a cop in Autre and why he would never take his badge off.

And then it hit him...if she could look *that* damned happy and relaxed and comfortable here, amongst all of *this*, then maybe she could stay here and they could make this work.

And then she'd smiled at him and he was done for.

The gumbo had never tasted so good.

"We've got nothin'," Spencer said two days later as he tossed his reading glasses on top of the papers on the table and leaned back in his chair.

Zander sighed. Spencer was right. They didn't know anything more about what was going on with Brantley Anderson than they had before Spencer had come to town and Max had handed over a mysterious envelope full of papers.

The papers clearly showed a group of men who had something in common having to do with money. But these were all rich assholes from New Orleans and the surrounding area. The money and business they had in common could be a million things. And it could even be legitimate.

Why it ended up in Caroline's suitcase they had no idea. They couldn't prove that Brantley had put it there and even if they could, they certainly had no idea why.

"We need to track Anderson down and talk to him," Zander said.

"If he'll talk," Spencer agreed. "But we don't have any reason to bring him in and make him talk. It would have to be his own choice."

"And if we brought him in for questioning, it would potentially throw up a red flag to whoever he's working for," Zander filled in.

Spencer just nodded.

"We can't even dive into these guys' bank records, can we?" Zander asked. "We don't really have reason."

"Not only that, but that probably wouldn't show us much," Spencer said. "These guys spend tons of money on tons of things. It's not like they'll have a line item that says *illegal lion cub*."

Zander ran a hand over his face. The emails that Caroline had collected from Brantley's computer hadn't given much more information either.

Spencer reached for the sweet tea Ellie had just refilled. They were camped out at the back tables of Ellie's with their paperwork spread out. It was fairly quiet this time of day, and they'd needed some space to work.

Caroline was at the animal park with Donovan and Max was up at the bed and breakfast working. Zander was trying very hard not to think about either of the women. He didn't think that Max was actually any kind of threat., but he did think she had the potential to be a complication if she got in the way. On the other hand, it didn't seem like there was much to get in the way of.

"There's nothing you can do, is there?" Zander finally asked Spencer.

Spencer blew out a breath. "Really sorry, man. There is nothing here to go on. I can keep poking and pulling at some threads. But if there's anything to find, it'll take some time. I can keep watch on these guys. But this list is long. I don't even know where to start."

"Good thing you have me."

They both pivoted as Max pulled the chair out between them and slid into it. Caroline was with her and Zander felt a stupid grin start to curl his lips. He stopped it before anyone could see it. Lately she just looked so happy. When she was at the animal park. When she was here at Ellie's. She looked at ease. Relaxed. And so fucking gorgeous that way.

And every time, he caught himself thinking things like *I want to make sure she looks just like that every day forever.*

Of course, he told himself that was a ridiculous huge jump, fueled by romance novels—though he'd stubbornly not picked one up since she'd come to town—and the way she looked in yoga pants. Forever? Really? He'd already added her to his list of people he was going to keep in a happy, peaceful bubble full of gumbo and bread pudding and cute, cuddly animals? But yeah, it seemed that way. And it wasn't about the yoga pants.

Well, it wasn't *just* about the yoga pants.

He tore his eyes from her as she took the chair on the opposite side of Spencer, putting the agent between the two women.

Zander did allow a half-grin to show at that.

Spencer narrowed his eyes.

Max reached for Spencer's iced tea, lifting the glass and taking a long pull.

"Why is you being here good?" Spencer asked her with a frown, taking his glass back.

"Because you're at a dead end, right? You can't find anything to move on based on what I gave you," Max told him.

"So?"

She crossed her legs and leaned in to rest her forearms on the table. "Well, it just so happens that I found out that four men on that list are having dinner together tomorrow night. At Octavia's. I figured it might be worth checking out. Who knows what topics of conversation might come up?"

Spencer's frown deepened. "And you just happened to find this out?"

"Yes." That was all she offered.

"Did you find out in a legal fashion?"

"I just—"

"You know what, never mind," Spencer cut her off. "Which four men?"

She leaned over to look at the papers. Then she pointed at the first four men on the list.

Zander and Spencer shared a look. Was it a coincidence that the first four names were men who regularly socialized with one another?

"I just thought I'd share the information. I plan to go to Octavia's tomorrow night. If I hear anything or see anything, maybe I'll let you know." Max stood, but Spencer reached out quickly, his large hand encircling her wrist. She paused and looked down at him.

"You just happen to be going to Octavia's tomorrow night?"

"Turns out I have a work assignment."

"Coincidentally, you have an assignment that's taking you to Octavia's tomorrow night?" Spencer asked.

"I don't think it's illegal for me to be at Octavia's tomorrow night so I don't really see why it's any concern of yours, Special Agent Landry," Max said.

Spencer looked at where he was holding her and let go. But he returned his gaze to hers. Finally, he said simply, "Be careful."

"Octavia's is one of the classiest restaurants in all of New Orleans and these men are all some of the most recognizable men in the city," Max said. "I don't expect any trouble. Plus, they won't even know that I'm there."

"You think you're gonna go unnoticed?"

"Of course. I'll blend in."

"Yeah, sure," was Spencer's muttered response.

Max gave him a slightly puzzled but also slightly pleased look. "I think I'll take that as a compliment."

Zander couldn't help but glance at Caroline, who gave him a little smile that made him want more shared secret moments.

Spencer opened his mouth to reply, but before he could say a word, the table was surrounded.

Zeke dropped into the chair to Zander's left, Fletcher took the chair straight across, with their cousin Owen grabbing the chair next to Caroline. He gave her a big grin and stretched his arms out across the chairs on either side of him—Fletcher's and hers. Their cousins Josh and Mitch commandeered the two remaining chairs at the table.

Zander groaned. He didn't know what this was about exactly, but he suspected it had something to do with him and a certain gorgeous blonde. Not that the redhead to his right hadn't caught some attention as well. But he knew his brothers and cousins would be more focused on the woman *his* attention was focused on. And he was sure it was very clear who that was.

"So you're dating a girl who showed up here in a wedding dress about a week ago?" Zeke asked him, as if that woman wasn't sitting right there. But Zeke's grin was hardly one of censure.

Caroline's eyes were wide, but she simply crossed her arms and legs and leaned back in her chair.

Max looked around the table and sat back down in her chair.

Clearly they were both settling in for the show.

Zander rubbed the middle of his forehead. This was so not what he needed. "What makes you think I'm dating her?"

"She's still in town, she's"—Zeke looked Caroline over —"wearing our girls' clothes." He winked at her. She ran a hand over her t-shirt with a smile.

"She's hanging out with the lion cub, she's doin' yoga with Paige, she's even answered the Goat Phone," Owen said.

Yeah, she was doing all those things.

See? It was not about the yoga pants. Not really.

Zander scrubbed the spot between his eyes a little harder but knew that would do no good to reduce the headache that was brewing. This was a twin-brother headache. There was no cure.

He sighed, dropped his hand, and looked at the six men who sat at the table with him. Not one of whom could be called good and chaste and a total gentleman. Every one of his cousins and brothers had been complete playboys in their time, some more than others, but until they'd fallen madly in love—something they'd all done now with the exception of Spencer—they had all enjoyed plenty of female company and very little of it had been called dating.

Then he looked at Caroline.

He wasn't dating her.

It was a lot more than that.

"She had a few really bad days," he finally said.

Caroline arched one eyebrow, but gave him a half-smile.

Fletcher, his older brother, grinned and nodded. "And you're the epitome of the perfect civil servant, right? Protect and...serve."

Zander knew he had to go along with this. He could not let them think that he'd actually been worried about Caroline. That would indicate that there was some danger around her, which might lead to questions about what she was messed up in and the people who had come looking for her.

Spencer had surreptitiously gathered up the papers and Max had held her bag open, so that he could slip them inside before anyone else at the table had noticed what was on them. But Zander didn't even want them knowing that there was an investigation going on or that Spencer was here for any kind of police work.

"Just doing my best to make sure that everyone who visits

Autre leaves with good feelings about the town," Zander finally said.

All the guys chuckled and Owen nodded. "Something I used to take very seriously myself, man."

Owen had done more than his share of entertaining the tourists who came to Autre for swamp boat tours. Ironically his wife was an Autre girl, so all of his work in the name of "tourism" had not really mattered in the end. Josh and Mitch, however, could both claim to have done their part to make sure visitors to Autre were quite happy and wanted to stick around. Both Tori and Paige were from out of town and it had only taken one visit to Autre to convince them to move permanently.

"Well, I'm so glad to hear that Caroline's feeling better after...everything," Zeke said, clapping Zander on the shoulder. He looked at Caroline. "How long are ya' stayin'?"

Zander started to respond, though he wasn't sure with what, when Max piped up, "Oh, Caroline and I are going back to New Orleans tomorrow. We have dinner reservations at seven."

Zander looked at Caroline with a brow up. Was Max saying she was taking Caroline to Octavia's with her? Caroline nodded, as if understanding his unspoken question.

Bullshit.

He knew he should be glad. Caroline leaving Autre was what he wanted. That had been the goal all along. The sooner the better.

But he wasn't ready.

That realization hit him hard. And he felt like a total asshole.

Still, it was true.

It was a bad idea, anyway. Max was going to the restaurant to spy on the men on the list and they'd probably all know Caroline. She couldn't just walk in there after dumping Brantley just a few days ago and hiding out from her family.

The wedding had been a surprise, to Caroline anyway, but no one wore a tiara and a huge-assed, jewel-encrusted wedding dress she could barely move in for a small, intimate wedding with only family. Everyone in their social circle had to know about the wedding. And Brantley being left at the altar.

That was what Zander was telling himself anyway.

It wasn't because he'd been planning on having more time with her. Or because the idea of her leaving suddenly had his gut tightening and his chest feeling like it was compressing his lungs.

Caroline was *not* going to Octavia's tomorrow night.

At least, not without him.

"Actually, the four of us are going out tomorrow night," Zander said. "Double date."

Max grinned at him and he had the impression that he'd just fallen right into her trap. Spencer, on the other hand, looked like Zander had just punched him.

"Wait. You're going on a *date*? Like a real date? Not a here-let-me-make-it-all-better-one-night-hook-up thing?" Zeke asked.

Zander looked from his twin to Caroline and opened his mouth, but Caroline beat him to it.

"Excuse me. Do I seem like a one-night stand type of girl?"

She didn't. She wasn't. And that was likely the biggest problem of all. He wanted her and knew he wasn't man enough to just leave her completely the hell alone. But he also knew if he slept with her, she'd take a piece of his heart.

"No. No, you don't." But Zeke was studying him carefully, and Zander knew that if anyone could figure out there was more going on here than he was letting on, it would be Zeke.

Zander turned his attention to Spencer and Max.

"And then Max, Caroline's best friend, came down to check on her and she and Spencer hit it off so we all decided to go to dinner tomorrow."

Again Max looked amused. Spencer did not.

"At Octavia's," Max confirmed with a nod.

Owen sat forward. "Holy shit." He looked at Zander. "We're clearly paying you too much to be our cop."

"Again, does Caroline strike you as the crawfish boil type?" He staunchly refused to look at Caroline until Owen did.

Owen slid Caroline a look. She lifted a brow, doing a very good impression of a haughty heiress completely insulted by the idea of being fed crawfish and corn on the cob on a paper tablecloth.

Zander wanted to kiss her. More than usual. Which was saying something.

"Not in the least," Owen agreed.

She really did play these roles well.

"Of course, she also doesn't seem like *your* type," Fletcher said. "You're more the crawfish boil type than the Octavia's type."

What he really meant was that Zander was more the one-night type than the date type.

And he was right.

Zander shrugged. "You all know exactly how this works. The right girl walks in and nothing else matters."

The other men at the table looked at one another and nodded.

"Well, damn, it's about time," Zeke said.

"Welcome to the club," Josh said.

"Wait a second." Max sat forward, looking entertained and curious. "You're all just accepting the fact that Caroline walked in here, in a *wedding dress*, told Zander she was over her fiancé, and now he's madly in love with her and it's fine? He's doing things totally out of character and you all just believe that it's true love?"

The guys all looked at each other again. And nodded.

"Happens all the time around here," Owen said.

"Doesn't that sound a little crazy?" Max asked.

"We specialize in crazy," Mitch told her with a grin. "Especially when it comes to love."

"Seriously?" Max looked at each of them. "You're all just big hopeless romantics?" She looked at Spencer last.

He held up both hands. "Not me. But yeah, the Autre Landrys are the stuff of legends."

Max looked at Caroline. Zander stubbornly did not.

"Prove it," Max said. "Tell me some of these legends."

"Well, there's Josh and Tori," Owen said. "He met her one night in a bar at Mardi Gras, served her a couple drinks, then sent her back to Iowa with only a kiss. They agreed to meet up the next year if they were both still single and interested."

Max grinned. "*An Affair To Remember*. Love that movie."

Owen nodded. "He waited a year for her. Not a single other girl in the meantime. Now they're married and have little Ella."

"Wow." Max nodded. "Okay, that's pretty good."

"Then there's me and Maddie," Owen said. "Our love story includes burning down a building and me in the hospital after her brother threw me through a window."

"I thought you threw *him* through the window," Mitch said.

"We kind of threw each other through it," Owen admitted.

"And don't forget how she almost shot you," Zeke added.

"Right," Owen said with a nod. "We're very dramatic."

Max's eyes were wide. "I guess so."

"But you took like twelve years to figure your shit out," Mitch said. "Me and Paige fell in love in a weekend."

"Maybe *you* fell in love in a weekend but you had to haul your ass back up to Iowa in *January* to convince *her*," Owen said, shaking his head.

"Saving her entire town's winter festival definitely helped." Mitch nodded. "But it all started when our eyes met over the back end of an alpaca."

Max laughed. "Love at first sight?"

"Pretty much."

"That was me and Jill too," Zeke said. "It only took me one night to sweep her off her feet."

"And a bunch of goats," Mitch said. "And I think it was *you* who were off your feet. Weren't you on your ass in the ditch under your motorcycle?"

"Details," Zeke said with a grin.

"Yeah, well, none of you grabbed an overnight flight to Vegas to go after your girl and then detoured through a wedding chapel so you could bring her home to Autre as your wife." Fletcher sat back, looking very smug.

"You?" Max asked. "Really?"

"Yep. My best friend got dumped by her boyfriend, on stage, during his big concert—"

"On TV," Zeke added. "I gotta admit, that was pretty fucking cool of you."

"Wait, on *stage* on *TV*?" Max asked.

"You know who Jason Young is?" Zeke asked.

Max nodded. "Sure."

"He was Jordan's boyfriend."

"What?" Max looked at Fletcher. "Wow, you stole a rockstar's girlfriend?"

Fletcher rolled his eyes. "It's country music, not rock. And he proposed to the wrong girl. On stage. I didn't need to steal her. She was done."

"Still..." Max grinned. "You flew out there and just married her right then?"

Fletcher nodded. "I flew out to be with her, but realized I had to tell her how I really felt about her and...that was it."

It hadn't been quite that simple for Fletcher and Jordan to just fall into wedded bliss, even as best friends since childhood, but they were definitely there now.

Fletcher marrying his best friend, Owen finally marrying the girl who got away, Zeke marrying the girl he—thankfully—

knocked up with twins, Mitch convincing his beautiful commit-ment-phobe to take a chance on him and his whole crazy family, Josh building a family with the girl who'd stolen his heart just by walking into a New Orleans bar, and all of the other love stories—and there were many—that Zander lived amongst every day was why he did what he did.

"Well, dang, I thought a runaway bride with a lion cub might be a little crazy, but sounds like that all fits right in," Max said.

"It's only fair Zander has a good story," Owen said. "He puts up with lots of crazy shit from all of us."

Well, *that* was true.

Max shook her head. "You all are really something." She looked at Spencer. "Except you. You seem boring."

He nodded. "I'm very boring. Don't be interested in me at all."

"No problem."

Zander watched Owen, Mitch, and Josh exchange knowing grins.

Yeah, Spencer had probably just sealed his fate.

He really should know better than to say stuff like that in Autre.

Zander looked at Caroline. She was watching him.

Speaking of sealed fates...he had a date. Actually two. They were going to New Orleans tomorrow night, but he had tonight with her. And he was going to take advantage.

14

"Hey, you hungry?"

Caroline was already smiling when she looked from the alpaca she was brushing to the hot cop in the truck idling along the road.

He'd pulled over to the shoulder by the alpaca pen and was leaning out the driver's side window. This was his personal truck, not his official truck. That meant he was off the clock.

"We're taking her to Bad Brews tonight," Jordan called to him from where she was brushing Alpacalypse, the alpaca she was grooming next to Caroline and Alpacapella.

"No, you're not," he said. He shifted his truck into park and opened the door.

Caroline and Jordan looked at one another. Jordan gave her a grin. Caroline felt her stomach flip. She didn't even really know why.

After Ellie's, Max and Spencer had headed back to New Orleans with plans to meet tomorrow night at Octavia's to check into these possible "acquaintances" of Brantley's. Zander had gone back to work and Caroline had come to the petting zoo with Jordan. They'd tended to goats, guinea pigs, rabbits, ducks, and now alpacas. She'd found it all strangely relaxing and fun.

But she and Jordan had not talked about going out tonight. To Bad Brews or anywhere else. Though a girls' night out with the Autre women sounded like a great time.

Caroline didn't really have girlfriends. Not *real* girlfriends. Other than Max. And when they hung out, it was at Max's townhouse or occasionally at the neighborhood bar around the corner from her place where no one knew who Caroline was. But they didn't want too many people in New Orleans to connect them and there were just too many places where someone who knew who Caroline was could show up.

Zander strode toward her, stopping on the other side of the fence. He propped a booted foot on the bottom slat of the fence and leaned onto the top, looking very much the hot country boy. He was dressed in blue jeans and a button down plaid shirt.

"Remember all that fun outside, moonlight stuff you've never done?" he asked Caroline.

Fishing. Skinny dipping. Crawfish. Fucking in his truck bed. Yep, she remembered. Her skin flushed and she nodded.

"You're doin' that tonight. With me."

Jordan laughed. "Did you mean to phrase that as a question. As in, 'would you like to do that tonight with me?'," she asked.

"Nope," he said simply, eyes still on Caroline.

"We've got burgers, beer, karaoke, and lots of great Zander stories to offer," Jordan said. "I've only told you a few so far."

Caroline glanced at her. She'd love to hear some more Zander stories. But she had this niggling feeling that her time with Zander might be winding down. From day one, he'd made it clear he didn't want her to stick around. She'd made it clear that the reason she was still here was because she wanted to make sure Brantley and the lion cub were being investigated. Now they were. She knew Zander expected her to be getting on with her life. And she should probably be expecting that of herself as well.

If she only had another night in Autre, and Zander was willing to spend it with her...doing all of *that*...then it was a no-brainer.

"I've had burgers before," she told Jordan. "I've never been to a crawfish boil."

Jordan looked at Zander. "Crawfish boils are Fridays."

Caroline knew that Ellie's had a crawfish boil every Friday that was attended by most of the town as well as lots of tourists and people from the surrounding area. It was a huge event with live music, lots of food and drink, and an event the whole family pitched in to make happen.

He nodded. "Special occasion."

"We're having a crawfish boil tonight for Caroline?" Jordan asked.

Caroline felt her eyes widen. They'd do that? For her? That was sweet. And, of course, meant that he *definitely* didn't expect her to still be here on Friday.

"*We're* not having a crawfish boil," Zander told Jordan. "*We* are." He moved his finger back and forth to indicate himself and Caroline.

Her eyes widened even further. And her heart kicked against her ribs. And her body got warmer.

He was going to make a private crawfish boil just for her?

"Ah," Jordan said. "Got it." She looked at Caroline. "Bad Brews can wait."

Caroline gave her a grin. "Thanks for understanding."

Jordan laughed. "I married a Landry boy in a Vegas wedding chapel the morning after I'd been dumped by my boyfriend of eleven years. I totally understand invitations you just can't turn down."

Caroline felt her cheeks heat, but she handed her brush over to Jordan. "I'll see you later."

She met Zander at the fence. He held out a hand. She put her palm in his and he helped her climb over, grasping her waist when she got to the top and swinging her over and lowering her to the ground in a swoony move that made her heart and stomach flip.

She kept her hands on his arms as she looked up into his eyes. "I've been hanging out here all afternoon. I should go change."

He looked her up and down and the corner of his mouth curled up. "You look gorgeous."

"I'm dirty."

"You're only going to get more so," he told her, his voice gruff.

The hot jab of desire hit her low in her belly. "My *clothes* are dirty though."

He gave a husky laugh. "Good thing you're not gonna have them on long then."

She felt her mouth curve. She loved the sexy, flirty side of Zander Landry. "Thought we were going fishing? Wasn't that on that list?"

"Yeah, but when a guy puts fishing on that particular list, it's just the excuse to get down to the bayou."

"And the skinny dipping?"

"Just the way to get you out of your clothes. You don't want to be skinny dipping in the bayou." He leaned in. "There are things that wanna take a bite of you that aren't nearly as pleasant as the thing that wants a taste of you in that truck bed."

The hot shivers that elicited were very welcome.

"Are there at least really crawfish to eat?" she asked with a grin. "Because I really am hungry."

"That and the moonshine are real," he said with a nod.

"And the bayou boy fucking better be real."

She saw the effect her words had on him. His body tightened and his eyes heated. "If I fuck you in the back of my truck, I'm not going to be able to have any other woman there ever again."

She lifted onto tiptoe and pressed her lips against his. "Good," she said against his mouth.

The next thing she knew she was backed up against the side of the truck and Zander was devouring her mouth as if he was starving. He cupped the back of her head, his hand cushioning the spot where her head would have pressed into the hot metal. He opened his mouth, sliding his tongue along hers and groaning when she met him thrust for thrust.

When he finally lifted his head, he just stared down at her for a few seconds. "I wanted to give you a bayou date night before we had a New Orleans date night."

She nodded, her lips still tingling. "Love that."

"You sure?"

"Zander, I *want* this. I...want you." She wet her lips. "So much. And neither of us really knows what's going to happen tomorrow night. I want to have tonight with you."

He reached up and brushed his thumb over her cheek. "The chances that anything major is going to happen tomorrow night are slim, Caroline," he said gently. "If you're expecting a mass arrest or a raid of a facility where a bunch of animals are being held or something, I need you to adjust those expectations. The chances are that nothing is going to be that different tomorrow night."

She understood that. On one level. But damn, that was frustrating and hearing him say it out loud made it more so.

She wrapped her fingers around his wrist and squeezed. "Okay. I still want the bayou date night tonight." She didn't want to pass up this chance. No matter what tomorrow night brought.

"Okay." He lifted her hand to his mouth and pressed a kiss to the palm. Then he tugged her around the truck and opened the passenger door for her.

As they drove down Bayou Road, Zander reached over and linked his fingers with hers, holding her hand on the middle console. Caroline smiled to herself. He was gruff and protective and could be downright stern, but he could be very sweet.

They turned off the main road just after the drive that led into the section of the animal park where the sloths, penguins, and tiger lived. They bumped over the narrow dirt road for a few miles before he turned again, taking them behind a line of trees and along the bank where the water was visible to the right side of the trail.

Finally, he turned onto a flat sandy area nestled amongst heavy bushes and trees. He parked and shut off the engine.

"Wow, this is really beautiful," she said, looking out over the water that moved so slowly it almost seemed to stand still, the cypress trees draped in Spanish moss, and the orange sun starting to dip on the horizon. She turned to look at him. "It's strange, isn't it, that we've been looking at the same water, but it looks so different."

"This doesn't look like your backyard?" he teased with a grin.

She laughed. "Not exactly. Our backyard is carefully manicured. Kept by people my parents pay and we never really see. And extends for about four miles behind our house. The river runs at the bottom of a cliff that drops about a hundred yards."

He whistled. "Damn."

She nodded. "But I would have loved *this* backyard as a kid."

"Hide and seek out here was fucking amazing," he said. "Zeke was good, but Owen was the champ. He had no fear. He'd climb up or into about anything. Sawyer won a lot though because he was patient as hell. Could sit and outwait them. Eventually they'd get bored or hungry."

"You didn't win much?"

He shrugged. "I played for the fun. To hang with them. I didn't care about winning so much."

She kind of loved that about him. Come to think of it, there were several things to love about him. She swallowed hard as that realization hit. Well, damn, that had happened fast.

"I miss the house where I played hide and seek," she said softly. "We lived there until I was thirteen and we moved to... where we live now. The house now just doesn't feel like home. I've never really *played* there, you know?"

He squeezed her hand. "I think I do. Me and my brothers and cousins have never really stopped playing. It's changed, of course, but we still let loose, have fun just to have fun. I think that's important."

She nodded. "I agree." She paused. She was glad he had that. He was protecting that too, she knew. "The grounds we have now aren't a place to play, but I do drive out to the river when I want to be alone and think. It's..."

"What?"

"It's going to sound weird out loud."

"Try me."

She took a breath. "It's the only place that belongs to my family where I can be *me* and not worry about putting on an act, or like I need to watch what my dad or brother are up to, or wonder who my mother is talking to and what they're filling her head with. It's one place that belongs to my father that's beautiful and peaceful."

His fingers tightened around hers again. "I fucking hate that you don't feel that anywhere else you associate with your family."

"Me too."

They just sat looking at each other for several seconds.

"I really wish you didn't already know all the bullshit that's out there," he finally said. "I'd love to wrap you in bubble wrap

—metaphorically, of course—and take care of you with home cooking and Cajun tall tales and crawfish boils and life in a town and a house that's been in my family, yard and all, for generations."

Unexpectedly a sob rose from her chest to her throat and she had to swallow hard twice before she could speak.

"You didn't happen to bring any moonshine with you, did you?" she asked.

"As a matter of fact..." Zander reached under his seat and felt around.

Caroline took the opportunity to sniff and blink hard and pull herself together a bit.

A moment later, Zander triumphantly produced a small Mason jar. "Never leave home without it."

She even managed a smile. "You never leave home without moonshine in your car?"

He chuckled. "This moonshine works for more than just getting a nice buzz real quick. In the winter it'll melt ice and frost faster than anything I've ever seen, can get blood out of almost anything, is the best lighter fluid I've ever used, and I swear it works as an antiseptic better than most things you can find in the pharmacy."

She laughed looking at the clear liquid in the unassuming jar. She was ninety percent sure he was kidding about...at least some of that. "And we're certain that it's safe to drink?"

"My grandparents and their friends have been drinking it for decades and they are definitely still kicking and their minds are working...as well as they ever have," Zander gave her a grin. "I promise their crazy doesn't come from this jar, anyway."

"So the all-purpose liquid is coming to the back of the truck with us?"

"Absolutely."

They carried the jar to the truck bed. Zander let down the tailgate and tossed in a couple of canvas bags she hadn't noticed. Already in the back of the truck was a large silver pot she assumed contained the crawfish. There was also a small cooler. He opened the canvas bags and started to unroll sleeping bags and blankets.

"Always prepared for anything?" Caroline teased.

"I've slept in this truck more times than I'd like to count."

"Just slept?"

"You have a question for me, Ms. Holland, just ask it."

"Okay, fair enough. How many girls have slept in this truck with you?"

"Like any good bayou boy, I've had girls in truck beds before," Zander told her. He turned to face her fully. "But..." He tugged the pot closer and lifted the lid. "I've never made a private crawfish boil for anyone."

Inside was not only cooked crawfish but also potatoes, corn on the cob, and sausage. She breathed deep of the spicy scent. "Oh my God. That looks and smells amazing."

He shrugged. "It's the best I can do. I'm not a romantic. I'm not sweet. I'm not lookin' for any of that so I don't usually make the effort."

But he was tonight.

Whether he realized it or not, this was very romantic.

Suddenly her hunger for food was gone. All she wanted, all she needed, was Zander.

She moved close. "I love"—She broke off just before she said the *you*—"all of this. Thank you." She took the front of his shirt and pulled him down for a soft kiss.

As they kissed, Caroline felt Zander's hands drop to her hips. He squeezed, then turned her so her back was to the tailgate. He pulled their lips apart as he backed her up, then lifted her. He stepped between her knees as she sat on the end of the tailgate. His hands slid down from her hips to her bare knees. With his eyes on hers, he separated her knees and leaned in, capturing her lips again. He stroked his big hands up and down her thighs, his fingertips dipping under the edge of the denim each time.

She ran her hands up his chest and over his shoulders, down to his biceps, where she squeezed as she arched closer.

"Please, Zander, I want this. I want it all."

Breathing hard, he stared into her eyes. "I'll give you all I can."

She knew he meant that. She knew that he wanted to give her more and just felt that he couldn't. She understood that he felt that way because of all the people he loved. Possibly even because of the way he felt about *her*.

She nodded. "Please."

He stepped back and took another look at her, his hot gaze sweeping over her. "Fuck, it's never going to be enough."

"But it's better than nothing."

He gave her a smile and shoved his hand through his hair. "There's no way I'm tough enough to just walk away from this."

She let out a breath of relief. She didn't know for sure if he meant just tonight or everything but either way, she'd take it. She'd take whatever she could get.

She watched as he started moving around the truck, grabbing additional supplies from behind the seat, and then returning to the truck bed. He climbed up inside and within minutes, there was possibly the most romantic scene she'd ever seen laid out in front of her.

The sleeping bags were stacked together like a thick mattress with a blanket over the top. On the edge of the truck bed were four lanterns that softly lit the area, and two insect-repelling fans sat on the top of the cab. The night was still warm, but there was a breeze that helped stir the heavy air. Caroline couldn't wait to get out of her clothes. For many reasons.

Overhead the stars were starting to appear and they were

surrounded by the sounds of the bayou gurgling by and crickets and frogs starting to sing.

"You really must camp a lot," she commented as he jumped out of the truck bed a final time and came to stand in front of her.

"I do."

"For fun?"

"Usually I'm helping Theo. When he's watching a campsite or tracking animals."

They all had one another's backs and she knew that brotherhood meant a lot to him.

"I have never considered myself an outdoorsy girl, but right now, in this moment, with all of this, I can't imagine anything better."

He lifted his hands and cupped her face, bringing her in. "This is not how it usually goes for me, Caroline. I need you to know that. This really feels different."

"You don't have to say that."

"I know."

He leaned in and she shifted and their lips met. The kiss was sweet. For about three seconds. Then they both moaned, her knees parted, he stepped between them, their mouths opened, their bodies leaned in, and his hands dropped to her hips while her arms circled his neck.

"Need to see you," he said huskily against her mouth. He lifted his hands to the bottom of her shirt and slid it up her body.

She leaned back and helped him pull it up over her head.

Then she unhooked her bra and let it drop.

His grin died quickly as he blew out a breath. "Holy fuck, you're so damn gorgeous."

She took one of his hands and lifted it to her bare breast. "And I'm all yours."

A little shudder went through him. But he ran his thumb

over the hardened tip and pulses of heat streaked through her. Her breath hissed out. "Yes, Zander."

He tugged gently on her nipple as his mouth found the side of her neck. He kissed his way to her collarbone, then nipped lightly. "I want to spread you out on those blankets. Naked under the moonlight. Crying out my name as you come harder for me than you ever have for anyone."

She straightened, almost knocking him in the nose with her shoulder. She grabbed his face, laughing softly. "Oh my gosh, I'm sorry. But yes. Yes to what you just said. All of that. Right now."

He kissed her. "Get your sweet ass up on those blankets then."

She scrambled backwards into the truck bed, her butt hitting the edge of the sleeping bags and sliding up onto them. When she was on her back, she kicked her shoes off and she unbuttoned, unzipped, and pushed her shorts down her body.

Caroline took a moment to just feel the sultry air caress her skin. She was sure her hair was already frizzing, and she could feel the light moisture making her skin glisten but she didn't care. It felt so amazing to just let go like this.

"What are you doin', cher? You're still a little ways away from being bare-assed naked."

She propped up on her elbows to look at Zander. He was standing at the tailgate. His eyes were fixed on her but his big, thick fingers were working the buttons of his shirt.

"I just got a little ahead of you. You need to catch up."

He finished unbuttoning and shrugged out of the shirt, tossing it onto the tailgate. She drank in the sight of his hard muscles and tan skin lit by the golden glow from the lanterns. The muscles bunched as he braced his hands on the tailgate and lifted himself up into the back of the truck. He crawled toward her on hands and knees and her heart rate kicked up.

He didn't stop until one hand was braced next to her hip

and one knee was between hers. He dragged his palm up her thigh to the center of the panties she still wore and cupped her.

Caroline gasped then arched closer to his hand.

Zander grinned a sexy, knowing grin that made her press up even harder, grinding her clit into the heel of his hand.

"You know that cliché move from novels and movies where the guy takes the woman's panties and tucks them in his pocket and keeps them?" he asked, his voice low and gruff.

She pulled her bottom lip between her teeth and nodded.

"I'm so doing that tonight."

She gave a little moan and started to reply but all thoughts flew from her mind as his thumb tucked into the top edge of her panties and he pulled, stripping the silk down her legs to her ankles. When she lifted her feet so he could unhook them from her heels, he gave a little growl.

Her eyes flew to his face, and she saw that his hot gaze was locked on the area between her thighs. She immediately grew hotter and wetter, aching right there for him. He tucked the peach silk he just removed into his front jeans pocket, as promised, then stroked his hand back up her leg from her ankle to her hip, causing goose bumps to ripple in its wake.

"Goddammit, Caroline, you're so fucking gorgeous like this. In my truck, under the moonlight, the bayou goin' by. It will never be better than this."

She realized that was exactly what she wanted. She wanted him to never find anything better than this. That was probably incredibly selfish of her, but she couldn't find it in her to be sorry.

Without a word, she reached for his face, pulling him down and kissing him deeply. His hands stroked up over her hip to her ribs and back down, squeezing and kneading and stroking. He kissed her hungrily. Then pulled back. "I have a lot of territory to cover here."

"What—"

But he rolled her to her stomach and pressed her into the blankets with one big hand on her ass and the other on her shoulder. He swept her hair up off the back of her neck and leaned in, kissing the exposed skin. He proceeded to kiss, lick, and nip down the back of her neck to her shoulder, across both shoulder blades and down her spine, taking time to kiss each rib and vertebrae on his way to the dip of her lower back. There he nuzzled his nose as he continued to squeeze her ass before moving down and nipping each cheek, causing her to gasp and squirm.

"You're fucking delicious. You smell amazing. God, you feel good." His words were rough and raw and came in short, unconnected combinations. It was like he was just letting himself feel and touch and talk without much thought.

He ran his hands down the back of both thighs, kissing his way down to her ankles. His thumb rubbed into the arch of one foot and she squirmed with the pleasure of it. He kissed each ankle bone and then began kissing up the inside of one leg. Caroline spread her knees apart, giving him more access and he gave a groan. She was wiggling as he made his way closer and closer to the point where she was hot and needy for him.

His hands gripped her ass again, massaging, and then he spread her even wider. His thumbs brushed over her inner folds and he ground out a low, "Fuck" as he touched her hot, wet center.

Caroline gasped, then moaned as the pads of his thumbs ran over her clit and then dipped inside her pussy. It was just the tips of each thumb, but she felt sparks of heat, and lust that she'd never felt before.

From her position on her stomach she couldn't see him, which almost made the sensations even stronger. He pressed one thumb deeper and she arched her back trying to get closer.

"God, I want you," he said. "This is incredible."

"Take me," she said breathlessly. "I'm yours."

Again with a little growl, he stroked into her with the thumb then withdrew. The next thing she felt was the hot wetness of his tongue against her. She gasped and cried his name as his tongue slid over her clit. "Zander!"

"I want all of you, all over my tongue."

"Yes." She wiggled her back trying to get closer to him, to his mouth, to everything he was making her feel."

He licked her again, then withdrew. Before she could protest, he flipped her to her back. With one arm braced beside her, he stared down at her, his breathing ragged. "You're everything. Need you to know that. I..."

She lifted a hand to his cheek. "I don't need the pretty words. You don't have to be something you're not. I want you. Just like this."

He leaned in and kissed her and she loved the dirtiness of knowing where his tongue had just been as he stroked it against hers.

Then he pulled back and began the kissing-her-all-over again. He ran his hand, his mouth, and tongue down her neck to her collarbone and over one shoulder, nipping and licking. His beard was soft and delicious against her skin and she wanted it brushing over her nipples. She arched, trying to urge him downward.

He chuckled. "I'm getting there, cher."

She cupped the back of his head and threaded her fingers into his hair. She loved his longer hair and the way it hung loose and also brushed over her skin. In the fading light, with the lanterns glowing, he looked even wilder and more rugged. She'd never been with a man like him before. He was a little rough around the edges, a little wounded, but loyal and noble, a warrior of sorts.

She ran her hands over his shoulders and down his sides, feeling the hardness under hot skin.

He moved his mouth across her chest and down into the

valley between her breasts, and then finally, *finally* took a nipple. He brushed his beard across the sensitive tip, then licked, before sucking, lightly at first, then harder. She arched closer, crying out. He sucked harder, then added a little nip and her fingers tightened in his hair. "Yes!"

He worked that nipple while he rolled and tugged the other with thumb and forefinger. She was writhing beneath him, just from the attention to her breasts so when he moved down her stomach and kissed over her ribs, then swirled his tongue in her belly button she almost begged him to return to her nipples.

But then he settled between her legs, spreading her thighs wide and gave her a long firm lick.

She cried out louder this time. "Zander!"

He licked again, swirling his tongue around her clit.

Sparks erupted from that point, shooting down her legs and up through her belly.

"Oh my God!"

He did it again, then again, then slid a thick middle finger into her pussy, pumping deep as he continued to tongue her clit, and it took less than a minute to shoot her up and over the edge into an intense orgasm.

As she started floating down from that high, he continued kissing down both thighs to her ankles again. Her heavy-lidded eyes opened slowly, and she found him watching her as he rubbed the bottom of her foot and kissed each toe.

She gave him a lazy smile. "Head to toe for real?"

"Head to toe. Every inch. Delicious, gorgeous, and imprinted on my memory forever."

That was a pretty sweet and romantic sentiment too. He was a lot better at this than he thought he was.

"Well, there's a lot of inches of you I haven't had a chance to get started on." Her gaze dropped pointedly to his fly.

He put her foot back down on the blankets and without a

word, unbuttoned and unzipped his jeans. He rose to his feet in the back of the truck and bent to take off his boots, then straightened and stripped out of his jeans and boxers and socks. All while watching her. All while letting her drink her fill of the sight of him stripping for her.

And what a sight. The man was absolutely made to be naked. He was hard muscle from head to toe. His tattoos stretched across his shoulders and chest and moved as his muscles flexed and relaxed. His hair hung loose around his shoulders, his beard and chest hair were exactly the right amount, and his cock hung heavy and hard between his powerful thighs.

Everything she'd been thinking about a wild warrior taking her in the outdoors and claiming her as his own continued to add up.

"This was a very good idea," she told him softly.

He grinned and dropped his jeans next to his shirt. Then he wrapped a big fist around his cock and gave it a long stroke.

"There's so many things I want to do to you," he said gruffly.

She nodded. "Come on."

He came back to the blankets, first kneeling and then stretching on his back, moving the arm closest to her to prop his hand behind his head. She rolled to her side, leaned on one elbow, and rested her hand on his chest. She began exploring, running her hand from his chest to his abs over his ribs on both sides, down his arms, inching down his abs, closer to his cock.

"Touch me, cher," he urged.

That she wanted to do. She wanted to give him as much pleasure as he'd given her.

She reached out and wrapped her hand around him, squeezing gently and then stroking.

He sucked in a sharp breath, his whole body tensing.

He was big, hot, and very hard. It'd been a while for her. She wasn't one of those girls who worried about fitting or if her body could take him. She understood anatomy and biology. She knew it would work. In fact, she was looking forward to it working. This was going to be so good.

"Let's start here," she leaned over.

He started to shake his head, but she stopped him. "Zander, I want you to have all the same memories I'm going to have. All the fantasies. All the different ways we can be together. At least as many as we can get tonight."

He looked at her for a long moment and sucked in a breath through his nose. Then he brushed the hair back from her cheek and slid his hand around the back of her head. He urged her forward and her heart thumped hard in her chest.

She moved the rest of the way forward.

She looked up at him. "Show me what you like."

"Anything you do."

She knew he meant that. She could see it in his eyes. Those weren't just pretty words.

She licked the head of his cock. He tensed instantly and again sucked in a sharp breath. But he didn't push her away. Or pull back.

She leaned in again and licked around the head, then took him partway into her mouth. His fingers tightened in her hair and his thighs tensed.

She took him further and could hear his ragged breathing.

For several minutes, she just licked and sucked and stroked and enjoyed giving him pleasure.

His breathing grew even rougher and his hold on her hair tightened as he began to guide her rhythm.

But then he tugged, pulling her off. "Enough. Need to be inside you."

She was all for that. She loved doing this to him, but she was aching and needy for him again. She started to lie back on the blankets, but he stopped her. Instead, he pulled her on top of him. They kissed deeply as he stroked his hands up and down her back, squeezing her ass and moving her so she was positioned over him.

"Need you like this," he finally said.

"Me on top?" she asked.

"These blankets aren't as thick as they look. If I'm on top, you'll feel how hard this truck bed really is."

Something about that sounded pretty hot. She grinned. "Not sure I'd mind. Or actually really feel it. Until maybe tomorrow."

He pinched her ass. "All you'll be feelin' tomorrow is these pretty thighs nice and stretched out and the happy aching in this sweet pussy."

Before she could even respond to that particular bit of dirtiness, he'd moved her so the tip of his cock was nudging against her opening.

"Here, help me with this." He held up a condom.

"You had that with you?"

"In my pocket all night."

She liked that. She took it from him and then pushed herself up to straddle his stomach. The new angle put a different pressure against her clit and she wiggled slightly. He clamped his hands on her hips. "Cover me, woman. I need inside you."

She loved how turned on he was and how clearly eager he was to get this moving. She unwrapped the condom and reached back to roll it down his length.

She'd barely tossed the wrapper away when he shifted her, moving her into position. She loved the way he felt comfortable just putting her where he needed her.

Once they were lined up, he looked into her eyes. "Thank you for this."

Her brows arched. "Thank you? Believe me, this is a pleasure."

"Thank you, for giving me tonight. I know this isn't the great romance you deserve."

She was already bracing her hands on his chest but she moved her right hand to cover his heart. "I'm not so sure about that."

Emotion flared in his eyes and the next thing she knew, he'd shifted her and thrust at the same time, sliding deep, joining them as intimately as two people could be.

She gasped as he filled her, every nerve ending in her body seeming to light on fire and her heart swelling to the point where she thought it might burst.

Physically this was the best she'd ever felt. But she wasn't sure she'd ever felt as connected and protected as she did at this moment either. Yes, Zander wanted her, but she knew that if he thought for a moment this would actually hurt her or somehow ruin her or actually break her, he wouldn't be here. He considered her strong and independent, and he trusted her when she said she wanted this. She didn't have to be anything with him but her absolute complete self.

Then he started moving. With his hands and hips he moved underneath her, getting them into a rhythm that hit spots that felt incredibly satisfying while also stoking an intense need. Caroline quickly found the tempo and began riding him, rocking her hips and taking him deep. They moved together, the crickets, frogs, and their own heavy breathing the only sounds around them.

All too soon, she felt her body start tightening and coiling in preparation for her orgasm. She welcomed it and dreaded it at once. She didn't want this to end.

"Come on, Caro," he urged, reading her. "Let go for me."

His coaching didn't help.

"I want it to last," she told him, her voice breathless.

"I need to feel this beautiful pussy milking me. You're too

good at this, too fucking gorgeous riding me like this, for me to hang on. And I'm not going until you do."

He reached between them, his thumb finding her clit and he pressed and circled perfectly.

She couldn't hold back, and her orgasm ripped through her as she shouted his name.

"*Fuck yes*," he said through gritted teeth. He gripped her hips and thrust up harder and faster. Then he held her tight and came, her name echoing in the heavy bayou air.

Trying to catch her breath, she melted against him, resting her cheek against his chest where his heart was thundering.

One of his hands cupped the back of her head. The other settled on her lower back holding her close.

As their skin cooled and their breathing slowed his hands started lazily stroking up and down her back.

Finally, she rolled to her side and took a long deep breath. That resulted in a yawn.

He chuckled. "Now *that's* the kind of satisfaction I like to see."

She kissed his chest and smiled. "I have a feeling I'm going to sleep very well tonight."

"Let me clean up a second." He shifted, sliding out from underneath her and moving to the end of the truck where he jumped out. He did whatever needed to be done with the condom.

When he climbed back up, he said, "How hungry are you now?"

She thought about it. "Starving."

"Good." He pulled his boxers and jeans on and tossed her his shirt.

She loved that. Wearing his shirt at his house the other day had been sexy and sweet. She pushed her arms into the sleeves and buttoned up as he pulled paper plates and other supplies from a box.

Within a few minutes, Zander had their dinner set up and was showing her how to eat crawfish "the right way".

Everything was incredibly delicious and they talked and ate and flirted as the sun fully set and lighting bugs started blinking around them.

When they were finished and half the jar of moonshine was gone, Zander said, without pretense, "I want you again."

She licked her lips. "Same."

"Here or my house?"

God, she loved talking so freely with this man. "I *loved* this. But...your house."

"Yeah?"

"I want a mattress so you can be on top."

His grin was downright wicked. "I can do that. If you do something for me."

"Anything," she answered honestly.

"Wear your tiara."

She stared at him. Then started laughing. "I can do that."

15

As she descended the staircase of the bed and breakfast the next evening, dressed in the only evening gown in her suitcase that really made any sense—the spaghetti-strapped solid black that hit just above the knees—Caroline had to admit that it was *all* worth seeing Zander Landry dressed in a charcoal gray suit, standing at the bottom of the stairs. Not to mention the hot look on his face when he caught sight of her.

"Fuck, yes," he said appreciatively as his gaze swept over her from the ringlet curls around her face to the strappy, three-inch heels on her feet and back up.

"Thank you. You look pretty *fuck, yes* yourself."

He gave her a grin and smoothed his palms over the front of his jacket. "Surprised I can pull off a suit?"

She thought about his question and let her gaze travel over him slowly as well. "Not really."

"Seriously? Most people would find it hilarious. I promise you some of the guys around here would find it hilarious."

"Then maybe they don't know you that well," she told him. "Because you're a guy who will do absolutely anything that needs to be done. Some things require blue jeans and boots and some things require suits. You are not only the guy to put any of those things on, but to completely pull them off."

For a second he looked surprised. Then pleased. He reached out and ran one hand down her bare arm from her shoulder to her wrist. "There are definitely a few things I want to pull off right now."

She gave a breathless laugh but she thought the heat in his eyes was as much about her words as it was about the dress. Though she was sure he noticed the way her nipples beaded behind the black silk.

Zander took the simple black shawl she carried from her fingers and drew it around her shoulders, covering her upper arms...and her traitorous nipples. But not before he gave her a knowing grin and wink.

"I'm sure you've had more men pick you up for dates in suits than in flannel and denim." His hand settled possessively on her lower back and she loved the weight as he escorted her toward the front door.

She nodded. "I have. But the butterflies I'm feeling aren't about the suit."

He hesitated before pulling the door open. "You have butterflies?"

She looked up at him. "I do."

"Why?"

"Because this is the first time I've gone on a date in a very long time where I *really* like the guy I'm going with and I'm really hoping for a kiss at the end of the night."

His gaze dropped to her mouth before going back to her eyes. "You're definitely getting a kiss at the end of the night."

A little shiver went through her and she let him see her wiggle. "Yeah, see? Butterflies like crazy."

"You haven't wanted the other guys to kiss you?"

"Not since high school. Maybe one in college."

His eyes narrowed and took on that familiar intensity. "Have you been kissed by a lot of guys when you didn't want to be?"

"Not exactly. But by guys I wasn't really into."

"Fucking hate that."

"I do too now."

"Now?"

"Now that I know what I've been missing."

The intensity increased along with the heat in his gaze and for just a moment Caroline was expecting him to back her up against the door and kiss her right then and there.

But he drew in a long breath. "I really..." He shook his head instead of finishing the comment. "We should go."

She nodded. They should. Spencer and Max would be waiting for them.

Zander held her hand during the drive to New Orleans and as they walked up the sidewalk in the French Quarter. They chatted idly as they strolled and it took Caroline about three blocks to catch on. But when she did, she wasn't surprised.

"This isn't the way to Octavia's."

"We're making a stop first."

Yeah, she should've been expecting this. In fact, she realized she had been. She couldn't show up at Octavia's with Zander. She couldn't show up at Octavia's at all. Not mere days after running out of her wedding and disappearing from her family. Easily half the patrons, not to mention the staff there, would know her. And Brantley. And her father. There would be nothing stealthy about them observing these men with Caroline in tow.

"I'm waiting for you somewhere else," she said.

He glanced over at her. "You don't sound surprised. Or pissed."

"You can't take me to Octavia's."

"Right."

"Why didn't you just leave me in Autre then?"

"Honestly? It's a completely selfish reason."

"I'm listening."

"I really wanted that moment when you came down the stairs dressed up like this for me. I really wanted to spend the evening thinking about stripping you out of that dress later on. I wanted to walk the Quarter, holding your hand, with all these other men knowing you're mine."

Her body heated and she realized that was a very good answer.

"But also because my family thinks we're going out tonight. And I didn't want them wondering what had happened and why you weren't with me. I would have wanted them to keep an eye on you as long as I wasn't in town and that would have made them suspicious that something was going on."

"And you would have had to admit that there might be bad guys in Autre and that there could potentially be trouble and that I might be in the middle of it. And you don't want them to know any of that."

He paused, but finally said, "Right."

She took a deep breath. Okay, these were all good points. She didn't like them—well, except for the coming-down-the-staircase moment—but they were legitimate points. "Fine," she finally conceded. "So where are we going?"

"This is Trahan's. Trahan's Tavern, officially," he said, stopping on the corner of Chartres and St. Peters. The restaurant and bar that sat facing Jackson Square had its big French doors open to the night air and music and laughter spilled out from the brightly lit interior. There was a short line to get a table but everyone seemed more than happy to wait.

"It's owned by a couple friends. Gabe and Logan. It's one of the most popular bars in the Quarter. You ever been here?"

She shook her head. "I've seen it though. It's always really busy."

He nodded. "It is. They're great guys, with great food and drink."

"And apparently good babysitting skills?"

"Listen, if I'm not with you and we don't know where Brantley is or what he's up to, I just feel better if you are with people that I know and trust. Would you rather be sitting alone at Max's? Or back at your mom and dad's? I didn't think you'd want to go home, but if that's what you want, I'll call you a car."

She shook her head. "No. You're right."

"And as soon as we're done at Octavia's, I was thinking we could have a drink. Maybe beignets." He inclined his head. Café Du Monde was across the square. "Or a horse-drawn carriage ride. Whatever you want."

She shook her head. How could she be mad? A horse-drawn carriage ride was definitely not a typical Zander Landry activity. But he was willing to do that for her. In a suit.

"Okay, let's go in."

He gave her a bright, pleased, and slightly relieved smile and settled his hand on her lower back to escort her inside.

Trahan's was a quintessential French Quarter establishment with floor to ceiling windows along both front walls, huge French doors, jazz music playing, and lots of laughter. It also smelled amazing and everyone walking out had huge smiles on their faces.

Zander led her toward the back of the restaurant where a group of four men were sitting with glasses of varying cocktails and several copies of the same paperback book on the table in front of them.

"Zander!"

"Hey, man!"

"Good to see you."

"Welcome."

The men greeted Zander with big smiles and handshakes. And very curious looks and smiles for Caroline.

"Caroline, this is Logan. He owns the place with his brother, Gabe. Who is over there behind the bar." Caroline looked toward the bar and a very good-looking man with dark hair lifted a hand in a quick wave.

"Hey, Caroline, welcome." Logan was equally good looking, with a smile that had a mischievous glint to it.

"Nice to meet you."

"And this is Caleb Moreau and James Reynaud," Zander said.

A big guy with a full beard and a more intense look offered his hand. "Hi, Caroline. I'm Caleb."

His hand was huge around hers and Caroline nodded. "Hi."

James was leaning back in his chair and gave her a big grin and a little two-finger wave. "It's *really* nice to meet you."

She lifted a brow. "Is it? Why is that?"

James's gaze slid to Zander and his smirk grew. "Oh, just that Zander's gotten real cozy with my girl. I'm very happy to have a chance to get to know his."

"Behave yourself." Zander's tone was firm.

"I'm a taken man," James assured him. "But I haven't forgotten all the times you flirted with Harper and made her all swoony over your deep analysis of romantic archetypes and plot devices."

Caroline looked at Zander with even more interest. "Character archetypes and plot devices?"

"Oh, Zander is quite the literary scholar," James said. "He cozied right up to my beautiful brainiac and took great pleasure in impressing her with his huge vocabulary."

"Yeah, it was my huge...vocabulary that Harper first noticed." Zander shot Caroline a look and immediately grimaced. "Shit. Sorry. Habit to give him shit about Harper. I have to remind him she's too good for him."

Caroline gave a soft snort. "Well, I just met James, but

judging by the uniform he has on, he's a firefighter? I'm guessing that Harper's plenty impressed by his...vocabulary."

Zander pretended to be shocked but it only lasted for a second before he grinned. "That's my girl."

James laughed. "Wow, thanks. I didn't even have to mention the fact that I'm a jazz musician too."

Caroline nodded. "Yeah, you're fine."

"Oh, and I'm amazing with dogs, babies, bearded dragons, and trees."

Caroline tipped her head. "Sounds like you have some good stories."

"Please sit. We have all evening." James indicated the chair right next to him and Caroline moved in that direction, but Zander caught her by the hips, pulled her back, and planted her in the seat next to Caleb. "*This* is the firefighter you should sit next to."

Caroline wasn't so sure. Caleb was very good-looking as well and, as she'd learned since she'd met Zander, she liked them a little intense and broody.

"And this is Matt LaSalle," Zander finished, indicating the man on her other side.

"Are you a cop? Because I'm a little surprised Zander is making babysitters out of two bartenders and two firefighters. He's a little more..."

"Wound up."

"Uptight."

"Tense."

Three of the men all spoke at once.

Caroline nodded. "Very." She looked up at Zander. "The cops in New Orleans don't like you?"

He narrowed his eyes. "Matt is home after several deployments overseas. Special forces."

Caroline's eyes widened and she looked at Matt. "Wow. Thank you for your service."

He gave her a single nod. "I've got your back."

Caroline leaned closer to him. "I feel very cared for suddenly."

Zander made a little growling noise, put both big hands on her shoulders, and leaned her *away* from Matt. "How are Lindsey and the kids, Matt?" he asked pointedly.

Both Caroline and Matt laughed. "Great. The boys are wonderful and our baby girl is the light of our lives," Matt said.

"Maybe I should tell *you* to behave," Zander told Caroline.

She met his eyes directly and wet her lips. "Well, only until...later."

It was clear he got her message. She didn't quite hear his growl this time, but she sensed it. And it was a whole different kind of growl.

"I'll be back soon."

She watched him stride across the bar and it wasn't until he disappeared through the door that she thought she should be more upset about being left behind. But honestly, what did she have to offer at Octavia's? And looking around the table she realized that she was going to be fine. Obviously well protected and in the company of some great men.

An arm reached over her shoulder and set a mug full of what appeared to be all whipped cream with a long straw down in front of her. She looked up to find Gabe grinning at her.

"Whiskey praline milkshake. Basically the reason my wife fell in love with me."

Caroline looked at it again, then back up at him. "I can see why."

He chuckled. "Glad to have you here tonight. Nice to meet you, and let me know if you need anything."

Okay, she was surrounded by handsome men and books and now had a decadent looking drink. She was going to make the best of the evening. After all, it was still going to end with her in this sexy black dress, Zander in his suit, and them alone in a bedroom.

"So what book are we discussing tonight?"

"Just happens to be a romance set here in New Orleans," Logan said.

"Are you a romance reader?" James asked.

"I am. Among other things," Caroline said.

"Great. This one's third in a series, but can be read as a stand alone. Though it's kind of fun to have read the first two. She was a teen in book one, where her dad was the hero. Now this is her book. She's a lower leg amputee. The heroine in book one was her PT," James said.

"Who's the hero?" Caroline asked, reaching for her glass.

"Works for her dad. Accompanies her to New Orleans when she comes for a bachelorette party."

"Is it sexy?" Caroline took a long pull of her milkshake. And holy hell was it good. "Because I only read books with open door sexy times."

Logan grinned at her. "You will fit right in around here."

"They're inside the bar."

Zander focused on Spencer, who was waiting for him on the sidewalk outside of Octavia's.

He really hated leaving Caroline behind. It was for the best, of course. There was no way she could come here and not be recognized. But he knew she felt left out. He had no qualms about her staying at Trahan's. The guys would not only take great care of her, but they'd make sure she had a good time. Still, he'd have to make it up to her later.

His body hummed with anticipation. Which was also selfish. But he wanted her more than he wanted his next breath, and if he couldn't let her be a part of this reconnaissance mission then he could at least show her a good time tonight. Trahan's would be fun for her and then they'd go do something fun before he took her home and fucked her until she couldn't move.

"Hello? Zander?"

He focused on Spencer. "It's just two of them so far?"

"Yeah, looks like they're waiting at the bar for the table to be ready and the other two to join them."

"Were you able to get us a table?"

"Yeah, but of course I have no idea how close we'll be to them."

"It'll be up to Max to get as much information as she can."

"Yeah, great. Our intel is in the hands of a cop-hating journalist who bribed us to tag along tonight," Spencer said dryly.

Zander laughed. "More specifically an *agent*-hating journalist."

"You think she likes *you*?"

"I think she likes me more than she likes you."

"She doesn't hate cops. Or agents. In general."

They both turned as Max approached them from the corner of the restaurant.

"She wouldn't like you no matter what your profession was. If that makes you feel better," Max said, coming to stand in front of them.

Spencer didn't reply right away. Because he was staring at her.

Zander understood why.

She looked amazing.

But Spencer frowned. "Seriously?"

She looked down at herself then up at him. "What?"

"I thought you were going for sad and pathetic and not noticeable."

She looked down again. She was wearing an animal print skirt with a silky black blouse and ankle-high black boots. Her hair was in two braids and she carried a large black nondescript bag.

"Don't worry, I've got this." She reached into her bag and pulled out a pair of glasses that she slipped on her nose. The black rims made her green eyes look even bigger. Then she withdrew a huge paperback book of crossword puzzles and a pencil that she tucked behind her ear.

"Crossword puzzles?" Spencer asked.

"I'll have you know that I'm a champion."

"A champion what?"

"A crossword puzzle champion."

"How does being really good at crosswords do anything for us?"

"I'm not just really good. I'm a *champion*," she told him. "I won the American Crossword Puzzle Tournament last year. And the year before. I'm also the champion of the Louisiana crossword puzzle league for the fourth year in a row."

"You don't even say that with a hint of humor."

"That's because I'm not joking."

Spencer just blinked at her. Max tipped her head and studied him.

"You don't think the skirt is a little on the nose?" he finally asked.

So they were done talking about crossword puzzles. Zander found all of this far more amusing than he should, he knew. But he couldn't wait to tell his brothers about Spencer having the hots for a girl who did crosswords for fun. And took her champion status very seriously. And probably had a vocabulary twenty times bigger than his own.

Zander wondered if she had trophies.

"I told you it was going to be a conversation starter," Max said, smoothing a hand over her shirt.

"You're just gonna walk up to them and start talking about cheetahs because you're wearing that skirt?"

"Probably not. Since this is a *leopard* print," she said with an eyeroll.

"For fuck's sake," Spencer muttered.

"I'm going to go sit by them at the bar with my earbuds in—without any music of course—and do my crossword puzzles and act like I'm being stood up. I'm going to just be a dorky girl who's not worth them even paying any attention to. Trust me, I've got this."

"But you think they'll talk about all of this animal stuff with you sitting right there?"

"I think my skirt will make them make some stupid comment which will lead into the conversation. But because I'm a young woman, who seems beneath them, it won't even occur to them that I have any interest in the conversation. Rich white men have a way of running their mouths, and their egos often get in the way of being careful."

"I think you're a little crazy," Spencer told her.

Max pushed the glasses up her nose with her middle finger. "Better men than you have told me that."

"I'm sure that's true." He sighed. "I'm going to say okay to this. Only because I don't have a better plan at the moment."

"I don't really care if you're okay with it or not." She turned on her heel and started for the door.

"And by the way," Spencer called after her. "Not sure you really understand the blending in thing. You look very...noticeable."

She shot him a grin. "I actually think that's just you, Special Agent."

Then she disappeared into the restaurant.

Zander watched Spencer watch her through the large windows. The entire way to the bar. Every single step.

Zander pulled his phone from his pocket and texted Caroline.

Does Max really not know she's gorgeous?

A moment later Caroline replied. *LOL. She really doesn't. Grew up the skinny redheaded nerd. Don't think she's really grown out of that idea.*

Well, Spencer's noticed.

And so have you, apparently.

Yeah, but just in passing. I go for blondes. In tiaras. Who steal lions.

That's too bad. I had a lion, but he wasn't stolen. He was a gift.

Zander was grinning as Spencer punched him lightly on the shoulder. "Come on."

Zander pocketed his phone and worked on focusing.

But twenty minutes later, he was restless and annoyed. Not only could he not hear anything the men were saying, but he'd just spent twenty minutes eating overpriced meat and drinking iced tea and watching Max work on crossword puzzles. And there was no way he was getting Caroline out of his head.

"Dude, what the fuck?" Spencer asked crossly.

"What?"

"You're like a little kid who needs to pee in the middle church. What the hell? Sit still."

"Sorry. Did you want me looking into your eyes lovingly so everyone thinks that we're in a deeply committed relationship?" Zander asked.

"We could...talk," Spencer said.

Zander snorted. "Well, let's not get crazy."

Spencer fiddled with his fork, his gaze on Max.

"So you're pretty crazy about her?" Spencer asked.

Zander looked at his cousin in surprise. "I'm going to assume you're talking about Caroline and not Max."

"Yeah, Caroline."

"I'm..." He let out a breath. "Yeah. I am. As much as I tried not to be."

Spencer sat back in his chair. "Because you can't put her in your happy bubble of bliss, right?"

Zander frowned. "My what?"

"The bubble of bliss. That place you keep everyone in Autre. Except for Michael and Theo."

Zander saw no point in denying it. "Yeah."

"Your brothers and cousins could handle it. They're not stupid."

"We've been over this."

"Yeah. And I get your points and I won't step over the line. They're your people and your territory. But I think you underestimate them."

Zander and Spencer had talked about this before. More than once. "Michael and Theo agree with me."

"Michael's as protective of them as you are," Spencer agreed with a nod. "Theo just doesn't want them getting in his way."

Zander gave a short laugh. That wasn't untrue. But Theo also had a pretty big wall up around his heart since losing his brother. He just didn't want people getting too close emotionally now.

"They could handle it," he agreed. "Of course. They'd want to help us fight off all the darkness and trouble. They'd be happy to stand up to anyone threatening our town and our people. They all feel the same way about the anger and hatred and greed and power. They'd want to keep it out. But that puts them in danger. We've got this."

"And as long as they know nothing about it, you can keep them from getting involved."

"Right. But once they know there's a threat, they'd jump right in. The same way they do with hurricane rescue and recovery. The same way they do with the animals coming to the park, or the people who come in needing someplace to land and feel secure. Hell, my family adopted Griffin and Donovan the minute they hit town. Even if Jordan hadn't married Fletcher, she would have been part of the family. Michael's family is as much a part of the Landry clan as those of us with the same last name. Knox and Fiona are the same. It doesn't matter who you are, if you need food or friends or family—or all three at once—you get it. I can't give them even a whiff of something bad going on."

"But Caroline already has that whiff. She knows that even when things look sunny and happy and solid, there's dark underneath. You don't have to worry about that scaring her off."

Zander nodded. "Yeah."

"So..."

"It's pretty great," he admitted. "I always thought I'd want a woman I was involved with happily..."

"Blissful. The word's blissful, man," Spencer told him.

Zander rolled his eyes. "Fine. Blissful. I'd want her living the happy, sunny, *blissful* life, feeling safe and secure and ignorant of the...crap. The dark and ugly stuff. But Caro..."

"She doesn't need that."

"No."

"And she must be pretty good at what she does," Spencer went on. "I mean, she *has* helped take down some guys doing some bad shit. She's clearly smart, patient, and careful."

Zander nodded slowly. That was all true. Caroline had been persistent and passionate, but she hadn't been reckless.

"Someone you can be yourself with, share your secrets with, but not worry about," Spencer said. "Sounds perfect."

Yeah, it really did.

Caroline knew all about the dark side of even the prettiest things, including that Autre wasn't always the happy haven it seemed. But that hadn't done anything except make her want to highlight the good—okay *blissful*—moments up on the wall at Ellie's and push him to keep working on this case. And she'd stayed out of the way. When Spencer had gotten to town, she'd left them alone to work. Tonight, when it had made sense that she needed to stay out of sight, she'd agreed to hang out at Trahan's.

Zander let that sink in. He'd never expected to meet someone like Caroline. He'd purposely been avoiding getting involved with anyone, not believing that a woman who knew crime and corruption personally could be sweet, generous, good-hearted, and careful.

He could have gotten involved with someone in law enforcement. There were plenty of amazing, kickass, smart, beautiful cops and agents and lawyers that he could have dated. But...he glanced over to where Max was still at the bar, seemingly unconcerned with anything going on around her, but only two feet away from one of the most powerful men in New Orleans...he would have worried about her all the time. Not because those women weren't highly trained and great at their jobs, but just because shit happened. Every day. He had a circle he worked with simply because he couldn't do it all alone, but he only got close to a very select few. And yeah, he worried about them. Thank God Spencer, Theo, Michael, and Wyatt were damned good at their jobs.

And he'd never been willing to expand that very tight circle.

Then again, he hadn't met Caroline Holland yet.

Zander took a deep breath. "You think we're about done here?" he asked.

Spencer nodded. "Unfortunately."

The two men at the bar had moved to a table across the room to join their friends who had finally arrived.

A couple minutes later, Max closed her crossword puzzle book and slid from her barstool. She slipped from the room by another door, making it possible the men wouldn't even have noticed her leaving.

"Well, I guess I'm gonna text her. See what she's got." He sounded very put out.

"Sounds good. I've got a date to get to."

"**E**verything okay?"

Caroline tuned back into the conversation and realized Logan was addressing her. She'd been paying more attention to her phone than she had to the book club for the past half hour. "I'm really sorry," she said with a grimace. "That's very rude of me."

"No problem. We know this wasn't how you planned to spend your evening."

She gave them a sincere smile. "It's just one of my friends. She's having some issues with the guy she's out with tonight."

That wasn't exactly *untrue*. Max was having some issues with the men she, Spencer, and Zander had followed to Octavia's. Her main issue was that she was getting very little information about or from the men.

Apparently, the other two men had finally shown up and they'd all been taken to their table for dinner and were now outside of range for her to hear their conversation. She had texted Caroline a photo of the men and she didn't recognize any of them as men that spent time with her father.

"I'm just going to step outside and call her real quick," Caroline said. "I just want to be sure she's okay."

"Sure. Just stick close to the front. Okay?" Matt asked.

Caroline nodded. "Of course."

She slipped outside the front doors of Trahan's. There was a short line of people waiting for a table and she walked to the end and stepped around the corner of the building but positioned herself in front of one of the windows so Matt wouldn't worry.

However, instead of calling Max, she texted her brother.

Do you know what this is? She attached a photo of the first page of the list.

His reply came back surprisingly quickly. *Where did you get that?*

Caroline: *I found it in my suitcase.*

Christopher: *It's Brantley's. You should get that back to him.*

Caroline: *I don't want to talk to Brantley. What is it? Is it important?*

Christopher: *Business contacts. Yes, important.*

Can I give it to you to give to him? She really wanted to know how much her brother had to do with this.

She held her breath as the little dots popped up as Christopher typed back.

No, I'm done with that project.

You were working on it with him though? she asked

For a little bit. But it's his baby. I'm done.

Well, that was something of a relief. *I guess I'll let him know I have it then.*

She waited for a moment to see if her brother would ask how she was, or even where she was. Nothing more came from Christopher, however. She tamped down the disappointment and sadness. She was glad that he wasn't involved with whatever this was. If he and Brantley had had a falling out, that could only be good for Christopher. But she was sad that she and her brother had grown apart, that they didn't really know each other anymore, that they didn't confide in one another.

She took a deep breath and then dialed the number she'd been avoiding for days.

Brantley answered on the third ring. "Caroline."

"Hi. I was wondering...can we meet?"

"You want to get together?"

She took a deep breath and pulled together all of her best acting talents. "Yes. I think I made a mistake. Can we get together and talk?"

There was a long pause on his end. Then, "Sure. There's something in your suitcase that I need you to bring to me too."

Caroline thought about how to handle the moment. Finally, she said, "Is it a list of names and phone numbers?"

"Yes. You found it?"

"Yes. I had no idea what it was. It's yours?"

"Yeah. Chris gave it to me the morning of the wedding and I stuck it in your bag at the last minute so I wouldn't lose it. I need it for a project I'm working on."

"Okay, I can get it back to you. Can you meet me at Octavia's? Tonight?"

"Tonight? Yeah. Why don't you just come over here?"

Well, shit...because she wanted it not only to be someplace public, but because she wanted to put him face to face with the men at Octavia's. And have Spencer witness him interacting with them.

"I have some apologizing to do. And...I just wanted it to be special." Caroline wrinkled her brow. That probably sounded stupid. Why would this need to be special? This was going to sound so fake to him.

But the next moment, he said, "Okay, sure. Octavia's is fine. How about twenty minutes?"

"That's perfect. I'll see you there."

"See you there."

Caroline disconnected and blew out a breath. Okay, she'd started this, now there was no going back.

She opened a text to Max and typed quickly. *We need to find out if Brantley knows those guys. Best way is to get them face to face. Brantley and I are meeting there in twenty minutes. Keep Spencer and Zander there.*

Max replied quickly, *Great idea. No problem.*

Caroline pressed a hand to her stomach and took one more deep, fortifying breath. Well, she wanted to be more involved with the good work that needed to be done. This was a good first step.

She returned to the table in Trahan's and gave the guys a big smile. "Hey, so my friend really needs a shoulder to cry on. This guy is giving her fits. I'm going to head over to meet her."

Matt frowned. "Zander made it sound like he wanted you to hang out here till he got back."

She laughed. "I live in New Orleans, Matt. I know my way around. I'm going to take an Uber over to her place and sit on her couch with her and a tub of ice cream." She felt a little bad about that lie, but she was heading to where Zander was. He wouldn't have to wonder where she'd disappeared to. "I'll text Zander and let him know where I am. If he shows up here before he gets my message, tell him I'm with Max."

Matt didn't look pleased, but he nodded. There really wasn't much he could do. She was a grown woman and he couldn't physically restrain her.

He could, however, text Zander that she was leaving and meeting Max. Still, by the time she was in an Uber and headed for Octavia's, Zander would figure out that she was coming his direction.

"Thanks for babysitting me, guys. It was great to meet you."

"Standing invitation to book club," Logan told her.

"I might just take you up on that." These guys were great. Just like all the other people in Zander's life. She understood why he felt protective of them all.

She made her way out to the curb just as her Uber was pulling up. She settled into the back and thought about what her next steps were. Getting Brantley face to face with the men from the list was a good start. Doing it in front of Spencer, since the FBI agent couldn't legally *make* Brantley come in and talk for any reason, was also good. But then what? She was going to have to wing it.

Brantley was already waiting in front of Octavia's when the car pulled up at the curb. Butterflies kicked up in Caroline's stomach as she got out of the car and pasted on a bright smile for him.

"Hi, Brantley," she greeted.

He leaned in to kiss her cheek. "You look gorgeous."

"Thanks. And thanks for meeting me. I feel like there are a lot of things we need to say."

"After you," he said, holding the door open for her and gesturing for her to precede him into the restaurant.

They had just crossed the marble floor of the entryway when Max met them at the hostess stand with a bright smile. "Welcome to Octavia's."

Caroline worked to not react. "Evening. Table for Brantley Anderson," Brantley told her. A name like his would get a table quickly and easily.

"Of course, Mr. Anderson, so nice to see you this evening."

There were no other hostesses in the vicinity and Caroline wondered how Max had finagled that. No doubt she'd made up some emergency or managed to spill something the hostess had needed to attend to when Max had seen Caroline and Brantley through the big front windows.

Max led them through the restaurant and Caroline had to stifle a small gasp when she spotted Zander and Spencer sitting at the table in the far corner.

She and Zander locked eyes and she could feel his shock, then anger as he recognized her and the man she was with. He started to get up, but Spencer put a hand on his arm and Zander sank back into his chair. His expression eased only slightly. Into disappointment.

Her stomach sank. But she had a job to do here.

She pasted on a fake smile. That, at least, was something she was really good at.

16

Max led them to a table across the room from Spencer and Zander, but easily in their line of sight. Caroline looked around and immediately recognized the four men sitting at a round table next to theirs. How convenient. She gave her friend a little smile. Max winked at her when Brantley wasn't looking.

"I hope this will do, Mr. Anderson," Max said, raising her voice slightly on his name.

"This will be fine."

He pulled the chair out for Caroline and just as her butt hit the seat, one of the men at the next table said, "Well, Brantley Anderson. How's it going?"

Brantley turned, and his mouth stretched into smile. Max carefully ducked behind him so the men couldn't get a look at her, not that they'd pay much attention to the hostess anyway. She gave Caroline a little thumbs up behind Brantley's back.

Yeah, this was going well. So far.

Brantley chuckled and approached the table with his hand outstretched. "Good evening, gentlemen." He shook each man's hand, greeting them all with familiarity.

Max and Caroline exchanged a look and then Max looked in the direction of Zander and Spencer's table. After a moment, Caroline also glanced in their direction as well. Both men were watching every move.

Brantley stood chatting with the men at the table and Caroline breathed a sigh of relief.

"Let me know if I can get you anything, Ms. Holland," Max said. She lifted a brow.

"We're fine. Thank you," Caroline assured her.

Max moved off, but Caroline knew she'd only go as far as the front.

Caroline reached for her tiny purse and pulled her phone out. She flipped through the various apps until she got to the recording app and hit record. Then she stood, smoothed her skirt, and approached Brantley.

She ran her hand up his arm. "Honey, I need to go to the ladies' room. Would you hold this for me?" She showed him her phone with the screen turned down.

Slightly distracted, he nodded. "Yeah, okay."

She slipped it into his jacket pocket and then kissed his cheek, giving the other men a quick smile. "I'll be right back."

She headed for the restrooms by way of the front foyer, where she passed Max and said quietly, "I have no idea what I'm doing."

"You're fucking amazing," Max whispered back, not lifting her head from her phone. The real hostess had returned to her station.

Caroline made her way to the ladies' room. She stood, staring at the mirror, taking deep breaths.

Max joined her a moment later. She checked the stalls and found them all empty.

"Okay, record as much as you can of any and all conversations Brantley has, then get him to go with you to my apartment," Max said.

Caroline nodded. Max lived within walking distance of Octavia's and it would be easy enough to convince Brantley that's where Caroline was staying now that she'd left home.

Max continued. "That way, he'll be there willingly. Spencer can't enter any of Brantley's properties, or any of his friends' homes or offices, without a warrant, but he can definitely enter a property where the owner lets him in. And it will be a private place where Spencer can assure him it's safe to talk."

Caroline smiled. "Got it. You'll make sure the guys are there?"

"We'll be *right* behind you, don't worry."

Caroline nodded. "I'm going to tell him he can have the list but it's at your place. I don't know how else to get him there."

"You could have promised him sex," Max said, with a shrug. "But yeah, the list works."

Caroline wrinkled her nose. Either way, the whole thing felt...manipulative. Because it was. She sighed. This was what she did. It's what she'd been doing for years. She played a part so that people would tell her things or do things she wanted them to do. No one ever confided in her or was influenced by her just being real. Would she even be able to convince someone of something without tricking them?

She thought back to the painting and redecorating they'd done at Ellie's. That was small. It wasn't significant in a national or global sense. But it had mattered to the Landry family. And it had happened because she'd been real and honest. And they'd listened.

What would it feel like to be open and genuine with someone in a truly impactful way? To really influence someone to do something that made a difference on a grander scale?

"Well, I think he wants the list more than sex with me," Caroline said with a shrug.

"I don't know. You look *hot* in that dress," Max told her.

Caroline smoothed her hand down the dress. "Zander likes it."

Max laughed. "Yeah, that guy is about to burn this place down and take you to his remote bayou cabin as his sex hostage or something, so you'd better get this thing with Brantley moving."

The idea that Zander was a little jealous gave Caroline a surge of bayou-sex-hostage-could-be-fun, but the mention of a remote bayou cabin made her think about his major concern for his family and town and she took a deep breath. "Yeah, let's get this over with. So my plan is to tell Brantley that I regret turning the lion cub over to the animal park and that I want another. I'm going to convince him that I want to buy another cub. I'm hoping that if I become a buyer, he'll tell me more about what's going on. Or, if he doesn't know, it can lead to me getting connected to sellers."

Max blew out a breath. "I don't have a better plan so let's try it. It's as convincing as anything else. We're kind of stuck here."

When Caroline got back to the table, Brantley had pulled a chair up to the table next to the four men and had a cocktail in hand. When he saw her, he laughed and said to the men, "My fiancée is back, gentlemen, and I have another type of business to take care of. It was nice to see you all."

"You too, Anderson," one of them said. "We'll be in touch."

Brantley moved his chair back to the table he was sharing with Caroline and gave her a smile.

"Who are they?" she asked as they settled in.

"Just some business associates."

"Should I know any of them?"

He shook his head. "I doubt it. Chris and I've been working with them more independently. Well, more me than Chris now. He's bailed."

She leaned in. "Does it have to do with the animals?" she

asked quietly. "Because that's one of the things I wanted to talk to you about."

He frowned. "What about them?"

She took a breath. Time to put the plan in motion. But just then she glanced toward Zander and Spencer's table.

Her gaze met Zander's.

And she couldn't do it.

She'd been real in Autre. She'd been able to let go. Be herself. Be accepted and appreciated and...loved for her real self. She hadn't had to trick or manipulate anyone there into trusting her or sharing their stories or bringing her into their inner circle. Zander had shared things with her that she knew he didn't tell many people. No, those people didn't have deep, dark, corrupt intentions and secrets, but...that was part of it too. They were good people. Doing good, honest work that did make the world better. Even in a tiny town in Louisiana, they were using their talents and hearts and support network to make a sanctuary for animals.

And people.

She wasn't the only one who'd come to Autre a little lost and alone and in need of a place where she could be her true self.

She felt her eyes stinging as that all hit her. She couldn't go back to lying and manipulating and playing these deceptive games with these people.

She focused on Brantley. "You have to stop what you're doing."

Brantley frowned. "What do you mean? What do we need to stop doing?"

"The transporting. You have to stop helping these people do what they're doing to these animals."

He frowned, then cast a glance in the direction of the four men at the next table. Caroline knew there was no way for

Zander and Spencer to see that particular reaction but it told her everything she needed to know.

"Caroline, let's just talk about us."

"I can't. This is what I care about," she told him honestly.

She slid her chair closer to him, put a hand on his arm and leaned in, whispering now as if they were two lovers having an intimate conversation.

She was sure Zander was going to love that. But she couldn't risk the men at the next table overhearing.

"Brantley, you're a good guy. I've known you for years. I don't know why you got mixed up in this, but you have to believe me when I tell you this is not good."

She leaned over and took her phone from his jacket pocket. She pressed the button to stop the recording. From here, Spencer was just going to have to believe what she told him transpired between her and Brantley. She opened her photos and flipped through until she found one of Mwanzo. She showed Brantley. "This is the lion cub you gave me. His name is Mwanzo. Do you see that dog he's with? That's his new mother. That German Shepherd is fostering him as if he's her own."

"No shit?" Brantley asked, staring at the photo.

She nodded. "That's pretty cool, right? But do you know what happens when lion cubs are taken from their mothers so young?"

She flipped to another photo of Mwanzo being held by Naomi. "The babies and mothers cry for one another for days."

Brantley frowned.

"It's very traumatic. They're supposed to stay with their mothers for two years. They're supposed to nurse. Being ripped away from their mothers causes stress—they suck on their paws, they self-mutilate sometimes in an attempt to self-soothe."

She flipped to a photo of him playing with Brinkley. "Even though *he* might be happier than most because he has a surrogate mom, he'll have long-term nutritional deficits like bone and teeth problems. And these people"—She pointed at Donovan and Naomi in the photo—"are wild animal experts. They work with abandoned and hurt and abused animals all the time. That's what they've made their life's work. Every single day. They rehabilitate them and some are able to return to the wild, but they can't fix everything. They can't fix all of his nutritional or emotional problems. They're not lions. They're not his mother. *That* is where he should be. And there are others in worse shape. Because of these people buying and selling and not caring at all."

She flipped to another photo. "There are farms in South Africa, Brantley, where they breed the female lions over and over to produce cubs for pets and petting exhibitions at low-rate zoos. They rip them away as babies and use them as exhibits and toys. And when the lions grow up, they turn them out for staged lion hunts."

Brantley actually looked bothered by that. "That's not happening here in the U.S., is it?"

"You tell me." She leaned in a little closer and met Brantley's eyes. "You have connections that could help us find that out. But even if not, these animals should not be bought and sold as pets."

Then she continued to flip through photos of Mwanzo with Brinkley. Then photos of the other animals that lived at Boys of the Bayou Gone Wild. She had photos of Donovan working with the animals, Griffin and Tori treating them, Jill taking care of penguins, Jordan with the alpacas, and more.

"These people are some of the *best*. He has a dog as a foster mom. He's a thousand times better off than most. But even this is really sad, Brantley," she said, the urgency and emotion in her voice completely genuine. "He was taken away from his mother so that some rich guy could have him as a pet to show off to his friends. You know these people as well as I do. None of them actually care that much about their own dogs. They certainly don't care about the plight of endangered wildlife." She flipped to a photo of the tiger the Autre group had rescued from a rich prick in Alabama. "Did you know that there are more tigers in captivity in the United States alone than are left in the wild? The people who own them consider them prizes and trophies. They're just toys to them. But these are living creatures."

Brantley didn't say anything for a long moment. "I'm not the one buying and selling them, Caroline."

"But you're contributing to the problem. And more"—She squeezed his arm—"you know who they are. Or you at least have ways of helping the authorities find out who they are."

He started to pull back, but she squeezed his arm again. "You can help shut this down." She knew when he looked into her eyes he would see how much this mattered to her. "Yes, maybe it would be just this one group. And yes, I know there are lots more. And if these guys can't get these animals this way, they'll probably find another. But that doesn't mean that we shouldn't try to shut this down. If we're not part of the solution, we're part of the problem, right?"

He was quiet for a few more seconds. Then he cleared his throat. "I started doing it just for some extra money. I took a loan out because I didn't want to go to my dad for money again. He always makes me feel like shit when I do that. But I wasn't able to pay the loan back as quickly as I should. So instead of making me pay it back, the guy had me do this job. It just kind of spiraled from there."

Caroline actually felt a flutter of hope in her chest. "I knew it had to be something like that. You're not a bad guy. Just help us figure out who's doing this so we can shut it down. We can figure out a way for you to get the money for your loan some other way."

"I'm in too deep. I don't want to get involved with the cops. I don't want to go to jail."

He cast another glance in the direction of the table of four men, but none of them were paying any attention. They were drinking and laughing loudly and talking about their own interests.

"Are they part of it?" Caroline asked softly.

He didn't answer.

"Brantley," Caroline said, pulling his attention back to her. "If you help us, you'll be an informant. You'll be working *with* us."

He frowned. "Us? What, you're a cop now?"

That little flutter in her chest turned into a *thump, thump, thump.* And it wasn't hope so much as it was excitement. "Not exactly. But I'm working with them. Helping them. And..." She shrugged. "Maybe eventually."

"You want to be a cop?"

"I don't think I'm really street cop material, but maybe I could be a consultant or...work for the FBI."

She braced herself for him to scoff. He might. Most people in her usual circle would.

The Landrys wouldn't.

That thought came right on the heels of the thought about the people she spent most of her time with.

No, the Landrys wouldn't. They would tell her to go for it. They would tell her to do whatever she wanted. To at least give it a try. And then she knew that if it didn't work out, she could show up at Ellie's and they'd feed her gumbo and sweet tea or maybe even a Pimm's Cup, if the occasion called for that. And they'd tell her hilarious stories and tease her, and within an hour, she would be feeling good again, refocused on what was most important in life—doing your best with the right intentions and surrounding yourself with people who loved you just the way you were, even when the way you were wasn't perfect.

But Brantley didn't scoff. "Well, you're smart enough for

that. And you've been putting up with a lot of shady assholes for a long time. You'd probably be good at white-collar crime."

Yeah, that's what she'd been thinking. She gave him a surprised but pleased look. "Thank you."

He sighed. "So, we're not going to have dinner, are we?"

She shook her head. "I'd rather go back to my friend's apartment to talk about this more. And invite a couple other friends over?"

He hesitated and she leaned even closer. "Listen, we *are* taking these guys down. Your only real choice here is whether you help us or you go down with them."

He lifted a brow, but it didn't look sarcastic or mocking. "Damn."

"What do you think will happen if one of those guys"—She tipped her head in the direction of the men dining next to them —"met me at a cocktail party and I told him that *you* told me everything about the buying and selling? They've seen us together tonight, being very close. And they've seen this dress." She lifted a brow. "Do you really think I couldn't convince them that there was some pretty intense pillow talk going on between us?"

Brantley's mouth formed a little "o". She wasn't sure if he was intimidated or impressed. Or both.

She didn't *want* to play games and manipulate people. But to save innocent animals? Or people? She definitely would.

"And now"—She lifted her phone, leaned her head on Brantley's shoulder, and snapped a selfie. With the four men clearly in the background—"I have something to remind them of the night."

"Okay, geez. I was going to cooperate," Brantley said. "You made a really good case even without the threats."

She gave him a smile. "Oh. Good."

He gave the menu a longing glance. "But I really love the scallops here though."

Caroline looked over at Spencer and Zander's table. The expressions on the faces of the men there said plainly that she and Brantley did *not* have time for dinner.

"We need to go," she told Brantley. "Like now."

"Fine."

They stood and Brantley put his hand on her lower back as they walked back through the restaurant to the front. They passed Zander and Caroline could swear that she felt the tension radiating off of him as he turned, watching them go.

Geez, could he be any more obvious? She risked shooting him a *knock it off* frown behind Brantley's back.

She read his return frown clearly. *I'm this close to tossing you over my shoulder.*

But maybe not in a totally good way. More in a *you're in very big trouble and I'm super pissed right now* way.

Crap. They were going to have to talk.

On their way out the door, Brantley slipped Max, their "hostess", a big tip for getting him a table that they ended up not using. Max thanked him and tucked the hundred-dollar bill in the front of her bra. Caroline almost blew Max's cover with the snort she had to pretend was a cough.

"You gotta calm down or I'm not letting you go in with me," Spencer told Zander as they strode down the sidewalk a block behind Caroline and Brantley.

They weren't close enough.

If Brantley wanted to hurt her, pull her into an alley, shove her into a car, or a million other things he could imagine—and was—they were too far back to do anything about it.

"I'm fine. Shut up," Zander muttered.

"We have to trust her. We're here as backup," Spencer said.

"This isn't an op. We don't know what we're here as," Zander ground out. "We don't have any idea what's going on."

"Caroline is getting us proof of a crime. Or an informant. Or both. We need to let her do her thing," Spencer argued.

"Since when does she have a *thing* to do? We didn't talk about this. This wasn't the plan," Zander said. Every muscle in his body was tight and his heart was pounding so hard he could practically feel the pulses of blood through his veins.

"You're being irrational," Spencer told him.

"Fuck off."

"He's *in love* with her and she's walking down a dark street with a guy who might be a criminal," Max said to Spencer. Very *unhelpfully*. "Give him a break."

"I can't believe you let her do this," Zander snapped at her.

"Hey, I didn't *let* her do anything. She's a fully functioning, grown-up human being. She can do what she wants," Max said. "But, for the record, I'm all in here. Team Caroline. This is awesome."

"This is *stupid*," Zander told her. "She could get hurt."

"Someone could mug her tomorrow. A hurricane could wipe us all out next month. She's safer with him than in a lot of other situations."

Zander just growled at her.

"Because *we're* right here," Max went on. "She's not stupid, Zander. She wouldn't be doing this without backup."

"And we've now got a hell of a lot more than we had before she showed up," Spencer added. "We've got a person of interest in a federal investigation seen by law enforcement interacting with other persons of interest. And soon we're going to have that person of interest holding evidence in that investigation." He looked at Max. "I assume he's going to have a photocopy of the list?"

"He's going to have the actual list."

"I thought *I* had the actual list," Spencer said.

"I gave you a copy."

He sighed.

"Hey, having the original is always more valuable."

"Yes. I know," he said dryly.

"Anyway, yes, the original list is at my place."

"And," he went on, addressing Zander and ignoring Max, "we're going to be able to enter the apartment where the person is without a warrant, because the owner of the apartment is going to let us in." He looked back at Max. "You are going to let us in, right?"

"Will you show me your tattoos if I do?"

He lifted a brow. "I'll—"

"Knock it off," Zander told them both sharply. Their banter-bickering bullshit was annoying as fuck. "Yes, she's going to let us in."

"The grumpy pants thing is *not* as hot when it's directed at *me*," Max muttered. Just as Caroline and Brantley climbed a set of steps to the front door of a townhouse.

Zander and Spencer pulled up short.

"Come on," Max said.

"We have to give them a little time," Spencer said. "Let them get inside. Let him get comfortable."

Zander was going to climb out of his skin. "Jesus, man," he said after what felt like twenty minutes and was really more like two. "I'm so sick of *waiting* on you."

"This is why you'd be a terrible federal agent," Spencer told him. "You're not patient enough."

"Yeah, well, sitting around doing *nothing* seems like a shit job I don't want anyway."

Spencer just shrugged.

"Caroline would be an awesome agent," Max said after a moment. "White collar crimes would be her specialty. You should totally recruit her."

"You think?" Spencer seemed to actually be pondering that.

"Oh for sure. She knows how they think. She can blend in with them. And she's got this thirst for justice. She needs to do more than what she's doing. She needs a real job. Where she can feel truly rewarded and fulfilled." Max turned to Zander. "Don't you think?" She stared at him as if daring him to disagree.

He didn't. Max was absolutely right.

"Let's go." He started for the townhouse. And this time Spencer didn't stop him.

"Hi, honey, I'm home!" Max called out as she let them in.

"Oh, hey."

Zander heard Caroline greet Max. Then he climbed the steps far enough to see her. She was sitting on the sofa, right next to Brantley. Looking so...happy. Proud. Excited.

"Hey, everyone," Caroline said brightly. "Great news! We have a plan! You're all invited to our re-engagement party!"

Zander stopped. Son of a bitch.

"What do you mean your *re-engagement* party?" Max asked.

But Zander already knew.

"We're going to pretend that we've gotten back together so our families can throw a big party and invite our usual circle... including the men from the restaurant. We'll put out the word we want to buy another lion cub and this time, I'll be in on any contacts we get from potential sellers," Caroline said.

Yeah. That was pretty much exactly what he'd expected she'd say.

Goddammit.

His chest felt tight and he couldn't draw in a deep breath.

She had *literally* left the safety of Trahan's, where she'd been surrounded by good people and friendship and laughter and entertainment, where he'd been able to provide her protection and a barrier from all of this corruption and depravity and darkness, to *seek out* Brantley and jump right into the middle of all of...*this*. She'd walked down an *actual* dark street, making a plan with a confessed criminal to get even further, *directly* involved in this case. *She* had made a plan with that criminal instead of waiting to consult with *him*—a goddamned law enforcement officer—or even Spencer, the FBI agent who had been *right there.*

And, worst of all, she was excited about it.

No, maybe what was worse was that it would very likely work. It was a pretty good plan.

Which meant, she'd want to do something like this again. And that would work. It would work the next time too. And the next time.

Because she was smart, and bold, and passionate, and, quite frankly, would be an amazing FBI agent. Just like Max had said.

There was no way she was ever going to be happy settling down in Autre with him keeping her away from all the darkness and danger.

So, he turned. And headed right back out the door.

He was almost an entire block away when she caught up to him.

"Zander!"

He didn't stop.

"Zander! Dammit! Running in heels sucks!"

He stopped and turned as she stumbled to a halt. "What?" he demanded.

"Where are you going?"

"Home."

"But..." She glanced back at Max's townhouse. "Okay, I'm sorry. That wasn't funny. You're right. Let me explain."

"*Funny?*" He suddenly crowded close. His heart was thundering and every muscle in his body was taut. "No, Caroline, nothing about any of this whole *thing*"—He practically spat —"was funny. What the hell?"

"I *had* to make this work." She reached out and grabbed his arm. "We *had* to come away with something we could use tonight. I knew if we didn't, there was a really good chance that Spencer would be assigned to something else that would have to take priority over this case. More animals would get hurt. More assholes would get away with crimes. This was a Hail Mary, but when Max told me you were getting nowhere at Octavia's, I texted my brother about the list and he said it was all Brantley's and he needed it back and the idea came to me and...I just went with it."

"Well, I don't like it."

"Why?" She dropped her hold on him, frowned, and set her hands on her hips. "Because it was a bad plan? Or just because it wasn't what you were expecting? Because Brantley's agreed to talk to Spencer. He's going to tell him everything. He does know those guys at the restaurant, obviously. And he expects we'll be contacted by several sellers within twenty-four hours of the party. He'll go from middleman to buyer and we'll get *actual* intel that Spencer can do something with."

Zander just stared at her. He'd left her at Trahan's to keep her *out* of this. Because she was the girl who just picked up on the little bits, the hints, the threads. She started things but she didn't finish them. She didn't get *involved*. And...he'd actually started to think that something could work between them because of that. She could understand him and what he did. She could be there. He could share things with her. But she'd be...safe.

And now...well, she'd fucking solved this entire thing. He'd been sitting in the restaurant, doing nothing, getting nowhere. And she'd walked in, got them evidence, a confession, and an informant.

Which shouldn't surprise him, he realized. He wanted her to sit safely on the sidelines but...Caroline Holland wasn't a sidelines kind of person.

She'd come to Autre and supposedly turned this whole mess over to him...but she'd stayed and reminded him every damned day that she expected results. She could have just given Leo and Ellie a throwaway suggestion for the bar, but not only had she given them a truly meaningful idea...she'd picked up a paintbrush and a hammer and helped them do it. She hadn't just stayed at the fence and watched the lion cub in his new enclosure...she'd gone inside and gotten grass stains on her pants helping Donovan get the cub and his new dog mom comfortable with one another.

"It's all...great," he finally said. "I'm sure it's going to work." Then he told her the further truth that she deserved to hear. And that almost killed him to admit. "It was a great idea and you pulled it off perfectly. You're bold and smart and gutsy and you have a huge heart and all of that turns me on as much as your gorgeous eyes and your sassy mouth and this body that I will, forever, lose sleep dreaming about."

Her expression went from surprise to touched to turned on.

But as she started to lean in, he said what also had to be said. "And now, I'm going home."

She stopped, frowned, and then her mouth formed a little "o" as understanding dawned.

"Because you can't wrap me in bubble wrap and take care of me with just Cajun tall tales and crawfish boils and life in a town and a house that's been in your family, yard and all, for generations," she said softly.

The words stabbed him in the heart as she repeated them almost word for word.

"Because you won't *stay* in that house and yard." Okay, that sounded bad, but she knew what he meant. "Because those tall tales and crawfish boils won't be enough."

She nodded. "That's true."

He felt the same painful jab in his gut then. He'd wanted her to deny it, he realized. He'd wanted her to say that no, if she could have all of that, she'd give up this idea of double-crossing rich pricks and saving exotic animals and exposing criminal activities of the wealthy and privileged.

"It would be an amazing addition to everything else," she added. "But I'd still want to do more. I want to be a part of something bigger."

"Bigger than family and home and community." He knew he sounded bitter. But he felt bitter. He spent his time, his energy, his *life*, protecting those things because they were big and were enough for ninety-five percent of the people he knew and loved.

Why couldn't they be enough for the woman he loved?

Why couldn't she be the superficial, high-maintenance woman he'd first pegged her for in Ellie's?

Instead, Caroline was gorgeous, feisty, and incredible, and she'd blown into his life and turned everything upside down.

She didn't speak for a long moment. Then she nodded. "I love Autre. I love your family. I love...you."

He felt those words deep in his bones. Not like a punch to the gut but like a long pull of his favorite bourbon. Warm and comforting, spreading through him, buzzing in his brain.

"But, yes, there's a bigger world, Zander. And you know it. You're protecting your corner and I get it. I do. I've been doing the same thing for my corner. But as much as I understand it and love you for what you do, there's more *I* want to do."

And that all made him love her even more. She felt alone in the world. She'd felt that she was fighting her fights alone—with Max's assistance, of course—for so long. Now, he was offering her a ready-made family and group of friends. With him she could lose herself in a world that was all happy and fun and supportive. He was offering her *him*. And he believed she loved him.

But she was willing to give that all up to do more. To stay in that darker world and fight. To be more. To make a difference.

He just wanted her to want what he could give her—

support, family, comfort—like he did everyone else. But that wouldn't be enough for her. He didn't know how to love her the way she needed to be loved...with the freedom to take the risks she clearly wanted and needed to take, without constantly worrying and being frustrated and angry. He'd thought he could do it. He *wanted* to do it, to make this work, to let her be bold and passionate, and not hold her back. But tonight had proven that he couldn't do this.

"I love you too, Caroline," he finally said.

Tears shimmered in her eyes. She pressed her lips together and nodded.

"I'm sorry I can't...be who you need me to be," he finally managed to push past his lips. "You're amazing. You're going to be...so damned kickass at whatever you want to do. I just want to protect you...from all the things you want to confront. You want to get out there and fight and I want to shield you from the reality that there is anything or anyone *to* fight. I just can't be the guy you need. I'm sorry."

And one tear slipped down her cheek.

He made a fist with the hand that itched to lift and brush it away.

Just then his phone rang. He wasn't sure if he should be pissed or relieved.

He pulled it out and glanced at the screen. It was Zeke. He immediately frowned. Zeke knew he was here in New Orleans with Caroline tonight. This had to be important.

He lifted his head. "I have to—" he started.

"I know," she said simply.

His gut in knots because of the woman in front of him and the incoming call, he lifted the phone. "Zeke."

"Hey, where's your floodlight?"

"My *floodlight*?"

"Dammit, Zeke, you weren't supposed to call him!" Zander heard Fletcher call from the background.

"Shut up, I'm just asking where the floodlight is. I'm not telling him why."

"You better not. He'll freak out."

God, Zeke couldn't even cover the phone so Zander couldn't hear this conversation? "Don't tell me what?" he barked at his brother.

"Nothing. I just need your light. Don't listen to him," Zeke told him.

"What are the chances I'm not going to listen to Fletcher?" Zander asked. If it was Zeke and Owen, or maybe even Zeke and Mitch, Zander might think they were just fucking around. But Fletcher, the oldest brother and upstanding, beloved third-grade teacher, was a little harder to ignore.

"Seriously, we've got it handled. Just enjoy your date. Sorry I called."

"You know at this point I'm coming home whether you tell me or not," Zander told him. He stoically avoided looking at Caroline. He was coming home because...his date, and his relationship, was over. "You might as well spill it."

He realized his hand was gripping the phone hard and his heart was racing. It was probably nothing. His brothers were probably just being stupid about something. They'd probably lost something, possibly something of his, and they were trying to find it before he got home.

But his gut told him it was more than that.

And he was feeling guilty. Not that he was away from Autre. Of course he left the city limits sometimes. It wasn't like he felt that he had to be there constantly. It was because he was completely indulging in...now he did glance at her...Caroline. Yeah. He'd been completely indulging in Caroline. In thoughts of last night and thoughts of tonight. And in thoughts of the future.

He'd made a reservation for tonight at the Windsor Court Hotel, the most expensive hotel in the city. He'd helped one of the concierges there with a problem two years ago and Gregory had said he was always available if Zander needed a favor. He'd wanted to take Caroline out both in his world and hers. And he'd actually been excited to surprise her.

He'd been looking forward to losing himself in the rest of the evening with her. Romancing her. Enjoying fucking being in love. Forgetting about his hometown, his family, and his job.

It wasn't that he never took time off or went out and got naked with beautiful women. But it had never been like this. It had never been with the desire to forget about it all. Sure, he blocked it out for a few minutes, maybe even an hour at a time, but none of it was ever very far from his mind. And that's how he preferred it.

Until now. Tonight with Caroline he wanted to forget. Completely. And now, not only was he feeling guilty, but he was feeling like a jackass for thinking it would work out.

"Fuck, fine," Zeke finally said. "Sharp's missing."

Dammit. Sharp had some shit going on in his life, for sure, and had been an angry asshole over the last few months. Zander didn't blame him. Having his son die and his wife walk out had understandably messed him up. But Zander had had no choice but to throw him out of Ellie's bar twice, out of the convenience store twice, and to pick him up for reckless driving three times. He was not Lionel Sharpton's favorite guy right now, but he didn't think Sharp had a favorite guy. He was mostly just mad at the world, and Zander had really been trying to help the guy out.

But Spencer and Zander had reason to believe that he'd been in contact with the guys who had holed up deep in the bayou. Possibly for a job. What they weren't sure about was if Sharp had agreed to take the job or not. And how the guys in the cabins had taken his answer.

"How long's he been missing?"

"Last time anybody saw him was about twelve hours ago.

He's not answering his phone and they found his truck down by the bayou about two miles north of Cutter's."

Cutter's was what they call the fishing spot just up from Gerald Cutter's cabin.

"I'm on my way back."

"No, don't," Zeke said. "Seriously, a bunch of us are out looking for him. And everybody's gonna be pissed at me because I told you."

"This is my job, Zeke. You *should've* told me. Someone should have told me a few hours ago. Where're Michael and Theo?"

"They're heading up the search. They've been up and down a lot of the bayou. They started out on their own and now called in some extra guys to help cover more area."

Fuck. That meant Sharp wasn't in any of the obvious, usual places. Sharp was either actually lost, in hiding, or had been taken somewhere he couldn't be easily found. Whatever the case, they had to figure out where he was and if he was alive, safe, and voluntarily there.

Zander's eyes went to Caroline again. She was watching with her arms hugged against her body. She looked concerned. And sad.

He'd never met a more gorgeous woman. It wasn't just her hair or her lips or her curves. It was her personality, her attitude, her humor, and her sweetness. There was so much more to her than first met the eye, and he was completely addicted. The sparks and chemistry had been there from the very beginning, but everything had only grown in the short amount of time he'd known her. He had the impression from the very start that he was going to fall hard and fast and sure enough, he was in deep.

"I'll be there as soon as I can," he told Zeke.

This was for the best. Having a reason to leave. It was also a great reminder to both of them that his job had to come first.

Autre would always pull him back. His sense of responsibility there would always have to come first.

He knew it was dramatic, he knew he overreacted at times, he knew that no one was *asking* him to put the town in front of having a relationship with Caroline. But even the idea of Zeke and Fletcher and the rest of his family out looking for a missing man, who was mixed up in God knew what, had his gut tightening and him itching to get back to Autre to take care of it himself.

He didn't think he would ever shake that.

"You really don't care that I'm going to be in trouble?" Zeke asked.

"You can just tell everybody that when you called I was already on my way back."

"They will never believe that."

Zander rolled his eyes. "They'll never believe that my date got cut short because I can't actually follow through on any kind of romantic commitment to a woman?" he asked, watching Caroline as he said it.

She just met his eyes, pressing her lips together.

Zeke chuckled softly. "Well, when you put it that way."

"See you soon." Zander disconnected and tucked his phone back into his pocket. He intended to ignore any more calls that might come in. "I need to head back to Autre," he told her.

"I heard. Someone's missing?"

"Yeah. And the bayou can be a nasty place. Especially at night. Not a great place to be out on your own in the dark. And if he's been drinking, it could be really dangerous."

She nodded.

How was he going to leave this woman? How was he never going to see her again?

He cleared his throat.

"Caroline—"

"I get it, Zander. You want to protect me the way you do

your family and town, but I won't be good and just stay on the sidelines."

"My brothers are going out looking for this guy," Zander said. "In the dark. On the bayou. Where there are all kinds of dangers. Not the least of which is a group of guys who might have recruited the man they're looking for. Or kidnapped him. Who might shoot first and ask questions later. Basically, they're going into a potentially unstable situation and if something happens to one of them, it will devastate every single person I love."

She frowned, clear concern pulling her brows together.

"So yeah, I'm a huge fan of metaphorical bubble wrap."

She nodded. "I'm a complication you didn't ask for."

"I didn't mean for anything to happen between us. I shouldn't have started any of this."

She shook her head. "Don't say that. I'm glad this happened."

He lifted a hand to her face and brought her in for a soft kiss. "If you ever need anything, call me."

"Don't worry," she said with a little smile and more tears in her eyes. "I will really try not to do that."

His heart slammed against his rib cage. He appreciated what she was saying. Her not calling would make his life a lot easier. But he also loved and hated the fact that she understood that.

"I do mean it though."

She nodded. "I know. And if I'm ever running away from another wedding or stealing another baby animal, don't be surprised to find me in Autre."

He knew she was trying to lighten the tone but the idea of her in another wedding dress, walking down the aisle toward another man, made everything in him rage. Whether she was running away or maybe even worse, not running, he hated everything about that idea.

But he had no right.

"Goodbye, Caroline."

"Goodbye, Zander."

He somehow turned and started down the block again.

She didn't follow him this time.

17

Michael and Theo were standing with a group of volunteers just inside the big doors where the fire truck was parked when Zander finally pulled into Autre.

"Tell me what the fuck is going on," Zander demanded as he approached.

The volunteers, all of whom Zander knew and half of whom he was related to, scattered. Likely because of the look on his face. He was not in the mood for...anything.

Michael and Theo turned to face him with frowns.

"What're you doing here?" Michael asked.

"Sharp's missing. Where the fuck else would I be?"

"On your date in New Orleans," Michael said, crossing his arms.

"You should've called me," Zander told him.

"Why? We're looking for him. There's nothing to tell you and you don't have any magical searching abilities that we don't have. It's okay for you to take a night off, you know. We have it handled."

"You handled it? Has he been found?"

Theo had his hands tucked in his pockets. But the much

bigger, much wider, ex-Navy-SEAL-now-game-warden drew himself up to his full height and managed to look incredibly imposing when he said, "We've got it handled."

"What you've got are my brothers and, I'm sure, a bunch of my cousins out looking for this guy instead of calling me."

"We just needed a little more manpower."

"For a lost fisherman, I might say fine. But this is Sharp."

Michael and Theo exchanged a look. Then Theo relaxed slightly from his I'm-two-seconds-away-from-kicking-your-ass stance and replied, "Sharp parked his truck down by the bayou, his boots are missing, and last anybody knew, he said he was going out fishing. I think he's drunk and floating."

So Theo thought Sharp had gone out fishing alone and possibly passed out, if not simply gotten lost, and was floating along waiting for someone to find him.

"You don't think you would have run across him by now? Zeke said you went up and down the main waterways."

"I did."

"And you're an ex-SEAL and the best game warden around here. If you can't find him, it is possible something else is going on."

Michael nodded. "We were just discussing that."

"He's not lost." Zander blew out an exasperated breath. "And I don't want my brothers out there looking for a guy who could be dead, or armed, or potentially being held hostage by people who are armed."

Theo's jaw tightened. "We only *suspect* Sharp's gotten involved with that group down the bayou. We don't have any hard evidence."

"Don't we need to assume the worst?" Zander asked.

Michael swore. "We went to high school with him. I don't want to believe that he's involved in that shit."

"There is no shit. They haven't done anything," Theo pointed out.

"Yet," Michael shot back. "But they're stockpiling guns and supplies for some reason."

"And they came to town looking for workers," Zander reminded them. "Just because we ran them out before they got far doesn't mean they're not doin' stuff we're not aware of."

"We've been keeping an eye out," Theo said. "I haven't seen any of them in town."

"Unless Sharp is working for them," Zander pointed out. "And is making the deals and recruiting."

"Fuck," Michael muttered.

Theo drew in a long breath through his nose, but finally nodded. "Yeah. Okay."

"You should have told us you suspected him of something more," Michael said. "I know that you keep it all from your family, but you can't do it all on your own."

Zander felt that statement hit him a little harder tonight. It wasn't anything they hadn't all said to one another at various times. They all tended to be the types that just handled things.

Theo had hauled a family out of a car that had gone into the bayou without calling for backup. He could have easily ended up sucked under with them.

Michael had been approached one night by a couple of guys who needed to be patched up after what looked like a pretty bad beating. They wanted it off the record and he'd treated them by the side of a dark backroad. Zander and Theo had chewed his ass about all the things that could have gone wrong with that.

They all needed to be reminded that they had a team at times.

"I was hoping Sharp would get his shit together. I didn't want everyone lookin' at him differently or bein' suspicious," Zander said. "But now that he's missing, it's different. My guys don't need to be stumbling across any guns or drugs or a dead body half eaten by an alligator."

His cousins, Josh, Owen, and Sawyer had already lost someone to the bayou. Tommy had been attacked by a bull shark. Sawyer, his best friend, had found him while he was still barely alive, but he'd died before they could get him to the hospital. It had messed with them all, especially Sawyer, for a long time.

Theo sighed. "Obviously we're not gonna put anybody in harm's way. But, we have a lot of space to cover now that the main areas and most obvious places have turned nothing up."

"We're pulling the volunteers back. At least while it's dark. The four of us," Zander said, indicating JD, the other firefighter and paramedic who was off with another group, "can handle this for tonight. If we need more hands we'll pull in some deputies. I'll call up to New Orleans where I have a bunch of people who owe me favors. Matt LaSalle will come down. He can bring some buddies."

Theo and Michael exchanged a look.

"You think I'm overreacting?"

"We trust you," Michael said. "If you think there's a chance that Sharp is out there with those guys, voluntarily or involuntarily, you're right, that's a whole different situation for us to be walking into and especially putting volunteers into. But you're not jumping to conclusions here just because you think that the second you leave Autre all things go to hell, are you?"

Normally, Zander would've lashed out at someone who suggested something like that, but Michael knew him well. As did Theo. And they actually tended to share his overprotectiveness and of responsibility toward their town.

"Maybe a little," he allowed.

Michael just gave him a nod. "Okay. The four of us will take two boats out. This could be a long night."

Zander nodded. He welcomed it. Maybe it would keep his mind off of Caroline.

"And," Theo asked, "do you know where your big floodlight is?"

The next morning, Theo spotted Sharp. He was on the dock of one of the cabins deep in the bayou. Which confirmed Sharp was mixed up with that group. Which pissed Zander off even as he was relieved the other man was alive. He was glad he'd pulled his brothers back before they'd found Sharp and started asking questions about those cabins and the guys inside. He was glad they hadn't wasted any more time or resources finding the guy. But fucking hell. Now any time he saw Sharp in town he was going to have to watch him like a hawk and make sure he wasn't pulling anyone else into anything illegal or dangerous.

And, though it seemed impossible, from there, Zander's mood continued to decline.

Two days later, he threatened to throw Charlie in jail for harassing a law enforcement officer if she didn't shut up about Caroline. Including talking to Jordan and Naomi about heading to New Orleans for a girls' night out. A conversation that hadn't even included him. She'd dumped a glass of sweet tea on him. But she didn't talk about Caroline in front of him again.

The next day, he stopped Maddie for going five miles above the speed limit through town. And ticketed her. Then he ticketed her again for failing to signal her turn at the stop light after pulling back onto the road and continuing on toward the Boys of the Bayou office. He also hung up on Owen when he called to ask him what the fuck he was doing. He also hung up on Ellie when she called. And he'd walked out of his office when Leo stopped to "check on him".

Two days after that, he put Beau up against the side of

Ellie's when Beau made a crack about girls in tiaras maybe being more work than they were worth.

The day after that, he pushed Zeke into the bayou because Zeke wouldn't shut up about how fucking happy he was being married and being a dad.

That one was unfair and he'd apologized later.

The worst part was Zeke had given him a one-armed hug and said he understood.

The truth was, Zander was miserable and he knew it was possible that was never, ever going to get better.

You have to stop texting me. I'm serious.

Zander glared at his phone. Spencer could be such a jackass.

Zander: *Just tell me how it's going.*

No.

It was Saturday, and Caroline and Brantley's "engagement party" was tonight, and Zander was climbing the walls.

He was sitting at the Landry table at Ellie's, surrounded by his family, most of whom were ignoring him because he'd been a dick to them all over the past week. Still, he was here with them because even when one of them fucked up, this was where they belonged.

They were all laughing and talking and eating. Happy, safe, taken care of, supported. Exactly what he wanted. What he worked for.

And he was miserable.

He looked at the newly painted wall and the colorfully framed photographs and felt...like shit. Caroline had done that. She'd realized how important those people, and those moments, and the lives that created those moments were. She'd fucking *framed them on the wall* so everyone who came in here knew how important they all were.

That wall was a huge, daily reminder of the way she'd impacted his life. She hadn't changed it. She'd understood that those photos represented what he worked and fought for, and she'd taken them, highlighted them with bright colors, and put them front and center where they truly felt like a celebration. And it made him smile. Instead of thinking about the dangers and the darkness, when he walked in here and saw those photos—new and old—he realized the light was winning.

And now she was gone and he understood that he needed her to help him keep seeing that light, to keep believing what he did mattered.

She knew that the animals she was currently rescuing were a tiny drop in the big bucket. But she was still doing it. And not because she was naïve or new to all of this. She'd been exposed to corruption and greed and cruelty longer and more directly than he had.

She still believed in doing what she could to fight back.

He couldn't keep her from that.

Zander shoved his hand through his hair. He was worried as hell about her right now. He ached with missing her. And he needed to know that *she* was happy and safe and taken care of and supported.

Zander: *I was thinking that maybe I could come up. I'll just stay with you. Keep an eye on things.*

Spencer: *Fuck no.*

Zander: *Come on, man.*

Spencer: *There is no reason for you to be here. And I've heard you've been a real dick this past week.*

He was right. On both counts. Professionally, there was no reason for Zander to be a part of the operation for Brantley and Caroline to get a direct seller on the line. He didn't even know the exact plan. He assumed that Caroline and Brantley would go into this party, put out the word they were in the market for another lion cub, and then wait for someone to approach them. He didn't know if there would be agents inside the party acting as servers. Or if Caroline and/or Brantley would be wired. Or all of the above and more. Or none of the above. Hell, the contact with the seller might not even happen tonight. It might happen as a phone call later or an email. They had no idea how the sellers contacted the buyers.

Correction, *Zander* didn't know.

Brantley had obviously bought a lion cub. He knew. And he'd told Spencer.

So Zander was the one in the dark.

Zander: *I just want to be there. As a friend. Help me out.*

Spencer: *I don't need a friend here.*

Zander sighed. *Fine. Not as your friend then.*

She doesn't need a friend. She's got me. And Max. And Brantley.

Zander prepared for the wave of jealousy. But that wasn't what he felt. All he felt was...discontent.

That wasn't enough. Three friends. Well, two and a half—he didn't trust Brantley enough to really call him a *friend*.

Caroline deserved more. She deserved to be surrounded by people who would love her loud and proud and unabashedly and unconditionally. All the more as she embarked on a career dealing with criminals and darkness and destruction.

He looked around the table.

She deserved to be loved by the Landrys.

She deserved to be loved by *him*.

Not that he had the unabashed and loud thing down quite yet, but he could get there. Because he did have the proud and unconditional thing. And he had a hell of a lot of examples of the rest.

He wanted her, and everything that came with her. He'd been miserable without her for the past week and he'd been worried about her even when she wasn't right here, even when he didn't know what she was doing, even when she was supposed to be out of mind because she was out of sight. Clearly not being with her didn't mean he wouldn't worry about her and be distracted by her.

He was going to worry about her no matter what. He might as well be a part of her life, right? Be the place she came home to after the op? The one she checked in with while they were brainstorming and planning?

But he couldn't shake the not-so-tiny detail of not being able to keep her safe.

He looked down as his phone chimed with another text.

Spencer: *Okay, listen. I shouldn't tell you this but she's not doing the party. So stop worrying. And texting me. I need to focus.*

Zander frowned. *What do you mean she's not doing it?*

Spencer: *She decided pretending to be back together with Brantley would be a huge can of worms she didn't want to open. Too dangerous. So Max is going in as his new GF. Still interested in buying. Should still work.*

Zander read the message twice. Caroline had pulled out? That...should make him feel better.

It didn't.

Zander: *Caroline would be the best. She knows them. She can sell this. Have her go in.*

Spencer: *It's decided. She's best on the sidelines.*

Zander felt a tightness in his chest. The sidelines was where a part of him wanted her. The part that wanted her safe and sound at all times.

But he still typed: *You want this to work? Caroline's your girl.*

Yeah, it might be safer for Caroline to have Max do it, but safe didn't always get results. Caroline knew these people. How they talked, how they thought, how they negotiated. She would be able to get more information out of them. She'd be able to tell who knew something and who was lying.

When people were willing to do shitty things to other people—or animals—you couldn't play nice and safe when you wanted to stop them.

Caroline wanted this to result in saving those animals and stopping whoever was behind this. She was smart. She knew there would be more dickheads doing terrible things. More animals at risk. She knew this wasn't going to solve all the problems. But she wanted to be a part of solving *this* problem.

If Max went in and solved it, Caroline would be happy, but she'd feel less than fully satisfied because *she* wanted to do this. If Max went in and it didn't work, Caroline would wonder if *she* could have done more.

Spencer: *Don't worry about it.*

Yeah, it was way past that.

Worry about it, about her, was all he'd done for a week now.

He couldn't just sit here. Zander shoved his chair back and stood. Everyone around the table looked at him, startled. "Sorry," he muttered. He stomped toward the kitchen with his dishes.

As he pushed through the swinging door and took his plate and cup to the sink, he realized he hadn't even finished his lunch.

"Finally."

He looked over to find his grandmother lifting pieces of cornbread from the pan just out of the oven into a basket.

"Finally what?" he asked, rinsing his dishes and loading them into the industrial-sized dishwasher.

"You're finally goin' up to N'awlins after your girl."

He turned to face her. "What makes you think that?"

"You look like a man who's finally figured out that it's his own fault that he's angry and pissed and feeling like shit and that he has to be the one to fix it and that the way to fix it is to go after the only thing that's gonna make it better."

He frowned. "I don't know what you mean."

She laughed. "Yes, you do."

He did.

She went on, as he knew she would. "You started this week off thinking everyone else was pissing you off."

"They were. As usual."

She shook her head. "No, baby. They were all just bein' them."

"Them bein' them often pisses me off."

She turned fully, wiping her hands on a towel, then tossing it aside. "Think about it. Think about how you *really* felt. Was this the usual pissed off? Or was this a soul-deep, everything sucks, nothing will ever make this better pissed off? Usually when they all piss you off"—She inclined her head in the direction of the dining room where a bunch of the family still sat —"you snap at 'em, write 'em a ticket, toss 'em in the bayou, and you feel better. You haven't felt one bit better in days."

Zander frowned deeper, opened his mouth, closed it, shook his head, and asked, "How do you do that?"

"Know what you're feelin' when you don't even know for sure?"

"Yeah."

"I've felt it all myself. And seen lots of other people feelin' it over the years. You know that bein' heartbroken because you did somethin' dumb isn't unique to you, right?"

He leaned back against the counter behind him. "You've been heartbroken because you did somethin' dumb?"

"More than I'd like to admit. And no, I'm not givin' out details."

"And you're pretty sure that's what I'm feeling?"

"Pretty sure," she said with a nod.

"I'm still one of your smarter grandsons, you know," he told her.

"Are you?" She didn't look convinced. At all.

"I knew days ago that Caroline was why I was feeling this way. But I have a good reason for not going after her."

"Do tell."

"She wants to work with the FBI. And I think she'll be amazing at that. It will be really good for her too. She needs to do...something big. Something more where she can feel fulfilled, feel like she's fighting the good fight. So, I think she needs to do it."

Ellie nodded. "I agree."

"But I can't keep her safe then. From the risks. From the..."

"Reality?" Ellie finally supplied. "The truth that the world is a tough place, and people can be really horrible, and there's darkness everywhere?"

He blew out a breath. Ellie was in her seventies. She'd lived through natural disasters, illnesses, a divorce and remarriage to the love of her life, the deaths of people close to her. Of course, she knew life wasn't always sunshine and roses.

"Yeah," he said simply. "So, I let her go. So that she can do what she needs to do without my dumb ass gettin' in her way, worrying, nagging her, distracting her, and making us both miserable."

"That's what you would have done?" Ellie asked.

"Yeah. Very likely. I might hold her back."

"You won't. Or if you try, she or one of us will call you on it and you'll stop."

God, she made it sound so easy.

"And you realize you're full of shit, right?" Ellie asked.

"I'm full of shit to think I'll be a pain in her ass?"

"No, I'm sure you'll be that sometimes," his grandmother said. "You're full of shit thinkin' you're my smartest grandson."

He rolled his eyes. "I said *one of*," he muttered.

"You don't understand what it means to keep someone you love safe," Ellie told him.

"Really?" He pushed away from the counter, frustration coursing through him. He'd been without Caroline for a week because of his dedication to this family. He spread his arms wide. "It's all I fucking do. It's what I've dedicated my entire career, my whole damned *life* to, El. Don't tell me I don't know about keeping the people I love safe."

She frowned at him and pointed a finger at his nose. "Don't

you get all sassy with me," she told him. "I was keeping this family safe before your daddy even had the first idea where babies came from or that he wanted to make some with your mama."

"Then you get it."

"What I get, Zander darling, is that there are lots of ways to keep people safe. And physically safe is not the most important way."

He just looked at her for a long moment. "What the hell are you talking about?"

"I can't keep you all safe from hurricanes. Or viruses. Or car accidents. Or falling off of ladders. Or cottonmouths or bull sharks in the bayou. Not fully." Her expression gentled and grew a little sad. Then she smiled. "But I can give you a safe place to *be*. A place to come to, no matter what. A place to be sad, and angry, and brokenhearted, and sick. A place to be happy, to celebrate, to hear *I love you, I believe in you, you can do it. That* is the way we keep the people we love safe. We...*are* safe. For them to be who, what, and how they need to be. Whatever that is."

Zander stared at his grandmother. He felt his throat tighten and he had to swallow hard. Memories rushed through his mind. Memories of her telling him and his brothers and cousins to slow down, to be careful, to mind where they were putting their hands, to stop, to "use their damned heads for something other than landin' on".

But they'd still gotten hurt sometimes. They'd still gotten sick. There had still been accidents, and illnesses, broken bones, and broken hearts. Owen's mom, Cassie, had raised him on her own—with help from the family, of course, but without his dad. Maddie's mom had been killed in a drunk driving accident and her dad had gone to jail. Mitch's mom had left when he was a baby. The big explosion when they were teens had killed a lot of people and injured even more. Tommy had died.

But Ellie still loved big and hard, and her arms were always open to welcome more people into the family.

People found their place here. In Autre. With the Landrys. A place to *be* exactly how they were, how they wanted to be. A safe place.

Zander couldn't breathe for a moment.

Ellie nodded, clearly reading his expression. "No one wants Caroline to be happy and fulfilled and loved more than you do, Zander. And that makes *you* her safe place, for all the ways she most needs to be safe."

He finally sucked in a huge lungful of air. "Yeah," he managed. But that was right. That was the only answer. Yeah. He could be that for her. For sure.

"Just to warn you though—protectors are given bigger hearts. That's where the instinct to shield comes from. You're one of those. But that bigger heart doesn't make it stronger. Knowing the bad things that can happen, the way people can hurt others, the evil and darkness that's out there...that will all chip away at it. A warrior's heart is bigger so that little bits can break off and there will still be some left." She paused. "But it still hurts when it breaks."

He swallowed hard.

"And Caroline is one of those too. And it hurts to see our people hurting. You gotta be ready for that."

He nodded. "Yeah. Okay. I am."

Ellie gave him a smile that was full of love and pride. She crossed to him and put her hand on his cheek. "Now go get your girl."

"Okay."

"And don't you forget where you got that warrior's heart from, Zander Landry."

He pressed his cheek into her palm. "Yes, ma'am."

She dropped her hand and started to turn away, but he

asked, "You know about the guys camping out down on the bayou, don't you?"

She looked back. Then nodded. "I do."

He shouldn't have been surprised. "Any advice?"

She simply smiled. "I love you. I believe in you. You can do it."

Then she picked up the basket of cornbread and left the kitchen.

He took a big, deep breath. She hadn't given him advice. But she'd reminded him that he also had a safe place. Right here. With the people he was protecting.

Well, except for one.

He pulled out his phone and texted Caroline.

You should be the one involved with this op. You need to be in that party with Brantley. Don't let Max do it instead. You'll be amazing.

He waited a few seconds, but got no response.

So he texted Spencer. *Put Caroline in that party with Brantley. I mean it. I'm on my way.*

Spencer: *Fucking calm down. I did. It was all perfect.*

Zander stared at his phone. He re-read the message three times. Then checked the time. Spencer had put Caroline into the party? It had been perfect? That all read as if it had already happened.

Zander: *What are you talking about?*

Spencer: *Party was last night. I was messing with you. Testing you. Thought you wanted Caroline sitting it out.*

Zander: *Changed my mind. Why last night?*

What the hell was going on?

Spencer: *Something with the caterer. Her mom changed it. No big deal. We got what we needed.*

Zander: *You didn't tell me.*

Spencer: *Not your op.*

Zander: *You're an asshole sometimes.*

Spencer: *Ditto. She's going to keep doing this, you know.*

Zander: *Good. She better. Where is she now? I'm coming up.*

Spencer: *Don't. We're heading out to celebrate.*

Zander again had to read the message three times. What the *fuck*? They were heading out to celebrate? Spencer and Caroline were going out? What did that mean? And he wasn't welcome?

What. The. Hell.

"Zander!" Zeke called. "Get out here!"

He really didn't need anymore...anything...going on. He was going to New Orleans. Everyone here was just going to have to deal without him for the rest of today. And tonight. If Caroline would let him stay, that was. He had some good old fashioned, romance-novel-level groveling to do first.

His hand hit the swinging door and he stepped into the front of Ellie's. "Look, I have to—" He pulled up short and the door, literally, hit him in the ass on his way out.

But he barely felt it.

The woman who had just walked into the bar was *I'll-fight-dragons-for-her* gorgeous. And she was carrying not one, but two pet carriers this time.

She was not, however, wearing a wedding dress.

But in that moment, he vowed to get her into one as soon as he possibly could.

Caroline had no idea how to describe the look on Zander's face when he saw her.

It was...shock and relief and *holy shit* along with a big dash of *I want you.*

And she wasn't sure he even noticed the people with her.

God, he looked good. Her chest ached with how much she'd missed him. She wasn't here to see him. Exactly. She'd *hoped* she'd see him. She'd hoped that they would be able to be friendly. She'd hoped he'd be happy to see her and glad to know the party had gone well and they'd rescued the animals.

But *that* was why she was here. They were bringing the animals they'd rescued to the animal park and sanctuary. The party had been a huge success. Not only had she and Brantley convinced everyone their engagement was back on and they were in the market for lion cubs, but they'd had five sellers contact them, three in person that very night, and they'd been able to use the information to track down where they were holding the animals and, with Fiona's help, take them all into custody.

She knew there were more. She knew she and Brantley wouldn't be able to pull this same setup off again. She knew there would never be a time when she felt like she had done *everything* she could. And she was okay with that. She'd felt good about what they'd done and she wanted to be a part of more. She was turning in her application to the bureau on Monday.

"So Caroline was just telling us that they shut down the entire operation where they were holding a bunch of illegally obtained animals that were being bought and sold—"

"Zeke?" Zander asked, cutting his brother off.

"Yeah?"

"Can you just shut up for a second?"

"But we've got two more lions, a leopard, three fennec foxes, another tiger—"

"Zeke?"

"Um...yeah?" Zeke was grinning widely.

"Just for a second."

Zander didn't even look in his direction. He was staring directly at Caroline.

"Yeah, okay." Zeke gave Caroline a wink.

Wow, Zander didn't even care that she, Spencer, Max, and Fiona were all standing in Ellie's holding five more pet carriers?

"Wait, how many?" Knox asked. "They're all coming here?" He looked at Fiona. And sighed. "How did *you* get involved?" Then he held up a hand. "Never mind."

"Knox?" Zander asked.

"What?"

"Need you to shut up too."

Knox lifted a brow. But he didn't say anything else.

"Caroline," Zander started. "I have something I need to say to you."

"Okay."

"Outside."

Oh. Was that good? Or bad?

"Hey, anything you have to say to her, you can say in front of all of us," Zeke said. His tone was still light, but he wasn't smiling now.

"This is between me and Caroline," Zander told his twin. He finally pulled his gaze from Caroline's to frown at Zeke.

"I don't think so. You've been an absolute ass for this whole past week. I'm not letting you at Caroline," Zeke said.

Caroline looked at Zander. He'd been an absolute ass this whole past week?

He sighed.

Huh. Evidently that was true.

"Fine," he gave in.

"No, it's okay," she said quickly. She trusted him completely. "Zeke, it's fine."

"No, this is..." Zander shook his head. "Caroline, I was wrong."

There were gasps from around the room. Caroline looked at them all. Wow, was that really that much of a shock? She met his gaze. He rolled his eyes, but also gave her a little yeah-it's-that-much-of-a-shock head tilt.

She pressed her lips together.

"I was wrong to think that I could let you go. That I couldn't keep you safe. I might not always be able to keep you from getting hurt or sick or keep you totally out of danger." He glanced at his grandmother. Ellie gave him a sweet smile. Then he locked his gaze on Caroline's again. "But you will never be safer than you are with me. With me you are fully free to be whoever, and whatever, you want and need to be. I love you. I believe in you. You can do whatever you want to do. And I want you."

There was a long moment of absolute silence. Caroline hadn't been in Autre all that long but even she knew absolute silence didn't occur often.

"You missed one," Max finally stage-whispered.

Zander frowned.

"I think she means you need to add, 'I'm sorry for always thinking I know best in every fucking situation no matter what'," Kennedy said.

Fletcher nodded, "Or 'I'm sorry for never giving anyone else a chance to have a damned opinion before making a decision'."

"Of course, 'I'm sorry for constantly bossing everyone around' would probably cover it too," Charlie said.

They all nodded.

"Or—" Owen started.

"*Okay*," Zander said. He sighed. Heavily. And looked at Caroline. "I'm sorry for...all of that." He paused. "And I'm warning you that all of that will probably continue. But I'll apologize for it when it does. At least some of the time." He looked at his family. "Because *some of the time I'm fucking right*."

They all just shrugged and rolled their eyes.

Caroline felt her heart filling to the point of nearly bursting. She wanted to cry and laugh. These people were so damned crazy. And she loved them. All of them.

One very stubborn, bossy, protective one in particular.

"Zander," she said, pulling his attention back to her. "You know what I would *really* love for you to do?"

He let out a long breath. "Anything."

"Take me fishing."

There was a beat. Then his face—hell, his whole body—relaxed, and he gave her a huge grin. "Really?"

"Really."

Twenty minutes later they were floating on the bayou in Zander's fishing boat, with two poles in the water, the sun shining down, without another person anywhere around.

Which meant no one talking anywhere around.

The water gurgled, a bird called off in the distance, insects buzzed. But mostly it was completely quiet for almost ten minutes straight.

Finally, Caroline took a deep, cleansing breath and said, "So this is fishing."

"This is fishing." His voice was deep and contented.

"Damn." She looked over at him. "This is pretty great."

His smile was so big and so sincere, she felt the impact to her very bones. "I really am falling madly in love with you."

She grinned. "And I'm falling madly in love with you." Her heart was full in a way she'd never imagined.

"By the way, if you get bored, you can always sit back and read," he said. He reached under the seat and withdrew a bag. From inside, he pulled a few books. The first he handed her was familiar.

She laughed. "Logan actually sent me the name of this one. I downloaded and read it the other night."

"Really?" He seemed surprised, and pleased.

"Yeah, I liked it."

"Oliver Caprinelli is a friend. His wife and Paige are close. They were all actually down here to visit a couple weeks ago. They left the day you arrived."

She nodded. "Logan said you had book club with him. That's pretty great."

Zander got a playful glint in his eye. "You might like this one then." The next thing out of the bag was a much smaller paperback.

She looked at the front. "*Gone Fishing*? Is this a romance?"

"My brothers, who think they're hilarious, asked Ollie to write me my own romance for my birthday."

She laughed. "You're kidding. This is your very own customized romance?" She opened it.

"Yep. I particularly like chapter three. Start there."

"But I won't understand the characters and plot."

"Trust me. You don't need to."

Grinning, she looked up from the first two paragraphs of chapter three. "Is it possible to have sex like this in this fishing boat?"

He shook his head, his eyes heating as his mouth pulled up on one corner in a sexy half-smile. "Nope. We'd definitely tip over."

"Too bad."

He chuckled. "Yeah."

She leaned back and flipped to page one. But, no matter how dirty or sweet or exciting a book was, nothing was as good as the man lounging on the other end of this boat.

She watched him over the top edge of the book. God, she'd missed him.

"When are you turning your application in?" he asked, catching her eye.

"My application? For the bureau?"

"Yeah."

"Monday." He understood that, right? This whole I-was-wrong thing and I'm-falling-madly-in-love-with-you thing and I-want-you thing was all still true if she went to work for the FBI, right?

"Good."

"You're sure?"

"I'm not going to lie and tell you I'll never worry. Or act like an overprotective jerk about things. But yeah, it's good. Of course. You're going to kick ass."

She smiled. "Thanks. And by the way, I'll worry about you too. And I might be a jerk sometimes too. Though that might be more about you not picking up your socks or drinking the last of the coffee and not going to the store."

He grinned. "That all sounds very domestic. You thinkin' I'm gonna let you live with me?"

"Well, yeah. I'm a spoiled heiress who has lived with her parents all her life in a big mansion with maids and cooks. What do I know about living on my own?" she asked, leaning back further and stretching her legs out in the boat.

He reached out and wrapped a big hand around one bare foot, running his thumb back and forth over the instep. It felt absolutely delicious and hot shivers ran up her leg.

"That can be arranged, of course," he said, his voice husky. "But you should know that blue-collar, small-town types do things a lot different from you rich folks. For instance, we do our own housekeeping. Naked."

She laughed. "Awesome. Can't wait to watch you dusting the house in that case."

He pressed his thumb into her foot and she moaned with how good it felt.

"Yeah, there will definitely be some negotiating of the 'chores'," he said, somehow making "chores" a very dirty word.

She was going to live with Zander. In Autre. And work for the FBI. This was...a dream come true. But a dream she hadn't even known she had.

"How about your parents?" he asked. "Have you talked to them? Do you plan to?"

She sighed. If he kept rubbing her foot like that, she could definitely talk about her parents without feeling tense or too sad. "I haven't really talked to them. I let them know I was staying with a friend in New Orleans and looking into a new job. I'll keep in touch. But..." She met his gaze. "We can't fix *everything* we'd like to fix in life, right?"

He nodded slowly. "Right. But some of us are programmed to keep tryin'. My grandma says those people have warrior's hearts. And they're bigger than most so that little pieces can break off and we still have plenty left."

Caroline felt a stinging at the back of her eyes and she blinked rapidly. "Wow. Your grandmother is...something."

"That she is." He paused. "She said you and I both have those hearts."

Caroline had to swallow hard. "Oh."

"So, I'm just sayin' that, if you *want* to keep trying with your family, I get it. Completely. And I support you. But if you don't, I get that too."

She gave him a small smile. "No, you don't."

He started to protest.

"But I love you for that. I love that you would support me *not* trying. But I also love that you *don't* understand not trying to protect and be there for people you love. So—" She took a breath. "Yeah, I think maybe my heart's big enough to take that on. And if it hurts once in awhile...there's always Ellie's gumbo to make it better."

He gave her a smile that was sweet and hot and proud and full of love all at the same time. "'Course your heart's big enough for that. And there's a whole ton of support around you." He paused. "Which is kind of like bubble-wrap, you know."

She felt her heart melt a little. Yeah, she did know. And she was glad he did too. She nodded.

"But the work you're gonna do in your life is gonna need lots of the pieces of your heart so...take your time deciding. Or try it and change your mind. It's all okay. The only person I ask you to keep on lovin' no matter what stupid shit he does and says over the next seventy-five years or so, is me."

She was going to cry. And laugh. And maybe burst with all of the emotions this guy made her feel. "Done," she managed to choke out.

A rumble of what sounded like thunder made her look up. Clouds were rolling in and the sky was darkening.

She frowned, sitting up. "Dammit, it's going to rain." The sun was already blocked out. She'd been so caught up in Zander she hadn't even noticed.

"It's no big deal. We can get back before we get too wet," he told her. He started pulling the fishing rods from the water.

"But it *is* a big deal." She felt the sharp stab of disappointment. "This was supposed to be your day off. Bright and sunny. A way to kick back in the quiet. But it's getting dark. I wanted to show you that there's always sun on the other side of the dark."

Zander dropped the rods on the bottom of the boat and leaned in, reaching to snag one of her hands. "But...you've shown me that, Caroline. Repeatedly."

She shook her head. "No. I've done the opposite. You were kicking back at Ellie's having lunch with your family...then I walk in with a lion cub and drag you into my big chaotic mess. You come out to help me and have a simple solution...then my brother shows up and almost kidnaps me. After that, things are fairly calm and we know when Spencer shows up things will be okay...then Brantley shows up and you get yanked out of bed in the middle of the night. Then we have an amazing date night and we have a plan to get the info we need...then I show up at Octavia's totally off script and turn it all upside down *again*. Every time you think things are sunny and warm, I roll in with clouds and rain on your plans."

He gave a little tug. She tumbled forward. The boat rocked, but he settled them in the middle, and it stayed upright. He wrapped his arms around her, tucking her against his chest where his heart was beating hard.

"No," he said gruffly. "You have *all* of that backward. Every time something started to look crazy or frustrating or dark, *you* were there to remind me there was a *reason* to fight through it. You were the light showing me the direction to go. Did you make my life crazier? Yes. But you made it bigger. You made it more meaningful.

"You could have just been this woman stranded by the road, who needed money to get back to New Orleans. Instead, you were this amazing person who needed someone to help her fight for a cause. You could have been this gorgeous woman I just took on a date and then back to a hotel. Instead, when someone had to step in and get something done with Brantley, *you* did what *only* you could have done. Without you, none of that case would be solved right now."

He took a deep breath. "You could have been some woman who was just here on vacation, taking a break from her hectic schedule, sight-seeing, and kicking back. Instead, you were this person who helped introduce a *lion cub* to his new foster mom and a whole bunch of people who will love and care for him instead of leaving him in the possession of rich dumbasses who would make his life miserable. And you mucked out alpaca stalls and saved a unicorn *and* a birthday party. And gave my family a gorgeous tribute to our lives and the people who have made us who we are."

His arms tightened around her. "No, nothing has been easy or simple with you, Caroline. Thank God. You've been *more* in every way, and you've made me and my life more because of it."

She was full-on crying now. She hadn't seen any of that but *God* she was so glad that was all true. Or at least that Zander felt it was true. She *wanted* that all to be true.

She looked up at him. "I love you so much," she told him as she sniffed.

"I love you too." He hugged her again. "And, you *are* my light. But..." He ran a hand up and down her back. "There can be some fun things about the dark."

Just then a big, fat raindrop hit Caroline's cheek. He lifted a hand and wiped the drop and the tears away.

"Yeah?" she asked, already feeling her body heating. She knew exactly what he was thinking with that look in his eyes. "Like what?"

"I can show you. Leo's fishing cabin isn't too far from here and it's got everything we need. And I think I might have just found an even better reason to come out to that cabin than fishing."

She gave a mock gasp. "That's the nicest thing you could have said to me, Zander Landry."

"Mean it with all my heart."

"And you think you're not romantic."

He grinned. "I think I'm learnin'."

"Should we call and let everyone know we won't be back for awhile?"

"Most importantly, that cabin has no cell service," he told her.

Zander being willing to go someplace with no cell service, where no one could get a hold of him if something went wrong, was huge. That was definitely romantic.

Her chest warmed. "Won't they worry?"

"We'll put out the 'Go the fuck away' sign on the dock. If they come lookin', they'll know exactly where we are."

She laughed. "How long can we stay?"

He looked at her with a hot gaze full of love. "Forever."

She gave him a soft smile. But shook her head. "We'll just celebrate the moments when things are quiet and everyone is safe and happy whenever we can. And we'll take care of them all the rest of the time. Together."

He held her gaze for a long moment. Then nodded. "Let's do that."

"And we'll go fishing as often as possible," she added.

He shifted her off his lap and onto the bench across from him. Then he reached to start the boat engine, pointing them down the bayou toward the fishing cabin. "And some of the time we'll maybe even *actually* fish," he told her with a grin.

EPILOGUE

Six months-ish later...

I *need a favor.*

Knox had two simultaneous reactions to seeing Fiona Grady's name flash across his phone screen as the text came in.

One, he sighed. The woman was a lot of work. She made his life much more chaotic. Something he did *not* welcome.

Two, his body tightened. Particularly one part right behind his fly.

Dammit.

Hearing or seeing her name made his body respond like he was a fourteen-year-old boy with a crush.

The woman had him twisted up. And worse, she knew it.

He picked up his phone and studied the message.

He was a twenty-eight-year-old man. And not just any man. He was a fucking grump. On purpose. And Fiona knew that as well. In fact, he was *especially* grumpy with her. She was an animal rights activist who had never met a furry or feathered creature she didn't want to cuddle and coo at.

It wasn't her love for animals that annoyed him, of course. It was the fact that she'd started bringing many of her rescues to Autre, Louisiana to live over the past eighteen months in the petting zoo that had slowly turned into an animal park that had slowly turned into a sanctuary for abused, abandoned, and neglected animals.

As Autre's city manager and right-hand man to the mayor, Knox's job had become more difficult because of those changes. There were more people underfoot now—visitors to the park, media, school groups, animal rights groups. There was also more paperwork crossing his desk with permits and licensing. There were more events too. Fundraisers, holiday parties, even a couple of protests from groups that believed all animals needed to be free in the wild. Hell, he even had more potholes to deal with now because of the increase in traffic.

And it was all Fiona Grady's fault.

She was so not his type.

So why did she turn him on more than he ever had been before?

Hello???????

He felt the corner of his mouth tip up as her next text came across his screen.

She turned him on because she had three very important things going for her.

One, she was fucking gorgeous. She had long, dark hair, sparkling blue eyes, and a smile that was quick, bright, and full of mischief. Which he *shouldn't* like but worked on him like a drug.

Two, she was fierce. She was petite and barely stood five-foot-one, but her personality and attitude were huge. She never backed down from his growls. He could bitch and bark at her and she hardly blinked.

For some reason he liked that.

She could always back her shit up. She might kick down a door to get to an abused animal and go toe to toe with the abuser, but she also knew the law, would have the correct permits, and would always win if someone tried to take her on.

Fuck, her boldness and her brain got him going.

Three, she lived almost seven hundred miles away. That was good. However twisted up she made him, most of the time she was too far away for him to do anything stupid about it.

I have a scar from the last time I did you a favor, he finally typed into his phone.

That was not entirely accurate. He had dirty fucking dreams from the last time he'd done her a favor.

And the favor before that.

It was the one before *that* where he'd been scarred.

Fiona Grady's favors had, so far, ranged from helping her unload a camel from the back of a truck, to tossing a hunk of meat over a fence to a hungry tiger, to helping bandage a gash on her lower back where a pissed off ostrich had tried to take a bite out of her, to letting her nap in his bed.

The first two, where he'd interacted with the animals directly, had been crazy—and definitely new additions to his resume—but it was those last two that had been haunting him.

To do first aid on the ostrich bite, she'd had to lower her jeans and show him a good portion of her sweet, well-toned left butt cheek. Not to mention the tattoo that curved over her left hip bone and read, *All great changes are preceded by chaos.*

He thought about that fucking tattoo every damned day.

She absolutely made him feel chaotic. When she was around, he felt it swirling in his head, his gut...his chest.

Then there'd been the day she'd napped in his bed.

Whenever Fiona came to town, she stayed with Griffin Foster and Charlie Landry but, in Fiona's own words, Landrys couldn't even take their shoes off quietly. She'd been wiped out from a huge animal rescue and then the long road trip from Georgia and she'd asked if she could sack out on his couch for a couple of hours. He'd said she should absolutely use a bed.

He hadn't specifically mentioned the *guestroom*, because he'd assumed she'd figure out that was where the *guests* slept at his house.

But no. He'd found her four hours later in *his* king-sized bed with the blackout drapes pulled over the windows. Under his sheets. Bare naked. Sound asleep the way only someone who felt completely comfortable and safe could sleep.

His pillowcase had smelled like her for a week. Sure, he could've washed it, but... then it wouldn't have smelled like her.

He hadn't jerked off that much in a week since he'd been a teenager.

Mine's bigger than yours, she replied in her next text.

He felt his whole mouth smile. It was true that the scar she had on her lower back from that ostrich was bigger than the one on Knox's hand from snagging it on the fence when he'd thrown twelve pounds of meat to the tiger.

His smile died a moment later as he realized that there was no way he was saying no to whatever Fiona was texting him about right now.

Which was a huge red flag. He had no problem saying no to *anyone.*

That included his boss, the mayor, Kennedy Landry. And his mother. And his *grandmother.* And the *mayor's* grandmother.

And he truly might be the only person to ever say no to Ellie Landry.

It wasn't an *easy* thing to do, he would admit, but he could do it.

Of course, whenever he did, he had to go without gumbo for a week or so. That meant he carefully chose his battles. Still, once in a while even Ellie Landry needed to have someone put his foot down.

So did Fiona Grady.

The fact that he had difficulty doing that made her living in Florida and him living in Louisiana a very, *very* good thing.

He liked her. He wanted her. And he absolutely did *not* want to be involved with her. Or anyone. But especially her.

Fiona Grady was...a lot. And Knox didn't want a lot. He very stubbornly and very purposely kept his life as simple as he possibly could. Fiona was gorgeous, funny, fascinating, smart, bold, and feisty. But she was not simple.

What do you need? he reluctantly asked.

It's probably easier if I show you.

He braced himself. She was going to send him a photo and God only knew what might flash across his screen next.

She'd never sent him naked photos, but a man could hope.

No, he meant a man could hope she *wouldn't*. He did *not* need a photo of Fiona naked. He had plenty of ideas in his head about what that looked like as it was.

And why did his mind keep going to dirty thoughts? She wasn't sexting him. They had a *working* relationship. Kind of. She had a partnership with the animal park and sanctuary in town (i.e., she was the one behind most of the animals that now called Autre home) and he was the city manager who got to deal with all the consequences of Autre now having an animal park and sanctuary.

Increased traffic problems. And road damage. And garbage. And noise and odor complaints from the locals.

Still, no, Fiona didn't work for him. Or with him. He would bitch at her because he blamed her directly for the fact that they had red pandas, a sloth, and lemurs in Autre. Because she'd literally brought them here herself. But she always had the paperwork in order, and if he complained about the traffic, the next day his phone would be ringing off the hook with all of the local businesspeople calling to let him know how much their bottom lines had improved as the animal park had grown and how happy they were with the increase in tourism.

He knew Fiona lobbied them to make those calls.

So, yes, their professional lives definitely overlapped—or, more accurately, butted up against one another—but this was definitely, probably not sexting. They'd never done that. They flirted in person, and over the phone, and via text once in a while, sure. But it had never gotten that serious. Why was he thinking it would now?

Because you've missed her, dumbass.

It had been a couple of months since Fiona had been to Autre. Which was unusual. For a while there, she'd come monthly or more to bring animals to the Boys of the Bayou Gone Wild. She had quickly realized that the Landrys, who owned and ran the petting zoo, were exactly the kind of people to welcome and care for abused and neglected animals that needed a place to live quietly and happily after what they'd been through.

Initially, they'd been building the business as a money-maker, of course, but Fiona had recognized bighearted animal lovers and had not-so-slowly introduced them to animals in need.

At first, the petting zoo had been fairly simple. Goats, a potbellied pig, alpacas, the usual. It had been a straightforward attraction. But they'd quickly added lemurs, a sloth, a colony of endangered Galapagos penguins, flamingos, a harbor seal, and various other animals ranging from hedgehogs to peacocks.

Yes, the animal park had been a headache for him nearly from the start, but when he'd realized that some of the animals —donkeys, camels, and some horses—had been rescued and were coming here as an escape from their previous abusive situations, he'd realized what Fiona was *really* up to.

He'd made her tell him about what she *actually* did at her

animal park in Florida. She had giraffes and a few other inter-esting animals people came out to see, but at its core, it was a sanctuary. And when she'd told him about the rescues she conducted, about the conditions they sometimes found, and the physical and emotional rehab they were able to do with the animals when they rehomed them in the right places...he'd fallen a little in love with her.

Fiona Grady was a force to be reckoned with.

And she was fucking gorgeous when she was passionate and riled up about something. Which was most of the time.

He was still waiting a minute later for a photo to ping his phone when his office door opened.

"Hey, Fitzwilliam."

God, he wanted her.

That was his first thought when he looked up and saw Fiona standing in his office doorway.

"Nope." He set his phone on his desk and strove to look nonchalant about the fact that she was in Autre and not seven hundred safe, can't-touch miles away.

Since they'd met and she'd found out that he went only by his last name and that no one knew what his first initial—F—stood for, she'd been trying to guess his first name. She hadn't landed on it yet and no one here in Autre knew. He'd always just gone by Knox, even in high school. Or F. Knox if it was something official.

He had no intention of telling her what his first name was. Simply because the more he got to know Fiona, the more he thought it was good to keep some secrets. He already had the very uncomfortable sensation of being wrapped around her tiny, sexy, pinky finger.

He purposely leaned back in his chair and laced his fingers together, resting them on his stomach. Calm. Cool. Unaffected.

As far as she knew.

He wasn't going to let her know that his pulse had kicked

up the moment he saw her smile, or that his fingers were itching to slide into her hair, or that his cock was hard and ready to go. How could she affect him this much with a simple greeting, standing twenty feet away?

"You're in town," he commented unnecessarily.

She spread her arms. "It's Christmas."

She wore ankle-high black leather boots and black leggings that molded to her legs, with a long red and black plaid shirt that just covered her hips and ass. Over that, she had a quilted black vest that gave a nod to the fact that it was cool outside but certainly not *cold*. Her hair was down and loose and she looked...gorgeous.

"Didn't know you were in town," he said.

"I like keeping you on your toes."

It seemed she was very, very good at that.

He glanced toward his office window. Sure enough, her gigantic purple truck was parked in front of City Hall.

And he was like one of Pavlov's dogs. That damn truck made his cock ache. They hadn't even slept together. But his body craved her and he got hard at the sight of her Ford F-150 XLT that was the color of grape soda and far too big for the woman he could have easily thrown over his shoulder and carried up the sixteen steps to his bedroom without even breathing hard.

Today, though, the pickup had reindeer antlers on top of the cab and a huge red ball for a nose between the headlights, that he assumed were supposed to be the eyes.

"You're a few days early for Christmas," he pointed out, turning back to face her, glad his desk was between them and blocking what was going on behind his fly.

Was she staying through the holiday? She usually only hung around for a day or so after delivering animals and saying hi to her friends in Autre. She had her own animals and life to get back to in another state. But it was only the twentieth. If she stayed through the holiday that would be nearly a week...

"No, we're heading home the day after tomorrow. So I wanted to come and give everyone their gifts before we left."

He frowned. She was heading home to Florida the day after tomorrow? "Where have you been?"

He was very aware that Fiona did a lot of things he wasn't privy too. Why should he be? And why should he care?

That was a question he always shut down as soon as he started to think it.

Well, *usually* as soon as he started to think it. When he'd found out that she threw herself into rescuing animals in the aftermath of natural disasters like hurricanes and earthquakes and wildfires, he hadn't quite been able to hold back. And he might have picked her up and carried her out of Ellie's bar and backed her up against his truck and demanded she tell him all about those rescues and her training and how she kept safe.

And he might have come within a centimeter of kissing her.

Even right now he had to consciously make himself take a deep breath.

He had no idea what she did on a typical Thursday night, either. He didn't know if she was safe or if she even thought about keeping herself safe or if the animals always came first...

Actually he *did* know. That's what made him crazy. She always put the animals, and other people, before herself. He worried. And he didn't like it.

He didn't need to know everything about her and what she did. He didn't *want* to know. What they had was...fuck if he knew. They weren't co-workers. They weren't friends. They weren't...anything.

She was a woman he was semi-obsessed with and trying very hard to *not* be even remotely interested in.

He should be glad she wasn't going to be here for the holidays. Every time he saw her around their mutual friends, he liked her more. She was warm and funny and smart and someone he could get very, very wrapped up in.

Fuck.

"I've been in Florida," she said.

"So how are you heading home?" he asked. "I'm confused."

"Oh, we're heading *home* home. To Europe."

He blinked at her. Europe? What? "You're from Europe?"

"That's where my family is. My mom and my grandparents."

"I—" He'd had no idea. "You're not an American?"

"Nope."

"You...don't have an accent." That was a stupid thing to say. But this was just one more fucking thing he didn't know about her and it made him just as crazy as everything else he didn't know and he didn't fucking want to be crazy. About her or anything else.

She gave him a little smile. "I got rid of it."

Oh, she'd put a little bit of... something in there. It didn't sound British. Maybe Irish? She was fucking Irish? What? He was *not* going to ask.

"Okay so, well, Merry Christmas," he said. He needed to get her out of his office.

"I stopped by for a reason, Fred." She gave him a grin.

His cock really liked that grin. It was full of naughtiness and a bit of I-know-I'm-getting-to-you.

"Nope," he said of the F name she'd guessed.

She rolled her eyes. "I need a favor, remember?"

How could he forget?

"What do you need?"

"Well..." She turned slightly and leaned over to pick something up.

And he heard the squeaking.

Oh. Fuck. No.

"Nope," he said simply. To whatever this was.

347

"Come on." She lifted a pet carrier with a bright red Christmas bow on top.

"Not doing it." Whatever this was.

"*Ferdinand*, they're just babies. They *need* you."

"I'm not the guy." He didn't even bother to tell her Ferdinand was way off.

"You *have to be* the guy."

"Why?"

She set the carrier on the corner of his desk. "Because I can't sleep with a guy who isn't willing to foster abandoned animals at the last minute."

That made him stop. Just for a second. But she noticed.

Her *gotcha* grin told him she'd noticed.

He narrowed his eyes. "What's in the carrier?"

"Three baby otters."

He did *not* want to be responsible for three baby otters. In fact, that might be the most ridiculous thing he'd ever heard. He didn't want to be responsible for any animals, period. He lived in a town *full* of animal lovers. And otters? They had an enclosure where a family of otters lived at the petting zoo. A family of otters that had adopted the Landry family way back. *He* did not need to take care of these animals.

Still, he knew he was fucking going to say yes to this.

Dammit.

"I do *not* want pet otters."

"Of course not," she said, as if *that* was a ridiculous idea. "I just need you to take care of them while I'm gone over the holidays."

"They're river otters," he pointed out. "They're not exotic or endangered. There are literally dozens along the bayou."

"But if you can't take care of three otters, I'm definitely not letting you near endangered lemurs or even recently rescued dogs that have been traumatized."

"Why do they need to be taken care of? Their natural

habitat is right outside the back door of this building." *Literally.* He could walk three blocks and plunk these babies in their natural habitat.

"These are newborns," she said, pulling one of the tiny animals from the carrier and holding it up.

He frowned. It was indeed a *very* young otter. It had to be less than four weeks old. It didn't even have its eyes open. "How the hell are there otter pups this time of year?"

"The mom and dad were being kept indoors as pets. We assume ever since they were very young as well." She scowled. "Because of that, we're thinking their...calendars...are messed up. Anyway, the babies can't just be put outside. Baby otters can't even swim without being taught."

Yeah, he knew that. Otters had to teach their young to swim. And fish. And...how to be otters. Obviously, the pups wouldn't survive without their parents. Or human intervention. Knox sighed. Fiona wouldn't let even a butterfly suffer without trying to help it. "You want me to give them swimming lessons?" he asked dryly.

"Of course not. They're not old enough for that. Yet."

Right. Not because it was *absurd* to think that he might teach baby otters to swim, but because they weren't old enough for that.

"These are going to need to be kept warm and protected and fed," she said, nuzzling the baby before putting him back in the pet carrier.

Then she turned a big smile on Knox.

"I'm not handfeeding three baby otters, Fi."

Her eyes softened at his use of the shortened form of her name.

He didn't do it often and he'd only ever heard Griffin Foster, the local vet and long-time friend of Fiona's—and the reason the woman had ever made that first trip to Autre at all—call her Fi.

The first time Knox had done it, it had been a total accident. It had just slipped out. And it had sounded affectionate. And sexy.

As it did now.

She braced her hands on the opposite edge of his desk and leaned in. "Please? The owners freaked out when their otters had babies. They thought they were both males. They were so upset, especially when two of the babies died. They dropped them off at the petting zoo in a shoebox with a note. How sad it that?"

"This is your fault," he told her.

"Probably," she agreed. "In part. Though, you all did have otters here before I ever showed up."

"But you turned that place into an animal park where people think they can drop off any stray or abandoned or unwanted animals."

"Good," she said. "I *want* that place to be somewhere animals can be safe and cared for and for everyone to know that."

Knox sighed. Right. "There's literally a dozen, probably more, people who can take care of those otters. Happily. Better than I can."

"It's not about who *can* take care of them. It's about if *you* are willing."

He narrowed his eyes. Why wasn't he just throwing her out of his office? He could. Easily. He could pick her up, toss her out, slam the door, and... think about her and wonder what she was doing in Europe and think about texting her the entire time she was gone.

Dammit.

"I promise you, once you're naked in my bed, you won't care how I feel about otters, Fi."

He regretted the statement almost the second he said it.

Heat flickered in her eyes and she tipped her head and gave

him a cock-teasing grin. "You're probably right...*once I'm naked.* But you have to get me there first."

His whole body responded to the challenge in her tone. "You think that's gonna be a problem?" Just as she'd added a little Irish-or-something to her tone, he brought out his Louisiana-boy drawl for that.

It worked. Her pupils dilated and her gaze dropped to his mouth. And stayed there as she said, "I think that if we're going to start sleeping together whenever I'm in town, I have to know that if I get a call or someone stops by with an animal, you're going to be okay with it and even willing to jump in."

If we're going to start sleeping together. She'd said the bit about how she couldn't sleep with a guy who wouldn't do this before, but this was more direct. This sounded like she had an actual plan.

He shouldn't have been surprised that she'd just put it out there like that. But he also hadn't been prepared for it. Or for the blast of heat that shot through him. Or the way his entire body seemed to suddenly strain toward her.

"Babysitting animals isn't really what I think about when I think about having you in my bed, Fi."

Yeah, his voice was lower and gruffer. It wasn't like she didn't know she got to him. She knew it too well.

Her eyes came back to his. "But when I'm here, it's always for something animal related. As much as I love flirting with you, I stick around for a day or two after bringing a rescue because I want to be sure the animal gets settled and the humans are comfortable. I have to be prepared to be interrupted for all kinds of reasons. And if you get upset or frustrated or act like an ass about it rather than jumping in to help, it'll be a huge turn-off and we won't be able to keep having our salacious, secret affair."

He pulled in a long breath through his nose. Even sex with this woman was going to be difficult. Great.

But not difficult enough for him to say *hell no* to the plan.

Because he and Fiona had been on a crash course to hot, sexy, fun, dirty sex since the first time their eyes had met in Ellie's bar.

The secret part sounded pretty good too, he had to admit. The friends they had in common were the Landrys. The Landrys were some of the best people on the planet. And they were crazy. They loved big, and loud, and hard, and had no problem falling head over heels in the blink of an eye. It was the same way they dove into the bayou—with a huge splash and very little concern for how dirty or dangerous it might be.

They also thought everyone around them should be the same way.

The second any of them had even the tiniest inkling that he and Fiona were doing more than flirting—everyone knew they were doing that and had been since the first second they'd met —they'd be pushing Fiona to move here and him to buy a huge-assed diamond ring for her left hand.

"You can't just keep those two parts of your life separate?" he finally asked.

"No, I can't," she said simply.

That wasn't a surprise. Fiona walked the walk, that was for sure. She didn't just love animals. She waded into flood waters, dressed up in fire gear, and climbed through building rubble to save them. She owned and operated a multi-acre animal sanctuary. She lobbied. She protested. She put her boots on the ground and backed up her words with actions, time and time again.

He'd never realized activism was one of his kinks.

He did now.

"So you're testing me," he said.

"Yes."

"I suppose we could just decide not to sleep together."

She thought about that. "Yeah. I guess we could do that."

He didn't respond. They just looked at each other, her standing, him sitting, his big, oak desk between them.

"Well, damn," she said after the clock on the wall had ticked several times. "But okay." She picked up the carrier, turned, and started toward the door.

Yeah, there was no way she was leaving with those baby otters.

"Fiona."

She stopped and looked back. "Yeah?"

"What do baby otters that age eat?"

Her smile was immediate and bright. "I have the instructions all written down."

"Okay."

Good God, he was going to be the foster dad to three baby otters. To get laid. By a woman he didn't want to want.

He really hoped those otters were still alive when she got back.

F eeling really good about everything in general, especially the part about sleeping with Knox, Fiona set the carrier down against the wall just inside his office door. "Excellent. I think you'll do a great job, Fritzy."

He just sighed and shook his head. She grinned. She really didn't think his first name was Fritz. She didn't really care what it was. She just loved teasing him.

The guy got to her. He was so not her usual type. She liked the charmers. The social justice warriors. The do-gooders. Not that Knox was a *bad* guy. But he was a damned grump. He was bossy. He loved to call the shots and seemed perpetually perturbed.

And she wanted to strip off his flannel and denim and lick him from head to toe.

"There is just one more thing I need to know before you jet off to Europe for the holidays with Colin," Knox told her.

She straightened and rolled her eyes. "Colin is just a friend. I've told you that. We let everyone think that he's my boyfriend because it's easier than explaining to everyone why we live together."

"Why *do* you live —" He broke off.

He did that all the time. He'd start to ask her a question about her life, but then stop himself before he got it all the way out. He talked about her work. He seemed actually fascinated —and concerned—about her work, as a matter of fact. Fascinated by the animal park in Florida and the lobbying and legal work she did. What he didn't seem to like was the protesting and going into disaster areas and facing down the assholes who illegally kept animals or abused them or both. When he'd found out about her work in Alabama post Hurricane Clare, he'd *demanded* she tell him about her training, how she kept safe, what she would do in a whole litany of situations he tossed at her. All while standing nearly on her toes and staring down at her as if he wanted to spank her. Or as if he wanted to strip *her* flannel and denim off and lick her from head to toe. Maybe after the spanking.

Yeah, F. Knox, the kind-of-nerdy, but also big, hunky city manager of a tiny bayou town had this dominant, naughty air about him that she *so* wanted to know more about.

And if he took care of these baby otters and was as sweet with them as she was certain he could be, she was absolutely going to toss her panties on his bedroom floor the next time she was in Louisiana.

"Knox?" Fiona asked. "Do you want to know why I live with Colin? Do you want to know where I'm going for the holidays?"

"No, I don't."

He really did seem to purposely throw up this barrier to

knowing anything too personal about her. That was...interesting.

"Okay, then what is it that you need to know about me before I leave?"

"I need to know how you taste."

Her eyes went round and all of the air in her lungs swooshed out. Heat flooded her system. And her brain immediately started chanting, *yes, yes, yes, yes, yes!*

She supposed she could do this *before* he babysat the otters. She was ninety-nine percent sure he'd still do that.

Okay, ninety-five.

He *might* pass the otters off to someone else.

But they'd still be alive and well when she got back to Autre.

And looking at him right now, practically oozing testosterone and heat and *I-want-to-eat-you-up*, she didn't care who gave the otters their tiny little bottles. She just wanted Knox.

And that told her everything she needed to know about how she felt about this man.

If he could cheat on his otter-fostering duties and she would still want him, she was pretty far gone for him already.

She swallowed hard. "Well, I..."

"Fi," he interrupted before she had to come up with something witty and flirty.

"Yeah?"

"Come here."

Her heart thumped, her stomach flipped, and her inner muscles clenched.

Whoa. She'd had an inkling that Knox would be a little dominating and dirty. Not that *come here* was dirty. But the gruffness in his voice and the look in his eyes were somehow crazy hot.

She wet her lips and came around the side of his desk. Without a word, he rolled his chair back, seemingly making room for her between his seat and the desk. She lifted a brow.

He just watched her. Fine. She wasn't going to play shy or hard to get. Shy simply wasn't in her DNA and hard to get was the last thing she was for Knox.

She slid her butt along the edge of his desk until she was positioned between his knees. They weren't even touching but she felt electricity crackling in the air.

Then he rolled forward and leaned in, resting his palms flat on the surface of his desk on either side of her hips, caging her in.

"Kiss me." The command was simple and gruff.

Her heart gave a hard *thunk* and she felt adrenaline flood her system.

She had to lean over just slightly to obey. And she was so not the type to be bossed around. But this guy also had her driving seven hundred miles on a fairly regular basis just so she could see him.

Sure it worked out that she could bring animals and that was absolutely a good thing—for the animals and the people involved. But she knew that the Autre animal sanctuary was growing faster because Knox was here.

He was also keeping her up late at night and had her replacing the batteries in her vibrator far more often than she had before she'd met him.

So him telling her to kiss him? *Yes please.*

She took his face in her hands, his beard soft against her palms, and locked her gaze on his. Then she pressed her lips to his. Softly at first, but the heat between them flared and the feel of his mouth on hers, after so many months of banter, and flirting, and sexual tension, and getting to know him, had her sighing and parting her lips after only a few seconds.

He felt like...*yes.*

That was the word that echoed in her head. This just felt *right.* It felt hot and thrilling and full of decadent promises. But it was also *satisfying,* like she'd finally scratched an itch that had been torturing her for months, while also filling her with a need for *more* that surprised her with its intensity. This kiss felt like something she'd been waiting for forever. It was strangely familiar, comfortable, and just *good.*

His lips were demanding against hers, but Knox sat with his hands still on the desk, not moving otherwise. His mouth moved over hers for several long, exquisite seconds, then he licked along her bottom lip, before stroking his tongue against hers. The firm, delicious thrust sent a jolt of heat through her and she was shocked by how thoroughly he could kiss her with no other part of his body involved.

But he was using plenty of chemistry, and their history, and lots of fantasy and longing on her side. She wasn't sure he knew just how much longing, but she wouldn't have been surprised if he suspected. She was a pretty open book...

That thought was what made her pull back.

There were things Knox *didn't* know about her. Things she thought she should tell him, but that fell in that category of things-he-seemed-to-not-want-to-know-more-about. I.e., her personal life.

She just stared down at him, breathing hard, shocked by the heat and emotion of the kiss, not sure what to say.

He studied her for a few seconds, then said in that deep, gruff voice, "I wasn't done."

Before she could respond, he came to his feet, towering over her and crowding close, his hands still braced on the desk.

She was trapped between his big hard body and the hard wood behind her. And she couldn't think of anywhere else she'd rather be. Except maybe with a soft horizontal surface behind her.

This time he was the one who took her face in his hands. His huge palms cupped the sides of her face, his fingers wrapping around to slide into her hair. Then he tipped her head and leaned down to seal his mouth over hers.

If she'd thought he'd kissed her before, it was nothing compared to this.

He *took* her mouth. Fully. With heat and intention. Lust and electricity zipped along her nerve endings and her entire world narrowed to focus only on this man and everything he was making her feel. Having his mouth against hers before had been amazing but having his mouth *and* hands on her and his body pressed against her was intoxicating. She felt dizzy, and full of happiness and warmth that was more than just lusty heat.

Though there was plenty of that too.

She moaned and grasped his biceps as she tried to press more fully against him. Their height difference was kind of hot. And kind of a pain in the ass.

He clearly agreed. A second later, with a little growl, his dropped his hands to her hips and lifted her onto the desk, stepping in between her thighs to press close. But again, he was too tall, or she was too short, for them to *really* fit together.

His growl was a little louder and more frustrated when he scooped his hands under her ass and lifted her as he sat back in his chair. She straddled his thighs now and, *oh yes*, she was now able to press right against the thick, hard bulge behind his fly.

This time they both groaned.

His fingers tightened where they still cupped her butt and the kiss grew even deeper. Her hands went to his head, her fingers sinking into his hair, holding him still as she pressed into his body from chest to cock.

She was really glad she'd worn only leggings today. The thin material let her feel everything from the impressive ridge between her legs to the big, hot hands holding her ass.

"God, Knox," she nearly panted as she came up for air.

He dragged his mouth along her jaw, his beard abrading her skin and sending goosebumps dancing down her neck and arms, tightening her nipples. She tipped her head back and his hot mouth trailed kisses down her throat until he got to her collar bone. He gave her a quick lick, and fire seemed to shoot from there straight through her belly to her pussy. She moaned and rocked against him.

He kissed his way back up her neck to her ear where he gave her lobe a tiny nip, then said roughly, "Yep. Exactly what I thought."

"What?" she asked, breathlessly.

"You taste delicious." He pulled back, pinning her with his gaze. "I want to eat you right up."

Her breath caught as she grew even hotter and wetter.

"Well," she said, her voice sounding thick and scratchy. "I think we should—"

His grip on her tightened and he shifted, but it took her a second to realize he was moving her *off* of his lap. He set her feet on the floor and rolled his chair back. With him still in it.

She waited for him to say something. When he didn't immediately, she asked, "Are we going to your place?"

"No." He looked around. "It's the middle of the day. I have work to do."

"But, there's lots more *tasting* to do."

"We're in my office."

She looked pointedly at the desk. "Yeah. And?"

"Do I seem like the type to have sex in my office on my desk?"

She thought about that. And took in the maps and charts on the walls around them. And the planner set to the side of the desk with the perfectly penciled in lines. And the pencil cup. And the file folders stacked up neatly.

And sighed. "No. You really don't."

"I told you I needed just a taste."

Her eyes rounded. "And that's really *all* you want?"

"Well, I need to be sure you're comin' back for those otters," he said.

And damn if the corner of his mouth didn't tip up *just* a bit.

"You think that *little* taste is going to bring me back?" she asked.

"Yes."

He wasn't wrong.

Fiona ran a hand through her tousled hair, tugged on the bottom of her vest, straightening it, licked her very-well-kissed lips, and lifted her chin. "Guess we'll see about that."

He full-on smirked then. And she almost fell over. Knox very seldom did much more than frown or glower or roll his eyes.

"Yeah, we'll see," he agreed, clearly not believing there was any doubt.

That full-of-himself look was really working for her.

"Merry Christmas, Knox." She rounded the desk and headed for the door.

"Merry Christmas, Fi."

God, she loved when he called her that.

She paused with her hand on the door. "Don't kill my otters."

"Trust me when I say I do *not* want to deal with you if you show up and those otters aren't totally healthy and happy," he told her.

She studied him. The hair that fell past his shirt collar. The full beard. The ink on his left forearm that dove under the rolled-up shirt sleeve. The biceps that made those shirt sleeves fit snug against his upper arms. All of those things didn't seem to jive with the perfectly-stacked-folders-and-sharpened-pencils-guy, but it just made him all the more interesting.

And then there were those eyes that seemed to see *her*—not just the things she did, but what those things meant to her and how they affected her. And that mouth...that said bossy, sarcastic, protective, even flirty things, and then kissed her like it was what he'd been put on earth to do.

Yeah, she didn't care if he passed those otters off to someone else while she was gone. She was still going to hurry back.

"See you soon, Fernando."

"I know you will."

Damn. He made her hot when he was a grump. When he was cocky? She was so in trouble.

"And Fi?" he called as she was pulling the door shut.

"Yeah?"

"Wear some panties with shamrocks on them next time. It'll remind me we have some talkin' to do when I see those on my bedroom floor in the morning."

Heat swept through her. But that also made her pause. He was going to get interested in her personal life after all? Well, at least it sounded like she was going to get an orgasm before she told him a thing or two that might send the likes-everything-neat-and-tidy-and-under-control grumpy, nerdy bayou boy running in the opposite direction.

"Sure thing, Felix. And hey..." She swallowed. "...don't hang out under any mistletoe, okay?"

That was as close as she was going to get to admitting that she was kind of crazy about him and would maybe be a little jealous of any other kissing he might do.

His expression softened slightly and Fiona felt her heart trip.

"No interest in mistletoe if you're not under it."

That made her heart flip all the way over. She gave him a simple nod. "Ditto."

Then she pulled the door shut between them... just as the baby otters woke up and started squeaking for their afternoon feeding.

The mischievous grin on her face as she left Autre City Hall would probably get her on the naughty list.

But there was no way Knox would be surprised about that.

Thank you for reading Zander and Caroline's story! I hope you loved it!

And don't miss the next book, **Kiss My Giraffe,** Knox and Fiona's book!

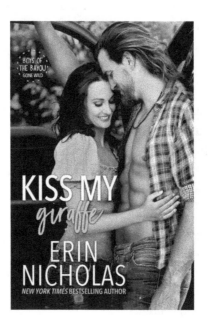

Enemies to friends to almost lovers then back to enemies...to lovers.

She's got a lot of baggage...literally and figuratively. And an entourage. And a freaking giraffe. For real.
For a guy who wants to keep things simple, this is anything but.
So why can't he stay away?

Knox and Fiona's story! Finally!

And yes! Spencer and Max are getting a book!

Look for book one in the **Badges of the Bayou** book, *Gotta Be Bayou,* coming fall 2022!

Sign up for my newsletter for that news (erinnicholas.com/contact) or join my Super Fan page on Facebook where you get all the behind-the-scenes looks and first peeks! Just search for Erin Nicholas Super Fans!

IF YOU LOVE AUTRE AND THE LANDRYS...

If you love the Boys of the Bayou Gone Wild, you can't miss the Boys of the Bayou series! *All available now!*

My Best Friend's Mardi Gras Wedding (Josh & Tori)

Sweet Home Louisiana (Owen & Maddie)

Beauty and the Bayou (Sawyer & Juliet)

Crazy Rich Cajuns (Bennett & Kennedy)

Must Love Alligators (Chase & Bailey)

Four Weddings and a Swamp Boat Tour (Mitch & Paige)

And be sure to check out the connected series, Boys of the Big Easy!

Easy Going (prequel novella)-Gabe & Addison

Going Down Easy- Gabe & Addison

Taking It Easy - Logan & Dana

Eggnog Makes Her Easy - Matt & Lindsey

Nice and Easy - Caleb & Lexi

Getting Off Easy - James & Harper

If you're looking for more sexy, small town rom com fun, check out the

The Hot Cakes Series

One small Iowa town.

Two rival baking companies.

A three-generation old family feud.

And six guys who are going to be heating up a lot more than the kitchen.

Sugar Rush (prequel)

Sugarcoated

Forking Around

Making Whoopie

Semi-Sweet On You

Oh, Fudge

Gimme S'more

—————

And much more—

including my printable booklist— at

ErinNicholas.com

ABOUT ERIN

Erin Nicholas is the New York Times and USA Today bestselling author of over forty sexy contemporary romances. Her stories have been described as toe-curling, enchanting, steamy and fun. She loves to write about reluctant heroes, imperfect heroines and happily ever afters. She lives in the Midwest with her husband who only wants to read the sex scenes in her books, her kids who will never read the sex scenes in her books, and family and friends who say they're shocked by the sex scenes in her books (yeah, right!).

Find her and all her books at
www.ErinNicholas.com

And find her on Facebook, Goodreads, BookBub, and Instagram!

CPSIA information can be obtained
at www.ICGtesting.com
Printed in the USA
BVHW071341100222
628586BV00002B/246

9 781952 280276